In the Manor of Heather Black

Carl D. Henry

ALL RIGHTS RESERVED

No part of this book may be reproduced or transmitted in any form or by any means, electronic or mechanical, including photocopying, recording, or by any information storage and retrieval system, without permission in writing from the author, except in the case of brief quotations embodied in reviews.

Cover Art:
MLC Designs 4U

Publisher's Note:

This is a work of fiction. All names, characters, places, and events are the work of the author's imagination.

Any resemblance to real persons, places, or events is coincidental.

Solstice Publishing - www.solsticepublishing.com

Copyright 2015

Gary D. Henry

In The Manor of Heather Black

Gary D. Henry

As always, this book is dedicated to my family and friends.

Live your life to the fullest. Create a wealth of memories in your lifetime, and relive them as often as you can because these are your riches when your allotted time on this earth is expended. Reflection will be your last greatest moment.

I would also like to dedicate this book to my sister, Belinda Bell who had tirelessly worked as my editor on many of my books until she lost her sight and eventually her life due to cancer.

Chapter 1
The Black Beginning

In 1848, newlyweds Cyrus Black and his wife Heather Blankenship Black moved into their new home. It was not just any home. It was a castle without the stonework, a sign of opulence, fitting for its regal inhabitants.

A handsome man at thirty-five, Cyrus descended from King George II of England who reigned nearly a century earlier; however, the royal life held no allure for him. He spent the majority of his young life under the watchful eyes of royal guardians who hovered over him to correct every mistake he ever made and to shield him from the horrors of life. He longed to own land in a place far away from his relatives' interference.

He wanted to be a simple farmer.

Cyrus hated being pampered. He wanted to choose his own friends instead of the highbrow elites forced upon him. When he was in his early twenties his parents began to pester him about marriage. He had the choice of every titled lady in England though none appealed to him. His parents chose most of the eligible ladies for him, except he wanted to be the one who chose. The women were all young and beautiful; however they seemed set on staying in England as most thought America was the land of the war lovers, peasants, and religious fanatics who would rather live in squalor than submit to the rule of Queen Victoria and her reign in their mother country.

Cyrus chartered a very large sailing ship, filled it to capacity with all his belongings and a ton of gold and sailed to New York, Britain's ex-colony. Cyrus' bold move upset his parents however they understood his desire to be free of the monarchy's adherence to the statutes and strictures of the royal family.

Cyrus landed on the shores of New York in 1845 and immediately purchased a small but livable country house on the Hudson River far away from the bustling city. Once he set foot on New York soil he replaced the dry goods dealer Alexander Turney Stewart as the richest man in the state.

He lived modestly among his neighbors and never mentioned his royal roots, nor did he flash his wealth around to invoke false friendships. However, a year later they knew that he was a man to be respected and he gained many friends.

***

He attended many parties in New York. Some were held to celebrate a business victory or other events that the wealthy held dear. However, most were designed for the rich to parade their successes in the business world and have a laugh or two at the plight of the downtrodden masses.

Cyrus hated the pompous affairs of the wealthy however, a year after he landed in New York, he felt restricted in the confining walls of his small house and wanted to find a larger house to live in. He wanted a spacious property to farm and enough land to ride his horses. His chance came when he attended one such party in order to meet the host, a wealthy landowner, who owned a five-thousand acre tract of land in northern Virginia with a large stately mansion built in the center of it. The property interested him. Cyrus drank glass after glass of Champagne as he haggled with the landowner until they finally agreed on a price. Once a deal was confirmed, Cyrus grabbed his hat and wanted to hastily leave the opulent affair. He noticed a beautiful woman who appeared to enjoy the company of dignitaries and business leaders.

All the while she glanced at the handsome man who was rumored to be quite wealthy. Cyrus couldn't resist the looks she gave him that night and he had to meet her.

Known as Heather, Hather Blankenship was the youngest daughter of a wealthy shipping magnate who resided in upstate New York. Named after the purple mountain flower "hather," she changed her name as a child to Heather because she decided it sounded pleasanter to the ear.

Heather stunned as a raven-haired beauty that, as her friends remarked, instantly fell in love with Cyrus. He was a handsome man and his money added greatly to his allure and for Heather that aspect of her affection far outweighed mere physical beauty.

They fell in love during the party, following hours of private conversations in the ornate parlor of the landowner's home, and made plans not just to meet afterwards but for months in advance. They dated for a long time. Cyrus always avoided the subject of marriage due to his own misgivings of the ritual that had changed so many of his friends.

Heather had different ideas about their relationship and insisted after two years of engagement it was time to wed-or else. A month later, Cyrus relented and requested her hand in marriage and she enthusiastically accepted his proposal. Cyrus wanted a small wedding though Heather wanted the world to know about her impending nuptials and invited a thousand guests and made the wedding a lavish and luxurious affair.

They were married on an April afternoon in a garden as the forsythia and cherry trees blossomed and flowers bloomed. Heather's closest female friends, as well as some of her acquaintances, gossiped that the main reason she married Cyrus was because her parents had cut her off from any inheritance years ago. They said she'd instantly tripled the wealth of her family by marrying Cyrus and no longer needed or cared about an inheritance from her father.

The women in town felt that her unfeeling and un-Christian ideas about people who had less than she had were the main reasons why her family dealt with her so harshly. She seldom attended church but when she did, she complained that her time was wasted there and the services bored her.

A few weeks into her marriage, she found out about the tract of land that Cyrus had purchased from the New York landowner. She wanted to visit it even though Cyrus explained that the two-day trip was a tough one especially in a horse-drawn carriage. Cyrus couldn't make the trip because he had to sell his small country house first, as well as the rest of his holdings before he left New York. He sent Heather to Virginia with plans to meet her there a few weeks later. After a rugged trip full of broken wheels, replacement horses and atrocious roads she arrived in Northern Virginia and checked into a hotel about ten miles from Cyrus' parcel of land. She contacted the land agent and he told her where the property was situated and drove her to see it. Heather had set her sights on living farther south and happily left the verdant meadows of the upper Hudson River Valley for good. She complained that the winters were too harsh for her anyway although the land agent told her that the winters in Virginia were also harsh at times.

When she saw the house she instantly fell in love with it.

***

She reunited with Cyrus three weeks later in a tiny town in northern Virginia called Leesburg. It had an interesting history. In 1814 the Constitution, and the Declaration of Independence were secretly moved to the small town before an imminent British attack on Washington, D.C.

Regardless of Heather's harsh view on those of whom she referred to as "the lesser people," she knew that they delivered a valuable commodity: to serve her lavish needs. Cyrus had not known of Heather's pretentious nature prior to their marriage; she had mastered the art of hiding her unsavory attributes to be able to capture a potential beau's heart.

Once captured, the hopeful young men wallowed at her feet and showered her with expensive gifts while giving her vacuous looks of undying affection. She accepted their presents and allowed them to dream only to suddenly dispatch them to her own "unwelcome" category if they started to demand too much of her time or attention.

It was the largest mansion in the state and was nestled in the middle of a five-thousand acre plantation just outside of town. Though it didn't have the stonework of a castle it impressively matched the size.

Constructed in 1804, the original owner's entire family died when part of the mansion caught fire thirty years after its completion; it had been vacant ever since. The enormous home stood majestically on the well-manicured estate with its fifty bedrooms, a spacious ballroom and dining rooms that ached for a party for the elite and well-bred citizens of the tiny community.

Although it had many trees the plantation also included acres upon acres of flat, clear, cultivated fields designed for farming.

All the locals agreed that the plantation's fertile soil far surpassed the other adjacent farms and that the best crops were grown there.

Heather loved the almost-fifty-year-old mansion, although Cyrus originally wanted a more discreet home to downplay his great wealth.

The plantation came equipped with all the modern implements along with forty slaves. The slaves greeted their new owners with skepticism however they were quick to find out that Cyrus was not like the previous owners of the manor.

Although Heather had different ideas, Cyrus did not want to be viewed as a man who owned people. To him, slavery went against everything he held dear and was a crime against humanity. He hated the fact that he owned slaves given his Christian upbringing and his overwhelming sense of human decency.

However, he couldn't free them immediately because he believed the slaves owned by his fellow farmers would probably revolt against their owners. Cyrus decided to release his slaves gradually to avoid the sneers and the inevitable questions as to why. However, those who chose to remain to work his fields were paid handsomely though they were still referred to as slaves to appease his neighbors.

Heather, on the other hand, enjoyed owning the staff as opposed to paying them because she relished the power she held over people.

Cyrus' conscience ate away at him at the notion of being a slave owner so regardless of his neighbor's morally deficient beliefs he eventually freed all of his slaves despite Heather's displeasure at the act. The former slaves loved and respected the new owner of the plantation because for the first time they worked as free men and garnered a decent wage for their efforts. They lived happily. They were now equals though only on the plantation and only in Cyrus' eyes. There were many slave owners in the state and he preferred not to inflict his views on others however, as he told Heather, his farm would not prosper on the backs of forced laborers.

The former slaves lived on the outer edges of his property on land that Cyrus gave them to do with what they would. They split it equally among themselves. The community was made up of dirt streets and hastily built dirt-floor homes made of castoff lumber and whatever wood the forest supplied.

There was a central meeting place where they gathered to talk about how to improve the living conditions of their newly formed settlement.

Cyrus convinced them to replace the old buildings with clean, small homes for them to live in. He supplied the lumber and they built the houses to Cyrus' standards.

To Cyrus, the slave issue damaged the supposedly Christian, newly liberated country. He noted the ambivalence from the clergy and wondered how people could own slaves and still be right with God.

He visited the new settlement many times and whenever he saw a problem he worked with the slaves to resolve it. Cyrus worked with them to improve their living conditions every time he visited.

The former slaves did all their laundry and cooked with water collected from the local creek however drinking it presented dangers to their health. Cyrus wanted to make the water cleaner to improve the overall health of his workers and their families. The camp needed a well because drinking the creek water made the children susceptible to diseases due to its questionable quality.

He hired a company to dig a community well right in the center of the settlement.

The drillers were puzzled by Cyrus' actions and were unable to understand why he wanted to help the slaves. However, he simply offered enough money for them to overcome their distaste for working around darker-skinned people. That still didn't stop the drillers from showing their prejudices by their words and actions. The slaves ignored the drillers' behavior because they rightly deemed the well too important to quibble over words. They had heard these words all their lives and had grown numb to the repetition.

The finished well brought an unlimited supply of clean water and enabled the women of the community to clean their clothes and cook their food and give fresh water to their children free from the threat of disease.

Some of the men in the slave compound made more money than some of the farmers in the area although spending it in the town proved hazardous at times. Dangers existed everywhere for former slaves with money in their pockets so Cyrus accompanied them each week to ensure the men's safety and to make sure the settlement had the supplies it needed. He visited the camp often and each time he saw changes that bettered the residents' lives. It warmed his heart.

The children waited for his horse and carriage to arrive. When it did they encircled him because Cyrus always had a pocketful of hard candy that he distributed among them and they happily accepted the sweet confections and thanked him for their gift.

Their parents told Cyrus they had suffered hardships that no man, woman, or child should endure and felt blessed to have him on their side, because it was the first time in their many tortuous years of toil, that a white man treated them as people rather than property.

The former slaves of the Black Plantation were the envy of the local slave population. Those slaves who worked for different masters on adjoining farms saw the changes in the living and work conditions on the Black farm and wanted a similar life. They were the scourge of the local white farm owners who didn't like the example Cyrus set for their slaves. Regardless of Cyrus' ideas about slavery, they liked, respected and admired him for his kindness in granting free water rights to all the farmers in the area.

Heather seldom visited the site with Cyrus because she did not want to associate with the slaves. Cyrus was perplexed by Heather's behavior. He'd hoped she would share his views and wanted her to work with him to alleviate the suffering and injustice. Cyrus, in turn puzzled Heather. She viewed them as servants in servant's quarters and with servant children.

Outwardly, she saw Cyrus' passion regarding the black people and feigned respect for them to appease her husband. The grimace on her face when they were around made it plain that she loathed them.

She had the best of everything; she used much of Cyrus' money to furnish and redecorate the manor to show visitors that they were indeed in a house built for a queen and admired anyone who gushed at the lavishly adorned home.

Gold fixtures abounded; inlaid precious wood walls gleamed throughout the house; ornate ceilings from the finest plaster artisans in England and grand chandeliers made of the clearest crystals the world could produce perched twenty feet above the fine Italian marble-floored main ballroom, dining rooms, sitting rooms, and bedrooms. The huge windows provided much of the light in the home. Colors of the rainbow shone through the crystals of the chandeliers and created colorful prisms of light against the walls.

Old World furniture from the finest craftsmen of both Virginia and England further enhanced the air of opulence. Spacious gardens surrounded the home, along with well-maintained lawns that made the visitors view the mansion and its grounds as a large green park.

Together, Cyrus and Heather hosted many formal affairs. The men talked of politics and the women liked to speak of their children and other wifely duties deemed mundane by Heather.

A new couple moved to town and Cyrus met them on one of his few visits to the local tavern. A wealthy banker named Tom Watts and his wife Karen equaled Cyrus' wealth though they lived on a smaller tract of land in a decidedly smaller home. They were respectable people who shared the same beliefs as Cyrus with regard to slavery and the outlook of the country. Heather met Karen but once again to Cyrus' regret, she ignored her. Karen and Tom had the type of wealth that normally made them acceptable in her eyes, however, Heather's coldness toward the woman betrayed the fact that she believed Karen's beauty had caught Cyrus' eyes more than a few times. It incensed her.

***

Unbeknownst to anyone, Heather had a dark secret, which she never revealed. She was a practitioner of witchcraft and given that the stigma of witchcraft remained a topic of ridicule in the nation, she didn't dare reveal her secret. No one suspected her because of her great beauty and her strong negative opinions on the subject. She constantly praised the efforts of the lawmakers and their torturous verdicts during the witch trials of Salem, Massachusetts in the late 1600s in an effort to make sure no one guessed she practiced the satanic art.

She learned the craft as a child.

Her childhood friend and mentor had given her a very old book of spells that she had kept close to her for all the years prior to meeting and marrying Cyrus. She secretly housed the book in one of the darker bedrooms of the mansion. A room not visited by anyone for decades.

Her friend's female ancestors had practiced witchcraft in Salem and suffered execution at the hands of the Puritans in the small Massachusetts town. The book passed down from mother to daughter until it reached the friend who, in turn, gave it to young Heather because she had no children of her own to pass it onto. The spells within the book helped Heather's friend when the world got too complicated for her. Later, subsequent bouts of depression and anxiety created an uncontrollable madness within her, and she took her own life. Heather never equated her friend's maladies with the use of the old and fabled book.

Now she had the enormous mansion and fifty rooms in which to hide her secret. She designated a private, locked room in the darkest part of the west wing as her practicing room and visited it often.

There, she conjured spells, mixed her concoctions, and spouted strange words in accordance to the books teachings — although nothing happened. The spells did not work.

She tried everything to make them work until she realized that the first two pages were stuck together; she had missed performing the initial procedure to unlock the magic within the book and bind the book to her forever.

The procedure would last five days. She had to recite a passage from the book, wait twenty-four hours exactly, return and recite the second passage, wait another twenty-four hours, then say the third passage, and then the fourth and the fifth. After the fifth passage was spoken, she had to prick her finger and drip one drop of blood on each page of the book.

Once she completed this course of action the book and all the magical spells within it would work perfectly for her and her only.

A part of her feared the book and wondered what dark forces would be unleashed if she opened that door and allowed the magic full reign. For this reason she did not perform all of the steps.

***

Heather loved to explore the expansive mansion in her idle time. Sometimes Cyrus joined her though he did not enjoy the home's vast and dark recesses. He seldom saw Heather because finding her in such a large mansion proved impossible given her desire to explore every room. He called out hundreds of times as he walked through the house trying to find her and eventually gave up after visiting twenty or thirty bedrooms.

When Heather finally reappeared, usually when the sun went down because of the dimmed light, he asked her where she had been.

"Heather, I've called you many times. Where do you go during the day?"

Heather did not want Cyrus to know of her secret place so she merely said, "There are fifty bedrooms in this house and I have to check all of them so I can direct the help to clean them. I won't have one of our guests stay in a room that is dusty or unkempt or has dirty basins and linens."

"Are you planning another party?" he asked.

"Oh, God no, those old biddies don't deserve to sponge off us any longer."

"Old biddies? Heather, I feel as if I have to remind you that those 'old biddies' are our friends. Their husbands are my friends. Sweetheart, why do you talk as if they are trying to take something from us? They're good people and have earned our respect."

"Respect? Most of them don't even have the means to support their families. Why should we supply them with a day of excellent food and drink when they can't reciprocate our goodwill?"

"Are you saying that you can't associate with them because they don't have the wealth that we do?" Cyrus inquired, as he removed his glasses.

"Well, yes, I guess I am. Cyrus, we are fortunate people, and I don't want our children to be brought up wanting for anything. I have a feeling that their children would be a bad influence on ours, should we decide to have them."

Cyrus wondered how his bride could be so cruel.

"Heather, when we have children, I would be happy to see them play among their children or any children. They are just children and we will allow them to associate with many types of people. Do you understand that?"

Heather, who had never heard her husband speak so decisively, looked confused. "Oh, dearest, I'm sorry to make it sound as if those others are not worthy to interact with our children. They are, of course."

***

Heather, oblivious to the fact that the women in town secretly didn't like her, invited them over for tea so they could marvel at her beautifully decorated house though many of the women thought that it appeared somewhat cluttered with too many expensive antiques. Most declined her invitations relaying various reasons, however, they enjoyed Cyrus' company and while they chose to be with their devoted husbands during all the lavish dinner parties, it was obvious to all that spending any time with Heather was not what the wives wanted to do.

The comment 'too pretentious' was whispered among them.

The men always talked of politics. They speculated on the possibility of the Old South fighting the North in hopes of solidifying the republic under one flag. Many of the men wanted the battle between brothers however Cyrus stood firmly against such a conflict. A man of great ideals, Cyrus considered the war, which would probably be fought on Virginia lands would destroy substantially more than the architects of war predicted. The fact that the proximity of his home was near to the Mason-Dixon Line troubled him. He knew wars were always the most intense near boundaries and his plantation lay only a hundred or so miles from this one. He feared that a great battle would certainly be fought on his land given that he owned more than his neighbors.

Although he lived in an area that people deemed part of the South he agreed with many of the North's stances with regard to slavery.

Yet the glorious South embraced its culture and had no intentions of changing to please the intellectuals of the North.

Heather did not want a war to happen either because she feared her property would be taken over by whichever side won such a war.

No one wanted their land stained with blood-soaked bodies and the remnants of gunpowder replacing the sweet smell of honeysuckles in the air. Cyrus and Heather had not come to this rich, green country only for it to be marred by war.

Cyrus had seen too much bloodshed in his own country and wanted no part of it in his new paradise. He made his views known to many of the plantation owners, which caused arguments within the usually cordial and gentlemanly conversations. However, before the end of the spirited if somewhat contentious debate they offered each other a hearty handshake and a thank you and parted friends.

Cyrus tried to discuss Heather's attitude towards people but to no avail. When she saw that her attitude had an effect on her relationship with her husband, whom she loved with all her heart, she attempted to change her ways.

To this end she invited the ladies over for tea, or a woman's meeting, as they called it and once again the conversations bored her and she prayed for them to end.

Try as she may she couldn't bring herself to like any one of the fine ladies of the town.

She explained to Cyrus of her attempt to interact with the local people had not succeeded.

Her failure in that regard incensed Cyrus. Heather seldom saw her husband's temper. That day he stormed out of the room and left her alone to contemplate why he was so angry with her.

Heather made yet another vow to change.

It was a change that wouldn't please her husband had he known what her plans were.

She walked to her secret room at the end of the darkest hallway in the manor, opened the evil book of witch spells, and determined to carry out the five-day ritual. She recited the passage as the oil lamps affixed to the walls ominously flickered dim and then shone brighter.

She closed the book, blew out the lamp and left the room. She returned at the exact same time the next day and performed the second stage. The oil lamps' flames were brighter than before.

At first she was unaware the brightness of the lamp had anything to do with the procedure, that is, until her third visit after she had recited the third passage. The heat generated by the lamps' flames singed the lampshades to an ugly brown.

The incident with the lamps scared her and she questioned whether to return for the reading of the fourth passage.

However, the next morning a rancher's wife sneered at her for no reason she could determine. That simple gesture gave Heather the courage she needed to recite the fourth passage. The lamps' flames ignited the shades and melted the small glass sleeves. Heather shielded her face from the heat and managed to turn the oil supply off and the flames extinguished. She closed the book and left the room, frightened, although resolute that the one sneer she'd received also warranted the final visit to the room.

Heather wished there was an easier way however her ego did not accept the status quo. Heather walked down the hall on the fifth and final day. She slowly entered the room, opened the book and recited the passage. The lamps exploded. They lay on the floor in a million pieces, but the flames magically blazed on their own without fuel supply or wicks. She uttered an additional phrase and noticed a slight wind swirling in the dusty, unlived-in room. She chanted more of the incantation; the wind grew in intensity. A tornado surrounded her in the closed room. Heather noticed that when the wind blew through various stones of the fireplace she could hear sounds, like words, which beckoned her to continue.

The walls of the room spun in the opposite direction of the wind, matching its velocity, as the floor remained stationary. Items in the large room were tossed around her and her long black hair whipped against her face with such speed that she felt the sting for many minutes. She secured her hair in one hand amid the swirling confusion the room created. She didn't feel fear as she battled the elements within the room. Resolute, she withstood the velocity of the storm as long as the end result delivered the desired effect.

The wind stopped, as well as the movement of the walls, and she looked around to see that all the flying pillows, sheets, and debris were back in their normal places. Even the dust once layered on the book returned to its original place. She silently read another incantation designed to affect anyone, other than herself, who should enter the secret room. According to the spell, the book was bound to her and her only and all the spells within were hers to conjure as long as the pages remained in the book. The unlocking procedure was completed and the book released its secrets. The lamps returned to their original state.

She searched the book for a spell she could use to coerce her husband's friends to like her. Heather viewed witchcraft as her only avenue to gain their respect. She had sought to change her attitude and soften her personality to allow the kinder, sweeter Heather to shine through however it hadn't worked. She also searched for a spell to make her husband see her as she saw herself, to love her and not scold her or make her feel bad.

She did not want to change and hoped she'd find a spell that could change other people and use magic to gain their honor and respect. She searched and searched until she finally found a spell she could use. It was an old spell that garnered the results she desired. The charm, originally conjured centuries earlier to make minions respect the kingdom's rulers, reversed the thinking of those who wanted to overthrow the ruling class.

Heather decided the spell fit her situation perfectly. She uttered the words:

"I summon the dark places to heed my request. I call to you, the Lord of the Book, to answer my plea! Change my husband and the visitors of this house to see my light and not question their minds. I call upon you, the Dark Lord, to make them view me as their Goddess!"

Afterwards she closed the book and walked out of the room. She strolled through the darkened hallways with only a candle to light her way because the oil sconces on the walls were devoid of oil.

Heather arrived back at the main room of the manor, where she sat at her writing table to address select invitations to a party. She planned to see if the spell worked. She sent out the invitations and they were delivered by carrier to every farm and to all the elite of the community.

Many of the women initially declined her invitation although the insistence by their husbands that they attend won over their objections. Once they entered the house, the spell took hold and they were enthusiastically pleased that they were there.

Their reaction upon entering her home convinced her that her spell worked perfectly. Everyone in the town attended the lavish affair. Cyrus and the rest of the men congregated in the massive oak-trimmed den, smoking cigars, telling war stories from their youth, and proudly comparing scars received from great battles.

The men heard laughter emanating from the room where their wives had gathered.

When the laughter became louder than the men's concerns of wars and political talk, curiosity stilled their conversation. The men investigated the boisterous laughter. Shocked, Cyrus saw his beautiful wife engaged in a raucous conversation with the other wives who actually appeared to like her.

Cyrus whispered in her ear. "I'm so proud of you, my darling. The women adore you."

"Thank you, Cyrus. I think that all your good husbandly advice has finally made me realize that I do like these women and they appear to like me as well. Now leave us because I want to continue to get to know them better."

Cyrus lovingly kissed her on her head and left the room. He smiled as if content that the difficulties they'd had were over. The other men followed Cyrus and scratched their heads in confusion. It was odd to see their wives cuddle up to a woman they'd said they despised just hours prior to their arrival.

The spell had had an extraordinary and profound effect on all the women in the room and Heather was happy to bask in their respect and ignored the fact it was due to mind-controlling sorcery.

Heather and her new friends talked throughout the evening. They hung on to every word she said and agreed with her views of the world. To her delight her beauty also suddenly and overly intrigued them.

Heather noticed that her spell carried over to the men as well and soon the gentlemen of the community admired her as much as they admired Cyrus.

At the time Heather did not realize that there was a price for the magic she commanded.

A few days after the party, a strange and unsettling concept came into her mind.

Something deep inside her told her to poison her beloved husband.

She quickly dismissed it and carried on happily with her newly acquired friends.

The evil idea was not stilled for long and weeks later the urge for her to accomplish her deadly mission grew in intensity.

As she prepared tea for Cyrus one afternoon, she saw a jar containing a spray of pretty flowers and green leaves were added to provide another color to the bouquet — hemlock. Her hands shook violently as she peppered his tea with the mashed leaves however couldn't bring it upon herself to put in enough to kill him. Something, even deeper within her, stopped her.

Even though Heather knew that she placed poison in Cyrus' tea, she couldn't prevent herself from doing so because for a fleeting moment, the urge to kill him overwhelmed her love for him.

Cyrus greeted her and she offered him the freshly made tea. The heat of the midday sun caused him to drink it quickly so she could not, and did not, stop him. He looked at Heather and told her, once again, about the pride he felt for her by allowing the town to view her as he did.

A few hours drifted by until Heather found Cyrus on the floor violently ill and writhing in pain. Although she knew the reason why he was ill, she did not dare confess her part as the cause of his condition, to him or anyone else. She had no way to summon the doctor so she ordered Hector, the manor's butler, to prepare the carriage to drive

Cyrus to town to see Doctor Silas Smith, a friend and drinking companion of Cyrus'.

Hector, one of the newly freed slaves, showed serious concern when Cyrus lost consciousness during the two-mile trip to town.

They arrived with the horses panting loudly. A strong man, Hector easily lifted Cyrus into his arms and quickly carried him into the doctor's office. Heather cried all the way to the door as she followed Hector inside the doctor's home.

He regained consciousness when the doctor applied smelling salts and he told Silas that he burned inside. The doctor had sewed Cyrus up after many a mishap around the farm and he didn't offer a single twitch of pain however, regardless of his high threshold for pain, this time he writhed in great agony.

"This man's been poisoned! Cyrus, did you eat something you shouldn't have?"

Cyrus began struggling for breath. "No Silas, I had a cup of tea. That's all! My stomach's burning up!"

"Heather, get those towels from over there along with that bucket and three glasses of water. Hector, take his shirt off, it may cool him off a bit," the doctor demanded. He reached into a glass cabinet and took out a bottle of brown liquid. "Cyrus, I'm going to give you this. You must drink it all down. Do you hear me?"

"Yes, I hear you," Cyrus muttered, between painful grunts.

Silas gave him an antidote designed to assist in many ailments within the digestive tract. He also gave him a lot of water to dilute whatever he'd ingested to cause his pain. He grabbed the bucket and gave it to Cyrus.

"What's this for?"

"You'll see soon; just keep drinking the water," the doctor requested.

Cyrus found out quickly what the bucket for as he vomited violently multiple times, which purged the poison before it could do any real permanent damage.

After a few hours of intense pain, Cyrus began to feel better and was able to walk, though still shaky. The more time passed, the stronger he became.

He told the doctor he'd probably ate uncured pork during dinner the night before. He stood up and told Silas that he felt well enough to go back to his home.

Heather was relieved he did not die and did not confess she'd poisoned him.

***

Hector drove Heather and Cyrus back to their house at a much more leisurely pace with Heather cradling her husband in her arms all the way home.

"I don't know what happened, Heather. I remember our dinner of pork roast but it didn't seem to affect you the way it affected me. You did eat some of the roast as well, didn't you?"

"Yes, I did. I do admit feeling a little unwell afterwards except not to the degree that it affected you. I probably did not have as much," she confessed.

Heather allowed him to think that tainted pork caused his illness and reiterated that she hadn't eaten as much as Cyrus. When they arrived back to the manor, Heather tucked him comfortably in his bed and allowed him to sleep.

She took the opportunity to go to her secret room and read more about the spell she'd put on all the women in town. She read of repercussions and side effects and noted that every time she used the chosen spell conjured to endear her to others she suffered an opposite reaction to the one she loved most dearly. The more she used the spell the greater her husband suffered by her hand from its evil intent.

She'd read that her evil intentions were penance paid for tampering with fate. The side effects dictated that she kill Cyrus however at the moment her inner love for him prevented that unwelcome end.

She reasoned that she could continue to use the spells because her love for him lessened the amount of the poison thus preventing Cyrus' death. Heather had to make sure that she did not use any spells again until he had completely healed and back to his old vivacious self. She felt that the value of the spell's results superseded the importance of her husband suffering minor bouts of sickness and as long as he fully recovered she accepted the risk.

***

There were new people settling in town all the time, and Heather enjoyed being the center of attention amid the townswomen. The positive attention from her neighbors acted like a drug to the new Heather and she coveted the attention of everyone in town including the town's most recent citizens. Though Cyrus had to pay a significant price for Heather's popularity he recovered quickly each time she used the deadly spell. He withstood the poisoning and the pain although the fact that his own body appeared to let him down perplexed him.

Two months later, Heather and Cyrus decided to get together once again with the townspeople.

The War Between the States seemed years away although that didn't stop it from being the main topic of conversation. The men were happy that Cyrus had recovered from his mysterious illness and each of them had their own notions as to why he'd gotten sick. The most recent townsmen appreciated Cyrus as much as his older neighbors.

The women sat down to tea and talked for hours, gushing over Heather's beauty and her worldly mannerisms. The six new ladies of the town did not appear to be influenced by Heather's spell. They did not care for her pompous attitude and couldn't see why the other women seemed mesmerized by her.

The ladies in the original group considered she emanated class, which demanded attention and envy, while the new people saw her as a spoiled woman who had a high opinion of her self.

The manifesting guilt Heather suffered from Cyrus' previous malaise made her decide to try to endure the ugly looks and scorn of the new members of their community without subjecting Cyrus to additional pain. Heather, addicted to the women showering her with respect and adoration, implored her possessed friends to make the new people in town like her. She wanted them to fall in line very badly because she felt awful about her unwilling attacks on her loving husband.

However, after two months, she could not stand it anymore and decided to return to the secret room to conjure the spell again.

Heather targeted the six women with the spell to make them like her and it was as if she had reached the point where she did not care that she had to put Cyrus through even more peril to achieve her desires.

Once conjured, the women fell under her spell. Now the entire female population of the town adored her. Heather had a few weeks of happiness because she had no ill thoughts of harming her husband. She basked in the unanimous love of everyone and her husband did not suffer further for it.

She enjoyed going to town with Cyrus now. They walked arm in arm down the avenue with waves of friendship and envy coming from everyone.

"The people seem friendlier these days, dear," Cyrus noticed.

"That's because they adore you, Cyrus," Heather said.

She guessed many of the salutations were for her because of the spells that she had placed on the people.

They walked to their favorite restaurant and received favored treatment from the staff and proprietor, who even went so far as to offer the couple their dinner gratis.

The number of people who came up to their table and wished them well amazed him. Most of them wanted Heather's attention and that made him proud to be with her.

Cyrus had the respect of men in town, whom he had never met before, for reasons unknown to him.

***

Four years after they moved to Leesburg the threat of imminent war, which worried Cyrus, was no longer mere fodder to give the men something to talk about over cigars and brandy. Sadly, Cyrus saw that his friends had already taken sides. To his mind the battle over states' rights versus federal control had begun years earlier although with words instead of bullets. His friends were not as gentlemanly in their beliefs as they were before and some even raised their voices in defense of the South. There were fewer in favor of the North.

Cyrus stood his ground against slavery; he also philosophized that one union stood much stronger than ten rogue states that made their own federal laws. He heard all the arguments and lamented that some of his friends made plans to venture North or further South to prepare to fight each other and nothing said in the small gatherings changed their decisions.

Heather did not like to discuss the possibility of war and refused to allow Cyrus to mention it in her presence.

The war loomed so Cyrus gave his freed slaves more of his land. He believed they would fare better during the war as landowners. Forty men and women worked on his farm and he gave five acres to each of them. Now they sowed their own fields and raised their children aware they were property owners and an important part of the community and the country. Cyrus believed that if a man owned land he owned his future and he wanted them to determine their future as free men and women.

As before most of the town didn't like what Cyrus had done with regard to his slaves and he didn't care. He was aware his ideals were in the minority in the tiny community however they did not dare fight him on the issue. Cyrus still held the mantle as the richest and most powerful man in town. The people knew it and they did not want to get on his bad side since Cyrus owned all the water rights for many of the outlying farms and they depended on his kind desire to see all the farms prosper as much as his did.

Heather had no such concern with the women in town because they all adored her and agreed with everything she said or suggested. As much as she enjoyed being loved and doted on, it inexplicably irritated her at times. However, as the town expanded she continually made its new citizens like her with magic.

It was as if the magic had a hold over her.

Just as before, the idea of killing Cyrus returned, except this time it suggested a different method to use to murder Cyrus. The idea tortured her because it seemed she needed to kill Cyrus through blood loss. She hated to see her own blood much less Cyrus'. The more she came to love him the greater the desire to kill him ran through her tortured mind. She didn't know how to accomplish the task although the idea of bleeding her husband to death made her cry uncontrollably.

Cyrus saw her in the parlor weeping and walked over to ask her why she hurt so.

"My darling, are you all right? Why are you crying?" he asked.

Heather had to think quickly because she could not tell him about the terrors which pounded at her head. "I just found out that one of my favorite horses died."

Cyrus hugged her and asked her which one had died. She said the first name that came into her muddled mind.

"Chief, the Appaloosa."

"I'm so sorry, sweetheart. There are plenty more to choose from. I promise that you will have the pick of the spring foals. Now, no more tears." Cyrus comforted his grieving wife.

He noted that Heather's sensitive nature had intensified over the years because when they had first moved to the manor the death of her favorite horse would've held no special meaning. She would have just picked another animal without as much as a tear.

Since Heather had told Cyrus that Chief was dead she had to make sure that her lie became reality. As soon as she could she left the house and went to the fields. She spied Chief grazing amid the high plains grass. The horse, upon noticing Heather walking toward him, galloped briskly and greeted her with great joy as he normally did.

She started crying as she hugged her loving horse. She pulled out a sharp knife and stabbed the great animal severing a main artery in his neck. The horse reared up and then stared at Heather as she cried and apologized for what she had done to her trusted steed. He took a few steps back and then fell to the ground. Heather could see her reflection in his eyes. They held the image of his cruel owner.

Chief died seconds later with Heather lying in the field and leaning on her fallen horse. She cried again as the wind blew his high mane around her face. She stood up and apologized to her friend once more and pulled the knife out of him.

As she walked slowly back to the house she realized that she still carried the bloody knife she'd used. She dug a hole quickly and buried it beneath the fertile yet fallow soil.

Heather walked back to the house. Hector met her at the door. "Mr. Black is looking for you. He wants to know where your horse fell so he can have it removed."

Heather pointed to a place in the field where Chief lay and then went straight to her bedroom to cry again as she remembered the look on her favorite horse's face when she betrayed him.

Cyrus ordered all reminders of Chief to be taken from the premises and told the stable people to move his saddle, reins, blanket, and everything once used on Chief before his wife saw them. Cyrus went to the fields with five other men to remove the horse's carcass.

He ruled out an animal attack because he had seen few large predators in his years in Virginia and knew that Chief could handle most of them anyway.

The men heaved and pulled the horse onto the cart in preparation for its burial as Cyrus unknowingly took the same path to the house as Heather had done earlier in the day. He took only a few steps when he looked up and saw Heather run toward him.

"Let me see Chief again before you take him away."

Cyrus stopped her because the men had used a few 'unmentionable' methods to get the massive horse onto the cart and he didn't want her to see her pride and joy in pieces.

She got down on her knees and prayed silently and hoped God and Chief would forgive her for what she had done.

Cyrus told her that he suspected Chief had jumped a fence and a post gouged his neck. "He didn't suffer," he said.

She knew differently and turned away from Cyrus as her guilt overwhelmed her and ran back toward the house. Cyrus ran after her and then stumbled over a groundhog burrow and fell. He hit the ground hard.

He saw that something had impaled him. He bled profusely from a knife wound. Heather, in her haste to hide the evidence of her earlier crime, didn't realize the knife she'd hidden deep within the soil, now protruded from Cyrus' right leg.

He called out to Heather. He saw her look back except she did not see him amidst the tall grass. The blood gushed. He applied pressure on the wound. He called out to Heather again. She followed his voice and then saw him. "Go back to the house and get Hector," he asked. "I need to go to see Silas again."

She stood frozen as she looked at the blood stream through his fingers.

"Quickly, Heather, I don't know if I can stop the bleeding! Where the hell did this knife come from?"

Cyrus ripped his shirt into strips and tied them tightly around his leg. He screamed in agony as he yanked the blade out. The blood kept flowing.

"Hurry. I need to get to a doctor, Heather."

Heather ran toward the house. The evil presence within her told her to slow down until she walked at a snail pace and then stopped suddenly. It was as if she forgot why she ran.

She waited for ten minutes before she turned and looked at the field and then the urgency of her flight came back to her. She wanted to stay. Her love for Cyrus won the battle being played out in her mind and she continued toward the house to get help.

Hector saw her and heard her wild screams for help. He went to meet her and she told him what happened. Hector called the men back to where they had collected Chief's body.

They found Cyrus still lucid however weak but he had managed to stop the bleeding although he lost an enormous amount of blood. The men immediately placed him in the cart and rode with him back to the carriage.

They then drove him to Silas' home and carried him into the doctor's office. The wound proved more serious and he screamed in agony as Silas cauterized the wound.

"You'll have to stay here for a few days. It's just to make sure an infection does not set in."

Cyrus replied, "A few days?"

Silas responded, "Yes, I don't have many medicines to combat a major infection. Those bandages need to be changed often until I see a clear sign that the wound is healing properly. Then you can go home."

Heather drove another team of horses to the doctor's office and almost burst open the doors to see her groggy husband. He reached out his arms to her as she ran toward him.

They embraced and he thanked Heather for saving his life. "Sweetheart, Doc Silas said that I would've been dead in another five minutes. You saved my life!"

The doctor agreed. "You lost almost half the blood in your system. As I said you will need to stay here at least for tonight and I'll check you again tomorrow."

Heather felt overwhelmed with emotion as she saw her husband on the bed white as a sheet, convalescing with his huge bandaged leg propped up. Luckily, Cyrus, full of morphine, felt very little pain.

***

The morphine wore off the next morning and Cyrus moaned. Heather, who had slept on the floor beside his bed at the doctor's office, woke up.

She wanted to ease his pain but had no way to help however, a few minutes later Silas entered the room and injected him with another dose of morphine. Gradually the pain dissipated and Cyrus settled back down and apologized to Heather for waking her up the way he did.

"What are you doing here, my turtledove?" Cyrus asked,

"I couldn't leave you, Cyrus. I had to be with you and I'll not leave here without you," she proclaimed.

The doctor removed the bandages to inspect the wound. He made an assessment of the wound. "I think that you'll be just fine, Cyrus. Your wound is healing nicely for just one day. How's the pain now?"

"It's not as bad as earlier. I think I can walk on it," Cyrus said.

Perplexed and scratching his head the doctor asked the question, which he said, puzzled him. "How the hell did you get a knife wound in the middle of a field?"

"I don't know, doc. I ran after Heather and then I stepped in a groundhog hole and landed on the knife. It stuck straight out of the ground. It went clean through my leg." He looked at Heather. "Sweetheart, you should go home and get some sleep. I know you must be tired because no one could sleep on that cold floor."

"I told you, Cyrus, I'm not leaving here without you."

He looked at the doctor. "Do you have a spare cot for Heather? I know from that look she gave me she will stay regardless of how cold the floor is. If you don't mind could she stay here with me?"

"Of course she can stay. I have a small cot; I'll go get it."

Heather asked, "Is there anything I can get for you? Anything at all?"

Cyrus mulled it over for a minute and then replied, "Well, I'm a little hungry. Could you go to the restaurant and get me something to eat?"

"Sure, sweetheart, I'll be right back."

Heather scurried away as the doctor came back. "Where did she go in such a hurry?"

"Oh, she's off to the restaurant to get me something to eat. She'll be back soon."

The doctor rolled the cot beside Cyrus' bed. "She sure is a fine wife, Cyrus. She's a little skinny for my liking but a fine wife nonetheless. I have to say that when I first met her I didn't quite care for her. I see how she dotes on you. I can see that she genuinely loves you and that's all that really matters, isn't it?"

"She has been getting better in that regard. Since I got sick a few years back, remember? I couldn't fault her as a wife."

"Oh, I remember that. You were sicker than a dog. Did you ever find out what made you ill? If I remember correctly you were very unwell. I remember now - it was the pork. That must have been one very sick hog to cause all that."

The doctor laid out some blankets on the cot.

"Thank God it never happened again after that. I never want to experience that again. It scared the hell out of Heather as well."

"Well, she's a good woman. I told my wife what happened to you and she came over here and talked to Heather. Of course after that my wife went on and on about how well-mannered Heather is while you are laid up here with that injury."

Heather returned an hour later with as much food as she could carry. They ate and laughed now that both of them knew Cyrus would be fine.

His wound healed quickly and he was soon back at the manor. He called the incident with the knife an accident and attributed it mostly to his clumsiness.

Heather vowed to ease off her desire to be well liked because each time she uttered the spell harm came to her precious husband whether by her hand or fates. That hurt her much more than any jealous sneers of the women in town were able to do. Her spells waned and people again started to wonder why they liked her so much. It was as if they all came out of their trance and saw the real Heather once more.

As much as she tried Heather could not change for the better. She didn't need many friends however, from the few she did have, she expected obedience.

***

In 1861, war broke out and it was only a matter of time before its effect was felt at the manor.

Cyrus vowed to protect his land regardless of which side invaded. He gathered up all his workers and allowed them to stay in his home to protect them from the oncoming war, a move that incensed Heather.

She didn't want them in her home living amongst the finery of such an opulent setting. It did not dawn on her that they were there to assist to protect the property. Cyrus bought an arsenal of guns and ammunition and as he planned the defense of his home from the massive living room, Heather had another plan for the manor's defense.

She went to her secret room and opened her book to find a recipe for a potion that she could use to protect the entire property. She perused the book for hours until she found one that might deter soldiers from setting foot on their estate. She procured and added the ingredients, stirred the potion, and said the magic incantation. With the potion made, Heather avoided everyone and left through the back door and crept to the stables.

She hitched up a horse and galloped to where her property ended and then rode along the line. She tipped out the concoction every few yards. Just mere drops of the magical liquid insured that anyone who had never set upon the property before could not do so now. She knew the war was near because she heard gunshots and cannon-fire in the distance.

Heather hurriedly sped around the property's perimeter and completed her task at the fence line up to the manor.

She then went to Cyrus and told him that the soldiers would not put a foot on their land.

Cyrus stood at the window with a gun barrel resting on the sill. "What are you talking about? This damn war has destroyed many of the farms in the area. What makes you think that they won't come here?" he asked

He directed the staff to the windows, their guns at the ready.

"I just know they won't. Now can you get all of these people out of my house?" Heather demanded.

"Heather, I don't know what you're talking about. Don't you hear what's coming our way? Those are gunshots and cannon fire and they are coming from opposite sides of our property. A great battle will be fought right here in our front field."

Heather, who knew that nothing would take place, grumbled, "No, a battle will not happen here. Perhaps a stray bullet here and there but no soldier will set foot on our property. You just wait and see if I'm right."

They saw soldiers from both sides advancing although strangely they stopped when they approached the property line. The same thing occurred on the other side of their property. The two armies fired at each other and never advanced onto their land.

Cyrus looked at Hector. "They're completely out of range! All of their bullets are simply falling in our fields. It's absurd!"

Cyrus stepped out onto his porch and sat on a chair. He watched in amazement as the two armies fought from a distance. He scratched his head and suddenly dropped to his knees as he felt warm blood escaping down his ribs.

He had been shot.

Hector pulled him inside the house to take off his shirt and saw the bullet's entry in his side. Luckily for Cyrus the bullet went right through the fleshy part of his side and out three inches from the entry point.

Heather ran from the house because she'd frantically tried to find a hiding place for the gun that she'd unconsciously used to shoot Cyrus. She hid the gun in the barn before she ran to him.

She had no idea why she'd shot him.

Hector, because he'd been doctor to the now ex-slaves, reassured Heather. "He'll be okay. The bullet passed clean through him."

Once again, Heather got to use the spell she wanted and managed not to kill Cyrus.

Incredibly, Heather realized for the first time that all the attention and adoration in the world meant nothing if she had to see her husband writhing in pain again.

Now she didn't want to visit her secret room. She rationalized her past actions because her love for Cyrus would not allow her to strike a fatal blow to him, even though she had crept ever closer to doing the deed.

She hoped that she would never need the book again as the war, which waged all around them, waned.

It appeared that Abraham Lincoln got his way and all the states flew just one banner. The battlefield did not see the final bullet shot. That final bullet came from a gun in a small theater in Washington DC that felled the great President in 1865.

A sad time for the country, but a happy time for both Heather and Cyrus because not only did they get to keep their massive mansion, it remained intact and not harmed in the least.

Chapter 2
Heather's Revenge

Three years later, Cyrus and Heather sat down to dinner. By this time they were inseparable. Heather had shelved the spells and Cyrus announced that he wanted to put a swimming pool in his backyard.

It would be a first for Virginia.

In England, Cyrus always had a swimming pool, and he wanted one on his estate. Heather loved the idea because she could cool off in the hot summer months and still have her parties. In the year 1868, with the Civil War long over, Cyrus and Heather experienced their happiest times as man and wife even though Heather was forty-five years old, and Cyrus was fifty-five. They never had children, due to an illness of Heather's, however that didn't make Cyrus less of a loving husband.

They had lived through it all, and now that the war had ended, they concentrated on more trivial things, like swimming pools and saunas. Although it appeared to Cyrus that there were some factions in the South that still fought against the fact that slaves had to be freed, life continued on as usual for the aging couple. The workers dug up the back yard and placed the pool under the huge sycamores that spread over the manor grounds. Their friends came in droves to see the pool and marvel at how they did it.

They all soaked in it, splashed around, and eventually wanted one of their own. The builders whom Cyrus hired had already returned to England, and they did not want to come back across the Atlantic for anyone except Cyrus. It thrilled Heather that she had the only pool in the state.

Her friends gossiped about how Heather picked and chose who she allowed to come over to use it. None of the younger neighbors were on the guest list and they wondered whether Heather feared they'd spend too much time flaunting themselves in front of Cyrus.

***

Even four years later, at the age of sixty, he still had all the appeal of a much younger man although Heather had not aged as well and perhaps the years of holding her secrets within her had caused worry lines across her brow.

Cyrus did not care that Heather showed her age, and even though he allowed the women to flirt, he still loved his wife completely and never considered leaving her for another woman.

He told Heather many times his views on the matter yet nothing he said made her believe him. Heather needed to be sure so she visited her secret room again and wiped many years of dust off the old book. She opened it to find a spell that would insure Cyrus always remained by her side.

She assumed that with any spell she conjured Cyrus would bear the brunt of the repercussions and needed to suffer a near fatal although survivable accident to satisfy her vanity. Heather did not feel bad because he'd survived so many close encounters with death; she felt that he had one more brush with mortality in him.

Heather searched her book to find the perfect curse, to not only make her young, but to make her cease aging altogether. And she found it. An immortality curse titled: Immortality: The Haunting House Curse. She turned the gilded page to where demonic figures dwelled and evil emboldened the cursed text.

It read:

For whoever should desire what time takes away in the living world, the dark world could make anew and everlasting the wishes of the few who desire to live a forever-flesh life. This journey should not be taken lightly, as consequences will have to be met. Six souls, who are loved deeply, will have to be taken, one in your lifetime and five in future lifetimes. Death will come to you. However, it will not be your end.

A husband, whom you must love without boundaries, will meet his fate by your hand. He would suffer many traumas before death will come to him, each by your doing.

After each event, you will have full recollection of your deeds, and suffer the consequences of that knowledge. Suffering is the dark world's salvation and with each event, the soul grows stronger, thus making it more valuable to us. Love cannot stop you from harming those whom you adore. Thoughts implanted will assist you in this pursuit. If, by the fifth attempt, you fail to kill your victim, or those after you fail, this prophecy will cease to hold. A relic must be taken from those whom you slay and be delivered to the place that houses the book and held over this page and allowed to drip its blood among these words.

Then you will form it into an object within a great room of the chosen home, until all six relics are retrieved, as it is necessary to perform a final curse. The true form of the hidden relic will not be observed, but will be displayed for all to see as an object one would normally see. The first relic being supplied in your lifetime, and the other five relics to be delivered by subsequent owners of the designated house in future lifetimes. The relics will supply the basis for the prophecy. Then, you will die and become a spirit with great power in the manor. Your victim's spirit will also haunt these halls. The spirit of your husband and subsequent future husbands will want to be at peace; however you must never allow that to happen, as your curse will dissolve, as well as your spirit, should they achieve their desired destination. Should the relic be reunited with its former master, your quest will take you longer to achieve. Should all six relics return to their respective spirits' resting place, you will dwell among the dead, and damnation will haunt you forever. The captured spirits will obey you, but they are not to be trusted.

You will curse future inhabitants to follow what you have done and take the life of the one most dear. They will bear your name and heed your commands unknowingly, but dutifully. When the six relics are delivered, and blood from each of them is spilt onto this page, you will be reborn and live normally, with full recollection of your past. You will reach your twenty-fifth year, and remain in that state for an eternity. Say the incantation below and become what you want to become.

She remembered the instances where Cyrus nearly died and wondered if that curse had anything to do with the one she had just read. Heather ignored the curse's warnings and settled on a simpler one, however the previous one intrigued her too much to be set aside.

She didn't really believe all that it said, yet uttered the incantation anyway, thinking it too preposterous to actually happen.

Heather found a simpler spell and used it on Cyrus. It made sure that even if his gaze roamed he would always view her as a goddess and be oblivious to the charms much younger women possessed to entice men away.

The door of the secret room was closed for the last time. At least, she hoped she'd seen the secret room for the last time. Heather also hoped that Cyrus wouldn't be in pain for long.

She spiked his tea and Cyrus again suffered agonizing pain as the poison coursed through his gastric tract, causing profound although non-life threatening damage. She remembered almost getting caught during that last attempt. She recalled the first time she'd placed something in his drink and how bad she felt to see the man she loved in such great pain. Heather realized too late that being nice could make people like her and that she did not need to use spells at all. As she became older she made friends naturally and found she didn't need everyone to like her, or to be around her, as she once had. Now Heather considered it a special night when the manor only had two people in it.

She and Cyrus splashed playfully in the pool, sipping Champagne and kissing under the Virginia moon. They loved soaking in the crystal clear water on a warm evening under the light of millions of shimmering stars. All of a sudden, Cyrus slipped and hit his head on one of the stone slabs on the side of the pool. He fell, unconscious, and sank to the bottom of the clear water.

For reasons unknown to Heather she allowed him to sink to the bottom. She just watched him drift down as a trail of bright red blood dissolved into faint pink, clouding the water.

The sight of her limp, lifeless husband at the bottom of the pool strangely mesmerized her. She struggled out of her trance, dived down to the bottom, and pulled him to the surface. She couldn't lift him completely out of the water but pressed his chest instinctively until she pushed all the water from his lungs and he began breathing on his own.

She placed a towel over the cut on his forehead to stop the bleeding.

He woke up, still in the water, and gasped for breath. Then he saw Heather. She supported him and helped him from the pool. She told him all that had happened, except she left out the part where she delayed rescuing him.

Happy that she did not have to call the doctor this time, Heather realized again that she could use the book to get whatever she wanted, because nothing appeared to kill Cyrus. The near drowning incapacitated him for a bit, but he remained alive and well. The event enhanced their love for each other.

However, Heather's luck, or Cyrus', ran its course.

When she noticed her looks fading, and every time she looked in the mirror, her resolve not to use spells, weakened. She wanted to perform one more spell. She remembered the incantation she'd whispered and wondered if everything that happened recently was because of that.

She wanted to be beautiful again.

Cyrus had withstood many calamities so she believed he could endure one more.

A few weeks later, she conjured up the spell again and magically she saw her wrinkles fade before her eyes. Her face and body firmed up and she couldn't wait to show Cyrus and see his reaction.

She searched for him, calling him throughout the house, but she couldn't find him.

She had an idea he might have gone to visit his foreman, John Brown, at his settlement. Heather, so fascinated by her beauty, found it difficult to pass a mirror. She had to stop and admire her beauty until finally she tore herself away from her reflection to look for Hector and ask him where Cyrus had gone.

He stepped back and said, "My, Misses Black, you look stunning!"

"Thank you, Hector, I feel great. Have you seen my husband?" she asked, while looking over the fields.

"Last I saw him, he was chopping wood out back," Hector replied.

"Chopping wood? Shouldn't you be doing that?" she asked.

"I wanted to, but you know Mr. Black, he likes to get his hands dirty. He's not a man who sits around watching other people toil," he replied.

"Yes, I know. I've been trying to get him to slow down, but he won't. Anyway, we're going to need a few chickens for dinner. Will you catch them and prepare them?" she asked.

"Will do, Misses Black. You want layers or roosters?" He grabbed his small butchering ax.

"Roosters. I'm getting tired of them waking me up too early." She walked out the back door.

She saw Cyrus in the distance, shirtless and sweating badly, but still quartering the logs with single powerful blows. The ax scared her, because she once had the odd idea of slicing Cyrus' arm with one. She hoped that he'd heal quickly when, or if, it happened.

He saw her from a distance and turned to split a final log, then leaned the ax against the stump as he wiped his brow with his shirt. "Hello, Heather. My, you look beautiful. In fact, I've never seen you look so good."

"Thank you, dear. Why don't you let the help do that? That's what we're paying them for."

She helped wipe his brow.

"I know, but I get very few pleasures and I enjoy this. Besides, Hector had other things to do. I can't get over how beautiful you look. What did you do?"

He stacked the splintered wood.

Heather smiled broadly at the compliment and explained, "I did nothing. Perhaps it's the sun. It is a beautiful day. Can we go for a buggy ride along the river?"

"I think we can do that. I have to stack this wood and get cleaned up a little first."

He looked at his dirty calloused hands.

I need to wash...

Before he could finish the muse, he turned around and saw Heather wielding the ax that he had rested beside the stump. She sent it flying into his right arm, nearly cutting it off completely at the shoulder.

He screamed in excruciating pain.

He grabbed the remnant of his arm and turned toward her. "Why did you do that, Heather?"

"I don't know!" she exclaimed.

He winced in agony as the blood shot out in all directions. She threw down the bloody ax and scrambled to assist him in stopping the blood flow, except it did not stop this time.

He lay on the ground while Heather screamed for Hector to come and help him. She certainly didn't want to cut off his arm; after all, the love she felt for him in the past had always stayed her hand. This time those emotions didn't make her stop. She pleaded with him not to die and that she would get help. She ran to the house but Hector had taken the carriage to his home to gather the roosters she'd requested earlier. There was no one to help; she ran back to Cyrus but it didn't make any difference. His breathing labored, Cyrus lay there in the back yard with Heather on her knees crying uncontrollably.

She screamed and cried, "This is not supposed to happen! You're supposed to get better, Cyrus. I'm so sorry, honey. Please wake up! Please, Cyrus, I love you!"

Cyrus did not answer this time. He died in her arms as the blood flow stopped when his seventy-one year old heart ceased beating.

She never looked lovelier however her beauty came at a terrible cost.

Later she discovered that the blood that smeared her new dress never laundered out. From that moment on, all her clothes had a splash of red in them and although it enhanced her beauty it reminded her of her evil deed. The memory of what she'd done could never be erased from her mind; the stain on her dress remained a permanent reminder of what vanity had cost her. The love of her life died and she bore all the responsibility, however she escaped the charge of Cyrus' murder. She told the authorities that Cyrus accidently axed himself somehow, and that she came across Cyrus after she heard his cries for help. At first the authorities appeared skeptical as to how Cyrus could have cut off his own arm and theorized that a gouge in a nearby tree lent credence that the ax may have slipped from his sweaty hand and ricocheted off the tree and into his arm.

***

At sixty-one years old, she was still a stunning beauty. Beauty meant nothing to her now without Cyrus in her life, and her personality changed drastically. She hated everything and everyone, although most of all, she hated herself and because of her self-loathing, lost all of her friends.

The authorities took Cyrus' body away, except they couldn't find his right arm. They searched everywhere but it had vanished. The magistrate asked Heather where she last saw it; she told him it was right next to his body and speculated that maybe a hawk or some other animal took it. The magistrate, satisfied with Heather's assertion, never asked the question again because of how it affected Heather emotionally.

Heather buried Cyrus in the manor's grounds in a park built specifically for his grave. Royals from his native country, as well as hordes of friends from his adopted one, attended his funeral. Conspiracy theories about his lost arm abounded in both countries though Heather knew the exact location of Cyrus' missing limb.

    She took the arm to her secret room and used it to make sure that his spirit would never leave the manor. She held the arm over the page and dripped blood on it and on all the rest of the pages, according to the book's demands. She spied his wedding ring stained with dried blood still on his ring finger where she placed it so many years earlier and shed a few more tears. She couldn't live without a remembrance of her deceased love and tried to remove it. It held firm on his swollen finger. The dripped blood from his arm fulfilled the prophecy of the book. She needed Cyrus around her, and if she couldn't have his mortal self, then she would have his spirit to talk to in her later years.

    She conjured his spirit and Cyrus appeared before her in a pale blue haze. His spirit begged her to release him but she defiantly rejected the request and never allowed him to leave the manor and followed the instructions from the book.

    Cyrus' capture was her final act of selfishness. She took his right arm and hid it in the house to adorn the manor forever until her final spell necessitated its retrieval. Every day she looked at the severed arm hidden in the manor to remind her of Cyrus.

    His trapped spirit did not satisfy her enough although she had a physical token of their time together. A lonely, bitter, old woman, she lived alone in the massive estate because she fired the entire staff, and the fields once filled with tall corn and plentiful peanuts, now stood overgrown with weeds and wildflowers.

    She spent her remaining years conjuring spells to protect the house and to make future inhabitants feel the pain she felt from being alone. She cursed the manor to allow only women with the same name as hers to live there and made sure that her spirit and Cyrus' spirit would haunt them into madness. She didn't realize the elaborate curse had taken hold and directed her very soul.

The future Heather Blacks would be subjected to the same thoughts and their husbands would suffer as Cyrus suffered and experience the exact horrors that the original Heather Black experienced.

Unbelievably, Heather never considered her actions were wrong. In her mind, the people with whom she interacted held the blame because they forced her to create potions and recite spells simply because they could not see her great worth.

Never did she feel that she had to change her attitude toward people. She wanted to manipulate people in her lifetime as well as all the other Heathers who would come after her. She spent years perfecting her spells and incantations for the future inhabitants.

She talked to Cyrus' spirit every day, and he continued to beg her to release him, except she never allowed it. He came to her in hideous forms hoping to convince her, or scare her, into releasing him. However, she stood firmly unafraid of anything the spirit conjured because she knew that she controlled it.

The spirit of Cyrus offered no threats to Heather. She could easily be rid of the spirit however that would also prolong her quest for everlasting life. To free Cyrus' spirit would negate the curse and she did not want to start over again. Heather wanted him around regardless of his efforts to drive her toward madness. To preserve the prophesy she added a curse to all the spirits that dwelled in the manor, including herself, to prevent them from telling future residents where the relic that Heather harvested from Cyrus and future relics were hidden in the great room.

She talked to the spirit as if Cyrus had never died, and it elated her that he existed, albeit in the otherworldly sense. She loved him too much to allow him to leave forever. Although she kept a physical remembrance of Cyrus, along with a spiritual one, neither satisfied her.

Dying was Heather's biggest fear, and she used magic to extend her life as long as possible. Though she was somewhat successful a price always had to be paid. The spells extended her life but made her angrier and more unpredictable; though death was necessary to fulfill her prophesy.

***

Heather died at the ripe old age of 104 years. In her final years she shunned all attempts to help her. Most of the people she knew had long since died and up to her final days she didn't allow people in her home. Even in death she did not release the spirit of Cyrus and took the secrets of the mansion and all of her crimes with her.

She placed one final spell on herself so that she could also come back as a spirit. To do that she removed a finger and performed the same ritual that she performed on Cyrus. She didn't realize it at the time, but the spoken prophesy accounted for her future in the spirit world, so severing her finger proved unnecessary.

The authorities had checked on the old woman weekly, until the week she died, which was the only time that she didn't curse at them and tell them to go away.

What they found gave them cause to run for the police. They entered the mansion and saw her in her bed, in a pool of blood, with a finger missing and a knife clutched tightly in her other hand.

They reckoned she weighed a mere seventy pounds judging by her skeletal appearance. Her long flowing gray hair extended well past her pillow, and her grossly long fingernails clutched her torn, unkempt gown. They noticed her missing finger but never found the digit. A blood trail led the detectives to the living area. The trail stopped as it went upstairs. As they stepped in the blood droplets they believed that she returned to her bedroom after some time had passed.

The police said she'd died not too long before the authorities had entered the house because a few drops of blood still dripped from the nub of the severed finger.

Her mouth and eyes were wide open, which scared even the seasoned officers investigating her death. An eerie feeling overcame everyone as they removed her body from the ornate bed.

Word got around the town that the old woman of the manor had died, and many were sad that their oldest citizen had passed; however, some of the descendants of the people who had known her well, rejoiced.

Their relatives had told them what she put her husband through and how she tried to manipulate them into liking her. Many people of Heather's time always believed that she dabbled in witchcraft and saw her as an evil vixen that caused her husband's death.

None of the town's citizens attended her funereal. They buried her quietly next to Cyrus in a family plot in the garden area of the manor, which she started with the death of her husband.

***

She left a will, written six years prior to her death, which stated:

> Who so wishes to purchase the property, I, of sound mind and body, bequeath that it be theirs without cost or burden. The land, the house, and everything in it, is bequeathed, however a caveat exists. Those who so legally possess my name shall be the only ones to occupy the manor.
> So signed,

Heather Blankenship Black
April 10, 1921

The managers of the estate did not know that only women with the name Heather Black would be allowed to live there. Heather wanted the opulent or the rich to own her manor and only those with the same name, as hers, could be part of her final elaborate scheme to become immortal.

That future Heather Black needed only to walk through the massive doors for the curse to take hold; then an unknown force would make her want the house and cause her to convince her husband to want it as well. The history of the manor could only be told after they decided to dwell in it.

Chapter 3
The Haunting Begins

The manor remained vacant until 1952 when a couple matching the will's requirements arrived at the manor.

It stunned Michael and Heather Black to discover their good fortune when the lawyer informed them that they already owned the beautiful property by virtue of Heather's name. Michael, an ex-actor from California, had made his fortune as a director and producer in Hollywood. Together with his young wife they longed for the country life and wanted an estate far away from the glitz and pressure of Hollywood.

However, before they moved into the home, the lawyer stated that the previous owner had cursed the mansion, and that they might see things that would cause them to reconsider living there. At first neither of them cared about the previous owner or any perceived curse that came with the expansive property. They considered themselves lucky to have walked into a gold mine merely because of Heather's name.

The lawyer told them the whole story, as dictated in the will. The more he read, the more concerned Michael became. He turned to his wife. "Heather, maybe we should look elsewhere."

Heather had a shocked look on her face as she retorted, "Are you serious, Mike? They are giving us five thousand acres and this beautiful mansion for free. We can't walk away from this."

She looked at the lawyer and said, "We'll take it!"

Mike remembered the somber tone of the lawyer's voice as he explained the curse and said, "That's easy for you to say. That woman put her husband through hell and according to legend, she killed him."

"Honey, do you actually believe all that rubbish? She seemed to be deranged and died a bitter old woman. From what the lawyer said, she wrote the will in 1921 and was obviously not only old, but also nuts. I'm not going to pass this up. Besides, I love it here," Heather retorted.

"Maybe you're right. I know that you don't possess the evil that that woman apparently had."

He looked at the lawyer. "Okay, we'll take it."

The lawyer presented them with the proper paperwork, and after both Michael and Heather signed it, the lawyer handed Michael the keys. Together they stood up and shook the lawyer's hand.

They walked out of the lawyer's office and immediately went to the property. The huge mansion stood in various states of disrepair and they knew that they had a big job ahead of them.

Weeds enveloped the property as well as the ancient pool in the back. The foliage inched through the marble tiles and permeated through the ornate stonework and the pool also contained a thick layer of green algae. They found an old barn, which housed antique farming implements that hadn't been moved in decades.

They were thankful that the property came free because they soon realized it needed millions of dollars of work to make the mansion into a livable home. They modernized the heating system, added a newly invented air-conditioning system to some of the smaller rooms, and replaced the old pool with a new more lavish one.

***

They added modern furnishings to complement the antique pieces already in the home. They anticipated moving in immediately except it had to wait until the completion of the renovations. The contractors had a little more work to finish.

In post-war America in 1954 people were happy that the war and rationing had ended. The country came back and the movie industry did its part. However, now Michael lived almost three thousand miles away from the industry he loved.

They had a home in Beverly Hills though the Virginia home proved to be their salvation when they wanted to get away from everything Hollywood. The fact that Heather wanted to give up her career in the entertainment business to stay in the Virginia manor year-round confused Michael. She was a classic beauty with long jet-black hair, the body of a goddess, and a pair of stunning blue eyes. Heather was more than just a pretty face; she possessed the ability to play any role to perfection and garnered high praise from industry elites. Heather used to love the glamour of her profession and that made her husband question her decisions.

"You're not missing California?"

Heather fiddled with her hair before she announced, "I'm not that impressed with California. The people there only talk to me because I'm your wife. I love it here and I want to stay here. You can do what you have to do with regard to your work but I'm retiring from acting."

Michael could not believe he heard Heather actually say that. "You're only twenty-six years old. You want to give up acting at twenty-six?"

"Yes, I'm not that enamored with the profession. The auditions, the twelve-hour filming sessions, the publicity tours… You didn't marry me because of my acting ability, did you?"

Michael, taken aback, conceded, "No, I married you because you're beautiful and fun to be married to. Not to mention our plans to have children and live worry-free."

"I don't want my children to be raised in Hollywood. I want to give them a normal life. You've seen how all those women give their children everything they want and how spoiled they are. I don't want that for our kids."

"Okay. Then I guess I'm going to have to get used to spending a lot of time traveling back and forth. I actually like it here as well. Maybe I can do most of my work here," he theorized.

"Sure you can. When do you suppose we can finally move in? I'm getting a little anxious."

"Oh, I think in a week or so. I went by the property yesterday and the contractors are making great progress. The furniture will arrive tomorrow and I know you want to be there for that."

"Yes, I do. That will be a fun day. Did you get everything I asked for?"

"Yes, all seven hundred thousand dollars-worth! I guess I can't complain about the cost of the furniture considering the property and land were free. Once it all gets set up, then we will be able to live in style."

***

A few weeks later, basic renovations such as indoor plumbing, conduits, and structural reinforcement were completed and ready for the happy couple to finally move into their paradise although, with the exception of ten bedrooms and the main rooms, the manor's other forty bedrooms in the west wing still needed updating. They motored up the newly paved driveway to the huge, covered front steps and decorative double doors.

Michael, being the gentleman, gathered up his bride in his arms and carried her through the doors, then set her down gently on the fine marble floor of the strikingly enormous foyer with a massive crystal chandelier hung majestically twenty feet above them. The spacious foyer matched the size of most homes in the area.

They ran to the living room to see that the stone-covered six-foot fireplace already had a blazing fire licking a few thick logs. They walked upstairs to their bedroom and again, Michael was amazed at the sheer size of it.

The ornate bed frame had come with the house though Michael and Heather had purchased a new mattress. They had a huge, completely renovated, bathroom and dual walk-in closets. The closets appeared to match the size of the foyer. Michael noted it was the only closet that Heather had some space left after all her clothes were in it. The room looked beautiful and was exactly the kind of room that she had always wanted. She hugged Michael and thanked him for what he gave to her.

The first night that they stayed in the house they experienced what the lawyer had warned them about.

Heather and Michael were sound asleep but something made her restless. She opened her eyes and saw a white mist hovering over her. Her hand went through it at first and then she felt something solid. The mist started to move. It transformed into a man with one arm. Frightened, Heather tried to scream however she mustered no sound, so Michael remained asleep. The eerie presence focused on Heather.

The apparition wailed, "Ascend to the fourth vertical and release me."

She sat up, terrified, and slammed her hand into Michael's ribs, which caused him to wake up in pain. "Why the hell did you do that, Heather?"

Heather pointed to the doorway as the ghostly apparition quickly disappeared.

She turned to Michael, and asked excitedly, "It's gone! Did you see it?"

"See what? There's nothing there! You were dreaming. Go back to sleep."

He irritably pulled the covers back over him and turned onto his other side and went back to sleep.

Heather muttered. "I didn't dream it! I swear it!"

Something else, just as strange, happened. Heather seemed to be in a trance. She got up, went over to Michael's side of the bed and stood and stared at him until he woke up. She had a terrible menacing look on her face.

Perhaps unaware that the spirit of Cyrus had haunted Heather moments before the spirit of the original Heather Black now used Heather's body to haunt Michael.

He sat up. "Heather, what's wrong with you? Get back in bed!"

Heather looked at Michael and asked, "Who are you? Why are you here? You don't belong here. I will make you disappear."

"Okay… Honey, I'm Michael, your husband, and I think you're sleepwalking."

"Sleepwalking? I see you and I'm perfectly awake. You will have to leave. My husband sleeps there."

Michael sat up. Heather continued to rant.

"You think I'm joking? You think I'm your precious wife? Think again!"

"Heather, I've got no time for games. I'm tired. I'm going back to bed. You can stay up as long as you like and play these games, but I don't have to. Goodnight!"

Michael covered himself up as he rolled over on his side, leaving his back exposed. Heather balled up her fist and buried it in the small of his back. After the impact he turned to Heather.

She had vanished.

He got out of bed, rubbing his side, and then saw Heather sound asleep on her side of the bed. Confused as to how she got in bed and fell asleep in just one second, Michael nudged her.

She woke up, yawning and stretching. "Why did you wake me up? It's still dark outside."

"You don't remember, but you were sleepwalking and you hit me in my side and my back. You said some very odd things, sweetheart," Michael explained.

"I don't sleepwalk, Mike. Odd things? What odd things?"

"You said that you were not my wife and that I had to leave the house."

"Honey, you're dreaming. What did I look like in your dream?"

Michael thought for a while then said, "You wore your nightclothes. Your hair looked perfect, styled as it always is."

"Well, look at my hair. Do you think this mop is perfectly styled? I mean, I wish I could wake up every morning with perfect hair, but it's not going to happen. You were dreaming, honey."

He realized Heather had made a very good point, and decided it was a dream. Heather lay back down and so did Michael. However, with his dream still vivid in his head and the memory of it, prevented him from getting back to sleep. Heather, on the other hand, drifted to sleep immediately.

***

She woke up the next day to see Michael wide awake and staring at her as she got out of bed and walked to the bathroom.

"What are you looking at?" she asked.

"Do you remember what happened last night?"

"What?"

"You woke me up and said that you saw a ghost. Then I opened my eyes to see you staring at me and then when I turned away you hit me in the back."

"Nonsense! I don't remember any of that. You had to be dreaming. Maybe the bottle and a half of wine you drank yesterday had something to do with it?"

"That's it! It must be that. Did I seem drunk last night?"

"Not completely. I think I drank just as much but I slept like a baby."

The morning sunlight blasted through the bedroom's huge bay windows and forced Michael out of bed as well. He met Heather in the bathroom and apologized for waking her up. A huge bruise had appeared on his back as a reminder of the previous night's adventure.

"What happened to your back, Mike?"

Michael looked in the mirror. "That is what I talked to you about last night. You hit me in the side, too."

She looked at it and giggled, "Mike, look at my hand, it's tiny. I weigh a hundred and five pounds. I couldn't have done that. I'm not that strong."

"Well, I didn't do it and we are the only ones in the house so how do you suppose I got it?" Michael retorted.

"You have a point there. I don't remember hitting you, but obviously, someone, something has done it. If I did it during the night, I apologize."

"No problem, it'll go away soon. It doesn't even hurt. What have you got planned today? I have to write a few scenes on my new screenplay in the den," Michael said.

Heather entered the shower as she replied, "I want to explore the house. There are fifty bedrooms, and I want to see each one of them. I need to make sure the rooms are okay for guests."

"Well, some of them don't have beds yet. I didn't think it necessary to make all the rooms bedrooms. I mean, we have never had more than ten overnight guests and most of our friends are three thousand miles away."

"That's true. I guess you're right but I still want to see all of them. It will probably take most of the day. There are so many. It will be like an adventure."

"Okay, I'll see you a little later, then. I love you."

"I love you too. I hope I find a few antiques in some of the rooms."

"Enjoy yourself. Oh, Heather, I forgot to tell you that I received a telegram from the studio. They said that they had told everyone where we moved to and gave all our friends our address and phone number, so you don't have to."

"That's great. By the way, when are they going to install the telephones upstairs? I'm sure that all the bedrooms need to have telephone wires as well. That's going to cost a lot of money."

"Oh, I know, but perhaps all the rooms won't need telephones. A lot of people will only bother to give a contact number for emergencies. When you go through the house, just write down the rooms you think should be wired."

"Okay, I can do that. I only want phone lines in the furnished rooms and two or three of the suites. Maybe one day we can get electricity and heating to each of them as well."

"One thing at a time, my dear."

Michael walked downstairs as Heather finished her shower.

She dressed and walked to the kitchen and fixed a quick breakfast of cereal and orange juice. She noticed the remnants of bacon and eggs on the skillet and guessed that Michael had already eaten. He'd left a few pieces of bacon in the pan. She smiled. He knew her penchant for fresh bacon.

Once she'd eaten she walked to the den to ask Michael if he was certain he didn't want to join her. He declined. "Got a lot of work to do, Honey."

Heather set out to explore the mansion. She entered every room and saw that most of them were already perfectly furnished with the finest Old World furniture available, though caked with fifty-year-old dust.

Some of the rooms were very large and had their own chamber rooms attached, but just like the bedrooms, they were in desperate need of an upgrade.

Heather had a blueprint of the property and she wrote notes for every room she visited.

There were five massive three-bedroom suites and noted that they would be perfect for their friends who had children. She saw nothing much that needed to be done to the suites, other than phone lines, and a little paint applied to the ceiling and walls.

She checked each room and found that most of the outer rooms were untouched nineteenth-century rooms and needed to be wired for electricity and telephones. To get the mansion up to date was a priority. Heather and Mike were the third set of inhabitants of the famous mansion and it looked in a poor condition.

There was writing on the walls of many of the smaller rooms from the previous mistress of the house confessing her love for her husband, Cyrus. When Heather read the name "Cyrus" it made her pause and wonder why the name seemed to mean something to her. She paused for a few minutes but soon discounted it.

As she ventured deeper into the chasm of rooms she felt as if she were being followed. The vast hallway did not have electricity however it did have empty oil lamps, that hadn't seen a match for decades, on the walls.

She had a flashlight to provide light for the areas where there were no windows. The eeriness of the hallway made her want to turn back many times but the thrill of the search beckoned her to continue. The further away she walked from the living areas, the darker it got, and soon she stood in pitch blackness in an area of the house that had not seen human presence since the early days of the first Heather Black.

Heather looked behind her many times, thinking that someone watched her every move. In the darkness she pointed the flashlight behind her and saw nothing -- then she aimed it straight ahead. A man was directly in front of her.

The spirit of Cyrus confronted her again.

She shrieked, dropped the flashlight and injured her knee as she fell to the floor.

She grabbed the flashlight and shined it on the one-armed mass of opaque flesh-like substance in front of her.

Cyrus Black with his hideous, deteriorating body stood five feet in front of her. Heather crawled to her feet and ran as fast as she could away from Cyrus' rotting, upright corpse. She looked back many times in her haste to get away however the spirit of Cyrus walked as fast as she ran and she could not get away from him. His jaw seemed to be locked open, as if trying to talk, though his utterances were incomprehensible.

He pointed to his missing arm but she didn't care. She just wanted to get away. She ran and ran and up ahead she saw something that made her stop in her tracks and fall again.

An old woman stood in her path.

She raised her flashlight and the light shone on the hideous specter.

Heather looked at the spirit as she struggled to get to her feet. The flashlight's beam flickered in all directions. Scared, she didn't want to shine the light on the spirit in front of her or the one behind her.

"Where are you going, Heather? There's no light at the end of this hallway. No sanctuary! So, have you given any thought on how you're going to do it?" the ghastly spirit asked.

"Do what? I don't know who you are or why you're in my house but I will make sure you are removed!"

The spirit of Heather laughed hard at the scared woman. "Removed? You're going to have me removed? I think that you may have it backward. You see, I'm the original Heather Black and you have to do as I say. You're in my house. This is my house! Now, have you figured out how you're going to do it?"

"Do what, you crazy old bitch?" Heather yelled.

"Why, kill Michael, that's what. You will attempt to kill him five times. I know you harbor thoughts of killing him. I know this because I placed those thoughts in your mind," the spirit replied. A crooked smile seemed to slice her withered face.

Heather snapped, "I love Mike. There is no way I would harm him."

"You keep thinking that. You're reliving my life. The book is making sure of that. One more thing before I leave you; what will you take from Michael's body once you've killed him? I know those things are streaming through the back of your mind as well. You will follow in line, as will all the other Heather Blacks who come after you. You and your husband will join us here eventually. There is nothing that will save Michael's life."

On that piece of ominous news, the spirit disappeared however the hideous form of Cyrus remained behind her. He swiped at the flashlight, sent it crashing into the wall, before it landed on the floor. Its light flickered and went out as the spirit disappeared in a cloud of swirling dust.

Heather, now in total blackness, screamed and cried as she felt her way down the long, dark hall. She did not know if the spirit of Cyrus or the original Heather Black would stop her desperate flight to safety. She ran until it became lighter and able to see clearly again.

Suddenly, thick black smoke filled the corridor. She screamed hysterically. "What is this? Michael! Show me the way out, Michael!" She kept screaming even though she knew Michael would be unlikely to hear her cries from his den.

In the darkness she'd felt the witch of the manor inject her murderous edict into her mind.

I'm afraid Michael can't help you. Perhaps it's better if Michael is not around Heather. I am here to teach you the things you need to know. The essence of darkness is penetrating your spirit and imparting directions to you. You will attempt to kill Michael. He will suffer at your hands and you will remove from him a relic that will haunt you for your remaining days. You will fashion it so only you will know its secret hiding place and he will come back to you as a spirit, like that of my beloved Cyrus. He will haunt all those who enter the manor and I will collect his soul and take it to the dark forces of the book. What's happening to you is far beyond your comprehension. The book of the dark forces cannot be denied. Do you feel its stinging tentacles penetrating your mind? Ah, yes, I can see its effect in your eyes.

The spirit of the original Heather Black laughed heartily while the present Heather Black placed her hands over her ears in anguish.

"Please, make it stop! I love Michael! I can't kill him." Heather pleaded into the darkness as the black smoke entered every pore of her body.

The spirit of Heather, now only a black, smoky face, explained, "Dearie, I'm afraid that's not your decision any more. You're Heather Black and soon the world will speak my name again. I shall live as I once did. I'm becoming younger as the dark forces take from you and give to me. Soon, I shall walk among the living again. Take heart, you will not be the last Heather Black to see these walls and be forced to explore the dark recesses of this manor. I made a pact with the dark forces. My wish is to be alive and beautiful once again so that people will look upon me with favor. Can you understand why I need you to complete your task? Only when I capture all the spirits I need will the book favor me."

Heather yelled defiantly into the smoky face. "I will not kill Michael! I will defeat you!"

"Defeat me? Dearie, I've already won, because right now poisoning Michael is the only thing in your mind. You see I've won."

The spirit dispersed amid the black smoke and dust in the hallway and spoke no more.

Now Cyrus moved toward her.

She ran as fast as she could. The hallway looked empty and free of obstruction and she ran right down the middle of it. However it appeared as if Cyrus became closer to her the more she ran.

In the distance she saw the faint light again and ran toward it. Cyrus caught up with her just as she reached the light. She fell to the floor and skinned her knee again. Then she looked up and saw Cyrus had vanished. A few feet away lay the flashlight, its glow returned. She had no idea how the flashlight got there. She'd run away from it earlier however she grabbed it and then shook it until the light shone brightly again. She saw nothing except hallway. All of a sudden the oil lamp sconces on the walls came on and brightly lit the entire hallway.

There were other things about the hallway that struck her as strange. All the doors to the bedrooms were open, except one.

She thought it odd. Just as she prepared to walk forward one of the doors slammed shut. And then another, and another until all the doors had slammed shut.

She focused on the only door left open.

Perhaps the door will lead to safety, she thought.

It was exactly the same as the other doors however she noticed that this one didn't have a doorknob and the wood felt very cold to the touch.

She backed away from the frigid door and continued running, favoring her injured knee. She finally found her way to the stairway, hastily ran down them and into the great room. She had to find Michael. She remembered where she saw him last, and ran for his den.

She opened the door and saw him at his desk reading some scripts.

"Hi, honey, what are you doing? Didn't you want to explore the house?" he asked.

Heather tried to catch her breath as she explained, "I did! Michael, this house is haunted!" She looked up at the clock on the wall. "My god! I've just spent the last three hours running from dead people!" Her terrified expression faded as if she felt safer being with Michael.

Michael removed his reading glasses. "How could that be? I just talked to you five minutes ago. You just told me that you wanted to explore the house."

Heather looked back to the clock and saw that three hours were erased from it. Heather looked at her husband strangely as she responded to his comment. "What? Michael, I tried to escape from a hallway in the far-west wing of the house for three hours! I saw two ghosts there, a man and a woman, and they spouted strange things about the previous owner. Three hours, Michael! I spent three hours running for my life!"

Michael put his arms around his wife, "Are you sure about the time, darling? You left this den about five minutes before you just came rushing in because I've only read half of the first page on the script that you just gave me."

"Really? Five minutes? Michael, I just experienced an evil presence in the hallway of the section of the house where there are no lights or electricity."

He decided to change the subject completely.

"Heather, I have to go back to LA for a few months. I want you to come with me."

Still confused she said, "Sorry, I can't. I have to get electricity all through this house. I can't let guests stay in those rooms without it. I'll be fine, honey. You go back to LA and get the movie done. I'll stay here and get the house in order."

Heather suspected that Michael didn't believe a word she'd said. Then she reasoned she'd returned safely therefore whatever she believed happened could not have happened. Perhaps it was all a dream.

However, if it is true then perhaps he needs to leave for his own safety, she thought.

Michael said she was obsessed with electricity and telephones but agreed to go. "Okay, a lot of the shoot has already been finalized in pre-production. Maybe filming won't take more than two months. When I get back we can have a house-warming party. Many of our friends want to visit."

"That's why I have to get this house fixed. I want to have the party as well." She paused for a moment as if in contemplation. "Do you want me to bring you some tea?" she asked.

Michael agreed that he would like tea.

Heather walked out of the den and toward the kitchen, still questioning her experience in the hallway, despite Michael's valid argument. Heather couldn't stop thinking about the door that didn't open or close in the hallway. She speculated that it didn't have a doorknob for a reason. Then there was the injury to her knee - that wasn't her imagination.

As she brewed a pot of tea, something strange came over her. She moved slowly as if her mind had been taken over. She stared at the newly brewed tea in her trance-like state although couldn't figure out what to do with it.

She heard a loud snap from behind the kitchen pantry door, which brought her out of her strange transfixion. She investigated where the noise came from, moving a few brooms out of the way, and saw an unlucky mouse in a deadly mousetrap with the slightest trickle of blood coming from its nose. Her screams brought Michael to the kitchen.

"What is it? Why are you shouting?" Michael asked.

"It's a mouse in the mousetrap and it's still moving. Michael, get rid of it, please! I don't want to see it again." She moved away from the pantry door.

Michael picked up the trap and placed the now-dead mouse in the garbage can and then walked back over to Heather. He laughed, at what he said, was her obvious overreaction.

She smiled and playfully slapped him on the arm. "Michael, stop making fun of me. It still twitched even though it was nearly snapped in half."

"Well, he's gone to mouse heaven now, dear. I need to get back to that script, and you're right, it is a good one. You have a great eye for talent. He's a new writer and his writing ability is not the best however the story is phenomenal. I can't wait to get to LA to promote it. I'll pitch it to the studio after I get the other movie done. Are you going to be okay?"

"I will be if I don't see another mouse splattered in a mouse trap."

Michael walked toward the cupboard under the sink and found a box of rat poison. "I'll place it carefully around the kitchen and replace the snapping mousetraps now you know what the startling sound means." Michael said he reckoned the sound frightened her more than the actual sight of the dead mouse. He kissed her then walked back to his den and continued with his work.

Heather poured the tea into a large pitcher, went to the cupboard, retrieved a large glass, filled it with ice chips, and poured the tea. She also found the sugar bowl because Michael liked his tea sweetened. She spooned sugar into the glass and stirred it up. To her horror, she realized that she hadn't spooned sugar into the tea, but the rat poison.

She poured it into the sink, threw the glass into the garbage and grabbed another one out of the cupboard. She poured the tea into the glass and something came over her that she couldn't control.

She knew that there were remnants of the rat poison on the spoon yet she couldn't bring herself to rinse it off. She used the tainted spoon to stir sugar into the tea. Heather knew the tea still contained traces of the poison but felt unable to do anything about it.

Michael drank the tea and she made no attempt to stop him. She had just poisoned her loving husband and yet something inside her prevented her from feeling concern for him. She picked up the empty glass and left Michael to finish his work however, had he noticed as she left the room, he would have seen there was a menacing smile on her face.

Heather cleaned and dried the dishes. Michael stumbled into the kitchen. Heather saw that he had a problem walking, and she knew why. This time she showed genuine concern for her ailing husband.

He placed his hand on the counter, bracing himself on the sturdy wood. "I don't know what's wrong with me. I'm very dizzy. Can you call Doctor Gray?"

"Sure I will, honey. Perhaps you should lie down. Here, I'll help you to the bedroom." Heather grabbed his arm and assisted him to the stairs.

"Please, call the doc, honey! I don't think I can make it to the bedroom," he begged. He gasped for air.

Heather dialed the doctor's number, but did it slowly, because she was scared she'd be found out. The love she felt for Michael won and the evil within her succumbed to its powerful force.

She told the doctor about her husband's illness. She also said that Michael had handled rat poison earlier in the day.

"He may have ingested some of it. Please hurry!"

"I'll be there in ten minutes. Do you have ipecac?" the doctor asked.

"Yes, I think we do. Do you want me to give it to him?"

"Yes, just in case. I'm out the door right now."

"Okay, thanks, Doctor Gray."

Just as she hung up the phone, Michael collapsed to the floor, foaming at the mouth. Heather got him to stand and helped him to the bedroom.

By the time she got Michael on the bed, the doorbell rang, and a harried looking Doctor Gray raced in to help Heather get Michael stretched out. He started his examination while Heather looked on.

"This man's definitely been poisoned, Heather! How did you say it happened?"

Heather looked down at her hands and then raised her head. "I told you he placed rat poison around the kitchen because we have a mouse problem here. I think he may have accidentally ingested remnants of the poison from his hands."

"Did you give him the ipecac?"

"No! He collapsed and I forgot."

"Well go get it and a bucket. I hope I'm not too late," Doctor Gray said.

"I'll be right back." Heather ran from the room and soon returned with what the doctor had requested.

He gave Michael the ipecac and it soon took effect. Michael vomited four times before he began to feel better and could talk about his experience.

"I've never felt this way before. Wow, I don't want to feel this way again." He gulped down lots of water and continued to vomit.

The doctor told Heather to keep Michael drinking water to purge all the poison from his system. He left when he felt confident that Michael had started to recover.

Michael fully recovered a few hours later nonetheless still felt nauseated and stayed in bed for the next five hours.

Heather joined Michael in their bed. Gently, she kissed him goodnight and he kissed her back. They both wanted to put the day's events behind them as they settled in to get a good night's sleep.

Heather hoped that by morning she'd be able to understand her temporary psychotic episode. As she waited for sleep she struggled to understand why she'd not only tried to kill her husband but why she didn't feel sorrow that he had suffered such excruciating pain.

Sleep proved difficult for her. She woke up a few times to see Michael sleeping soundly. She rolled over and tried to drift off. Once asleep, she had vivid dreams of the old legends of the storied manor, and about her own paranormal moment in the dark hallway of the mansion. The spirits of past residents woke her up many times throughout the night. During the times when she was able to sleep, something infiltrated her thoughts and tried to guide her toward an unimaginable evil.

***

Michael felt better the next morning and wrote the whole experience off as an accident. His energy level returned and he asked Heather if she knew what had happened. "Do you know how the poison got in my tea? I mean, did you see me accidentally put it in the tea?"

"No, I thought that you may have had some residual powder on your finger and possibly stirred the drink with it. You always do that," she said.

He snapped his fingers. "I bet you're right. I do remember doing that before I drank it," he said.

Heather had offered a reasonable explanation and Michael smiled. She smiled, even though she knew that she'd unconsciously spiked the drink.

***

The next few weeks went by without incident however Michael started seeing things as well. He saw blue glowing silhouettes and they told him that his wife tried to kill him and would do so again. The voice continued until he punched himself in the face to wake him up. He hoped the blows would stop the all too vivid dream but resumed when he fell back asleep.

"She will come to you with a knife. She will remove your hand and you will allow it to happen," the voice repeated.

"Bullshit!" he screamed.

"When it happens you will not have time to ask why because you will have already died and be dwelling with us."

The spirits dissipated in a wisp of blue mist.

Michael woke up and realized that he'd dreamed it all although he felt a welt on his face. That part wasn't a dream. He showered and then went to his den and Heather followed him. He told her exactly what happened to him and paused before he asked her what was on his mind.

"Have you had any thoughts of killing me, Heather?"

"What? Are you serious?"

"I've read up on the house. The authorities thought that is what the first Heather Black did. In my dream, the spirit told me that you intend to kill me. Crazy stuff, huh?"

"It is crazy. I would never harm you. I love you." She kissed him softly on the forehead. "What happened to your face? Your cheek is swollen."

"I don't know," he said. He didn't want to admit that he had hit himself.

Heather turned his head, balled up her fist, and suddenly with great force, struck him in the head. Michael was in a trance-like state and could not move to avoid Heathers blows. He had no expression on his face as Heather hit him again and again. She continually pummeled him for an hour. Her knuckles were cut to the bone. Michael's face became hideously deformed and he lost his front teeth because of all the massive blows. He continued to take the blows until the sheer jarring of his brain made him fall to the floor.

Heather sat on his stomach and continued striking him in his unconscious state. The knuckles on both of Heather's hands were devoid of flesh as she got up off Michael and casually walked to the kitchen. She sat down on a kitchen chair, looked straight ahead without blinking, as if she waited for additional instructions. She suddenly started blinking and looked down at her hands and noticed that they were barely recognizable. She screamed.

"Michael!"

She went back to the den and saw her husband holding his face while trying to get to his feet. "Michael, are you okay?"

"Don't come near me, Heather! I couldn't raise my hands to you before but I swear I'll kick your ass now if you lay a hand on me!" He stumbled behind his desk, holding his hands over his face.

"Did I do all that? Well, look what I did to my hands!" She held out her hands for Michael to see except he looked blank. "What the hell is going on here? I saw my bones protruding through my skin earlier and now they're perfect. Michael, remove your hands. Let me see your face."

"Hell, my hands are the only thing holding my face together. What does my face look like? Why did you hit me?"

"I don't know why I did it. It's as if someone took over my body." She walked over to Michael and gently removed his hands from his face. To her amazement she saw no injuries other than the welt from the night before.

"Your face is fine, Michael."

"What about my teeth?" He opened his mouth wide so she could check.

"They are all there. I think both of us had the same nightmare. I dreamed that I beat you to a pulp and you dreamed the same thing,"

"I don't get what's going on around here. I'm tired and I need to go to bed. I want to forget this day. I wonder if this has anything to do with me poisoning myself a few weeks back."

"Perhaps you're right. It is associated with that. Michael, I don't feel safe here anymore. I think we made a mistake moving here. I want to go back to California tomorrow. Would that be okay with you?"

Michael agreed. "Sure, we can go tomorrow morning. I should make quite a profit on this place with all the renovations we did and the fact that the house and land were free."

"Well, we didn't finish the west wing or parts of the east wing, but for all that we have done, we should do well."

"Curses. Of course we won't make a profit. This place is a gift. And what a gift," Michael said.

They went to bed thinking about what happened.

Michael went straight to sleep although Heather had problems once again. She fell asleep for only short periods of time because she remembered every blow she'd delivered to Michael's head and it terrified her.

Each time she woke up she tried to stop the thoughts however every time she nodded off, the thoughts returned, urging her to do their bidding. Heather woke up at three o'clock in the morning and felt warmth at her side.

The moonlight lit up their bedroom enough to see a bright red liquid permeating her white satin nightgown. She threw off the blankets and saw blood all over them and didn't register that she carried something in her hand.

Once over the shock of finding blood all over she looked at her left hand. She carried a twelve-inch kitchen knife and in her right hand she held a bloody severed left hand. She threw it across the room in horror. The limp, bloody hand landed in the middle of the room. The moonlight shone brightly here and the bright red blood, still oozing from the severed hand, glistened.

She threw the knife away and screamed violently for Michael. He'd vanished however the severed hand she'd tossed across the room appeared to move from its original spot. It inched forward two feet and a trail of blood provided proof it had moved, albeit at a slow crawl. She jumped back onto the bed crying violently and screaming for Michael.

She looked around the room, then at her bloody hands and tried to wipe them clean on the bed linens.

She noticed a dark figure sitting calmly on a chair in the shadowed corner of the bedroom. The figure did not move. She screamed. "Who are you? What did you do with my husband?"

Semi-obscured by the gloom cast by an errant cloud over the bright full moon the figure became familiar once more. She recognized the figure. It was Michael, her loving husband, slumped in the chair. His eyes had an open evil stare fixed on Heather. As she watched, his body slowly slumped over and fell to the floor in the patch of blood where his hand used to be.

The severed hand had now vanished but the trail of blood ended at her bedside. She jumped off the bed, ran to Michael, turned him over and propped him against the chair. His bright blue eyes were wide open as if staring at his now frantic wife. His eyes held no reflection.

Michael had died and she couldn't bring him back.

Horrified, she desperately tried to remember what happened during the night. She had no recollection of the night's activities even though all evidence implied that she had done the deed.

She went back over to the bed, picked up the bloody knife and tried to remember how it came to be in her hand when she woke up. She cried as she stared at her husband's motionless body propped up against the chair, his head hung low though she knew what she needed to do.

She called the police and they came in great haste to the famed manor. She answered the door.

Afterwards it was judged that she had suffered a psychotic event. Heather couldn't remember opening the door, her hands and gown drenched in blood, as she collapsed in the foyer into the arms of a detective.

***

She woke up in hysterics on a hospital bed with her hands and feet tightly bound. The experiences, suffered a few hours earlier, were forgotten until memories slowly trickled back into conscious thought.

The nurse and doctor rushed into the room. The doctor injected a sedative. A few minutes later she calmed down. In a drug-induced stupor she talked incoherently; however the drugs prevented her from causing any harm.

An hour later Heather lay awake and appeared quieter to her doctor so he allowed the police detective to ask her some questions about the death of her husband.

"Be careful how you question Mrs. Black. She is very frail," he said.

"Misses. Black? Hello, I'm Detective Barry Simpkins. I'm here to ask you some questions about what happened three nights ago at your home."

Heather said nothing for a few minutes and as the detective and the doctor stared helplessly at each other, it was she who asked questions. "What happened at my house? I don't remember what happened. Why am I here?"

The detective realized she couldn't remember the night or the morning. He said he hoped she would soon recall events.

"You called us to your house because of an injury your husband had suffered."

Heather cried out as the memory of her husband's bloody death returned to her addled mind. "He's dead! My husband is dead! I don't remember how he died. I remember trying to wake him up, but I couldn't. That's the last thing I remember."

Heather's eyes rolled back into her head and she began laughing uncontrollably. "Yes, I killed him, so what?"

"Mrs. Black, did you just confess to your husband's murder?"

The detective, and the doctor, moved closer to Heather to hear her answer. Her voice changed to that of a much older woman.
A deep, dark, throaty voice emanated from Heather, causing them both to take a few steps back.

"Mrs. Black, are you okay?" the doctor asked. He had a concerned look on his face.

"Yes, I'm Heather, but not the Heather you think. The Heather you're speaking to is helping me come back into the breathing world. I have her now and she will be with me for the rest of her life. She does my bidding. I can kill her whenever I want, but that would set me back a Heather, so I won't kill her. However, you can!" she shouted.

"Why would I kill her? Or you? I don't make those decisions," the detective asked.

"I'm not talking to you. I'm talking to the doctor," she said. "You want to kill her don't you, doctor?"

The doctor, without saying a word, walked over to her bedside and began strangling her. The detective called for help as he rushed over and subdued the doctor.

The other police officers carried him out as he screamed. "I have to kill her! I have to kill her!"

Other medics arrived on the scene to sedate the demented doctor.

"What about you, Detective Simpkins? Do you want to kill her too?" the voice asked.

"No, I don't. Stop! You are planting thoughts in my mind. I don't want to kill this woman." The detective shouted the words as he eased his hand off his gun.

Heather continued to speak. Her expressive face was now disconcertingly blank. "Why not? She killed her husband. I have already confessed. She killed him. I mean I killed him. I planned it years ago and I'll state that in court."

The detective knew the woman he spoke to was no longer the same person. He fired off one more question for Heather.

"Where is your husband's severed hand? We scoured the house and couldn't find it."

It wasn't Michael's Heather who answered.

"That is the question, Detective Simpkins. You'll never find it because the house absorbed it. It will never be found, but I know where it is, as well as other artifacts. I'm collecting them. I've made a vow and by the time I achieve my goal, you'll be long dead. Two down, four to go," she said. An eerie smile lit her face.

The detective called for yet another medic because Heather's deranged mind concerned him. After a sedative was injected into her arm she drifted to sleep. However, her blue eyes remained wide open and fixed on the detective. Concerned she had died the doctor checked her pulse and waved his hands in front of her eyes. Her lashes moved slightly interrupting the blank stare.

He gently closed her eyes.

"She's just sleeping."

However, as they looked back at Heather, her eyes were again disconcertingly wide open. Heather's mind had not been invaded by the old witch of the manor, but suffered from dementia brought on by countless attacks on her mind at the manor. She just recounted what the witch put in her head prior to her leaving the mansion and it stayed there. She suffered a real psychotic event without the witch's invasion into her addled mind.

***

They interred Michael in the manor's grounds just a year after he and Heather moved in. He was placed in the same area as the original Heather and Cyrus Black. Heather did not attend his service because she stood as the prime suspect for his death and was still sedated in the hospital.

The authorities never located Michael's severed hand and Heather offered no further information about it. Eventually, the court ruled Heather to be criminally insane and sentenced her to spend the remainder of her days in a psychiatric hospital.

She was never to be seen or heard from again.

She died in 1995, forty years after Michael's death, at the age of sixty-nine, and even though it outraged the public, the authorities buried her next to her husband on the grounds of the now neglected mansion.

Chapter 4
David Challenges His Fate

Heather's claim to the manor ceased with her death.

The property and all its curses were left to Michael's younger brother, Paul, a widower with a young son.

Paul never moved into the manor because the lawyers disputed the inheritance although he continued to maintain the grounds 'just in case'. Finally he took the matter to court and to his surprise won the long battle to allow his son, David and his now fiancée, Maggie Brockton to take ownership.

Even his lawyer showed surprise. "Never thought you had a cat in hells chance," he said. "Those deeds were very explicit. You want me to investigate further?"

"No. We've won. Let's not ask the reason why."

As David walked around the spacious grounds he came across the cemetery and saw the four graves of the manor's-predecessors. They were adorned with huge marble monuments. He viewed it as a strange coincidence that both of the wives had identical names but knew that his wife would not follow the pattern because he didn't know anyone named Heather. He and Maggie planned to marry soon.

His father pleaded with him. "Please be careful son, this house has a murderous history."

David replied, "I'm not concerned dad. I really don't believe all those legends surrounding the manor."

His father rubbed his chin. "Legends? History is history and the time is marked by those graves."

"Dad, I wonder if I can have those graves removed."

"No, they are protected by the original will. Money has been placed in a trust to take care of the graves and additional graves to be added later."

"So I can be buried there?"

"I don't see why not. However you have a lot of living to do before that happens. Have you chosen a college yet?"

David responded, "Not yet. There are so many to choose from. I will narrow it down soon."

"Okay, but I don't want you to completely discount the manor's history."

"I don't believe all those silly stories. There's always an explanation for everything."

David discovered that four million dollars in cash was included in the trust.

This had been money unused by the previous Heather Black. As she'd been in a mental institution most of her life with no kin to inherit any monies, the authorities deemed, stayed with the house.

His father knew about the money but explained he'd not disclosed the information until he felt David could handle his sudden wealth. As Paul wanted David's wedding to Maggie to be the first event held at the manor the money was given as a wedding gift to the happy couple.

David and Maggie moved into the manor a few weeks after he took ownership and her immediate thoughts gravitated towards redecorating the house.

"I want to put my own stamp on the manor," she said. "And of course I'll consult you as well." She added the latter almost as an afterthought.

While they unpacked David cautioned her about spending too much. "We need to be careful, Maggie. The manor is so large we don't have enough money to redo everything. We have to live off the capital. The furnishings are all very old, but they are in great shape and I think we should keep them."

"Oh, I agree, these things are priceless. But we have to at least spend some money to add electricity to all the rooms. We can sell some of the antiques to supplement the costs. The lawyer told me that the entire west wing has not changed in over a hundred and forty years. We can't have guests stay in those rooms as they are."

He laughed. "Do you think that we have that many friends?"

"No, not that many perhaps but I still want it done."

"Yes, I agree, but let's do that first and see where we stand. I still have to find out what the taxes will be on this place."

"Honey, your father said all the taxes have been paid and fixing this up will be paid out of the trust. We will never get a bill for renovations. You are a worrier!"

Arrangements were made to have electricians come to the house and assess what needed to be done in the far west wing of the mansion. The next day, Eduardo Perez, owner of Perez Construction Consultants, and two of his apprentices showed up. There were a total of fifty bedrooms in the mansion however forty of them had never been lived in. Those forty rooms were still locked in their original time frame with oil lamps and very old wallpapered walls. A few suites even had chamber rooms with their original ornate pots and washbasins. There were no bathrooms in the entire west wing. Eduardo and his crew spent three days assessing the house.

Eduardo said, "This is not going to be cheap. After going over everything you want us to do, it's going to cost about two million dollars."

David said, "You're right that's not cheap but it has to be done."

"When we get done this place will be completely wired on the east and west wing."

Eduardo looked over his paperwork and explained his estimate. "This will be a big job, Mr. Black. We were able to get in all the rooms—except one. I looked over the plans of the house and there's supposed to be a room right here." He pointed to a room on the drawing.

Eduardo continued, "Peculiar thing though, there's no door knob on the door, or hinges. We tried to get into it, but we couldn't without damaging the door."

David said, "Okay, we'll just forget about that one then. After all, fifty rooms? I told my wife I didn't think we had that many friends."

The contractor agreed with David's suggestion. "There is something else I should mention," he added.

"What's that?" David asked.

Eduardo organized his paperwork again and paused. "The guys told me that they heard voices of a woman. I know what you're thinking and I didn't believe it either but when I investigated, I heard it too."

"What did the voice say?" David forced his lips into a tight smile to keep from laughing.

"Mostly, it told us to get out. Then I heard a man's voice say, 'Ascend to something or another.' It was only said once. Needless to say, my crew is a little freaked out."

"Are you trying to tell me my house is haunted?"

"No, I'm not. I'm just telling you what we heard. Maybe just creaking joints or age. I'm just saying that if you contract us to do the work, we'll only be able to work in the daytime. My guys are very superstitious and don't want any surprises."

David now queried the estimate. "You boosted the price because of this so-called haunting?"

Eduardo slammed the paperwork onto the table. "Listen, I'm a reputable electrician and I'm very good at what I do! I would never pad an estimate!"

"Okay, okay. Calm down. I believe you. When can you start and how long do you think it will take to get the job done?"

Eduardo took a breath. "We can start tomorrow and it should take about three to five months. However, I'm warning you, if I feel my guys are in some sort of unknown danger, I will pull them out and void our contract. Do we have a deal?"

"Okay, it's a deal. Do me a favor, if something strange does happen, tell me before you pull them out. I want to hear these 'voices'."

"I can abide by that. We'll get started tomorrow morning. Is that okay?"

David shook his hand. "That will be perfect, thanks."

Afterwards David went to the pool to tell Maggie that the crew would start work the next morning.

Maggie blocked the bright sunshine with her hand and asked, "Did you give him the key to the wing?"

"Dammit, I forgot! I'll unlock it now and then give it to him tomorrow morning."

"Good. I don't want to be awakened that early by a knock on the door and all the clanging and noise."

"Noise? They're going to be a mile away from us. Well, maybe not a mile, but the west wing is a long way from our bedroom. Trust me, you won't even know they're here working on the house."

***

The next morning, David looked out and saw three trucks parked in the driveway.

Maggie said, "We are finally going to get those rooms fixed up. I can't wait to buy the furniture for the rooms"

David said, "More furniture equals more money!"

"Yes, I know but we have it!"

"I'll be right back."

David walked to where the trucks were parked.

He didn't see any workers but assumed they were working somewhere else on the property so placed the key on the front seat and clipped a note on the windshield of the biggest truck.

David and Maggie had things to do the entire day. Maggie had to go to the wedding planner and David went to the golf course with a few buddies. Maggie returned first and David finished his golf a few hours later. He saw Maggie typing away on the computer.

"I see the contractors are still working. Have you seen any of them or heard any noise?"

Maggie smiled at David's sarcastic remark. "No, I haven't. They have been very quiet. It's a good thing, too, because I didn't need to hear it today. This wedding is getting on my nerves a little."

"It will be fine, sweetie. Stop worrying! It'll be great."

"Easy for you to say. You've been off golfing all day. I met with the wedding planner, the flower shop, and when I went to try on my dress, the woman messed it up! So now I have to go and get it resized."

"Resized? Are you putting on a little weight, honey?"

Maggie stared at David. "No! That's not it! Do you think I'm fat or something?"

David laughed. "You must be joking. What do you weigh, about one hundred ten pounds?"

She stopped ranting and smiled as if aware David was joking. "I weigh one hundred seven pounds, and it had to be resized because she made the dress too big."

David hugged her. "I'm sorry, sweetheart. I just wanted you to smile. You know I can't resist that pretty smile of yours. Hey, why don't we forget about all this and take a swim. It's going to be a nice night for it."

Maggie logged off of her computer and started undressing right there in the den. As she left the room, she threw her last bit of clothing in the hallway. "I'll meet you at the pool."

David followed her lead and, quickly disrobed.

Because the evening was nice and warm, David and Maggie sat by the pool. A slight breeze made the night a one to remember. They swam and talked all night, made love under the stars and then settled into their deck chairs to sleep as if they didn't have a care in the world.

***

The next morning Maggie went to make their breakfast. When she looked out the window she saw the contractors' trucks in the distance. "David, the contractors are here," she yelled out.

He peered out the window and said, "Wow, he told me they were the best. It's so great to actually get workers who do what they said they were going to do. I'll have to visit the west wing to see how much progress they've made so far."

Maggie said, "Oh, I want to go too. I want to make sure that they put enough outlets in the rooms."

David agreed, "Sure honey."

Maggie said, "I just realized something, we need to put bathrooms in as well, to replace the chamber rooms."

David smiled. "Yes, we don't want our guests to have to come all the way downstairs just to take a shower and besides we don't have someone to come in and empty all the chamber pots."

"Chamber pots? No way! It's the 1990's David. Those rooms need full bathrooms."

David shook his head. "I knew you were going to get to that sooner or later so I've already decided to add six or seven of them after the electricians complete their work."

"Six or seven? David, there are forty bedrooms that need to be renovated. We are going to need more than that," she stated as she placed his breakfast in front of him.

"That will cost a fortune. I know some of the rooms are big enough to equip them with a bathroom, but that will be stretching our reserves. The electricity alone is going to cost at least two million dollars, or more," said David.

"Honey, it's okay, I'll ask my daddy to put them in. He asked me what I wanted for a wedding present, well, now he'll know I want bathrooms installed, one for each bedroom," Maggie stubbornly stated.

David asked, "Does he have that much money handy? I mean, I know he's rich, but is it going to make him sell some of his stock?"

"Oh, he's got that much just hidden in his house. Twenty-seven bathrooms will be nothing for him. I'll ask him next week, okay?"

"It's okay with me if it's okay with him, but I hope he's got a few million dollars that he doesn't want anymore, because it will be expensive," he confirmed.

***

A few weeks went by and neither David nor Maggie had visited the west wing but every so often Eduardo gave him an update as to their progress. David told her that they would be there for at least four months and to plan a celebration after the completion of the work.

"Let's make it a two-day affair to allow our friends to explore the property," she enthused.

David read a book as they lay in the bed and Maggie typed on her computer.

Suddenly he closed his book. "Oh, damn, I forgot to move the car into the garage. I parked it in the rear driveway."

Maggie kept on typing. "Do it tomorrow, David. It'll be fine."

"I just had it polished and it's supposed to rain tonight. I'll be right back."

"Honey, take the flashlight. That back driveway light is out. Oh, and while you're out, could you move mine into the garage as well?" she asked.

"Sure, give me your keys."

She threw her keys at him and he caught them easily. "Nice catch," she said as she typed on her keyboard.

David put on his robe and left the bedroom.

He drove Maggie's car into the spacious ten-car garage and then walked to the back of the property to put his away. A few sprinkles started to fall when he arrived at his car but his brand new Mercedes getting wet changed to a secondary concern. He saw the electricians' trucks still parked in front of the west wing. He shined his flashlight on his watch to confirm the time. It was eleven thirty five. Then he realized something else — the trucks had not moved in weeks. They remained parked in exactly the same spots.

The increasingly heavy rain pelted him as he walked slowly toward the trucks.

The now faded note that he'd clipped to the windshield weeks earlier flapped in the pre-storm breeze. Inside the truck the key to the west wing still rested on the front seat. He walked over to the west wing and shined his flashlight into one of the windows. There were no lights or movement. Nothing.

"Shit, something's very wrong here," he muttered.

Soaking wet, with rainwater dripping from his hair, he burst into the bedroom. "Maggie, call the police! Something is very wrong! The contractors' trucks are still in the driveway."

"They must be working late. It's only 11:45. Why are you so upset?"

"Maggie, you don't understand, it looks as if the trucks haven't been moved in weeks. I placed a note on the windshield and put the key to the wing on the front seat, and they are exactly where I put them, a few weeks ago."

The look of horror on David's face frightened Maggie. "Do you think that they are staying in the bedrooms to get them done faster?" She struggled to find a reason why the trucks had not been moved.

"No, the owner said they would never do that. Plus, they have wives and kids, Maggie. Why would they stay in rooms that have no electricity and no bathrooms? And besides all that, I swear they haven't removed any of their tools or supplies from their trucks. It's been weeks!"

"Oh my God, I hope they're okay! I'll phone the police! Get out of those wet clothes and then we'll find out what's happened."

The on-duty desk sergeant, Terry Moore, who answered Maggie's distressed call, said, "We'll be there as soon as we can."

Maggie and David were at the door, with flashlights, when the police arrived forty-five minutes later. The torrential rain came down hard as they saw the familiar blue lights pull up. They directed them to the rear driveway where the trucks were parked. David and Maggie followed and met them there.

Sgt. Moore and his two officers arrived with their collars drawn up covering their necks but that didn't protect them from the razor sharp drops stinging their exposed skin, which dripped down their backs. David handed Sgt. Moore the key to the west wing.

"Thanks, Mr. Black, we'll go in and investigate. Where were they supposed to be working? Could you tell me a little about the wing?"

"There are two floors with twelve bedrooms on each floor. The rooms are numbered. The electricians arrived several weeks ago but we didn't see any of them.

We had a few reports from the boss, Eduardo Perez, but they've stopped now. We don't even know how many workers the owner of the firm has with him, or if he is part of the crew. All I know is that those three trucks haven't moved in weeks. The men have to be in there somewhere," David explained, as he pointed to the west wing.

The officers investigated the three trucks first and two of the officers, Ken Knies, and Joe Reynolds, reported back to Sgt. Moore.

"Mr. Black is right. These trucks haven't been moved for a while. There is at least two weeks' worth of dust on the steering wheels and the tires. Also, the trucks are still filled with supplies, and even their tools appear to be here."

"Thanks, Ken. You and Joe can start with the upper floor. Remember, I don't want you guys to split up. I'll call headquarters to get a few more officers down here."

Officer Knies said, "I don't think that's necessary, Sergeant. Joe and I got this."

"I know you do, but you don't know what you're dealing with. Those men are missing and presumed to be in there. How do you know that a murderer is not lurking inside? I'd feel better having a few more guys here," Sgt. Moore replied. "You guys got your flashlights?"

Officer Knies answered, "Yes, we do. I also have my night vision visor. We'll find the workers."

Sgt. Moore noted that Ken possessed equipment that he had never seen before. "Night vision visor? Is that police issue?"

"No, sir, I got it at an Army surplus store and have been waiting for an opportunity to use them. I also brought my AR-15 and my Glock, just in case," Ken replied.

"When we get back to the station, remind me to have a sit-down with you to discuss why the hell you're carrying an arsenal," Sgt. Moore said.

"Because you never know, Sergeant," Ken explained.

Sgt. Moore smiled. "Okay, there's the country you're going to invade." He pointed to the house. "Call me on the radio when you get to the second floor and I want you to call me when you finish clearing every room. The owner said the rooms are numbered."

"Roger that, Sergeant," Ken said. He looked at Joe. "Let's go, Joe. You take the rear."

Joe said, "Okay, you just keep that rifle pointed away from me."

The officers made their way to the door. David followed along with his flashlight when the officers stopped him. "Where are you going?" They asked the question in unison.

"I'm going in with you."

"Beg your pardon, Mr. Black, but we don't know what's in there. My men are trained to enter buildings where a possible crime may have occurred. Allow them to clear the building first and then you and I will enter," Sgt. Moore said.

"Hey, it's my house. I want to go in!" David demanded.

Maggie spoke up. "David, let them do their job. I don't want you going in there if it's not safe. Please?"

He listened to Maggie's plea and relented. "Okay, Maggie. I'll wait."

Chapter 5
Heather Shows Her Strength

Joe and Ken entered the building. Joe immediately called Sgt. Moore on the radio. "Sergeant, we're on the stairs. It's very dark in here, and I can barely see my hand in front of me. Ken's got his night vision on so he may be able to see a little better than I can."

Ken responded, "Yes, I can see everything. I can tell this place hasn't been lived in for quite a while."

The officers made it safely to the second floor. Each step on the hardwood floor echoed throughout the broad, dark hallway. A lone rat startled the two trained officers as it scurried down the hallway. They came to the first set of doors opposite each other and decided to clear one room at a time. They kicked open the door and it blew up a cloud of dust. Their flashlights trained on everything in the room.

Joe saw a laser beam darting everywhere. "Really, Ken? A laser?" Joe shook his head.

They saw another door and positioned themselves in front and to the side of it, pushed it open quickly, only to see an empty closet. They left the room and were then startled to see that the doors for each room opened out in the hallway.

"What the hell, Joe? These weren't open when we went into that first room! I've never seen door open outward like that."

"I know! Kind of eerie, eh? Scared?"

"Hell no! I'm not afraid of anything! I'm ready to tackle the second room!"

Joe radioed in. "Sergeant, room 101 is clear. We're going to room 102 but the weirdest thing just happened; all the doors just opened by themselves."

The two officers heard a strange sound at the other end of the darkened hallway.

"Ken, did you hear that? Can you see anything?" Joe asked, nervously.

Ken said, "I got nothing, Joe. It sounded like a door slamming at the end of the hall."

"Sergeant, we heard a door close at the end of the hallway, permission to investigate?"

"Negative! Clear the rooms to that point. I don't want any surprises. I want the rooms behind you cleared as you make your way to the end," Moore demanded.

"Roger, sir. I'm leaving Ken at the door and I'll clear the next room."

Joe walked into the room and decided to put a scare into his partner. Ken looked as if he was freaked out by his surroundings.

Joe suddenly screamed bloody murder and hid behind the bed. Ken ran into the room and Joe jumped out from behind the bed. Ken reacted immediately. He dropped his gun and swung his fist at whatever had jumped out at him. The wild punch missed Joe who laughed at his partner now quivering with fear.

Ken was pissed off at his partner's irresponsible joke.

"I could have shot you…you blasted fool."

When Joe saw how much the fright had jolted Ken, he apologized quickly. Ken turned away from his partner but Joe reckoned he was more scared than angry. No one spoke until they walked back into the hallway but it was only to contact the Sergeant.

Joe relayed information to the Sergeant. "Room 102 is clear."

As they slowly and methodically walked to the next set of doors they heard eerie noises that sounded like laughter. Suddenly a door slammed loudly and echoed down the hallway, followed by another one after it.

Ken couldn't see anything. "I hate these cheap goggles," he muttered. He removed his night vision goggles and turn on his flashlight. The eerily quietness of the hallway, paneled with wooden ornate walls and adorned with antique oil-fueled sconces every ten feet, caused a considerable amount of fear in the two men.

They cleared the next set of rooms and moved on. The silence continued as they approached the third set but they entered the rooms and cleared them as well. Ken sweated profusely and it made Joe regret his practical joke.

"Sorry about back there, Ken. I frightened myself!"

Everything changed again. It went from silence to unearthly noises.

"I've still got the heebie jeebies and this doesn't help."

The doors slammed and eerie noises made the job terrifying but they persevered. Then something happened that they didn't expect. Joe glanced behind.

"Ken, didn't we close those doors?" Joe whispered.

All the doors that they had cleared were now wide open. They shined their flashlights on the doors.

"Yes, we did. I remember doing it," Ken acknowledged. His flashlight cut into the darkness behind them.

"Then why are they open now?"

"I don't know. Joe, I feel we're being watched, but not from afar. I feel as if something is walking with us."

"There's no one around us, Ken. Maybe the wind blew them open."

"Wind? Do you see an open window anywhere? There is no wind, Joe. There are no windows."

Joe suggested, "Maybe we should go back to the rooms and check them out again."

Just then, the sergeant called on the radio. "What's up, guys? Talk to me."

"Sir, we cleared six rooms and closed the doors behind us but now all the doors are wide open. We closed them behind us. I know we did," Joe said.

"Are there any environmental reasons for that?" Moore asked.

"Negative, sir, we're going back to investigate," Joe replied.

"Okay, but be careful, both of you," Sgt. Moore said.

The two officers took one step toward the open doors when all six slammed shut with a bang, loud enough for the sergeant to think that they had fired a shot.

"I heard shots, guys. Are you engaged in gunfire?" The sergeant shouted on the radio. He demanded a response. "What's happened?"

"Negative. The doors slammed shut on their own, Sergeant. All six slammed shut at once. I don't know what the hell is happening!"

Ken tugged at Joe's shirtsleeve. "Joe… Joe, turn around. Look at the hallway."

"Hold on, Sergeant."

Joe turned around and saw an amazing sight. The rest of the doors of the unvisited rooms in the hallway were now wide open. Ken and Joe took a defensive stance as they inched closer to the un-cleared rooms. They could still not see the end of the huge hallway.

"Joe, what should we do?" Ken asked.

"I don't know but I'm getting a bad feeling. There's someone or something in here but I'm not really anxious to see it. Are you?"

"Hell no! I think we're going to need backup. We need to come back here when it's light outside. I can't see shit in here!" Ken whispered.

Joe looked around and said, "Okay, let's backtrack, slowly."

The two officers cleared each room again with military precision as they backed up to the top of the stairs.

Just as they were to go back to the first set of doors, the sergeant called on the radio. "Joe, tell me what's happening," he demanded.

"Sergeant, we have to backtrack. Strange stuff is happening in here that we can't explain," Joe said.

The sergeant heard the fear in the officer's tone. The men had never requested to leave a building before.

"Okay, back away, Joe. You and Ken come on out and we'll assess it further. I've already called for backup."

"Negative, Sergeant. I don't advise entry again until daylight hours because it's pitch black in here. Even with the flashlights, we can't see much, and Ken's night vision visor appears to be defective. I would request a full SWAT team with everyone equipped with night vision. There are no windows in this hallway and when the doors are closed, it's unbelievably dark in here. We can barely see each other."

"Okay, acknowledged. Now, come on out of there."

Ken said, "Will do, Sergeant."

"Well, you heard him, Joe. Let's get the hell out of here."

"Let's clear these last two rooms. Can you see the top of the stairs?" Ken asked.

"Not yet. You take the one on the left and I'll take the right."

"Roger!" Ken whispered.

They cleared the rooms and closed the doors behind them. Ken noted the quietness of the space. "I can hear your heart beat in here, Joe. Let's get going. There's the stairway."

Ken pointed just ahead of them. "Wait, Joe... Do you hear that?"

"Yes, it sounds like something is running toward us. Put your night vision on. Quick!" Joe shouted. He held his revolver out straight, pointed down the darkened hallway.

Ken stopped. "Joe, I heard something else!"

Joe squinted his eyes and tried to look down the darkened hallway. "What?"

"I heard a woman's voice and she screamed, 'Kevin!'"

"Kevin? Were any of the workers named Kevin?" Joe asked.

"Not according to the missing person's report, anyway," Ken said.

Ken put on his night vision visor. "Better than nothing," he mumbled. He pointed his assault rifle, with its laser darting in the darkness, down the hall. Suddenly, he fired multiple shots and screamed out. "It's a goddamn lion! Joe, it's a lion!"

Ken fired five more shots. The animal fell to the ground. He looked up. Two more fully-grown lions growled fiercely and ran full force directly at them. Again he fired his weapon and killed the beasts.

"Ken! Stop firing! What the hell are you doing? Those aren't lions, they're men! They're men! What the hell has gotten into you?"

"Men? Bullshit! I saw them, Joe. I saw three lions barreling toward us! I killed lions, not people! Please, God, tell me that I killed lions."

Joe, with his revolver trained on whatever Ken killed, said, "Well, we can't really tell from here. Let's go."

"Joe? Ken? Are you taking fire?" The sergeant's voice squawked over the radio.

"Stand by, Sergeant. We fired the shots. We're investigating now. We'll get back to you," Joe stated.

"You need me in there, Joe?" the sergeant asked.

Joe replied quickly, "Negative, Sergeant."

Joe and Ken cautiously approached the mounds of flesh still twitching in the center of the hallway.

"Joe, is it a lion? Please, tell me it's a lion!" Ken begged.

"Sorry, according to this nametag, it's Eduardo Perez. Ken, it's one of the missing electricians." Joe placed his gun back in its holster.

Ken dropped his weapon as if he didn't care where it landed and removed his night vision goggles to see the bearded man struggle for breath. Tears flowed as he tried to comfort the man. The man looked at Ken and mumbled three words that confused both Joe and Ken.

"Thank you, son," he murmured. A small trickle of blood dripped out of his mouth and his eyes closed. He died without telling the two officers why he thanked Ken for killing him.

Ken and Joe went to check on the other two men but they were dead as well.

"Ken, are you okay?" Joe asked.

"No, I'm not okay. I just killed three unarmed innocent men. I've never even fired a shot while on the job in ten years."

Joe sensed the hurt and confusion on Ken's face and tried to console him. "Ken, it is dark in here and you didn't know. We'll get through this, I promise you."

"Thanks, Joe. You're a good friend and a good man, but all the friendship in the world can't take away the faces of these men who died by my hand. I veered from protocol, Joe. I fired shots into the darkness and allowed my fear of the situation to cloud my vision. I was sure I saw something else. I will turn myself in to the sergeant when we get out of here."

Joe saw a broken man who made a grievous mistake and knew that he would dwell on it for rest of his life. Joe vowed, regardless of the consequences, to stand by Ken. The man had earned his friendship and whatever the future might hold, Joe would be there. Joe wished there were extenuating circumstances because Ken bled police blue and would never allow Joe to fabricate evidence to make his action appear justified.

Joe called the sergeant on the radio. "Sergeant, the scene has been cleared. The missing contractors have been found and are deceased."

"Deceased? How so? Come out, guys!" the sergeant demanded.

"I shot them, Sergeant. I didn't know who they were. Lions were running at me. I shot them," Ken stated. He spoke slowly and sounded full of sorrow.

"Sergeant, we're on our way out now," Joe informed him.

"Ken, pick up your rifle. Let's go."

Ken did so as he glanced at the dead men. Then, he heard Joe call out.

"Get down here, Ken! I don't know what the hell is going on?"

"What's wrong, Joe?"

"The door, it's gone! The fucking door is gone! It's supposed to be right in front of the staircase!"

Joe and Ken stared at a blank wall. "We are not going back up there. Ken, how many rounds do you have in your rifle?"

"I have about twenty-five, and another thirty-bullet clip, why?"

"Blast that wall, Ken. Blast a hole in it so we can get the hell out of here," Joe said.

Ken pointed his rifle at the wall. "Okay, Joe. Get out of the way. I'll put a hole in it."

"What are you talking about Ken? I'm right here behind you. Blast it!"

"Joe, you're right in front of the wall. Move out of the way," Ken pleaded.

"Dammit, Ken! I'm behind you. You're seeing things. Put your night vision glasses on and look behind you."

"Oh, there you are. I must be going nuts because I could swear that you were in front of the wall."

"Look at the wall. Do you see me now?" Joe asked.

"No. Okay, hold your ears because this is going to be loud."

Ken blasted the wall but then something happened that he didn't expect. The wall didn't seem to get the full impact of the bullets. He removed his night vision glasses, only to see Joe lying on the floor with blood gushing from the many holes that he'd just put in him. He'd shot his friend.

He turned around and saw a vision of an old woman cackling and laughing as she dissolved into a mist while talking with Joe's voice. "You don't belong here. I see you."

Ken turned around and emptied his magazine into the mist while he heard laughter emanating from the hallway on the upper floor. He heard the loud bangs of doors opening and closing again. He ignored the sounds and the visions within his mind of the three dead men. Ken gathered his friend up in his arms and leaned him against the wall. Ken removed his hat, placed his hand over Joe's heart and said a small silent prayer. He remembered how his partner of ten years had taught him how to be a fine police officer. He also remembered how the man he loved as a brother had saved his life on two occasions and stayed his hand in countless other stressful situations.

Ken stood up expressionless, replaced his hat on his head, and walked through the newly appeared door. He left Joe where he sat. He didn't question why the door had magically appeared.

Then he saw the sergeant run toward him.

Ken had the fresh blood of his partner on his hands. He held up his hand to stop the sergeant. The man stopped and waited for him to speak.

"I did it, Sergeant. I killed them all. The three contractors, and Joe."

The sergeant looked down at Ken's other hand and saw the blue steel of his Glock. Drops of blood from the barrel pooled onto the ground giving contrast to the thick green grass.

"Sergeant, you and Joe are great men. I don't deserve to live amongst such great men."

Three of Ken's friends and fellow officers, Randall Smith, Daniel Purdy, and Barry Green, joined the two men.

Barry asked, "What the hell happened in there?"

Ken smiled and said, "Barry, don't worry about what happened in there. Worry about what's happening here and now."

Barry looked at Ken strangely. "Here and now?"

"Yes, Barry! Here and now!"

Ken raised his Glock 40, and in the blink of an eye, blasted a bullet through each of their heads. Randall and Daniel died before they hit the ground but the bullet glanced of Barry's skull. Ken fired another shot.

"Courtesy shot, Barry," he said.

Ken raised his weapon to his head. His sergeant, pleaded with him. "Don't do it, son. Lower the weapon. Please. Ken, don't do it!"

Tears of anguish ran down Ken's face. "I'm not doing it, Sergeant. She is…" Ken pulled the trigger, sending a .40-caliber bullet straight through his head.

The sergeant took a few steps back, then asked, "She is? Who's 'she,' Ken?"

Ken didn't answer. He died instantly and left the question unanswered.

Moore called the medical examiner's office and told them that he had five officers down. He gave them the address of the manor. He went to the door and saw Joe slumped against the wall with more than ten bullet holes in him. He forgot about the other three men after he witnessed Ken commit suicide, along with finding Joe dead. He just went over to the step and sat in the rain at the break of dawn, waiting for the backups and the medical examiner to arrive.

He heard static on Ken's radio. He walked back to Ken's body and heard a woman's eerie voice. "They were easy to kill. You will be even easier if you come into my house." The mysterious voice whispered over the radio.

"Who is this?" he demanded.

"This is Heather Black and you have no power over this house."

Let's see how well you do against the entire police force, whoever you are! We'll get you! Mark my words! We'll get you!"

The voice simply said, "Look up!"

The sergeant looked up to the second floor windows of the rooms just before they exploded. The bodies of four men blasted out of the windows with such incredible force that they landed fifty feet away from the building. The sergeant ran to one the mutilated bodies and identified it as Joe. He assumed that the other three men were the electrical contractors.

The sergeant, a veteran of many wars, didn't scare easily but even he with his nerves of steel, backed away and unconsciously bit his lip and stumbled back on his now wobbly legs. He stared forward with glassy eyes and instinctively grabbed his gun from its holster. The other officers saw his hand shake terribly as he tried to get his gun back where it belonged. The Sergeant noted the missing radio on Joe's lapel. He looked up to see the backup officers and the medical examiner's truck rolling up the long driveway, with their sirens and police lights cutting the early morning mist.

He grabbed his radio and repeated his threat. "We will destroy you!"

George Sells, the medical examiner, and his assistants ran with gurneys to the bodies and placed them all into body bags while the sergeant directed the other officers to surround the building.

He took to the radio and said, "We are ready to show you how strong we are. Are you ready?"

The female voice whispered, "Look around. My power is unmatched. All of you living creatures will die. Look around you, I say. Is something missing? Your power, perhaps? You have no idea what real power is."

Then a shrill laugh diminished as she sent the police radio that was once attached to Joe's belt out toward the sergeant. The radio stopped in mid-air and floated directly in front of him. He grabbed it and then threw it toward the house but it returned and floated effortlessly in the morning breeze right in front of him. Fascinated by the dangling radio, he grabbed at it again, then let it go and then stared, as it stayed afloat near his face.

Then the medical examiner ran to him. "Where did the bodies go? We put all of them in body bags, then I called my guys over for a meeting and afterwards when we went to collect the bodies, they'd gone. All eight of them have disappeared!"

The sergeant didn't answer. He saw lights flashing on his squad car dash; an emergency call from headquarters. The medical examiner followed him.

"But where the hell did the bodies go?" The frantic medical examiner repeated.

"Shut up!" The sergeant balled him out. He had no time for the medic's questions. He walked to his car but the medical examiner followed.

"Are you sure your officers didn't remove the bodies from their body bags."

"No, they didn't remove them. Go check again. They have to be there!" the sergeant demanded.

He answered his car radio. "Moore here!"

"Sergeant Moore, there is something very strange happening here. I just received three frantic calls from the wives of those missing contractors at the Black house. Their husbands just appeared in their beds when they woke up this morning. All of them have been shot multiple times."

"Impossible! They're here at the Black manor!"

"No, they are at their homes. I just sent officers out to each location and they acknowledged that they are the missing men. I called the M.E.'s office and they said that they were at your site…. Hold on, I have a new notice coming in. Oh, No Shit! I can't believe this!"

"Believe what? What's happening there?" The sergeant looked down to see all of his other telephone lines were also lit up. "I'm sorry, but I have people waiting on other lines."

"I'm sure you do. I'll let you get to them, but I have to warn you, it's not good news."

He took the first call. He heard hysterical shrieks. "What the hell? Betty?" Then the command officer's voice came through in gasps and sobs.

"I…I…I can't believe it… Ken and Joe are dead!"

"Yes, I know, but how did you know? I haven't called it in yet."

"You didn't have to." The frantic officer screamed over the wire. "We found them at their desks and, dear God, Ken is missing most of his head! That's not the only thing! We looked at the office cameras and it showed how they just appeared instantly!"

"Calm down, Betty. That's not possible. I just saw them here at the Black mansion! Are you sure?"

"Yes, I am. I've known Joe and Ken for ten years. They are here! There's something else, Sergeant, they each had a pen in their hand and wrote a strange note."

"That's also impossible! You've told me Ken has half a head. How could he hold a pen and write anything? What does the note say?"

She read the note. "'Bring on your power. I've shown you mine.' Does this mean anything to you, Sarge?"

The sergeant looked around for the medical examiner and then waved him over to his squad car. "Did you find them?"

The M.E. scratched his head. "No, they are still missing. They are nowhere, and I've checked the entire field. They have simply vanished."

"I think I know where they are. Go to headquarters. They are there!"

"What? That's impossible!"

"I said they are at headquarters. Dammit! Go there now!"

He returned to his call. "Betty, the ME is on his way there. Is the captain there?"

"I can't seem to catch my breath I'm so scared. Yes, I called him and he just arrived," she said.

"Put him on, Betty."

"Terry, what the hell is going on, and why do we have two dead officers sitting at their desks?"

"Frank, I don't know. We've encountered something that can't be explained. I think I've just stumbled upon the answer to the question about whether heaven or hell exists. Never mind - I'll explain when I come in. Right now, I'm leaving this place and pulling all my cops away from here. I also decided to take up your offer for that early retirement. Frank, we can never come back to this place. As I said, I'll explain later. I've got to clean up this area."

"Okay, get here as soon as possible."

Sergeant Moore called three tow trucks to tow the contractors' vehicles back to headquarters, then assembled his officers and told them to slowly leave without sirens or lights, and to meet back at headquarters — his last official act as a police sergeant.

As the cars and tow trucks left the scene he looked at the manor. "You win. I guess there are some mysteries that are not worth solving. I don't know you but I hope hell takes you away."

***

David and Maggie were up most of the night but had no idea of the events that had taken place in the west wing. As soon as the morning sun shone through the bedroom window few hours later they woke up. They wondered what the scene looked like at the west wing so they went to find the sergeant. To their amazement, the police cars, the contractors' trucks, all the officers were gone with nothing to indicate that anything had happened the night before.

Confused, David asked, "What happened here? Where is everyone?"

Maggie looked up at the second floor of the west wing. "I don't know, but look," she said, pointing above her. "Four windows are broken out."

David saw the damage. "I'll call the sergeant."

David went into the garage, grabbed his car-phone and called the police station. "Hello, can I speak to Sergeant Moore?"

"I'm sorry, but Sergeant Moore is no longer here. He retired this morning. Can I direct you to someone else?"

"Yes, this is David Black. He and his officers were here last night investigating three contractors who went missing on my property. What did they find out?"

"Is that the property in between Hemlock and Broadway, the Black manor?"

"Yes, that's my house. Can you tell me what happened here last night?"

"No sir. I'll connect you with the captain."

A few minutes went by and then another man answered the phone. "Hello, this is Captain Frank Bellows. How can I help you?"

"This is David Black. Can you tell me what happened at my home last night? I woke up this morning and the police were gone."

"Ah, yes, Mr. Black, the contractors were found at their homes so we closed up the scene. The trucks were removed this morning," the captain explained.

"They just left the site without telling me anything? I'll have to call Eduardo and see what happened," David said.

"I'm sorry to tell you this, but Misses Perez found him dead this morning. His men are dead, as well. We're investigating it. Mr. Black, we believe their deaths had nothing to do with what happened at your residence."

"They're dead? All of them? That's horrible! Something must have happened here. I mean how did my windows get broken?" David asked.

"I have no information on that. That huge storm that passed through last night could have blasted through them," the captain suggested.

"The wind did all that? Well, I guess it could have happened. Okay, thanks for the information. I guess I'll have to find another contractor. Thanks, Captain Bellows."

David hung up the phone. He saw that the police had placed the key on the doorstep, which irritated him.

Why would they leave a key to their home outside in the open like that? he thought.

David told Maggie what he had found out. "It's all so odd. I got a strange feeling that he was trying to get me off the phone. Every time I asked a question, he tried his damnedest not to answer it."

"Why wouldn't they answer your questions?"

"No clue. Oh, well."

"Where are you going, David?"

"I've got to go see if the broken windows will damage anything inside. You want to come?"

"Yes. I want to see how the rooms look now. I hope there's no damage."

David and Maggie opened the door and noted that the electricians hadn't gotten very far with the work. It was very dark inside the west wing compared with the bright sunshine outside.

They walked in and saw blood splattered on the walls. They walked upstairs. Maggie instantly felt strange. She held tightly onto David's hand. They walked to where they guessed the windows were blown out and opened the doors.

David said, "That's odd. Where are the broken windows? Hell, where are any windows? I'm seeing nothing but old furniture along with the uninstalled light fixtures and electrical components and a lot of dust. I know I saw windows outside and I know we're in the right room. So where are the windows?"

Just as they were about to turn and leave, the door shut behind them. They were in room 101 when they both heard a voice. The man's voice struggled to get his words out to the couple but then there were two voices that delivered an equally strange message.

David heard, "Ascend to the fourth vertical."

However, Maggie heard a completely different voice, with a completely different message. She heard, "Surrounding the master, the con to stay holds my soul."

Scared, she pleaded with David to leave. "David, there's something here. I want to leave. Let's get out of here."

Just as she said that, the door opened and a mysterious wind picked up. Then a completely different and more forceful voice simply screamed at them.

"Get out!"

David and Maggie ran through the whipping wind and flew down the stairs. They both turned around to face the door when it slammed shut, which sent them running toward the larger part of the house.

They entered the foyer and David said, "Maggie, I don't know what happened, but I heard someone say, 'Ascend to the fourth vertical.' I have no clue what that means."

"I also heard a voice but it said something completely different. Honey, maybe we should move out because I don't like being scared. I feel that we're not wanted here and the house is warning us that if we stay, something terrible is going to happen."

"This is our house and we're staying! I don't understand what's happening, but we're staying! I'm not going to let anything beat us out of this house!"

"Look, David, one moment the windows are broken and then they're okay. What the hell is happening here? Honey, what is going on here? I'm frightened," she said. She began to cry.

"What's got me spooked is that the rooms didn't have any windows in them, but when we walk outside and look up, there they are. It'll be okay, sweetheart. There has to be an explanation for all of this."

David put his arms around his scared fiancée.

***

When David and Maggie went to bed that night neither of them found sleep easy. She held on tightly to David and eventually they both nodded off.

Maggie tossed and turned. Her dream started. She opened her eyes, looked up, and saw a vision of an old woman crawling on the ornate twenty-foot-high ceiling. The woman moved slowly across until she looked down, and in a flash, swooped down to two inches from Maggie's face.

"You are not welcome here. You will not be allowed to stay. I will kill you if you stay! Your precious husband will die in this house, by your hand. There will be no more warnings. Go."

Maggie woke up. She gasped for air. David woke up as well and tried to comfort her. Frantic, David asked, "What's wrong, Maggie?"

She had her hand on her throat. "Can't breathe! I can't breathe!"

She got up out of bed and ran toward the living room. David followed her.

"What's wrong, honey? Please tell me!"

"David, I had a bad dream and it took my breath away. Honey, I can't go back up there. There is something about that room. I heard a woman's voice and when I looked up I saw her crawling across the ceiling. She said that I didn't belong in the house and that she would kill me if I didn't leave."

"Maggie, you've just had a bad dream, that's all. Come back to bed, okay?" David pleaded.

Maggie breathed hard. "David, I can't. I just can't."

David hugged her. "Okay, we'll stay here for the night. Honey, you're bleeding!" he said. He pointed to her gown.

She looked at her satin gown and saw blood droplets. "Where did it come from? David, help me find out where the blood came from. Help me."

David started to help her undress. "I am. Maggie, I can't find any place where you'd be bleeding. Are you on your period?"

Maggie, irritated by David's question, said, "No, I'm not! Even if I were, I wouldn't have blood on my chest! It has to be coming from somewhere else."

"Well, I can't find anything. Maybe it was already on your gown."

Maggie said, "Yes! That's it! I remember blood from a hangnail when I did the laundry. It's from an old wound. That's how it happened. I guess I'm being silly about all this. I actually may have had an anxiety attack. That's probably why I lost my breath but I'm fine now. Let's go back to bed. I'm going to change my gown first. I'm sorry about all this."

David realized she was embarrassed by everything. "Okay, don't worry. I'll be waiting for you. Wow, that scared me too. I hope you feel better in the morning."

Maggie returned to bed wearing a new gown. David had already fallen asleep. She nestled next to him and as she went to sleep she vowed to dream of her wedding day. In her mind, she walked down the aisle; then a gentleman stopped her and whispered in her ear.

"Ascend to the fourth vertical."

Maggie immediately woke up and saw the sun shining brightly through the open window. The wind billowed through the linen curtains, creating a snapping sound that woke David. He kissed her good morning but noticed splatters of blood still on her nightgown.

"I changed my gown, David. How could this happen? What is going on here? David, someone or something doesn't want me to be here."

"Nonsense, Maggie, you just forgot to change your gown, that's all," he said.

"No, I changed it, David! This is fresh blood! Look!" Maggie yelled as she touched the droplets and smeared the blood over her gown. "See! The blood hasn't even penetrated the fabric yet. I've got to go to the bathroom and check myself out."

Maggie came back after a few minutes in obvious distress and crying. "I can't clean the blood off me. It won't come off. It's all over my face. My pores are bleeding and I can't get it to stop! I need to see the doctor, David! Oh dear, what's wrong with me?"

David noticed her tears diluted the blood from her ducts into a light pink. "Let's go, quickly. There's blood dripping from your face. Hurry!" he exclaimed. He tried to stop the blood flow.

He and Maggie got in the car and sped off to the hospital and drove faster than he had ever driven. His reaction time and depth perception waned as he struck curbs and spun the tires around sharp turns, jostling Maggie from her seat a few times. He swerved to avoid other cars on the way to the hospital. Maggie frantically tried to stop the blood flow from the pores on her face with a towel but the towel turned bright red and she seemed to be bleeding to death right in front of David.

He took her up in his arms and ran into the hospital. She kept the towel over her face to cover it completely as they ran through the ER doors. A doctor and a nurse met them and immediately placed Maggie on a gurney. Her face was still covered by the blood-soaked towel.

They all ran into the examining bay. When the doctor removed the towel, he took a few steps back, horrified at what he saw. The nurse screamed at the sight of an ax embedded in Maggie's face and blood gushing from the gaping wound.

David, unable able to see what the doctor saw, asked, "What's wrong? What do you see?"

The doctor smiled oddly and said, "Ascend to the fourth vertical. You must help us."

Maggie woke up in a sweat. Her gown clung to her body and her skin felt clammy to the touch. Her side of the bed was drenched but the dampness did not wake up David even though it had soaked to his side of the bed as well.

She let out a scream that sent David almost tumbling to the floor as he woke taking the wet blankets with him. He saw Maggie examine her hands.

She screamed.

"Where did the blood go? I had blood all over me."

David stood up, grabbed Maggie, and hugged her.

"Sweetheart, you had a bad dream. It's okay now. You're fine."

"I have to have a mirror! Please, get me a mirror, David."

David ran to the bathroom to get a mirror. He skidded and nearly fell to the floor a few times in his haste to get back to her. When he returned Maggie was fast asleep. He then realized that she had not had the bloody dream — he had.

Maggie woke up to find David with a broken mirror in his hand. Sweat literally dripped from his body.

"What's wrong, David?"

"Wow, what a nightmare I had."

"What did you dream about? And why do you have that broken mirror?"

"I don't want to tell you. Let's go back to sleep, or, at least you can go back to sleep. I won't be able to for quite a while."

"Come back to bed, dear. You had a bad dream. It'll be okay."

"Too many dreams, dear."

David got back into the bed. The wind blew the curtains away from the window, so he got up to shut it, calming the white curtains. He looked up at the ceiling while Maggie's arm stretched across his chest and uttered, "'Ascend to the Fourth Vertical'."

Startled, Maggie sat up in bed. "What did you say?"

"Ascend to the Fourth Vertical. That's what a doctor told me in my dream. We've heard this phrase so many times. I wonder what it means."

"Oh, my God! I've dreamed the same thing except at our wedding. The exact quote! How can that be?"

David looked at her. "We must be dreaming the same things, but that's impossible. What the hell is happening to us?"

"I don't know, dear, but I can't sleep now. Do you want some tea?"

David, already knowing the history of the house, and tea, said, "No! No tea. I want something a lot stronger. I'm going downstairs to the bar. You want to come?"

"Yes, I think I'll join you. It'll give us a chance to compare our dreams - or should I say nightmares. Something is happening here. Honey, there's something that I haven't told you. I didn't want to upset you, but I've been having very strange dreams since we moved in. I dreamed about the original Heather Black. She wants me out of here. She said that I didn't belong because my name isn't Heather."

"That's about as ridiculous as my dream. In mine, you were bleeding from the pores of your skin and didn't know why until we went to the hospital and the doctor found an ax in your face."

"My God, David! We've got to get out of this house! Now!"

"No. We are not going to allow whatever is in this house to dictate our departure. It's ridiculous, Maggie, to think that the original Heather Black is here, haunting us. I don't care if the previous two tenants had the same name and their husbands died mysteriously, this is my house and it's soon to be yours as well."

Maggie poured another shot of whiskey. She held the bottle towards him. He nodded. "Okay, David. We'll stick it out, but can we at least sleep in a different bedroom? That big one gives me the creeps." She handed the drink to him.

"Thanks. Yes, we can do that, and if spirits invade that room, then we'll just keep moving until we can put up with their haunting and not allow them to scare us."

The joke was weak. They smiled as they made the toast. They drank until both of them passed out on the front porch. David sat on a chair and Maggie lay on the chaise. The balmy weather and the gentle wind drifting by made the environment perfect for sleeping.

In the morning David gently nudged Maggie to wake up but she didn't move. Her head rested on a cushion and her housecoat covered her face. As David moved to pick her up the wind blew her housecoat away. She had a small hatchet buried in her face. She was dead.

"Oh, dear God in heaven! What happened last night?" he screamed. "Maggie! What happened?"

He checked for a pulse but felt none. He stayed in the chair unable to move, as she lay calmly on the chaise. He tried to understand what he saw as his hands shook in terror. He wanted to believe this was still a dream. He did not remember what had happened the night before, after they drank the whiskey. David wandered about the house.

"Did I kill Maggie?" he muttered, and he shivered.

He knew that he didn't do that to her and figured that the house had delivered the blow to Maggie just as his dream had depicted. Dazed and confused he tried desperately to remember the previous night's events.

He walked round and round in nervous circles but then he saw something he could not understand. He stopped. A stream of blood on the fine white marble trickled from under his den door.

As he opened the door he saw a decapitated male body on the floor near his desk its bloody head perched menacingly on the poor man's chest. David moved the desk and what he saw completely horrified him. There were two things he recognized very well: one, a gold-encrusted watch on the dead man's wrist and the other, a previous amputation to the first knuckle on the pinky finger of the man's left hand. David sat on his chair and stared at the dead body.

He began to cry because he didn't see an anonymous murder victim - he saw himself.

Maggie's mother called many times that day and was worried when her calls went unanswered. She phoned the local police department but they refused to go to the Black Manor again after the Ken Knies incident. The police eventually succumbed to threats from Maggie's mother and sent four squad cars to the mansion.

They instantly called for backup when they saw the hatchet buried in Maggie's face on the front porch. After the previous time at the mansion they hesitated to enter the manor and waited for the entire police force to get there.

Ten officers walked through the front doors and after fifteen minutes they noticed the stream of now dried blood coming from the den. They entered the den and saw the decapitated body. They searched as much as they could but stayed far away from the west wing.

Five hours later, they removed the bodies and informed David and Maggie's family. Until the wee hours of the morning, they took photos and compiled evidence about what happened.

However, a brash new detective, Artemus Bocanegra, fresh from Virginia State University reckoned he'd already pieced together what had happened.

Captain Bellows asked, "So, I hear that you know it all?"

Artemus cleared his throat, "Yes, I do. A murder-suicide."

"Really? How do you think his head came off after he killed his girlfriend?" the captain asked.

"No, sir, it's the other way around. I contend that Maggie Black decapitated David Black and then slammed the small ax into her own head."

"That's an interesting theory. Can you prove it?"

"I can't prove everything the evidence suggests but I can prove that she killed her boyfriend. First let me tell you what I can't explain. An uneven floor did not cause the blood to stream from the den. I contend that the woman decapitated him and carried the boyfriend's head out of the den thus creating the stream."

"That confused you? A man is decapitated just inside the room. It's obvious that the blood streamed out of the room. Perhaps the floor is uneven. That stream led us to the body."

"What confused me is not where the stream of blood came from, it's that I can't explain why the woman carried her boyfriend's head upstairs and an hour later walked back down the stairs and placed the head on the boyfriend's chest. Here are the photos of the staircase."

"Yes, I saw them, but why are the footprints just as prominent coming down as going up the stairs? I assumed that a human head would run out of blood to drip before an hour had passed. We noticed drips of blood on the hallway runner carpet all the way to the west wing, but none coming back."

"You're right. The severed head eventually ran out of blood. However, when she got to the top of the stairs, she paused. I don't know why she paused, but she did, because a large swath of carpet about three feet in diameter sopped up a lot of blood dripping from the head.

When she returned, she stepped into the pooled blood that hadn't dried. Hence the footsteps leading down the stairs."

"That's amazing police work, son, but how do you know she did it?"

"That's the easy part. The woman had blood on her bare feet. I had it tested and it matched the boyfriend's blood type. She walked through his blood so she had to be alive after he'd been decapitated."

"Okay, I agree with all that, but does it prove that Maggie actually cut off his head?"

"Factually, without video footage of the act, nothing is definite. Her hands had her blood on them but a thin layer of dried blood matching his blood type lay directly underneath her blood. Also, she had his blood and hair under her fingernails. His hair fused with the dried blood on her hands. The hair came from his head as she carried the head up the stairs."

"So you are saying that she buried the hatchet into her own head?"

"Yes, she did. She didn't need much force to drive the razor sharp ax into her head. Her hands fell perfectly apart on her lap. Plus, we found splinters in her hand that denote she had to swing it with great force to bury it as deeply as she did."

"That's astounding, Artemus! Just an amazing piece of reasoned police work."

"Thank you, sir."

"Hey, as long as it didn't conform to the legend of Heather Black. You see all the murders and deaths associated with this house, had a Heather Black living here. I didn't need another Heather Black dying here."

"Well, sir, there is one more fact that I haven't imparted to you."

"What is that, son?"

"When Maggie turned eighteen, she changed her name from Heather to Margaret because of the legend. So her birth name was Heather Brockton, soon to be Black."

"Shit! Let's keep that out of the report. Dammit! Another Heather Black! That's three!"

The captain made Artemus' theory factual by reporting it as the official cause of death of both the young victims.

***

The somber double funerals for David and Maggie were held a week later. The Black family allowed her to be buried in the family plot next to David.

David's father Paul, respected Maggie's family and because they knew Maggie they were sure a terrible and unexplainable mental crisis had occurred.

After the service they walked with the coffins out of the church and drove them to their final resting place in the family plot on the grounds of the famed estate.

A gentle rain fell, causing the pallbearers to slide as they heaved David's heavy coffin toward his grave. One of the pallbearers slipped on the slick ground and fell, which caused the others to fall like well-dressed dominoes because the remaining pallbearers could not manage the weight of the coffin.

The coffin lid fell open as it hit a rock.

The women shrieked in horror at what they saw.

The men were also shocked to see David's body thrown into the mud. His head was gone. Some women fainted and all the men gasped.

"What the hell?" Paul uttered the question in shock. "I swear to all of you! I saw him in the coffin last night at the church. You all saw him in his coffin today. But it's gone now. How can that be?" He turned to the funeral director. "You dressed him! You embalmed him! You didn't notice that his head was missing?"

Behind him, the pallbearers put David's body back in the coffin and quickly closed the lid.

The funeral director tried to offer an explanation that seemed plausible. "I did have a hard time dressing him and I had to sew his head back on. It's possible it broke loose when the coffin fell because mere thread held his head on his shoulders."

"Okay, where's my son's head, then?" Paul asked.

"The coffin hit that rock pretty hard, so much so that it broke the lid, so perhaps his head fell out of the coffin and is around here somewhere."

They looked for hours amid the now torrential downpour but the searchers had no luck and decided to bury David's headless body beside Maggie. Everyone wanted the funeral over. The people walked slowly away in the mud as the gravediggers filled in his grave, all the while they watched for the missing head amid the piles of dirt.

No one ever spoke of David's missing head, or of David, again.

***

There were many tears shed for David and Maggie, but everyone knew that the curse of the manor never allowed its past inhabitants to live or leave. The few remaining relatives of the past inhabitants of the manor shed tears as well, as they walked among the monuments, but they never offered an opinion as to what really happened for fear that the witch of the manor would haunt them as well.

Paul reported the missing head to the local authorities. The police captain assigned Artemus Bocanegra, the young detective, to find David's head or at least determine what happened to it.

Artemus called the funeral director to come to the police station for an informal interview. He wanted to interview Jonas Hector, the funeral director, because he said he'd closed the coffin for the last time early on the morning of the church services and burial. After exchanging pleasantries he sat down with Artemus.

"You say that you sewed Mr. Black's head on during the embalming process?"

"Yes, sir, I did. The viewing was all last week, and we took the bodies to the church for the services early that

Monday morning. They had the service and we brought the coffins to the manor for burial."

Artemus wrote every word Hector said, trying to piece together what happened. "About what time did you close the coffin?"

"I remember opening the coffin to check on the condition of Mr. Black's body in case the family wanted an open coffin service. I was informed that they did not. That was the last time it was opened, I believe."

"What did you do after you closed it?"

"I left the coffin there, just in front of the lectern, while I settled up with the florist. I remember seeing and talking to an old friend at the church, the pastor."

"What did you talk to the pastor about?"

"The service and what to do with the bodies afterward. Oh, and he told me that the church had been broken into again. He told me that it has been robbed five times in the last month."

"Five times?"

"Yes, he said that he was so disgusted that they installed a videotape system to nab the guy. He thinks it's just one guy involved."

Artemus closed his notebook. "So the church has a surveillance system?"

"That's what I said. The church is ten miles from here!"

They both drove to the church. It cut through time, and red tape, as the funeral director knew the pastor. All three watched the video. Its lens focused on the main aisle. David's coffin stood in state in the center, slightly obscured by the pastor's pulpit. They didn't see the whole coffin but they'd seen what they needed, when the lid to the coffin moved, suddenly opening and then closing quickly.

"There! It moved!" Hector said.

Artemus and the pastor took steps back from the monitor.

"Aren't you scared at what you're seeing?"

Jonas Hector said, "All I know is that Mr. Black's head was stolen."

Artemus asked, "By whom?"

The funeral director looked back at the screen and saw no one there. He rewound the tape and watched it three more times and finally realized what the pastor and Artemus already knew.

"Oh damn! How the hell did that happen? There's no one there!"

Artemus could not logically explain what he saw so he ripped up his notes and said, "This cannot leave this room. I don't ever want to hear of this moment or this controversy again. I do not want to work on this case anymore and if they make me, I'll quit!"

He mentioned his findings to his employer and the police Captain and they all agreed to keep the secret.

Chapter 6
The Haunting Returns

The house stayed vacant until 1997, three years after David and Maggie's horrific deaths. The caretakers maintained the outside but legend and superstition kept workers and lawyers out of the massive manor's interior. During this time Paul, David's father, suffered a heart attack and died suddenly before the mystery of David's missing head was solved. He was buried at the local cemetery beside his wife.

The Black family trustees, David's uncles George and Charles, lawyer Monty Ferris and bank president Dan Burk met to decide what to do with the estate, given its murderously evil history.

George said, "I want the place leveled. There's an evil there that can't be vanquished any other way. My nephew didn't kill his wife-to-be and she didn't kill him. The house did it. I'm convinced of it."

"We can't just level such an expensive property. We don't really know what happened to David and Maggie. I say that we sell it and let someone else deal with its past," Charles said.

"No, we can't tear down a property worth several million dollars. Hell, no! My bank has millions of dollars invested in this property through upkeep and repairs. The land is only worth a few million and we are not about to take a hit. I don't care if Satan himself rises from hell and decides to live there, we are not tearing it down!" Dan said.

George stood up. "I know how much the land is worth but did you know that there is over one hundred million dollar's of art and furnishings in the house? Maybe more; that would certainly lessen your loss."

"How do you know that? Have you been in there recently? Who's going to go in and get it? I'm certainly not. I know the history of that house," George commented.

"No, no one has been in there since my nephew's death. Well, except the cleaning crew two years ago, but I know the art is there because David told me so," Charles said.

"The cleaning crew? Are you serious? You know the story? They cleaned and covered the main rooms' furnishings, cleaned the east wing and the den, then most of them went missing when they started cleaning the west wing. Twenty people went in and only four came out. The others were never found again and the survivors went back to their own countries. We don't know what's in there, and the only ones who do are dead. I still say we demolish it."

Dan said, "My bank will not allow that to happen. It's too much money to lose. Listen maybe we can get the police to go in with us to retrieve the art and furnishings."

George said, "The cops will not go inside regardless of the manpower or firepower. I'm telling you all, there is an evil in there that can't be described. Perhaps our only hope to get rid of it is to tear it down. How many more people have to die?"

Monty looked up from the papers he'd brought regarding the house. "I remember the David Black incident at the manor. I knew Ken Knies. The most gung-ho, hoo-rah, ex-marine I've ever known but he unbelievably blew his brains out just because, as legend tells it and police reported, the witch of the manor told him to do it. That's not the strangest thing that happened because I saw a secret police memorandum on the event. It stated that Ken Knies and another officer disappeared from the manor site and reappeared at the police station with his head blown off yet he still wrote something on his desk pad. I'd like to tear it down."

"Listen, my bank has the most at stake here and we're not going to eat the costs. The manor will not be torn down period!"

"I agree with Dan. Our family has a stake in this as well and I'd rather see a percentage of two hundred million rather than a percentage of twenty million. No one will go in there and collect the artwork. No one is stupid enough to do that," Charles said.

"Charles, are you saying that we sell this to someone knowing what we know? Do you want to commit the new owners to what's in there?" George asked.

"George, it's not our problem if we sell it. The bank gets their money and we get ours. I have bills to pay and I know you do too. We can't just allow this property to be destroyed."

George relented. "Okay, Charles, I see that I'm outnumbered. Sell the damn property! However, if anyone asks me why we sold it knowing what we know, I'm going to send them right to your door. Got it?"

Charles smiled as he replied, "I can live with that."

George stormed out of the room, muttering to himself, then swiped everything off the hall table onto the floor and slammed the door behind him.

"Well, he took being an instant millionaire well, don't you think?" Dan asked.

"It's all set. I just have to get the other family members to agree and then we can put it on the market. Monty, if you can drag yourself away from that file, you can do it."

Monty had contributed little to the conversation until now. He tapped at a paper he'd read.

"I'm afraid to disappoint you boys but we cannot pull down the house or sell it on to just anyone. Legally it will be passed to the next Heather Black. You'll have to contest it by law if you want to alter this fact," he said.

"That damn legal clause," George said.

"I'll do as you bid and call the real estate agent tomorrow to market the house," Monty suggested. "However unless they're associated with a Heather Black – they'll never get a look in."

"But remember—don't give the real estate agent or any prospective viewer too much information. By the way, anyone associated with my family is off limits. If I had my way I'd get this albatross away from all of us Blacks," Charles said.

Monty stood up and gathered his papers. "Good luck with that. I'm not sure who will want to view it but I'm pretty sure it will be a Black and also, the chances are very good that he'll have a wife named Heather!"

***

Five years later, in the year 2002, another Black inquired about the house, and strangely his wife's name was also Heather. She and her husband were unrelated to the unfortunate Black family.

John Black and his wife, Heather, were second-generation immigrants from Germany. They were vetted by the family, who found out that they were not related to the new homeowners so didn't feel compelled to tell them the history of the storied manor.

John Black, a fifty-year-old world renowned author, had found another property in Pennsylvania, but his much younger and indulged wife Heather, did not want to buy any other place but the Black Manor as history named it. The house mysteriously drew her to it, and John always gave way to what ever made his beautiful wife happy.

It also made John happy when Monty Ferris informed them that the clause in the deeds made it possible for Heather to have the property for free.

Monty glossed over the manor's history.

They were there for only two months when Heather noticed strange ideas pumped through her head. She'd never experienced thoughts of death and evil before they moved into the mansion but now strange morbid ideas surfaced.

John, whose books had been read by millions, always searched for interesting stories to write and was certain the manor presented ample opportunities for ghost stories. He and his wife loved mysteries. The scarier the better and the manor did not disappoint.

John loved to explore dark places. The house presented many areas ripe for his storied imagination. They ventured many times to places where people had not set foot for a century. He noted that some of the rooms still held the scent of an earlier time.

John found the secret room accidently. He leaned against a panel in the ornately decorated, wood-trimmed hallway, and the wall gave slightly. He opened it the rest of the way as cobwebs broke.

The dark, windowless room had a thick layer of dust on the bed and furnishings. He noticed writings on the wall but the scribbling made no sense to either Heather or John. Three quotes were prominent and repeated many times on the wallpapered walls.

"Ascend to the fourth Vertical," and "Surrounding the Master, the con to stay holds my soul." The author had written the third quote eight times. "The vessel of the mind sets the President of the time of people's rights."

Heather asked, "What do you think they mean?"

John scratched his head and said, "I haven't a clue but it's as if someone wrote these things for a reason. I sense that we're being told to do something. This last one is more recent."

Heather flashed her flashlight beam on the wall.

"How do you know that?"

"It's simple. You see, the first saying is written many more times than the second and third. The author wrote the second passage many times but the third only eight times," he stated.

"I didn't even notice that. You're right. I wonder if the number of times they are written mean anything."

"I don't know. I think it means that the first passage held more importance than the other two, or it could be older than the other two."

"Demarking time?"

John rubbed his shoulders. "Possibly. I'll write them down and think about it later. I'm getting chills in this room. Do you feel it?"

"Yes, now that you mention it. I'm feeling a breeze although I'm not sure where from."

"I am too, but there are no windows in here and the door is closed."

John wrote down the last words when they heard a creaking door opening somewhere in the room. They pointed their flashlights toward the sound and saw a large closet door opening. Inside stood a lectern with what appeared to be a large book on it.

Just as they walked toward the closet a huge gust of wind caused the pages of the book to flutter about. The dust swirled around them as the wind's velocity increased. They abandoned their desire to see the book and wanted to get out of the mysterious room with its own internal weather system. They had to feel their way along the wall because the dust blinded them and the flashlights were useless. Heather found the inside doorknob. She grabbed John's jacket, pulled him and both fell through the doorway. Then she saw that it isn't John who she'd pulled from the room.

It was a headless man.

The door shut tightly behind them.

On the floor Heather immediately scooted away as fast as possible from the terrible specter.

"Who or what the hell are you?"

Her screams echoed round the mansion.

The hulk stood up and motioned with his hand toward the room. Heather cowered in fear against the far wall of the hallway. She whimpered now unable to shout for John. The man, dressed in a dusty suit, pointed toward the room repeatedly.

She heard a loud scream from the end of the darkened hallway and instantly the thing vanished into a blue mist.

Heather heard something approach her.

Was it whatever haunted the place?

She found her flashlight and pointed the beam toward the endless, dark hallway but saw nothing. She stood up. John languished in the mysterious room and she tried to find the door to free him.

Then again she sensed something approached her.

A dim blue light in the distance got larger. It was closer. Suddenly she heard footsteps, a sound so loud, it hurt her ears.

The pounding caused her to drop the flashlight and cover her ears tightly. She leaned against the wall and slowly slid down. She was in agony because of the booming, pounding steps. She closed her eyes tightly. Then, as the pain in her head became unbearable and as suddenly as the sounds came, they stopped.

She opened her eyes to see an old woman dressed in a typical flowing Victorian gown. The broad dress brushed against her face.

She looked up and saw a horrible sight. The aged face, framed by gray, stringy and sparse hair, spoke to Heather.

"You're very pretty, but you won't be for long. Are you ready to do what's in your mind?"

Dust flew from the decaying face.

"What have you done with my husband?" Heather asked. She crawled backwards away from the specter.

"Why. I am the original Heather Black, my dear. Your husband is marked. He will die. He will soon walk these halls oblivious to what's happened to him."

"No, he won't. You will not kill him. I'll stop you," Heather said.

The other Heather laughed. "You'll stop me? Why, my dear, you'll be the one who kills him. Isn't that what your mind is telling you to do?"

"Stop it! Stop it! Why are you doing this?" Heather shouted.

"We're both women. Wouldn't you do anything to remain beautiful? I found a way to do it and you're going to help me."

She laughed.

"Never! I'll never help you. If you think I'm going to kill my husband, you're crazy!"

Now she got to her feet, suddenly unafraid of the decaying spirit in front of her.

"No, I'm not crazy but I am most assuredly dead. That will not always be the case but I am now. I grow stronger with every soul I take, and soon my beauty will return to me. You will do as I demand. There is nothing that can prevent it. The souls of my past beckon only to me and they will make your life a living hell until you cannot take it anymore and deliver to me another soul to rule.".

Just as she uttered those final words the light vanished and so did the spirit of Heather Black.

***

The younger Heather Black grabbed the flashlight and walked back to the wall to find the hidden door to the room. She found it, and as she entered the room she saw everything back in complete order with John in the closet reading the ancient book, the flashlight in his mouth.

"Heather, come in here. This book is fascinating."

"John, stop everything. We need to get out of here!" she begged.

"What? We can't leave yet. This book, I think, dates back to the beginning of the sixteenth century. It's amazing. Apparently it's some kind of witch's handbook."

"I said put it down, John! We have to leave now!"

She screamed the words. It caught his attention. He pointed his flashlight at Heather. It highlighted her pale terrified face. "Easy, honey, what's wrong?"

"John, I know you won't believe me but I've just encountered a headless man and had a conversation with the original Heather Black. We need to leave now!"

"Okay! Okay, we'll leave but I'm taking this book with me."

"I'm afraid that she won't let you do that," Heather said.

"Bullshit, I'm taking it. Now where is that door? Funny, I can't find it. I distinctly remember it being here. Heather, help me find the door."

"John, place the book back on the lectern and the door will appear. She will not allow you to leave with the book," she said.

"How do you know that?" He continued to look for the door.

"Because she's talking to me now and she's angry. Please, John, put the book back."

"She's speaking to you now? Prove it! What have you got in your hand, dear?"

"They're scissors I got from the table." Heather gathered a huge hunk of her flowing blonde hair in her hand and started cutting it.

"What the hell are you doing?"

John's flashlight illuminated his wife. He looked at a horrible sight. Her eyes had blackened as she continued to cut off her hair. All of the sudden a deep gravelly voice came from Heather's mouth.

"I'm destroying your precious wife's will. Once all her hair is gone she will cut her scalp off and continue until she digs into her brain. I'm going to tell you one more time to put the book back. Remember, one chance!"

"Okay, okay, I'll put it back. Just don't harm my wife."

John ran to the closet and gently placed the book on the lectern and then ran back to the room to find Heather's hair intact.

Is all this an illusion? he wondered.

He found the door and they both ran out of the room. John still had the written phrases he copied from the wall in his pocket. He hoped the specter had no knowledge of the act. They arrived at the main room and hugged each other.

"We have to leave this place," she begged.

"I'm afraid that won't be possible. We must fight her. Maybe these phrases can help us," he reasoned.

"John, I don't want to fight her. I talked to her. I know what she's capable of. Even now she talks to me."

"What's she telling you to do?" he asked.

"She's telling me to kill you."

John stared at her. "Me? Why does she want me dead?" he asked.

He pulled the small piece of paper from his pocket.

"I don't know, honey. I just know that we have to find a way to get out of here," she replied.

Heather never wanted to venture toward the west wing of the manor again.

They were never able to leave the huge mansion except for a few instances when they needed food.

They never mentioned their tortured existence to their friends and family and changed the subject whenever the manor's evil past crept into the conversation.

***

Heather fought her desire to kill John but it continually haunted her thoughts for the next two years.

The original Heather haunted her daily but Heather told her husband whenever a murderous thought tried to control her brain.

John, aware of the danger of possibly being poisoned by Heather, prepared his own meals.

The evil was always there but nothing prevented Heather from telling John what her plans were. Sometimes, it slipped his mind that his wife wanted to kill him, like the time he took a sip of a Jack and Coke that she made for him while he wrote his latest mystery novel.

That time he was lucky. The next time could be fatal.

John and Heather lived on the edge.

Nevertheless they vowed to live their lives as best they could and hosted lavish parties to take their mind off their fearful day-to-day existence.

***

Five more years went by but the witch of the manor cared little about time in her quest for everlasting beauty and immortality.

The need to poison and to kill, which had once permeated Heather's mind, became weaker. They decided they were wrong to think that the woman still wanted Heather to kill John.

Slowly their everyday life returned to normal after years of non-stop worry.

Yet the phrases John had copied from that room remained a constant mystery to him. He couldn't solve them but he believed they were important and wanted to leave them for the future inhabitants of the manor. They might be able to decipher the meanings.

He framed the piece of paper with the written phrases on it and placed it on his wall, with the phrases facing the backing of the frame.

The framed clue appeared to be only a small blank piece of paper and only he knew what lay on the other side. He'd memorized the phrases and every time he glanced at the wall he wondered at the riddles' true meanings. Finally he decided he lacked the intellect to solve the secrets of the writings.

He went back to that mysterious room several times, without his wife's knowledge, and noticed that the phrases written on the wall increased over time.

He always left quickly because he didn't want to push his luck too much. John began to spend most of his time in his locked den. Heather believed that whenever that occurred John was deep into research for his next novel. Now Heather's haunted mind with its deadly plans scared her and she needed to be near John where she felt safe. In the past, she'd helped him while he wrote many of his bestsellers.

Eventually, interrupted for the tenth time one day, John realized that Heather felt left out. He explained his project. He could no longer exclude his wife.

"Heather, I need your help on this. We both know that you're being haunted and I need to know what you're feeling."

Heather cried. "She doesn't always attack my mind but when she does it usually has to do with me killing you. I've tried to stop her many times but I can't always do that," she confessed.

John said, "I know that dear but I also know that your love for me has stopped her insidious plans. I don't know why she wants you to kill me, but through my research, I'm starting to find out. I'm writing a book about this house and its history."

Heather wiped her tears from her face. She told John she hoped being involved in writing the book would stop her murderous notions.

"It's a great idea. What can I do to help?" she asked.

"I just need you to tell me what you're thinking. Or rather, what she's telling you to think," John said as he began to type.

"I promise. I'll tell you everything."

"If you're able to do that, then I may live long enough to figure out not only why she wants me dead but why it's so important that you do the deed."

"I want to know that too. I think we need to go back to that room," she said.

She vividly remembered the terror she felt watching things spin around at great speed. She remembered shaking with fear when she left.

"I didn't want to tell you this, but I've been there three times this month. Each time, I saw something unnatural. I didn't tell you because I didn't want you to worry. I gathered some ideas for the book but the spirits wouldn't allow me to stay long," he confessed.

"You went there without me? How could you do that? John, we are a team and I'm the one being haunted. I want her out of my head."

John hugged her.

"Hey, I'm the one she wants dead. I was certain that if I went there alone, I could gather more information."

"I'm sorry," she said. "So what did you find out?"

"Well, they built the house in 1804, and it's had only a few owners since, and believe it or not, all had your name, except for the man who built it. Or rather, two of the wives were named Heather Black but one was named Maggie. However I researched her and found out that she was originally named Heather as well."

"That's odd. Are these people related to us?"

"No, they aren't, as far as I can tell, but I really haven't completely explored the genealogy of the story. I'm interested in the strange things that occurred within the house. There is a lot written about the house." He glanced at his notes. "It appears to have started with Cyrus and Heather Black just prior to the Civil War. Cyrus died tragically," he said.

"What happened to him?"

"Blood loss, I think. The death certificate records an accident. His arm was severed while he chopped wood. But some gossip has it that his wife did it. What ever happened the local police never found the arm. Something else intrigued me."

"What's that?"

"His wife took him to the local doctor on two previous occasions. Once for poisoning and the second time for accident in a field. Each time, it appeared to the writer of the articles, Cyrus' wife seemed unconcerned about her husband's injuries." He paused. "I think there's a reason why the authorities never found his arm."

"What does a missing arm have to do with this story?" she asked.

"I don't know yet. Apparently, Cyrus' wife obsessed over her looks and the speculation at the time was that she practiced witchcraft and used her husband's arm to perform some sort of spell to make her beautiful. I know it sounds odd, but I believe this is where it all started. Many women used to be accused of being witches when something happened if a simple explanation couldn't be applied. I found this stuff in the archival writings of a slave who worked on the farm, prior to the Civil War."

"You lie, John Black!"

Heather's eyes opened widely and she did not blink. A vacant stare replaced her normally expressive face. Her sudden yell caused him to stop typing. He stepped away from his desk and turned on his tape recorder to capture the words of his obviously possessed wife. He spoke to the spirit.

"I've found out something important, I see. Why are you haunting my wife?" he asked.

She stood up.

"She means nothing to me. It's you I want," she said.

"Me? I knew it! You need me to die, right?"

"You will die. Your wife cannot resist me. I am relentless. Your wife has a strong love for you but I will break her. Many have tried to resist me. They all eventually succumb. You'll be dead soon and she will take a relic. You'll be among my minions!"

Then Heather fell and hit her head on the corner of the desk, opening up a gash on her temple. John immediately went to help Heather and applied pressure to her head wound. He called Doctor Hugh Phillips at the hospital.

After the head scan, Doctor Phillips told John that there was no internal damage. He stitched her wound. The doctor told John that Heather would need to stay in hospital overnight for observation but otherwise she was a very lucky woman.

Fifteen minutes later, Heather woke up.

"Why did you hit me, John?"

John heard the fear in Heather's voice and sought to reassure her.

"Hit you? I'd never do that! You fell and hit your head on the corner of the desk."

"No, I distinctly remember you yelling at me and your eyes widened as if you were possessed, then you hit me with something. What's going on?"

"That didn't happen, sweetheart. I recorded what happened. When you come home tomorrow we'll go to the den and I'll play it back for you."

* * * *

The following day, after discharge from the hospital John persuaded his reluctant wife to return home.

They both went back into the den.

Heather noticed the pool of blood on the floor and a bloody towel cast over the back of a chair. One of John's awards lay broken on the floor.

"That's what you hit me with. Your award! See? If I fell, why is your award on the floor covered with blood?"

"That's odd, why is that there?" John picked it up and examined a chip in the finely polished wood and the bloodstains. John wiped the blood away and placed the award back on his desk.

Heather made a move towards the door.

"I have to go, John. I can't stay here."

He said, "I don't know what's going on but I hope that this will tell us. Please stay here and listen to this with me. Maybe we'll find out."

He pulled out the recording device on the desk and hit the play button. What it had captured shocked him.

"Heather, I think that you are playing me for a fool. I'm tired of you trying to kill me and me lying awake at night wondering how you're going to do it! Maybe I should kill you first!"

"What are you talking about, dear? You're scaring me. Why are you yelling at me? I'm not trying to kill you. I love you!"

"Bullshit, Heather! The only way I can sleep is for you to die!"

In the recording Heather screamed and begged John not to hit her anymore as static replaced the voices on the tape. John pushed the button to stop the tape, slumped down at his desk, and cried.

"What did I do?" he muttered. He rested his head on his hands.

Heather, upset by her husband's distress, walked over to him and placed her arms around him. Gently she reminded him of the many strange things that afflicted both of them. "Perhaps the spirits in the house have manipulated this event.

"That's right, Heather. You know that I would never harm you. I saw how that witch possessed you and you saw something completely different. I'm sorry I attacked you, sweetheart. I understand what's going on now. She's trying to confuse us and she doesn't want me to write this book. I'm finding out too much," he reasoned.

"I think you're right. She seems scared that you are doing something that may go against her plans. This Heather ghost told me that she could wait forever to get want she wants yet I get the impression that she's impatient. I don't think she's happy about the fact we keep resisting her invasions into our brains. I wonder where all this is going. It could get worse."

"We need to continue despite what happens. I feel it's as important as ever."

Heather smiled at John as if reassured. "You bet your ass we'll continue. She can't beat us."

"Sadly, I think she could win. She's made me do something that I'd never believed I could do. Added to that I was completely oblivious to everything. If she could make me strike you, she's capable of anything. We have to get this book written and published before we die. It's just too important."

"Well, let's get it done then, sweetheart."

"Okay, I will do this, but only if you stay with me at all times, and I want to give you this, just in case I ever raise my hand to you again." John handed her a pistol.

"What's this for?"

"It's for protection."

"This will not do any good against a spirit."

She handed the gun back to John.

John refused to take it. "Heather, it's not for shooting the spirit. It's for shooting me if I ever threaten you again."

"No. I don't want it in the house. Don't you see? It will give her another way for me to kill you. John, we have to be smart about all this. Maybe we should leave."

"We can't leave here. Not after all the time we've spent fighting her evil." He took the gun and placed it back in his desk. "You're right about the gun though. I'll get rid of it. If you won't use it on me, then it can't help us."

***

For the next three months John and Heather researched and wrote about how the house and how it seemed to change the behavior of its inhabitants. They also found out how each owner met their fate. Yet the reason for the missing body parts of the victims escaped both Heather and John.

John stared at the framed piece of paper on the wall and agonized over the meanings, who wrote them and why. He remained convinced they were key to solving the mystery. The messages baffled Heather as well.

Although he was unable to resolve the mystery John still included all the information in the book. Everything from historic records to interviews with local people was recorded for future reference. His research found that they buried Cyrus Black without his right arm, Michael Black without his left hand, and David Black without his head.

All of their wives were named Heather. His research also revealed that the original Heather lived until the ripe old age of 104, but she'd lost a thumb or a finger but like the appendages of all the dead husbands it was never found. The research wasn't clear about when she lost the appendage. John however felt the importance of mentioning it in his book.

***

When John finished the manuscript three months later Heather asked to read it.

"I'm sorry, dear, I've already sent it to the publisher."

"I didn't even get to read the last chapter."

"I know. You'll understand later because I'll be dead in a few days, maybe hours," he said.

"What? What are you talking about? She hasn't been around us for a long time. Maybe she forgot about us."

"No, she's won already, Heather. The book is finished and you know how I celebrate a finished book."

"Yes, single malt Scotch on the rocks. It's right there in front of you. I didn't make it for you so I couldn't have poisoned it."

"No, you didn't spike my drink. I poured it straight from the bottle, but you did give me the ice cubes. Did you put poison in the ice cubes?"

"Yes, I did. I put poison in the ice cubes. Oh my God! I put poison in the ice cubes! John, we must get you to the hospital!"

Heather grabbed the phone and fumbled with the numbers, but with shaking hands, it proved to be futile. So she started all over again until she got through and told the dispatcher, "Please hurry! My husband has been poisoned."

"Poisoned?"

"Yes, please hurry!"

The dispatcher told her that an ambulance was on its way. Heather was so distraught she hung up the phone without giving any more information. John sat down calmly in his chair and sipped the tainted drink. He placed his fingers over the phone to stop her futile attempts.

"It's too late, dear. I can feel the poison attacking me. Here is something I wrote weeks ago. I just have to put a date on it."

To my wife Heather, I leave all my possessions. I write this in hopes that she will understand why I had to end my life. I took poison because I didn't want to deal with the pain of death. I hoped that it would ease my passing, as I've been depressed over the last few months. I do hope you forgive me for this. I love you, as you know. The last chapter of my last book will explain why it's necessary to find the truth. Our secret code applies.

With all my love from our world and the world I'm about to enter.
Your loving husband,
John Black
4/10/2010

"What's this?" she asked, as tears ran down her face.

"It's protection from prosecution. I need you here to solve the many mysteries."

He gasped for air.

John loved Heather and with each book he published he placed a hidden message to her in the final chapter, using a code that they both knew, to thank her for being so patient while he wrote the book.

He wrote the secret message because of all the hours they spent apart. It was a love letter to his wife. Once the first book had been published he'd shown her how to decipher the code. It usually consisted of a one-page sonnet written just for her. She never told any of her friends or family about the message in John's books, because it was their special secret.

"Please, hang on, John, the ambulance is on its way. Please don't die, my darling!"

She pleaded with him to breathe as her tears flowed down her face and onto his.

"I'm afraid I can't hold on. The last chapter, Heather, remember the last chapter and our code. I will try to help you solve these mysteries. If my research is correct, then I will return as a spirit. My spirit will not be able to leave this house. There are things I know that I've kept from you, to protect you. This is a necessary step. I have to see the other side of life. I hope I'm right. Goodbye, my precious Heather," he murmured, and then gasped his last heaving breath.

John died in her arms.

She gently closed his eyes.

Heather phoned the hospital once again.

"Don't bother with an ambulance," she said. "My husband's dead."

The medical examiner came to pick up John's body. He, and his crew, refused enter the house because of a direct order from the police captain due to previous unexplained events.

"Misses Black, I apologize, but we can't go in this house," he told her

"What? Why not? My husband is dead! You want me to carry him out here? He weighs two hundred thirty pounds. I can't lift him," Heather explained.

"I'm sorry, Mrs. Black, but we have our orders. This house and our department have a history that we don't want to revisit. We'll wait at the door for you."

"Okay, I'll see what I can do."

She pulled John, still seated in a chair, onto the large throw, which covered a sofa. She dragged his body over the fine smooth marble flooring, through the huge double doors to reach the hallway. It was a struggle to get John this far and she cried all the way.

The police then carried him down the steps to the driveway. The coroner gathered him up and placed him in a body bag and then he and three men lifted his body onto a gurney.

"I want him buried in the Black plot over there. Do not cremate him," Heather said.

"Okay, I'll place that in my notes," he said.

They placed his body into the ambulance and transported him back to the morgue. John's limp body was finally placed onto the embalming table to conduct an autopsy.

The body presented the coroner and his assistants with a few shocks. It had already been opened up and a rib removed. He reported his findings to Detective Bill Jones. Detective Jones immediately called Heather.

"Mrs. Black, I'm sorry but I have to ask you a strange question."

"What do you want to know?"

"Well it's obvious to us that Mr. Black committed suicide. What I wanted to ask you…um…do you know what happened to Mr. Black's rib?"

"His rib? What? Isn't it in his body?"

"He is missing the fifth rib on his left side and it appears that it was removed soon after death."

"What are you talking about?"

"I talked to the coroner and he said that someone removed it prior to him picking up the body. You say you don't know anything about it?"

"I don't know anything. You're crazy. Are you suggesting that I took it?"

"I'm saying that it's gone, that's all."

"Are you sure the medical examiner didn't lose it during his autopsy. Why would I remove one of his ribs?"

"Okay, thank you. If we have any more questions for you, I'll call."

"Sure. You're not going to search the house for it...just in case I've hidden it away? Is he missing anything else? An arm or a leg possibly?"

"We aren't allowed to enter that house because of an incident that happened many years ago. We have the suicide note. There's no need for an investigation. I would like to know about this secret code that he mentions in his suicide letter, but we can leave that for another day. I'll talk to you later, Mrs. Black"

"The code is private. It will remain a secret between John and myself," she said.

"Okay, are you going to be home for the next few weeks?"

"Yes, I'm not going anywhere."

"I'll need to talk to you again once the medical examiner has finished his autopsy."

"He poisoned himself."

"That's true, we have his suicide note, so that will go into our report. We'll need an official cause of death."

"Remember, I want him buried here at the house. I've already told the medical examiner."

"When he finishes the autopsy he will hand over Mr. Black's body to you for burial.

***

Three days later, Detective Jones called her again to tell her that the autopsy did reveal that John died of acute poisoning and they were able to release his body to her for burial at the manor.

A few people from John's family attended. Several of his most ardent fans, John's close personal friends and some of his publishing associates also paid their last respects.

Heather walked slowly with John's casket to the graveside and noticed the monuments to all the other Blacks buried there.

Cyrus, Michael, and David Black, together with their brides Heather, Heather, and Maggie. She imagined that one day she would join them. An idea came to her.

There are three cryptic messages and three dead husbands, she thought. *I wonder if these messages came from them.*

The ceremony ended and she stood near a mound of dirt covered with flowers along with the monument maker measuring for John's tombstone. She threw one last rose on the pile and walked slowly back to the house.

***

Heather wanted to read the last chapter of the book. She turned on John's computer. However, just like all his other books he deleted everything once it was sent to the publisher. She looked for a back-up file in the drawers but found nothing. She knew she'd have to wait for the publisher to return the manuscript.

She didn't know what to do for the next few weeks. She accepted the responsibility for John's death. She also accepted that she couldn't bring him back. She cried most nights. On other nights she felt angry for not being able to combat the evil meanderings within her mind.

One day she spied the blank piece of paper that John had framed. She took it down and out of the frame. She read it over and over again, trying to figure out what the cryptic messages meant.

No ideas came into her head.

Chapter 7
John Returns with Warnings

The following days and nights seemed to last a lifetime for Heather. She studied the messages over and over but still could not decipher their hidden meanings.

It has to be here somewhere! Think, Heather.

She focused on what John had found and felt her survival depended on her solving the mystery. Then one night as she turned in, the lights flickered.

They are flickering in a pattern, she thought. *Oh my God, could it be a message?*

Heather's hands shook as she turned on the laptop and looked up the Morse code alphabet. Sure enough someone had sent her a message using the lights.

The light switch jumped up and down as the pattern matched the flickering light. She couldn't decipher it fast enough so she turned on the laptop camera and caught the flashes. She had to find out if it's a message or simply a faulty light switch, although she'd never seen a switch move on and off, at will, without someone operating it. She studied the flashes for the next five minutes and then they suddenly stopped in the "on" position. Just to be certain, she walked over to the switch and turned it off; the lights went off. She turned the lights back on, walked back to the laptop and played the video. She had to play it many times before the fragmented message made sense.

She wept as she deciphered her beloved husband's cryptic words. The message puzzled her.

Old Heather controls me…Supposed to torture you… can't resist her…She makes me hurt you…Needs your soul...Other husbands are here…Riddles are pleas for help…Spirits seek relics…Warning…Leave now, sweetheart… John

Heather looked up - her tears dried.

"No, John, I will not leave you here to be controlled by that bitch. I'm not afraid to die now that I know you will be there for me! I will stay. But John, what did you mean about the relics?"

Tired, she walked to the bedroom and resolved to create a plan the next morning. To leave the manor was an option for her only after she received the author's copy of his book. She needed to read the last chapter to find her secret message. Until that time, she stayed to solve the puzzle and try to free her beloved John. She laid everything aside and settled under her covers to try to get a good night's sleep.

Heather tried to make sense of the cryptic messages in her bed. She yawned and eventually sleep overwhelmed her.

That night the torture John warned her about started. It began with the blankets being slowly removed causing the cool night air to brush against her bare skin. She kept her eyes closed as she grabbed at the blankets. She tugged at them. It turned into a tug of war as they were pulled from the foot of the bed by a stronger force. She opened her eyes to see the blankets being eaten by something beyond the end of the bed.

Her grip slackened on the sheets and followed them. She crawled to the foot of the bed as the blanket completely disappeared. Heather, frightened by what it could be, didn't want to see what hid there. She stepped as far as she could away from the bed then kneeled to look underneath. She saw nothing there except her comforter and sheet.

Bewildered, she rushed over to the bed and grabbed the sheets and blankets from the floor. She withdrew in horror as she felt something solid and menacing within the mass of bed linen.

"What do you want?" she screamed. "John, is it you?"

She heard no response. Something moved within the mass.

"Who are you? What do you want?"

She heard three voices reciting the same thing.

Now I lay me down to sleep.

It's time for bed, Heather.

The voices were haunting and eerie. Then a loud laugh bellowed out and the blankets crawled toward her. They stopped before they reached her feet. She waited. They flew toward the ceiling, spreading out flat, before drifting down over her head. She grabbed frantically at the sheets as if fighting a demon and ran toward the bedroom door.

Heather looked back to see the sheets now flat on the floor. Apparently whatever caused the event had left. She cautiously gathered them off the floor and placed them back on the bed.

"Is that all you got, bitch? It's going to take a lot more than tricks to get me out of here."

Suddenly a loud, ear-piercing reply echoed throughout the massive manor.

"So be it!"

The voice screamed.

The sound burst Heather's left eardrum.

A small trickle of blood oozed out and through her fingers. She went to the bathroom to stop the blood,

The voiced still screamed yet the sound was muted. Helen feared the high-pitched noise had damaged her hearing.

Determined not to be daunted or afraid, she turned off the bathroom light, climbed back in her bed and tried to sleep even though she worried that the witch was not finished with her.

She sat up and called out to the witch of the Manor, "You won't make me leave. John's spirit will never hurt me."

She hoped, despite John's warning, his spirit would keep her safe while she slept.

She awoke next day and felt relieved that she was still alive. She walked to the kitchen and made breakfast, and for the first time she felt lonely in the huge mansion. She called her friend, Sally Richards, to ask if she would come over and keep her company for a few days.

Sally answered before she'd finished her first bite of the bacon sandwich she'd prepared.

"Heather, I was just thinking of you. How are you doing? I haven't seen you since the funeral."

"I'm doing okay, but it's kind of hard sleeping alone. I hate it. Can you spend the next few days with me? I mean this place is a lot closer to your job than your apartment," she reasoned.

"Sure, I'd love to. Well, as long as you have the pool open and margaritas. Can I bring my dog?"

"I have both and of course you can. I miss Jester. I loved it when we took him for walks. In fact, stay as long as you want."

"Wow, that's great. Why don't we get the whole gang together for an extended stay? LeAnne is in town and perhaps Sharon could come as well?"

"That's a great idea! I wonder if Diane and Marty would like to join us. "

"They will. As long as the husbands are invited as well."

"That's fine. This house is big enough for an army. I just don't want to be alone."

"I understand. When I lost Dave, I didn't do anything for a year. I felt so miserable."

"If you can call LeAnne and Sharon, I'll call Diane and Marty to see if they're interested."

"Jester will love running in the fields there. Have you been to the west wing yet?" Sally asked.

"No, not since John and I moved in. Those rooms haven't been lived in for over a hundred years and the west wing is haunted. I'm not going back there. Sally, you are my best friend and I need to confide in you about this house. I'll tell you when you get here."

"Okay, I have to pick Jester up from the vet and I'll start packing."

"One other thing, we'll have to do all the cooking and stuff," Heather said. "I can't get any staff to work here now."

"That's okay, we'll take care of it and the boys can take care of the grounds. This is so exciting! I must explore the west wing."

"I'm not sure about that...we'll discuss that when you get here, okay. Hurry, the margaritas will be ready soon."

"Don't start without me!"

Heather called Diane and Marty and they confirmed that they'd love to visit.

"Our hubbies can ride their ATVs on the grounds and tap a few golf balls on the putting green," Marty said.

A knock on the door announced Sally's arrival about two hours later and Heather greeted her a hug and a kiss on the cheek. Jester jumped up to Heather and licked her face.

Sally said, "Hi, Heather, sweetie, I found this on your porch."

Heather read the label on a small package. It was from John's publisher. She tore it open to see John's new, freshly printed, leather-bound hardcover book. She wanted to read it immediately, however since she had guests she placed it in John's den to be read later. She just wanted to have fun now, and not think about death, spirits, or the threats against her.

The next day the rest of her friends arrived, and after she greeted them all, they immediately went to the bar and took drinks out to the pool. The pool area with its huge Olympic size pool and attached Jacuzzi amazed them. The group talked about their travels and the many events that had happened in their lives. Dan, Marty's husband, manned the barbeque and soon the aroma of chicken and steaks wafted toward the women. After the women changed into their string bikinis they lay on loungers soaking up the sun and making plans for the next few days.

Sally still wanted to explore the west wing intrigued by Heather's stories about the mysteries of the house. Dan, and Diane's husband Bill, wanted to test John and Heather's theories of the mysterious west wing.

Bill was a scientist who loved exploring history's secrets. A large man, who feared nothing and welcomed intrigue into his life. Likewise Dan, a professor at the local college, also enjoyed adventures into seldom traveled places. He wanted to see the rooms that had been locked in time and to observe how people lived a hundred years earlier.

"I'd love to view the art, the furnishing, and all the history preserved within them. You say there are about twenty rooms that have never been entered since the manor's construction, Heather?"

"That's true, Dan. There is no plumbing or electricity in those rooms. In fact, I think that they still have the old chamber pots there."

The group went quiet.

* * * *

They had all heard the legends of the mysterious mansion, but found it difficult to believe. John had spoken to them often about the manor; nevertheless they were convinced that John, an author with a love of drama and the paranormal, inflated the legends' value. His stories of spirits of dead husbands floating around the manor and creating havoc for those who dared to doubt their existence was definitely the creation of a fertile mind.

They wanted to see it with their own eyes before they believed such fantastic tales of spirits and the infamous witch of the manor.

Dan said, "Heather, we needed this vacation and I want to thank you for inviting me and Marty."

Heather picked at her salad. "It's my pleasure, guys. You all are welcome here anytime you want. In fact, I thank you for coming. It's a lonely place since John passed away. You know he's buried here on the grounds?"

Bill said, "I know. Diane told me and I apologize for not being here for the funeral. I traveled to Cairo and couldn't get back fast enough."

"Oh, I know. LeAnne couldn't attend either, but we're all here now; well except for Sharon. Her flight should arrive soon. She'll text me when the plane is about to land and I'll send a car for her. Oh, speaking of cars, if any of you want to take a drive, feel free to pick out one of John's cars. Virginia is beautiful at this time of year. We never appreciate where we live, do we? I think we ought to pretend to be tourists. Take a good look at this wonderful place."

Dan said, "That's fantastic! Maybe we should all go to DC one night and hit Georgetown. I hear the bars are amazing."

Heather responded, "I want to go, too! That's a great idea! I'll get a limo to take us to all the great spots."

"Okay, time for a swim, Marty?" Dan picked up his wife and threatened to throw her in.

"Wait, Dan! No! Not yet. Please put me down!"

"Sorry, sweetheart. I want you to remember I love you."

He jumped in with his wife in his arms and they splashed around. She faked anger until he came up to her and kissed her. The others followed suit and jumped into the pool and laughed and played for the rest of the beautiful summer day.

Heather didn't have a chance to dwell on mysteries, relics, torment, or cryptic messages with her friends there. She just wanted to enjoy her life and live freely in the moment. She didn't fear the unknown and later as all her friends settled down in front of a bonfire they'd built out of fallen branches, old packing cases and even a couple of broken chairs, it seemed like the perfect time for Heather to tell her friends the real truth about the house and its horrors.

"I'm happy that all of you decided to come. I have to tell you why I wanted you here. I'm scared," Heather confessed.

"Scared? Scared of what? You've never been afraid of anything," Marty said.

"Usually I'm not, but what John told you is true. I've seen it with my own eyes. The witch of the Black Manor has talked to me and made me do strange things. I even think that she made me poison my husband," she confessed.

"What? Are you saying that you killed John?" Dan asked.

"I don't know, but she made me do strange things and…" Heather said.

Sally interrupted the conversation. "Bullshit, Heather! I've known you since grade school. You would never do such a thing."

"You're right, I wouldn't. I loved my husband. You haven't seen her. I know what she's capable of. If any of you want to leave, I'll understand."

"You've seen who, the witch?" Bill asked.

"Yes, I saw her when John and I explored the west wing. We found a secret room with strange writings on the wall. They were cryptic messages left by all the dead husbands from the manor's history. Do you know all the wives who have lived here were named Heather?

Bill said, "What? I didn't know that"

"We also found an odd book on a lectern in the closet. It appeared to be a book of spells and charms used by her. Well, John speculated that the ex-husbands are still here. They are now spirits that roam around the mansion. I believe him."

"Do you know where the secret room is? It sounds like a place I'd like to visit." Dan asked.

LeAnne said, "Guys, this is a little creepy. I don't think this is just a scary story Heather's telling

"It's true, LeAnne. John was the author, not me, yet even this was beyond his imagination. When we were in the room it started spinning and we couldn't get out until John placed the book back on the lectern. I swear to all of you, it's true."

Heather looked around at her friends; their faces bleached white by the firelight. "You must believe me."

Bill, with an extraordinary thirst for knowledge, asked, "So, the book is still in there?"

"I guess so. John read some of it and he told me that the original Heather Black lived in the 1800s and made a pact with the evil book to deliver souls in exchange for everlasting beauty and immortality. She had to deliver the souls of all the dead husbands. The catch was the wife had to be the one who killed her husband. John researched the history and found that the wives all had the same names, Heather, with the exception of the original owners. I'm just the latest one who possibly unconsciously killed her husband."

Bill said, "Heather, we all love and respect you, but I for one, need to see it with my own eyes. You couldn't have killed John."

Just as the conversation reached its pinnacle, the doorbell rang loudly. Heather didn't hear it.

"Heather, you've got some more company." Marty said.

Heather said, "Dammit! The witch took the hearing in my left ear a few nights ago. That's another story to tell you about. I'll be right back. It's probably Sharon, although she promised to text me."

She walked back into the house.

The conversation continued after Heather left.

"Do you believe her, Dan?" Marty asked.

Dan responded, "I don't know. I can't believe she'd tell us this if it isn't true. I know John told me some wild stories about the house. It is kind of scary and also intriguing to me. I want to go find that secret room."

"I'm game," Bill agreed.

Diane frowned. "I don't know, honey. I mean, we've done some crazy things before, but the way she described what she saw is kind of frightening."

"I know, but Heather's our friend and I don't want to leave her here. Not if all this is true. John told me that he wrote a book about all this," Bill said. "I wonder if he finished it."

Heather came back to the poolside.

"Everyone's here now!"

Sharon greeted everyone with hugs and kisses.

"Okay, what did I miss?" she asked.

Marty said, "Well, you missed Dan's excellent barbeque, a pool party and a scary story that Heather told us."

Sharon asked, "Is the scary story about the house?"

"Yes, how did you know? You just got here," LeAnne asked.

"I work with John, remember? I'm his editor. Heather, did you get his book yet?" she asked.

"Yes, it came today. I forgot all about it,"

Heather sat down in front of the crackling fire.

"It's an amazing book. I had to edit it myself. That's why you got a fully proofed copy Heather," Sharon said. "I just couldn't wait to get here to check out this place myself."

Heather took a sip of her drink before she looked at her. "What? You've been here a dozen times."

"Yes, but not as an investigative reporter, I want to explore the things John wrote about in his book. He told me that it's all true, but it seemed too fantastic to believe."

Bill said, "I know. Heather's been telling us about it."

"Well, when are we going there?" Sharon asked.

"Going where?" Heather inquired.

Sharon poured a margarita and then sat down beside Heather. "To the secret room in the west wing. I want to see it with my own eyes."

"You guys don't believe me, do you?"

Dan said, "We want to, Heather, but you have to admit, the story seems a little far-fetched."

"Okay, tomorrow morning we will all go, but be warned, you'll see things that you wish you hadn't and I'm not sure how she will take being invaded by all of you."

Sally changed the subject and commented on the home's marble floors and the millions of dollars' worth of original artwork that lined every wall in the great foyer.

The mansion housed the works of Rembrandt, Renoir, Henri Matisse and many more of the masters' works. Sculptures and statues by Gian Lorenzo Bernini, Donatello, Constantin Brancusi, and all the famous artisans of Italy, Spain and France adorned the hallways and stood proudly as a sign of great opulence. Presidents were featured in the President's Room, where artifacts from all the presidents were proudly displayed. The friends moved from room to room in utter amazement at what they saw. It especially invigorated Bill because of all the history displayed in the manor.

"This is utterly amazing, Heather. How did John collect all this?" asked Bill.

"Most of it came with the house, but the rest we brought in. We had it all appraised for insurance purposes and we found out that the artwork is nearly worth more than the house. I wouldn't dream of selling any of it though. It's all so beautiful," she said, as she proudly escorted the group throughout the house.

"Well, we have a big day tomorrow. Has everyone picked out a room?"

They all nodded except for Sharon. "I just got here, so no, I haven't."

"You have about twenty to choose from, Sharon. Just let me know what the room number is. Everyone is staying in the east wing's rooms."

"Not me!" Sharon interrupted. "I want to stay in the west wing. I want to experience what John experienced."

"John never stayed in the west wing as far as I know"

"Read his book, Heather; he stayed in a few of the rooms when he researched the story."

"I don't know if I want you to stay there, Sharon. It's dangerous, and should you need us, we will be a long way from you."

"I'll be fine, Heather. I have my cell phone if I need you." Sharon picked up her suitcase. "I'll be fine. I have Mace and my revolver."

"Okay, but call me if you see anything strange. Do you promise?"

"I will. Where do I go?"

"I'll take you. You guys know where your rooms are?"

After saying goodnight to everyone, Heather led Sharon to the first room on the second floor in the west wing.

"This is far enough," Heather said.

Heather left Sharon and walked to John's den. She had waited all day to see what special message John had written for her in the last chapter of his new book.

At John's desk she opened the cover to reveal a beautiful drawing with the house mired in black smoke. She turned to the last chapter, decoded his special message to her, and read what John wrote for her eyes only.

Heather cried when she read John's final words:

To my lovely wife I say that I do not want to die but I will to save you. I think I've unlocked the code and will try to save both our souls from this hell house. Just know that if I die trying, I will come to you. I will break every protocol to have my words reach you. In the void of death we will find each other and show all in that realm how eternities are supposed to be lived. I love you with all my being, Heather.

John

She vowed not to allow her soul to be captured by the witch of the manor. She wanted to be with John in the afterlife, so she had to solve the mystery, break the spell, and send the witch back to the depths of hell where she belonged.

She closed the book and wiped the tears from her face then walked slowly to her room, wondering what the future held for her. Too late she realized her friends might be in danger as well. Her desire to have company had perhaps completely clouded her judgment.

She resolved to end her friends' vacation the next morning. She could deal with her own fate, but she did not want her friends to be involved, or be harmed by the witch's twisted hauntings.

She dressed in her favorite white satin nightgown, and then settled into bed. There she started to read John's book from the beginning with the hope his research would defeat the witch of the manor. She read page after page, but to no avail.

She managed only a few chapters in the book before she fell asleep. Her dreams were colorful and happy, filled with images of her past, a far cry from her previous dreams.

She speculated that John had a hand in making her have beautiful dreams once more.

John's words took her back to the first time she read one of his books. She'd fell completely in love with his words and later with him. She awoke often that night and as she thought about the most memorable times, she hugged her pillow as she cried and tried to get back to sleep.

Deaf in her left ear, she did not hear the faint sound of John's spirit as he tried to defy the witch's spell by speaking directly to his beloved wife. He beckoned her to acknowledge his sacrifice. Instead, she heard the scream of an anguished spirit being tortured.

Finally Heather fell into a deep sleep regardless of what she heard or saw in her room.

***

The next morning she awoke to find Sally beside her.

"Wake up, sweetheart. We are all by the pool waiting for you. Well, except for Sharon. We don't know where her room is."

Sally cuddled her best friend.

"Is it morning already? What are you doing in here?" Heather yawned.

"I'm here to wake you up. We want to go to DC for the day and we want you to come with us."

"DC? Oh, yeah, of course. Wait, did you say that you couldn't find Sharon?" she asked.

"Yes, you put her in the west wing, but we didn't know where," she explained.

"Did you try her cell phone?"

"Yes, but she's not answering it. Get dressed and we'll all go get her up and ready. It's a beautiful day outside. So, get up!"

"Okay, okay. Remind me to lock the door next time."

"Oh, come on. You know you want me here cuddling you. Besides, you're hot!"

"Oh please. Are you going lesbo on me?" Heather asked jokingly.

"Maybe later, but not now, we want to see the museums and the monuments."

Heather relented. "Okay, I get the message. I'll get up." She took a quick shower, got dressed, and met all her friends at the pool eating breakfast.

"Here's the sunshine," Bill said, as Heather walked to the pool. "Breakfast is served."

Heather looked at everything on the table as she sat down to a buffet of eggs, bacon, potatoes, ham, sausage, fresh fruit, and orange juice. "Wow, you guys did all this? What a spread!"

Dan asked, "Where's Sharon?"

Heather replied, "She's not here yet? I guess she slept in."

"I've got an idea, let's all go and knock on her door at the same time. That will shock her awake," LeAnne said.

"That sounds great, but not until I've eaten. I'm starving and it all looks so great, I want one of everything," Heather suggested.

They ate, and then Heather, guided all the friends to the west wing towards Sharon's room. They stopped in front of her room and knocked loudly. They heard nothing through the closed door. There were no sounds to suggest that she would be out soon.

Concerned, Heather grabbed her master key and opened the door.

To her horror, they saw Sharon, nude and suspended in mid-air with blood oozing out of her ears and every other orifice of her body. The blood didn't fall to the floor. It floated out, surrounded Sharon's body, and dispersed into a pink mist. She raised her head. Her eyes rolled up into her eye sockets as she started laughing, spitting blood and teeth.

The friends vomited, almost as a group, at the horrific sight. Heather took a few steps toward Sharon. Her friend started spinning slowly and Heather stopped. Gradually Sharon spun faster and faster. Blood shot everywhere, coating the walls and everyone's clothing.

She spun so rapidly, her legs and arms detached from her body and flailed toward the group. They ran from the room. The door slammed behind them.

They stood together with blood dripping from their frightened faces in a silence, which seemed to mock them, and attempted to wipe their blood splattered clothes. LeAnne and the rest of the women wept. The men hugged their wives. They all looked questioningly at Heather, but she stared, a blank look on her face. As they turned to leave, a voice echoed through the hall.

"None will leave here."

All the doors of the rooms opened and then shut.

"What the hell happened?" Diane asked. "Honey, I'm scared."

"I am too. We need to get out of here," Bill replied.

They heard whispering coming from Sharon's room as the group started to leave. They stopped as they heard her words.

"Help me."

Sally asked, "Did you hear that, Heather? She's alive. Sharon's alive."

Her body shook with fear.

"That's impossible, Sally! You saw her arms and legs being hurled at us. She can't be alive! Look at us. We're covered in her blood!" Heather said.

Again, the voice of a woman whispered to them.

"Please God! Help me."

Dan said, "That's Sharon's voice! Open the door, Heather. Or give me the key and I will!"

Heather's hand shook as she opened the door.

The door flew open. Marty, slightly to the side of Heather, got sucked into the room right before it slammed shut again.

"What happened? How the hell did that happen?"

"Let me out! Let me out! Dan, help me!" Marty shrieked.

Dan pulled at the handle. The door would not budge. "Give me the key, Heather! The rest of you stand back."

When he finally opened the door he saw his precious wife standing rigid in a darkened corner with her back to Dan and the group. Sharon's torso still hung in mid-air and the walls were still splattered with her blood.

"Marty, please walk to us! We'll get you out!" he called.

Marty just stood in the corner and ignored Dan's pleas. He left the safety of the hallway as he ran into the room. He slid and fell on the blood-soaked hardwood floor. Mere steps from her, he stopped when she whispered.

"Too late."

Dan stood and tried to hold his wife. He managed to grab only half of her. She had been sliced down the middle from her head to her feet. Dan fell with only the back half of his wife in his arms. Her entrails fell to the floor. The front part of her body still stood in the corner devoid of her back and inner organs.

Suddenly what was left of Marty, turned around.

"I told you that you were too late," she said.

The door shut. The group of friends heard death screams from Dan. They imagined a mammoth struggle being fought in the room.

Mere seconds later, silence.

"Let's investigate," Sally suggested.

"We need to get the fuck out of here!" Bill and Diane yelled.

"Come on, Heather! Let's get the hell out of here! You watched them and saw how fast they were killed!" Bill repeated.

They all ran toward the stairs and flew down the steps, skipping many of them.

"Where's the fucking door? Heather, how do we get out of here?"

"It's supposed to be right here. Now it's gone. I don't know what to do."

"What's down at the other end of the hallway up there?" Sally asked.

"We can't go there, she lives there!" Heather said.

"She? She who? Heather, who lives down there?" Bill asked.

"I told you. It's the witch of the manor. She lives at the end of the hallway upstairs. She's the one John wrote about and the one who did that to Sharon, Marty, and Dan. She won't let us leave now."

"Bullshit! I'll tear through these fucking walls!" Bill roared.

They all stopped and stared at the flight of stairs. They agreed they couldn't get out that way and walked back.

"Let's hope we find another way out."

"I'm sorry I don't know if there is another door upstairs or not," Heather apologized.

They all peered down the long darkened hallway and heard noises. They heard a thumping noise as if something was being thrown against the walls toward them.

"Oh my god. Something is coming in our direction," Sally said.

The closer it got, the louder it got. Finally, they saw the object rolling toward them through the darkness of the hallway. They stepped back and watched as it passed and bounced off the wall behind them. They shrieked out when they realized that the thing that finally stopped before them was Dan's severed head.

LeAnne, Diane and Sally cowered in a dark corner, while a scared Bill and Heather frantically tried to find the way out.

"What are we going to do?"

Bill looked around for a weapon; anything that he could use to defend them from whatever threatened their lives.

Heather and her friends were in grave danger. She had no idea how to protect them. John had previously told Heather the witch wanted her to kill herself and therefore commit her soul to the darkness. She would die. She had to save them.

"We have to go down the hallway and find the secret room. I think it may lead us out of here," Heather said.

Bill asked, "There's a secret room? What secret room? I'm not going down there. Did you see what just came from there?"

Heather said, "It may be the only way out, Bill."

"We can't see a foot in front of us. How are going to find this secret door?"

"I found it once and I'll find it again. We just have to stay together and we'll be fine. Follow me."

Heather walked toward the darkness, feeling her way along the wall. The friends held each other's hand as they walked slowly toward the unknown. Heather noticed that the further they walked down the hall, the colder it got, and the musty smell of many forsaken rooms wafted in the air.

After they walked fifty feet, Heather reached up on the wall to find an oil lamp. She lifted it from the wall, and shook it gently to hear if oil sloshed around within it. She heard oil in its tank. She asked Bill if he had a lighter.

Bill searched his pants pockets to find a lighter. "I used to light many a happy cigar with this," he said.

Heather lit the lamp and they were thankful they could see at last. When they shined light in the hallway it looked normal, almost too ordinary, with doors on both sides and a hardwood floor and a carpet runner in the center of the hallway.

They continued to walk hand-in-hand when Sally suddenly stopped. "LeAnne! She's gone! Oh my God, She's gone! I held her hand and I felt her hand getting colder and when I turned around I saw that I held just her arm. LeAnne's arm! What the fuck is happening to us?"

Heather moved the lamp nearer the floor and saw the arm. It lay by the wall after Sally had thrown it across the hallway.

"How do we know it is LeAnne's arm?" Diane asked.

Heather walked nearer to the severed appendage and shone the light on it. "It's hers. She's wearing a ring I gave her," she explained. "Sally, didn't you hear anything? I mean, there had to be some sort of noise when her arm was ripped off."

"No, I heard nothing. Oh dear God, what's happening?" Sally slumped to the floor. She hid her face with her hands. "I don't want to see anymore," she said.

"Sally, you'll make us all panic if you lose it. We have to keep our heads or we'll die here. I believe the room is close. Please, I know you're upset, we all are, but we have to find the room! I really think the answers are there! Now, how long were you carrying her arm?"

"Okay, Heather, I'll try to keep it together. Please get us out of here. I don't know how long I carried it! I remember talking to her about fifteen minutes ago. I never let go of her hand, until I saw what I held."

"Guy's, the wall over here just moved. Is this the secret room? Heather, listen to me! Is this the room?" Bill asked. He made an effort to pry the door open.

"That's it, Bill. Can you open it?" Heather asked.

"I think so. There, it's open. Do we go in?"

Heather said, "Yes! Let's go now!"

The room had dust covering everything. Heather again saw the messages on the wall and how many times they were repeated. She remembered how John speculated on the riddles by the amount of times the cryptic messages were written, and told the group about it. Though, even John said that they were only assumptions on his part. He reckoned he could tell who wrote each one by the amount of times displayed.

The spirit of Cyrus Black wrote, Ascend to the Fourth Vertical, because the first Heather Black sacrificed him and thus he had been in the spirit world longest.

Michael Black wrote, Surrounding the Master, the con to stay holds my soul. The third message, written seventeen times, by the spirit of David Black, read, The vessel of the mind sets the President of the time of people's rights.

Then a new message appeared on the wall.

It appeared once.

Released from my cage, seek the stilled flow where rainbows once harkened the sun. 9 11 66 45 23 5 28 45.

"It's from John. I'm sure it's from John," Heather whispered.

Bill asked, "What does all this mean?"

"They are clues and this one right here is from John." She pointed to the last message."

"John? John's dead, Heather. You said that if we found this room we'd be able to get out of here. Help us! We're still alive," Diane begged.

Sally defended Heather. "Diane, Heather is my best friend. She would never allow her friends to be placed in this kind of danger. She's here with us!"

"I know! I'm sorry, Heather. It's just that I'm just so scared."

"We all are, Diane," Heather said.

Bill stared at the walls. "Heather, do you know what these writings mean?" he asked.

"Not all of them, but I know what the last one means. It's from John."

"What do the numbers mean?"

"It's our code. I'm sorry. I'll explain. In every one of John's books he wrote a special message to me in the last chapter. He's done it here as well. The numbers mean 'Fountain'."

"Fountain? How do these numbers mean 'Fountain' and how is that going to show us the way out of here?"

Bill began to walk toward the small room that housed the lectern with the book. He halted as writing appeared in the dust on the floor.

"Look at this," Bill said. "What is it?"

"Someone's trying to tell us something," Heather replied.

The words read,

"Rip page thirty from the book and run with it through the hall. Go now! Burn the page at the end of the hall and a door will appear. I love you."

Heather ran to the lectern with the lamp and counted the unnumbered pages to thirty and ripped it out.

"Come on, let's go now. Diane, get up! We need to go!" Heather begged her friends to follow.

"I don't want to go back into the hall, Bill. Please, go without me," Diane said.

"Diane, get the fuck up! We have to go! We have ten seconds to leave this damn room! We will die here!"

Bill said, "Stop yelling at my wife, Heather. She's scared!"

"We're all scared, Bill. Are you two coming or not? Heather and I are leaving," said Sally.

"Go then, Diane doesn't want to go. If we're going to die, we're going to die together right here in this room." Sally said, "Come on, Heather. Let's go!"

Heather and Sally took the lamp. They ran out of the room and through the hallway. Suddenly a huge wind blew against their faces as they ran. Heather held on to the ripped page and the lamp. "We're almost there, Sally."

The wind slowed them down, but they still made it to the end of the hallway and down the stairs.

Heather checked her pockets. "Oh shit! Bill has the lighter! I gave it back to him."

"What are we going to do?" Sally asked. "I don't have a lighter."

"Stand back, Sally." Heather smashed the lamp against the wall. It exploded into flames. She threw the ripped page into the fire. The fire immediately disappeared and the door magically reappeared for Heather and Sally.

They opened it quickly and escaped.

They hugged each other as they looked back at the west wing. Then they went to John's den. Heather added John's quote to the others on the wall, reframed it and replaced it neatly on the wall between the Picasso and the Matisse.

Sally shook with fright at the remembrance of what just happened to her and her friends. The memory of the blood soaked room made her stomach churn. "What are you doing Heather? We have to call the police."

"They won't come, Sally. They will not set foot into this house because of an incident that happened with David and Maggie Black. I'm afraid our friends' deaths will not be explored any time soon."

"Then we should call the press. They will come," Sally suggested.

"Yes, they would. They will want to go to the west wing and when they get there they will die as well. We had one chance to escape and took it. Will there be another chance? There is no longer a page thirty to get us, or anyone else, out of there. Look, it's dark outside; we've been in that hallway for nearly twelve hours. I'm tired. I think it's time for me to leave here. It's just too much to take on and I'm in way over my head. I feel that I've let John down."

"John? John's dead, Heather, but I agree, let's get out of here."

Sally hugged Heather.

"Tomorrow we'll leave. I've got to get some sleep first and I feel strange about leaving our friends. I think we'll be safe until tomorrow and then we can decide what to do about Dan and the others. You may be right, though, we can't just let all our friends down. They are dead and the world needs to know why and how they died. I just hope the world believes us."

"Okay, perhaps the press won't believe us, however if they go into the west wing they will."

Heather replied, "They will not be able to write what they see because they will be dead."

Sally said, "I'm sleeping with you tonight because we have to stay together."

"Okay, I'll have a shower. Go grab your things and bring them to my room."

Sally went to her room and gathered up all her belongings and then went into the bathroom while Heather showered.

Heather asked, "Sally, is that you?"

"Yes, it's me. I don't want to be alone. Oh, fuck it, I'm coming in with you." To Heather's surprise Sally disrobed and stepped into the massive shower.

"My, you've got a hot body there, Heather."

"Sally? What the hell? Our friends have just died, I'm scared out of my mind, and you're coming on to me?"

"You think I don't know that? I'm sorry, but sex takes my mind off stuff that's haunting me. You're right, though, I know you're right."

Heather grabbed Sally and hugged her. She stroked her hair to calm her down until she smiled, but as she looked into her eyes, Sally kissed her gently on the lips.

"Oh, God, you've gone lesbian, haven't you?"

"Hey, after all I've been through today, it's just refreshing knowing that I can still get turned on at all," Sally said.

Heather turned her back to Sally to catch a stream of warm water on her face. Sally hugged her from behind, resting her head against her back.

"Are you getting turned on? Okay, it actually feels pretty good to be held again. Hey, since you're there, I'll let you soap my back." Heather suggested.

Heather sighed when Sally's hands touched more than just her back. She returned the favor, except Sally didn't turn around, so Heather could feel her breasts and everything else as well. "Wow, you have extremely soft skin, Sally. John and I always talked about this but I always nixed the idea. John would get a kick out of seeing us in the shower together. Let me shampoo your hair."

Sally reached out and kissed Heather on the lips again and they embraced for the next minute.

The hot water had started to run cold when they finally emerged from the shower holding hands as each took turns drying the other off.

Heather dressed in a fine satin nightgown and got into bed. Sally followed suit, but snuggled against Heather completely nude. Sally did not want to sleep.

She massaged Heather up and down her body. Heather, partially asleep, allowed Sally to stroke her legs right to the tips of her toes. Sally got on top of Heather and began to rub her body against Heather's and then Sally's lips caressed her face.

Heather's eyes opened, she momentarily resisted, then allowed Sally to kiss her before eagerly succumbing to her advances.

As Sally kissed her, John appeared, in spirit form, at the foot of the bed and implored her to stop.

"Heather, it's not Sally!"

'Sally's' eyes went black as she thrust her hand backward toward John's spirit. He recoiled in agony then disappeared. Heather watched as the person she supposed was Sally turned back to her. The eyes were black as night. Although Heather struggled something held her rigid and allowed the witch to force her body into submission.

Heather lay there helpless as 'Sally' licked Heather up and down her body. She concentrated on Heather's toes. Suddenly, 'Sally' bit off her big toe and spit it out on the floor.

The intense pain Heather experienced was expressed by the tears, which flowed down her face. Blood dripped from Sally's mouth. She moved towards Heather's other big toe and bit that one off as well. Blood soaked the white sheets. Sally moved to the other toes, and one by one, she bit them off. Heather felt the pain of each injury but as before she was unable to react or cry out.

John's spirit re-emerged and began to attack 'Sally'.

'Sally' resisted. "Go away, spirit! I command you!" She turned away as if to continue Heather's torture.

"You will not torture her, you old hag." The spirit of John spoke in a loud, booming voice. "I'm sorry, my dear wife. I will have to take your life or she will eat you all the way up your body. Forgive me!"

'Sally' confronted the spirit of Heather's beloved husband. "You'll do nothing, spirit."

As the battle raged, Heather gained her body back. She got up out of the bed and limped toward the stairs. Blood smeared the floor with every step of her badly maimed feet. She made it to the top of the stairs. Then, as she turned to look back, she fell forward, as if someone had pushed her from behind.

The fall broke her neck and killed her instantly.

The spirit of John appeared at the top of the stairs.

"Sleep well, my love. I hope I'll be able to join you soon."

The witch captured him. She caused his gentle blue aura to turn bright red. It made him scream with pain and he exploded into dust.

The 'real' Sally, finally able to eradicate the old witch from her mind, ran to where she saw Heather at the foot of the stairs.

Then the witch tripped her. She tumbled down the stairs, and broke her back as she landed on Heather's lifeless body. Sally did not die right away but had to watch as the witch descended on the two of them.

The witch broke Sally's neck with such force that her vertebrae bulged from the skin. She picked up the now lifeless body and threw it across the room and smashed it into the far wall.

***

Heather's family grew concerned when she had not returned any of their calls. Finally, her mother called the police and made them investigate. The police told her mother that they could not, would not enter the house. She threatened a lawsuit.

They relented but took military support.

They also had missing person's reports for all of Heather's friends.

Once they saw Heather at the bottom of the stairs, along with Sally's body strewn all over the foyer, the police realized that all of the friends were in the manor somewhere. They didn't want to search the rest of the house, even though the National Guard, with all their weaponry, was mere feet away.

***

They retrieved Heather's body. Although her severed toes were missing, among other strange things, it did not compel the authorities to investigate whether Heather had been murdered. They didn't want to investigate any part of the manor. It didn't take much persuasion to convince the medical examiner to record that Heather died due to an accident at home.

They buried Heather beside her husband John, on a bright sunny day at the immaculately manicured family cemetery. They released Sally Rogers' body to her family for burial in Florida, while Dan and Marty Wright, Bill and Diane Morrison, LeAnne Burber, and Sharon Butler were listed as missing and presumed dead.

No search for the missing friends was conducted because of the history of the manor's destruction of police officers and whole departments. The families sued for many millions of dollars.

The police department deemed it a small price to pay.

No one wanted an investigation into the latest Heather's death.

Chapter 8
The Next Relic

Two years passed before the manor attracted another family to live in the home. John's brother, Ben, who bore a striking resemblance to John, took on the manor. The legal clauses of the will were finally circumvented because the authorities washed their hands of the estate.

A wit proclaimed, "Let the original Heather Black contest it!" No one laughed.

The locals informed Ben of the horrors associated with the estate. He also did not believe the stories. He'd read his brother's book and believed it to be mainly a work of fiction.

The executor of the Heather Black estate felt relieved that Ben's wife was named Rianna and not Heather. Heather wasn't her first or middle name so he was confident the manor's history wouldn't affect them.

***

Three weeks later the moving trucks came and the couple moved in. The executor, Ethan Robb, met them as they arrived so he could give them the keys and a tour of the property. The Blacks' limo pulled up to the front door and the chauffeur opened the door. Ben Black got out.

"Hi, Ben, glad to see you," Ethan said.

"Hello, Ethan, what a great day. I've always admired this place. This is my wife, Rianna."

His wife emerged from the car.

"Hi, Rianna, nice to meet you." He extended his hand to greet her.

Rianna looked at the huge estate. "Honey, we're going to need a lot of help for the upkeep of this place. It's enormous! Oh, I'm sorry! Where are my manners? Hello, Ethan, I'm sorry, I'm just amazed at the size of this place."

"That's okay. It is an amazing property, isn't it? Your property line is as far as the eye can see. Shall we go inside and I'll give you a short tour?" Ethan ushered them both toward the front door. "Although you'll know it Ben from your previous visits."

"Never seen all of it, Ethan," Ben replied.

"Wait, Ben. Come on out of the car, sweetheart."

"And who is this cutie?" Ethan asked. A young girl appeared from the car.

"Hi, mister, I'm Heather and I'm ten years old."

"Her name is Heather? My God, what have I done?"

"What are you talking about, Ethan?" Ben asked.

"I knew you had a daughter, I just didn't know her name. Heather, right? Ben, can I speak to you in private?"

Ben smiled at Rianna and Heather and said, "Sure. Rianna, take Heather in and get settled. Ethan and I will catch up with you later."

"Okay, come along, dear. Let's go look at your room." Rianna and Heather entered the house.

Ethan showed Ben into John's old den and closed the door.

"Ben, you read your brother's book didn't you? Aren't you afraid for Heather?"

"Yes, I read it, and it appears the legend pertains to wives named Heather. We'll be fine," Ben said.

"You know about the manor's history, right, especially the last few years?"

"I know all about it. I even knew many of John and Heather's missing friends. I'm sealing off the west wing because we don't need it. In fact, I may just rip it down. It'll make the place look kind of off-kilter, but we'll never set foot over there. Rianna knows all about it as well," Ben said.

"You know those bodies are probably still over there, don't you?"

"So what? I don't do research like my brother. I don't care about the house's past. Plus, I own ten guns and I know how to protect my own," Ben said.

"Guns? Do you know how many men walked into the west wing with guns and died anyway? Do you also know that the police will never respond if there is any trouble here?"

Ben shook his head. "I know all of that. Listen, Ethan, I appreciate your concern, but we'll be okay."

"I held that belief until I met your daughter, Heather. Strange things happen to all the Heathers in this house," Ethan said.

"It won't happen to my Heather. We're splitting our room and she'll stay with us to keep her close. She'll be safe."

"I'm worried about all of you. Well, I have to go. Is there anything else you need to know about the manor?"

Ben stood up and shook Ethan's hand. "No, I think I know enough. I'm going to seal the west wing tomorrow with the help of a few friends. There are only three doors leading to it, so it shouldn't be that big of a deal."

"Okay, I'll check in with you later. I've got to go," Ethan said.

The next day Ben did as he promised. He removed all the doors leading to the west wing and walled them over.

He seriously contemplated demolishing the west wing and rebuilding it. He hoped it would repel all the ghost hunters who chomped at the bit to spend time there.

The word spread around the Internet about the "Manor of Heather Black," as they called it. John's book spurred on other books that also explored the legend of the original Heather Black.

For the first few months, nothing out of the ordinary happened and Ben thought that he had eradicated any possible evil within by sealing off the west wing.

He did have a few concerns about his young daughter, Heather, who met and played with an imaginary friend. Children do have imaginary friends but this was something different.

She was in the back yard in her sand box when Ben first noticed that Heather talked to herself.

"Who are you talking to, sweetheart?"

"I'm talking to my friend, daddy," she said.

He watched as she loaded another pail with sand.

"Does your friend have a name? No wait, let me guess, Casper?" he asked.

"Nope." She smiled. "Guess again, daddy."

"Is it Shrek?"

She giggled. "Daddy, Shrek's not a ghost. He's a green monster man."

"Okay, I give up. Who's your friend?"

"It's Cyrus. He only has one arm because his wife chopped it off."

Ben stepped back and then gathered Heather up into his arms. Scared, he looked all around outside and then ran inside.

She began to cry. "Daddy, I want to play. I don't want to go in the house."

Ben sat her down inside at the kitchen table and gently dried her eyes. "Did you say Cyrus? Honey, I need to know everything about your friend and what he said."

"Yes, Cyrus. He's a nice ghost. Daddy, can we watch Shrek on the television?" she asked.

"Sure, dear. Did Cyrus say anything else?" he asked.

"Yes, but I don't know what he means. He said 'Ascend to the fourth vertical'. Daddy, what's vertical?"

"It means up and down, sweetheart. Could you do your daddy a favor?"

"Yes."

"Can you tell me whenever you talk to Cyrus again?"

"You want him to be your friend too, daddy?"

"Yes, I want to be his friend," he said.

They went to the theater room to watch Shrek together. Heather fell asleep halfway through the movie. He moved her into the living room and placed her on the couch.

Rianna came in later.

"Have you noticed that Heather talked to an imaginary friend?" he asked.

"So what, she's has many imaginary friends."

"I bet she didn't have one named Cyrus Black."

"Oh dear God, no! I believed you when you said it was only a glimmer of truth inflated by your brother's fiction. Ben, we have to leave. You know the history of this house and also who Cyrus Black was. How would she know that name if he wasn't haunting it?"

"I know. This is our house now and I'm not going yet. I promise you that if it gets any worse, we'll leave. Heather loves it here. It'll break her heart if we leave. Maybe we should get a dog?" he suggested. "Yes, that's it. A dog. They have a keen sense about paranormal things. Perhaps it could warn us."

"Okay, I trust you. What kind of dog do you want? I love Golden Retrievers and they are great with kids."

"Golden Retriever it is. I'll see if the animal shelter has one tomorrow. I'll feel a lot better having the dog around her when we're not near. Besides, maybe she'll spend so much time with the dog that she'll forget about her imaginary friend."

***

Ben brought home two Golden Retriever puppies and Heather named them. At first she wanted to name them Cyrus and Michael but Ben talked her out of those names so she settled on Bingo and Bongo.

Her invisible friend continued to concern Ben especially now she knew another Black with an evil past, Michael. The spirits hadn't made themselves known to Rianna and Ben. They seemed to concentrate their efforts on young Heather. Ben didn't know what they could want with her so he retrieved some of John's research on the house.

To his horror he discovered that blocking off the west wing did not prevent the witch of the manor, or her minions, from haunting the estate's newest residents. It just prevented people from entering the wing.

Ben vowed if one more spirit contacted his daughter they would leave and give the manor to someone else. Thus far, they noticed nothing else out of the ordinary. Ben and Rianna kept a keen eye out for any paranormal activity.

"Honey, do you think these ghost hunters are legit? I mean, do you think they can really eradicate spirits from a house?"

He asked the question one night as he and Rianna sat in bed looking at ad's for paranormal companies that could come in a eradicate the threat.

"I could call one of them. Loads of them have left messages begging to explore the west wing," Rianna said.

"I know, I'm thinking about it. I don't want to be on camera, or want publicity, and I don't think we should allow Heather to be involved. I just want these spirits out of here. The dogs bark all the time for no reason and perhaps they sense the spirits around us. Heather appears to be able to see them."

"Yes, I noticed that. And I agree, I don't want to be on camera either."

Then Ben pointed to her foot. "What is that on your ankle?"

"No idea. I don't know what that is. My whole foot ached this morning and that open sore just appeared," she said. She dismissed it and began to read her book. "Probably an insect bite. It really doesn't hurt that much, though."

"All the same, you should call Doctor Bell."

"I'll get an appointment for tomorrow. Can you watch Heather? Is that okay with you? I'll have to leave really early to get there on time. I wish his practice was closer."

"Sure, no problem, He's been your doctor for a long time. There's no reason to change now."

He turned off the light on his side of the bed.

***

The next day, Heather came in their room, scared because she said she'd had a bad dream. Ben comforted her while Rianna got up and took a shower, since she had managed to get an early appointment with the doctor. Heather slept for another hour. Rianna kissed them both before she left for her appointment.

Ben woke up later. Heather was still asleep and he put on his slippers. He took one step, then winced in pain and threw his slipper off. A dead scorpion flew out of it. He noticed the scorpion's stinger still in him as he sat in the nearby chair to pull it out. He knew he had to get to a doctor so he woke up Heather and told her get dressed, quickly.

Ben did not know the poisonous nature of scorpions so he gathered up the dead animal and took it with them to the doctor's office.

He limped into the doctor's office with Heather's and met Rianna in the waiting room.

"Still waiting on blood tests?" he asked.

"The question is, what are you here for?"

"Look at this. It's a damn scorpion. It stung me in my foot and it's swollen. It stung me when I put on my slipper," he explained. "I need to see the doctor just in case it's one of the deadly ones."

"Take my appointment dear," she said, as she looked down at Ben's swollen foot.

"I'll ask if he can see both of us. This hurts like hell and the swelling is spreading. I hope the doc calls us soon."

Rianna went to the reception desk to tell the nurse a scorpion had stung her husband and the swelling had started to spread to his ankle. The nurse immediately admitted him to a room. Rianna and Heather went with him.

The doctor came in and looked at Ben's foot.

"Did you happen to see the scorpion?" he asked.

"Yes, I have it in this box. It's dead. I didn't know there were scorpions in Virginia."

The doctor opened the box. "Oh, there are a few varieties, but not this one. I went to school at Arizona State University and I've seen many of these. This looks like a Sculptured Scorpion and it's very deadly. I'll call Reston Hospital and get them to deliver some antivenom as soon as possible. I'd send you in an ambulance, but they aren't that far away and the swelling isn't progressing too fast. I'll place a tourniquet on it until it arrives. Strange that this species is here in Virginia," he commented, as he applied the tourniquet. He injected him with something to ease the swelling.

The doctor then inspected the sore on Rianna's foot.

"We'll have to take a culture. It looks as if you've been burned. I'm a little concerned that the rest of your foot is red as well. I'll swab it and send it to the lab. We should know more in a day or two. For now, we'll clean it, apply antiseptic cream and then bandage it up. Let's see if it gets any better with antibiotics. It may just be an infection of some sort."

He finished bandaging her foot.

"Well, at least you two are consistent. You both have ailments on your left foot." He stooped down to say hello to Heather. "How's my little Heather been?"

He gave her a lollipop.

"I'm doing super, Doctor Bell. My mommy and daddy are sick this time," she said.

She opened the lollipop and put it in her mouth.

"Has it been ten years since I delivered you? My, time's blasting by. You certainly are a cutie."

The antivenom showed up ten minutes later. Dr. Bell immediately injected Ben and then told him to call if the swelling didn't go down overnight.

They all left with both Rianna and Ben's left foot bandaged up. The doctor kept the dead scorpion because he wanted to send it off to an expert to determine exactly what kind of scorpion stung Ben. To him, it looked like the deadly Sculptured Scorpion. He puzzled over how one of the non-lethal ones indigenous to Virginia had ended up in Ben's slipper.

A few days went by, and Rianna noticed sores appeared on her right foot as well. She called the doctor. He informed her that she seemed to have contracted an infection but he did not know what kind. He'd chase up the results.

A few hours later, the doctor got his answer, to the problem with Rianna's feet. They were acidic burns, not an infection.

"Acid burns? How is that possible?" she asked.

"I don't know. It's a weak nitric acid. Do you wear socks?"

"Yes, all the time, why?"

"Well, it could be that the laundry detergent you're using is slightly acidic and it could be causing the burns, especially if your skin is sensitive to even the weakest of acids. Change your detergent and we'll see what happens," he suggested.

"Okay, I can do that."

"Call me if you see no changes. How's Ben's foot doing?"

"Oh, he's doing great. The swelling is completely gone and he's in no pain. What did you find out about the scorpion?"

"It's as I said, a Sculptured Scorpion, a particularly deadly one as well. It shocked my expert to hear that you found one here in Virginia. He said that some people buy them as pets and either let them go after the novelty factor has worn off or they escape."

Rianna accepted the doctor's speculation.

***

A week later, Rianna showered with Heather playing nearby in the huge bedroom. She poked her head out of the shower.

"Honey, could you hand mommy the lotion in the blue bottle right there on the shelf?" she asked.

"Is this it, mommy?" She handed the bottle to Rianna.

"Yes, dear, that's it. Go and see what daddy's doing, okay?"

Rianna applied the lotion to her body.

Heather went to Ben's hobby room and saw him cleaning one of his many guns.

"Mommy told me to come and see what you're doing. What is this, daddy?" she asked. She pointed to one of his pistols.

Ben picked up the unloaded pistol. "This is a nine millimeter Glock, sweetheart."

"Can I shoot it?" she asked.

"Of course, baby. I'll have to show you how first."

He continued to oil his revolver.

"Don't tell your mother though. She still thinks you're too young to shoot but I had just turned ten when my father taught me. I still remember my first hunt with him when I got my first rabbit. Those were the days."

"You killed a bunny, daddy?" she asked.

"Yes dear, but it suffered. You don't like to see animals suffering, do you?"

"No, I love animals. My teacher told me that animals have feelings too," she replied.

"Your teacher is probably one of those anti-hunting nuts. Animals suffer when they are sick or in pain and sometimes we have to put them down when they are hurting, to spare them the pain they are going through."

"So…we kill them so they won't hurt anymore?"

"That's right, dear. Do you remember Old Blue, at our other place? Remember when he broke his leg? I had to kill him so he wouldn't suffer."

"I liked my pony Blue. I didn't know he hurt," she said.

"No need to get upset, sweetheart. Old Blue loved you even more because we eased his pain and he went to heaven with the other ponies. In heaven, all their pain is taken away," he explained. He gave her a hug. "I tell you what, if you don't tell mommy, we can go shooting today. There are some sick rabbits and groundhogs way down by the river. I'll show you how to shoot them."

"Thanks, daddy. Can we go now?"

"Sure, sweetheart. I have a little gun just for you."

He handed her a small two-shot derringer.

"This is my gun?"

"It will be when I show you how to use it."

Ben and his daughter set out on an ATV to the far reaches of his property. Ben hoped the sounds of the gunshots would not reach the manor. Rianna hated guns and tried to talk Ben out of having so many with a young child in the house but he possessed a stubborn regard for his guns, and at times, obsessed over owning as many as he could. Ben had an irrational fear that the country neared a civil war. Ben loved his family life. Rianna said his fears sometimes clouded his fatherly instincts.

Ben and Heather drove his ATV to the site near the river and they immediately saw a groundhog digging a hole. He told Heather that the groundhog suffered pain and needed to be killed.

"Put these on." He handed her earplugs. "It's going to be loud. Now watch, Heather."

He aimed his rifle and blasted the groundhog.

They walked over to look at the mortally wounded groundhog. "See, he's not in pain anymore."

"Daddy, he's bleeding. He's still moving. Help him!" she begged.

Ben aimed again and shot the groundhog again, killing it instantly.

"See, Heather, he's not in pain anymore. He's in heaven with the other groundhogs."

"But daddy, didn't you cause him to be in pain by shooting him the first time?" Tears rolled down her face.

"Trust me, he suffered no pain," he explained.

"I don't want to do this anymore. I want to go home." She walked over to the ATV and sat there. Her lips pulled into a scowl. "I don't want to kill animals!"

Ben gathered his gear and felt disappointment as he drove back to the house. Ben knew he'd traumatized her, and tried to justify the killing all the way back to the house, but Heather was not to be pacified. Ben wondered if he'd made a terrible mistake. He should not have allowed his young daughter to see the destruction of the groundhog.

He guessed his wife would hear about the adventure and he readied himself for the onslaught from a very angry wife. He took his guns back into his hobby room and locked them up, but he forgot about the little .22 caliber two-shot derringer that he had given to Heather. Suddenly, Ben heard loud shrieks from Rianna's bedroom.

He picked up a gun and ran towards the noise.

She lay in her bed with burns all over her body. She writhed in agony. Ben called for an ambulance and frantically sought to help his beloved wife. He didn't know how to comfort her.

Heather ran into the room and called out, "Mommy, mommy!" She saw her mother's blistered skin. She reached into her pocket, got her shiny .22 caliber derringer, and shot her mother in the arm.

"What did you do, Heather? Why did you shoot your mother?"

Ben grabbed her by her small shoulders and tried to shake an answer out of her. Ben's yells, and the shakes, just caused her to stare at him. Heather seemed unbelievably calm as her father continued to yell hysterically.

"Mommy is in pain, daddy. I don't want her to be in pain. I want her to go to Heaven."

She raised the weapon again. Unaware of his actions Ben raised his gun toward Heather.

"Ben, what are you doing? You're not going to shoot your daughter!"

"She shot you! She's got one more bullet in that gun!"

"Lower the gun, Ben! Do not shoot Heather!" his injured wife begged. "Heather, dear, I'll be fine. Don't shoot me again."

Heather lowered her gun and Ben lowered his. Then he took the gun from her.

"Mommy, daddy told me that if animals are in pain then we have to shoot them so they won't be in pain anymore and they can go to Heaven and play."

"Ben, you son-of-a-bitch, did you tell her that?"

"Well, yes, but I didn't mean for her to shoot you."

"You and your fucking guns! When are you going to grow the fuck up? Every one of those goddamn guns had better be out of here by the time I get back! You will not teach our daughter to be a fucking terrorist! Do you understand me?"

He shredded his shirt and tied it around her arm tightly to stop the blood flow and then called the medics. He didn't want to argue with his angry wife. "I understand, but it's not the gun's fault she shot you."

"Shut the fuck up, Ben! It's not the gun's fault; it's your fault. You did this! Not Heather!"

There was a knock on the door that broke the tension.

Ben let the paramedics in and they immediately saw that Rianna had burns all over her body and a gunshot wound to her upper arm.

"Who shot you?" one paramedic asked.

She pointed to Ben. "My husband. It was an accident."

The paramedics relayed Rianna's condition to the hospital. "We have a woman in her mid-thirties with various thickness burns over ninety percent of her body and a gunshot wound to her upper left arm. We're transporting her now."

Ben and Rianna listened to the reply.

"Okay, bring her to the burn unit as fast as possible."

He apologized as they placed her in the ambulance, "I'm sorry. I'm so sorry. I vow to be a better father and husband."

The doctors deemed her condition critical and immediately placed her in intensive care. They quickly examined the burns and were shocked to find that she had been burned by a concentrated nitric acid. They minimized the damage to her skin before they removed the bullet from her arm.

The doctor came into the waiting room. Heather was asleep but he told Ben that Rianna had suffered mostly first-degree burns with a few second-degree spots. "She should be okay once we determine her recuperative abilities Mr. Black, I understand that you accidentally shot your wife?"

"Yes, I did. My gun went off in my haste to get to her to help her. She screamed and seemed to be in quite a bit of pain."

"I have informed the police. There has to be an investigation. They are here and have some questions for you," the doctor said.

A police detective came in and questioned Ben but he seemed satisfied that the shooting appeared accidental and wrote it in his report.

"We'll have to speak to your wife but the doctor said she'd told them it was an accident as well."

"Yes, it was an accident. Detective, I need to get my daughter home. Can this wait until later?"

"Oh I think it can wait; in fact I think that's all I need to know, Thanks, sir."

Ben took his sleeping daughter home. He carried her into the house and placed her gently into her bed. He sat down near her bed, placed his head in his hands, and cried as he remembered that he had consciously pointed his gun at his precious daughter and seriously pondered the idea of pulling the trigger and sending a round into her head.

"Oh, dear God, what have I done?"

Ben and Heather visited her daily. She rewarded them with a big smile every time they came. Eventually, the burns healed perfectly. The doctors informed her that only a few would leave a scar. The redness subsided and she could see, in the mirror, her beautiful skin slowly return to normal.

She stayed in the hospital for another week and planned a party for her return to the manor.

Ben drove to the hospital to pick her up and take her home. When they arrived Heather, and all of Ben and Rianna's friends, were there to welcome her home. They partied and laughed the rest of the night never bringing up her gunshot wound.

She felt elated when Ben told her he had destroyed most of his guns, but not all of them. Rianna knew Ben had a sickness but she believed that he tried hard to conquer his fears.

She didn't know why Ben suddenly changed his world perspective however she welcomed the change and allowed him to heal. Although she still was skeptical about his resolve.

***

One night as his wife slept peacefully in her bed, Ben walked in to see Heather in the room. He noticed that she played with a ball, which she rolled, to the other end of the room.

"What are you doing sweetheart?"

"I'm playing with Cyrus," she answered.

"I don't see Cyrus, honey. Are you sure he's here?"

"Yes, he's here, see?"

She pointed to the ball. It rolled slowly to her.

Ben stepped back.

"You can't hurt him, daddy, because he's not real, and you can't shoot him because he's not in pain." She rolled the ball back into the dark unlit corner of the room.

"Why would I want to hurt Cyrus?"

He saw the ball return to her.

"He doesn't like you, daddy. He tells me that you don't like mommy and that you burned her." She pushed the ball back.

"I didn't burn your mommy, Heather! Cyrus is lying to you."

The ball rolled towards him this time. In anger he kicked the ball back into the darkness. The ball returned. It had been burnt to a crisp and disintegrated in front of him and Heather.

"He's mad that you burned the ball, daddy," Heather said.

He picked up his smallish ten-year old and said, "Listen, I did not burn the ball and I did not burn mommy."

"He said you did. You put acid in her socks and her lotion. You are trying to kill my mommy, aren't you?" she asked.

"No, that's not true. I love your mommy. Tell him it's not true."

"I can't because he's gone now. He and Michael think I'm a grownup. They can't see that I'm little, but they can see you and mommy." Her eyelids closed. "Daddy, I'm so tired. Can I go to bed?"

"Of course dear, do you want to lie down next to mommy?"

"No. Mommy's dead. I don't want to sleep with mommy."

Ben walked over to Rianna. She opened her eyes.

"Why are you staring at me?"

"Do you feel all right?"

"Ben, I'm fine." She yawned and went to place her arms around him. Then she squealed with horror. "What have you done to Bongo?"

Confused, Ben looked at his hands and saw that he held a bloodied Golden Retriever by its neck. He threw the dog aside. "I had Heather in my hands, not Bongo. What the fuck is going on? I swear to you, I held Heather," he explained.

Heather had followed Ben into her mother's room. She stood at his side. He didn't mean to but he dropped the dead dog at his daughter's feet. Her face turned white, as she looked first at Bongo and then at her father.

"Daddy, why did you kill Bongo?"

"I didn't kill Bongo!" Frantically he wiped the drops of blood from his hands.

"Then who did, Ben? Come here, Heather, come to mommy," she said.

"I didn't kill Bongo, dammit! Do you think I'm mad?"

She covered Heather's ears.

"Go away, Ben, and take Bongo with you. Bury him out back and we will talk later about this. Can't you see what you've done to your daughter?"

Ben picked up the dead dog. He looked towards his wife and daughter but they turned away.

"There you go, sweetie. It'll be okay." her mother comforted her trembling daughter.

"Why did daddy kill my dog, mommy, like he killed my pony? Daddy doesn't like my friends, does he?"

"Honey, have you seen Bingo?"

"No, daddy probably killed him, too. Why does daddy kill things?" She hugged her mother.

"Your daddy is having problems, dear. I'll talk to him later. Do you want me to read you a story?"

"Yes, read me about the brown squirrel again. I like that book."

"Okay, go and get it off the shelf over there." She pointed to the bookshelf.

Still confused as to what happened in the bedroom, Ben dug a shallow hole in the garden, placed Bongo in it, and filled it in. He placed the shovel in the ATV and looked back at the grave. He noticed movement and suddenly a paw poked through the ground. Ben ran to the grave and dug the loose dirt away as the dog struggled free itself. Ben helped the dog, but then he noticed the dog's collar. He'd buried Bingo instead of Bongo.

"What the hell is happening to me?" he mumbled.

He attempted to clean the dirt off the dog as Bingo licked his face happy to see his master. Afterwards Ben went back to the house and to the bedroom to see Rianna happily reading to Heather.

He sat in a chair near the bed. "Honey, I think I need to see someone. I think I'm going nuts."

Bingo ran into the room as Rianna closed the book and Heather got out of bed to hug Bingo. The dog licked her face.

"Don't touch Bingo, Heather. He's muddy, Ben. Take him outside and clean him off. How did he get so muddy?"

Ben looked around the room but did not see the dead Bongo. Ben didn't want to tell her what he'd done, so he took Bingo outside without an explanation. Heather went with him. He spied a large jar with grass in it sitting just outside the back door.

"What's this?" he asked, as he got the hose out.

"Those are mommy's bugs. She said that she used them to kill spiders," Heather replied.

She brushed the mud from Bingo's coat.

"Spiders?" He held the jar up to his face.

"Yes, she saw spiders in the kitchen," Heather explained. He looked in the jar and saw two large Sculptured Scorpions, the same variety that nearly killed him. Then Heather told him something that made him wonder. "I saw mommy put one in your shoe, daddy. She said a spider walked in there."

"What? She put one of these in my shoe?"

"Yes, she told me not to tell you," she said. She continued calmly to brush Bingo's coat.

Ben left Heather after he cleaned the mud off the dog and then went to confront Rianna.

He held up the jar. "Why do you have these and why did you put one in my shoe?" he asked.

"Why would I do that? I hate crawly things and you know that I don't have a clue about scorpions. If we're into accusations, Heather told me earlier that she saw you put acid in my lotion."

"What is going on here? She also told me that she's been playing with her imaginary friends. You know, Cyrus and Michael. I wonder if the house is doing this?"

"Oh, dear God, do you think that they are telling her to do these things?"

"I don't know, but something is going on here. When I buried Bongo it turned out to be Bingo."

"What are you talking about? Bingo is with Heather and Bongo is right here under the bed," she said.

Ben looked under the bed and Bongo came out wagging his tail. "Something very strange is happening to us, honey. I think the witch of the house is haunting our daughter and us. We're getting out of here. Are you well enough to travel?"

"I'm doing okay. The sores on my legs haven't healed yet. If something is haunting us, we need to leave now!"

"My brother saw the signs, but he stayed and we know what happened to him and his wife. I'm not taking any chances."

***

They watched their young daughter. The attention she received from the spirits frightened them. Ben explained to Heather that they had to leave the estate.

"No," she said, "I don't want to go. I like it here."

"We have to, dear. There are things happening that you do not understand."

"Mommy's not well so we can't leave can we?"

"We'll manage. We'll both help mommy. Now go play with your dogs."

Heather stormed off and took her dogs with her.

Ben explained that Heather appeared angry about leaving.

"She'll accept it later. You know I'm still perplexed as to where all this nitric acid is coming from. I've checked everything and nothing has acid in it."

"Well, I don't know. I know Heather accused me, but I didn't do it."

"I know you didn't. Honey, do you think Heather could have done this?"

"No way! She hasn't a clue what acid is or what it does to skin."

"You're right, of course. What am I thinking? It's getting late. I'm a little tired. Tell Heather it's time for bed. We'll go tomorrow, okay?"

"Yes, you rest up. I'll send her to bed."

Heather ignored her father. She went to her bedroom without a word. Ben attempted to kiss her goodnight but she turned away. He left her clutching her doll with an angry look on her face.

They settled in for a good night's sleep. However Ben woke up abruptly from his slumber when his wife screamed. She held her ankle. Ben saw the white linen sheets were bright red. Her ankle spewed blood. He wiped away the blood from the gaping wound and saw that her Achilles tendon had been severed.

Heather was in the doorway. "Did you do this?" Ben snapped.

"Do what, daddy? I heard mommy scream. Are you hurting mommy?" she asked. She started to cry.

"No, I'm not hurting mommy, but someone is. I'll ask you again. Did you do this?"

"No, daddy, I didn't do anything!"

"Ben, stop blaming Heather and get me to the hospital. We'll figure it all out later."

The doctor who met them at the emergency room expressed surprise to see them again.

"Another mysterious injury?" he asked.

"I don't know what happened," Ben said.

The doctor returned to the waiting room an hour later. "Fortunately we were able to reconnect the tendon and sew up her wound. It appears as if some sort of wire cutter was used. It is a clean, quick cut," the doctor said.

"Could a little ten-year-old girl do this?" Ben asked.

The doctor frowned. "Are you assuming that young Heather did this? That little girl over there wouldn't do such a horrible thing; besides, she's not strong enough. It took some strength to do this."

"I'm just asking. I know I didn't do it and Mrs. Black obviously didn't. Heather is the only other one in the house."

"What about your help? Could one of them have done this?"

"They're all day workers. They go home at night," Ben said.

He walked with the doctor to Rianna's room and discovered Heather on the bed beside her mother, crying.

She confronted Ben, "Why are you being so cruel to Heather?"

"Cruel? Think about it! Who else could have cut your ankle?"

"You could have!" she said.

"Me? I was sleeping beside you when you screamed! How could I have done it?"

"I don't know, but I know that my angel didn't."

She held Heather tightly.

Ben stormed out of the room. He did not like being accused of something like that. He went to the cafeteria to calm down, and an hour later he returned to apologize to Heather and Rianna.

When he took Heather home, he tried to mend their shaky relationship with ice cream and cake and an offer to watch her favorite movies with her.

Heather watched a cartoon, but Ben saw something completely different, something that scared the hell out of him.

An old woman came on the screen and whispered, "We've got you, Benjamin! You'll not see many more good days. The prophecy will continue. A relic of Heather's choosing will be taken. We have her now. You cannot leave the manor and you will not survive, nor will your pretty wife. You cannot leave the manor now," the spirit said.

The image dissipated into the happy cartoon.

Ben jumped up and ran, so frightened for his life, he fell over the leather-bound theater chairs. He did not realize he'd left his young daughter alone. He ran to his hobby room to collect his guns and carried them to his bedroom. Deranged with fear, he lay down on his bed with his eyes trained on the open bedroom door poised to blast the first thing he saw.

It was Heather who came to the door.

He instinctively fired a shot. It barely missed his daughter but the bullet splintered the door jam and sprayed a huge part of the wood into Heather's face. He watched her recoil in pain as he came to his senses and realized what he had done. A huge splinter pierced her cheek; blood spurted out of the wound and her mouth. She was hysterical and when Ben came to her aid she shouted at him.

"I don't want you to touch me, stay away from me, daddy!"

He ignored her protests as he gathered her up and took her to the emergency room to get stitched up. He didn't want to tell his wife what happened. Unfortunately the same doctor who treated his wife sewed up his daughter.

"Mr. Black I don't believe this little girl is safe in your care, I don't know what's happening at your house, but this is the last straw. I've called the police and they are on their way. I think you did this to this little girl. Social Services will take Heather until her mother is well enough to bring her home."

Ben protested but realized the doctor's decision presented the perfect opportunity to get his possessed daughter out of the house.

Chapter 9
Ben's Mental Demise

Social Services informed her that they would take Heather into their care until she got out of the hospital. They had serious concerns about Ben's mental state.

Ben agreed with their decision.

"No, she is his daughter, and he loves her. I will not allow my child to go into foster care. I will fight this even though my husband won't," she replied.

"Mrs. Black, Heather's face was just stitched up because a piece of wood got impaled her cheek in your husband care. Do you want to take the responsibility if he were to harm Heather?" the social worker asked.

"What?"

"She's fine now, however the doctors had to stitch both inside and outside her mouth. Your husband said that it was an accident."

"He'd never intentionally harm our daughter. Sure, he has a few minor issues, but they can be worked out. I'll talk to him. Is that okay? Bring me my daughter!"

"We do not need your permission. If we feel that the child's in danger, we will take her into our protection. Mr. Black appears to have the notion that little Heather is a real danger to you both," she said. "It's all in this report."

"He'd never harm her, how many times do I have to say that? Heather is only ten years old. How can she be deemed a threat to us?"

"Okay, I'll get a judge to release her to her father, but we will be checking in on them until you are able to return to the home. Is that agreeable?" the woman asked.

"Yes, I'll agree to that. I will talk to him as well."

"Very well, Mrs. Black, good day," she said, as she walked toward the door.

"Thank you. If my husband is out there could you please tell him that I want to talk to him?"

"Sure, I believe he's in the waiting room with Heather."

"Thank you."

Ben walked in with Heather and Rianna immediately noticed her bandaged cheek. He asked her why she talked the social worker out of taking Heather for a week.

She called her over to her bedside. "Oh, sweetheart, does it hurt?"

"No, mommy, it doesn't hurt anymore, but Daddy shot his gun at me," Heather reported.

"He did what? Sweetheart, can you go talk to Nurse Jackie? I think she's got some lollipops behind the counter. I need to talk to daddy." She kissed Heather on the head.

"I'll take her. I'll be right back."

Ben held Heather's hand and walked her to the nurse's station. When he returned to Rianna's room he could tell that she seethed with anger.

She struggled with the words. "What the hell are you trying to do? Heather is our beautiful child. How could you shoot at her, you son-of-a-bitch?"

Ben held his head low and got ready for the barrage of insults and accusations.

He confessed, "My mind is not right! I know that and I don't know what to say. I do know that I'm sick and need a mental evaluation. I think that Social Services should take her for a week, or until you're released."

"How could you just give her away? Collectively, we are worth nearly a hundred million dollars. How'd that look to the press if they got wind of it? What were you thinking when you shot at her?" she shouted.

"It would only be about a week. There is something not right with her. I see it in her eyes. She's trying to harm us. I can just sense that she is stalking us and using her sweet nature to hide it. I shot at her, yes. I viewed her as something evil. I don't know why, but I see my error now."

"Are you listening to yourself? She's our child. She weighs seventy-five pounds and is four and a half feet tall! How can she harm us? Get a grip and suck it up for a week or hire someone to look after her, but she will not go into foster care! Got it?" She waved her finger at him.

"Okay. Okay, I'm sorry, I'll watch her. I apologize. You're right, of course. I feel so ashamed of myself." He shook with fright as he relived the entire chain of events in his tortured mind.

The nurse brought Heather back in the room and Ben hugged her and asked her if she wanted to go home.

"Can we stay with mommy some more?"

Rianna answered the question. "Of course you can, sweetheart. Come to momma."

She held out her arms to receive her beautiful daughter. Heather walked over to her bed and she picked her up and sat her beside her on the bed.

"Do you miss Bingo and Bongo?" she asked.

"Oh, yes, Bingo came back to life," she responded.

"Came back to life? What do you mean, dear?" she asked.

"Daddy buried Bingo and he came back to life," she said.

"How the hell did she know that?" Ben whispered.

"What did you say, Ben?"

He hadn't realized he'd spoken out loud.

"Nothing," Ben lied.

He noticed Heather smiled menacingly at him. "He killed Jose too and he buried him down by the river where the blue flowers grow," she added.

"Jose? Our head groundskeeper?" she asked.

Ben raised his eyebrows at that statement. "I did what? Heather, you're lying to your mother."

"Now, Heather, you know that your father wouldn't hurt Jose. He likes Jose. We all do."

"He did, mommy. He showed me his gun and he told me that you should shoot anything that is in pain. That's why I shot you. You were crying and in pain. Daddy gave me the little gun."

"I shot a groundhog! Heather, you know I shot a groundhog!"

"Is everything else true, Ben? Did you say that and did you give her the gun?"

"Well, yes, but I didn't tell her to shoot you. I did give her the gun and I forgot to get it back before I locked up the safe."

"I told you to get rid of those damn guns!"

"I did destroy many of them, but I didn't shoot Jose," he said.

"Daddy, I saw you. You buried Jose. I said that he's still moving and you shot him again and then you buried him. I know where you buried him." She stared ahead as if remembering the scene.

"Who taught you to lie like this, Heather? Your father didn't kill anyone!" Rianna supported Ben.

"But mommy…"

"I don't want to hear any more about it! Now apologize to your father!" she demanded.

"Daddy, I'm sorry." She hugged her father and then went back to her mother.

"She's just embarrassed, Ben. Where did she learn how to lie like this?"

"I'm not lying, mommy. I will show you where he buried Jose!"

The conversation ended as the doctor walked in.

"Visiting hours are over but you can both come back tomorrow. Your wife needs some rest now."

Ben kissed his wife affectionately and Heather did as well.

"Bye, sweetheart, and no more fibs about your father. Ben can you bring her back tomorrow?"

"Sure, honey. Come on Heather, let's go home."

"Okay, daddy, bye, mommy. I love you!"

"I love you too dear."

Ben took Heather home and all the way back he reminded Heather that he had killed a groundhog.

However, Heather stuck with her story.

"Sweetheart, when we get home I'll take you to where I buried the groundhog and show you."

"Okay, daddy, I want to pick some blue flowers for mommy."

"I'll help you sweetheart, okay?"

She said, "We can pick a lot of them."

Ben drove up the long driveway and went inside to get a drink and to fix them both some dinner. They ate sandwiches with milk and talked while they ate. Ben hated the fact he didn't trust his daughter yet he felt happy that his wife had talked him out of allowing Social Services to take her. His wife had called him a monster and he felt it necessary to prove her wrong. Obviously, she'd re-evaluated his parental skills and considered they'd taken a backseat to his fears of the manor's past. His brother's epic journey into the paranormal only aided those thoughts and although he held strong doubts about many of the circumstances surrounding the grounds of the old house, he was not about to discount them, either.

Ben drove Heather to the ornate and elaborate flowerbed where he had buried the groundhog and started digging.

Soon, Ben saw something that took his breath away and made him sink into a heart-pounding panic so severe; he believed his heart had exploded right out of his chest.

A hand, a human hand protruded from the rich soil. He frantically moved the dirt away from where he reckoned the head lay and eventually revealed the body of Jose

Rivera, his trusted landscaper and friend. The deeper he dug, the more insane he felt. He sat back when he saw the bullet hole in the dead man's side. He moved Jose's shirt up to see another bullet hole positioned directly over Jose's heart.

He cried. "Rianna is right. I need psychiatric help."

He became aware of his sweet daughter's stare.

"I told you, daddy," she said, as she picked a few of the blue flowers.

Ben frantically dug up the flowerbed looking for the dead groundhog, however there were no groundhogs. He fell to his knees and placed his dirtied hands over his face as he cried. His panic calmed as he resolved to believe he'd done the evil deed. His precious daughter had been right.

Ben did what he had to do. He dug up Jose and placed him gently into the ATV and then covered his body with a sheet before taking him back to the house. He knew that he'd need to have a long talk with his daughter and wife before he turned himself in to the authorities.

* * * *

Before he did that, he dropped his daughter off at her friend's house. Then he returned to the mansion alone. He cleaned off Jose and dressed him in one of his own finest and expensive suits. He combed the dead man's hair, then fashioned a makeshift coffin and placed Jose in it. He wanted Jose to have a fitting end. He acted as if he had lost his mind and instead of immediately calling the police, his muddled mind told him to bury poor Jose. He drove the ATV through the darkness to the cemetery on the estate's grounds and began digging under billions of stars.

He worked hard. He never tired. He hoped that by burying Jose in the cemetery graced the man with the honor he deserved, given that he had no family. For hours, Ben dug non-stop. He felt no urgency in burying Jose, nor did he feel a sense that he hid his ill deed. A proper burial was the proper thing to give his friend.

He still did not remember shooting Jose. The evidence was plain enough. It terrified him that his daughter not only saw him shoot a trusted and well-liked worker, but also inhumanly deliver the kill shot.

"I need help." He repeated the words over and over again as the hole got deeper and deeper.

He thought, I'll never get enough help to overcome the memory of this night.

He climbed out and gently eased the box, holding Jose's body into the hole, said a few words over him and hoped that Jose somehow knew the sorrow he felt. He filled in the hole until exhaustion caused him to stop. Tired, he knelt down on his knees and prayed for forgiveness. The flat brown patch among the green grass existed as a remembrance of his deed.

He went back to where he'd discovered Jose's body and retrieved as many of the flowers as he could hold. He'd frantically thrown them to one side when he'd believed he was searching for the dead groundhog. He carried them back to Jose's grave and planted them, carefully covering the bare brown patch. A simple wooden cross, emblazoned with Jose's name was all that remained for him to add.

The wooden cross looked odd and out of place among the ornate stone and marble monuments installed for the affluent. It was the best he was able to provide.

Ben wanted to sleep well that night, so he did what every man did to forget or to ease a memory's destruction of his soul. He drank. He hoped the alcohol made his decision easier for him to carry on.

The loaded Glock, which he'd saved despite his wife's demand to destroy the guns, lay on the desk in front of him, along with a half-bottle of Jim Beam. Many a time when he went to fill his glass he touched the gun first. Yet he felt something powerful direct his shaking hand away from the pistol.

Ben felt depressed, so much so that he seriously contemplated the end of his life. Anything to avoid telling his beautiful wife and child that he was the monster they believed he portrayed. The picture of them finding him dead in a pool of blood prevented him from committing his final act. It could have been his faith, or the memory of his child's face, that steered him away from the easy way out of his situation. Whatever stayed his hand caused him to stow the gun in the drawer and all thoughts of suicide left his mind. He decided to stand up to face his fears and his ultimate punishment for what he'd done. He could have easily covered up his crime. Jose didn't have any family members to ask questions; however, he knew a deed memory as monumental as this couldn't be hidden for long.

Ben eventually put the stopper in the bottle and staggered to the bedroom where he lay in bed and stared at the ornate ceiling. He dreaded the next morning's sunshine. He decided to ask the parents of Heather's friend if they could keep her for another day because he wanted to confess what he'd done. He knew that he couldn't put it off forever however he wanted to consider all his options. If Heather were here they might decide to hide his dark secret forever.

Then circumstances changed.

Rianna called to tell Ben that the doctors had released her early and he could pick her up at noon the next day.

"I'm so excited. Can you bring Heather with you? I've missed you both so much. I want to get back to some sort of normalcy."

"Okay, I'll be there at 11:30 tomorrow. We'll pick up Heather later. There's something I need to discuss with you first."

"You sound depressed, honey. Is there something wrong?" she asked.

"Yes, there is, but I don't want to discuss it over the phone."

"Oh God. Wait! You said Heather wasn't with you. Has something happened to Heather?"

"No, Heather's fine, she's over at the Adam's house. I'm the one with the problem. I'll talk to you on the way home, okay?"

"I hope you're okay. God, I hope I never see another hospital again. The doctor said that I should be able to walk in a few weeks."

"That's great, dear. I miss you too. I know Heather does as well," he said.

"You're scaring me, Ben. Whatever it is, we'll get by. We've always persevered. We love each other and we have a beautiful child and a lovely home. We are living the American dream."

"I know. You're right as always. I'll see you tomorrow."

"Okay," she said.

Ben put the phone down.

She doesn't know that our life together is over, he thought.

* * * *

Rianna hadn't a clue what was wrong. She'd never heard Ben sound so down.

Everything will be fine once I'm home, she thought.

The next morning she waited for him at the front door of the hospital in a wheelchair.

"There's my bride."

He helped her into the car.

She sensed a difference in Ben. He didn't turn on the ignition, just sat there. He looked down as if studying the steering wheel. She placed her hand over his.

"Okay, tell me what's wrong?"

"Do you remember when Heather told you that I shot Jose?"

"Yes, of course. It's not something one could easily forget."

"Well, I went with Heather to where I thought I shot the groundhog, to dig it up and show her. Apparently, I must have had a mental episode because I actually shot and killed Jose," Ben explained.

"What? Are you fucking serious? You killed Jose?"

"I dug up Jose. I shot him twice."

"There has to be a mistake! You can't possibly mistake a groundhog for a grown man. It's just not possible! Think about it, Ben!"

"I have thought about it! For two damn days I thought about it! It's the house!"

She asked, "The house?"

"Yes, the house! You read John's book. You know what he wrote! I didn't believe it at first because I considered it to be fiction; that's changed. I believe it now and it's making me crazy."

"Okay, calm down. We have to keep our heads together and think about what we need to do. Where is Jose's body?"

"I buried him in our cemetery. I've already decided what I'm going to do."

She asked, "What have you decided?"

"I'm going to turn myself in to authorities. I can't live with what I've done. Tomorrow, I'll call the police and confess."

"We have lawyers, Ben. Perhaps there is another way out."

"If there is, I can't see it. I'm afraid that there is nothing we can do. My life is over and I want this to be out in the open and done with. I will go to prison for the rest of my life. I want to shield you and Heather from as much embarrassment as possible. I think that's the best approach."

There was a silence between them. He started the car to drive to the manor. Tears rolled down her face and she hugged Ben as he drove toward their driveway and through the huge iron gates.

"Dear God! Heather! I hope she understands what this all means," she said. She wiped at her tears.

"I just want to spend the rest of this day with you. Heather is at her friend's house. Can you do this for me?"

He grabbed her hand.

"Of course I can, and I will be with you throughout everything, even though I still think it's a mistake to turn yourself in. Whatever the outcome, please know that we love you and will always love you." She squeezed his hand.

"Thank you. I love you more than you know."

She replied, "I love you, too."

They spent that night together and woke up to an uncertain future. They picked up Heather. Once back home they sat her down, and told her the reality of the situation. They didn't know how she would react when they told her; it was a complete surprise.

"That's not going to happen, daddy. You can't leave us. I saw Jose today," Heather said.

"No, you didn't, sweetheart. Whoever you saw just looked like Jose. I told you Jose is buried over by the blue flowers," Ben explained.

"No, daddy, I saw him today. Why don't you believe me?"

"Because I buried him. You were right, I accidently shot Jose instead of the groundhog." He lowered his head in shame.

"Mommy, do you believe me?"

She climbed onto her mother's lap.

"I'm sorry, but your father knows what he's talking about." She hugged Heather tightly.

Heather cried and Ben grabbed her to him. "I'm so sorry, honey. I will always love you."

After she'd calmed down Heather went out to play with the dogs. Ben decided it was time to call the police and confess his crime.

He shook, and obviously in distress he slowly dialed the number. A police officer answered the phone. He introduced himself as Detective Jones.

"Detective Jones, I have a confession to make. I accidentally shot and killed my landscaper, Jose Rivera."

"You killed your landscaper? Is the body there at your home?"

"Yes, well, not in the home, I buried him in our cemetery," Ben explained.

"You moved the body? Mr. Black, you shouldn't have done that. You destroyed evidence!"

"I destroyed evidence? I just confessed I shot him accidentally."

"I suggest that you get a lawyer." The detective cautioned Ben as he made arrangements to visit. "We'll have to exhume him. Please don't touch the grave."

"Okay, I'll take you to the body when you get here."

The police set out for the manor. They were very wary of going inside however entering the home did not appear to be an issue. Ben Black had told him he'd shot the man outside and buried him far away from the manor. They arrived with a backhoe, a body van, and four cruisers with blue and red lights blazing. Bad news travelled fast. The press had already amassed outside the gates.

Ben and Rianna led the way to the site on their ATV. The grounds were smooth enough to allow the cruisers and medical examiner to drive to the cemetery over the freshly cut green grass.

Ben showed them where he buried Jose. A spot marked by the wooden cross. The police handcuffed Ben then made him stand near the police cruiser.

"We don't want you involved in the exhumation," Detective Jones said.

"Is this necessary?" Ben asked. He held up his handcuffed hands while he was patted down. "I'm not going anywhere!"

"Sorry, Mr. Black, it's just standard procedures. We have to determine whether you're armed. If you did what you said you did, we have to protect ourselves."

Ben leaned against the police cruiser.

"Okay, I understand."

The backhoe started digging and digging. They didn't find a body. They were already well past where Ben had dug and still there was no body. A police officer called the detective over.

"We found something, sir."

Detective Jones walked over behind the big pile of dirt. He asked Ben, "There isn't a body in there! Are you sure this is the spot?" he asked.

"Yes, I know it is. You dug by the makeshift crucifix? He's there."

"We found a dead groundhog. That's it!"

"Oh my God! You found a groundhog? Did you see bullet holes in it?" Ben asked.

"Yes, looks like that's how it died," Detective Jones said.

"I must have made a horrible mistake. Detective Jones, I apologize and I'll pay for your time and everyone else's time," he said. "I know I didn't kill Jose. It was my imagination!"

"It's not about the cost, Mr. Black. My officers could be out saving lives right now."

"I know and I'm embarrassed. Will I be charged with wasting police time? I will pay any fine."

"You seem happy about all this." Detective Jones had a scowl on his face.

"When I called you I was certain I'd killed someone. Now I know I didn't. Wouldn't you feel happy that you didn't do such a horrible thing?"

"I guess you're right. I don't think we'll charge you with a crime." He took off the handcuffs. "However I do recommend you seek help, Mr. Black."

"I will certainly do that, sir."

Ben smiled and turned to hug Rianna. As Ben tried to explain what happened, or what he believed happened, Rianna noticed Heather being led from the cemetery by a smiling and very much alive Jose Rivera.

"See, daddy, I told you I saw Jose."

"Jose, you have no idea how good I feel to see you," Ben said, smiling.

"Mr. Black, I'm sorry I missed the last few days. I had to fix something at my house. What's going on here?"

"Nothing, Jose! How about coming here and making a garden out of this area? I feel that this place should be tended to."

"I'll start tomorrow," Jose said. He shook Ben's hand and left to go to his car.

"Heather, I should have believed you. Will you accept my apology?" Ben asked.

"Sure, daddy, I told you that I saw Jose but I've got a secret to tell you."

"What's that, dear?"

Heather whispered, "I know who really killed Jose."

Ben looked at her. "Jose's not dead, sweetheart."

Heather whispered, "That's really not Jose. That's Cyrus. I know who killed Jose. Don't tell mommy because she will cry. Do you promise?"

"Yes, dear, I promise not to tell anyone."

The hairs on Ben's neck bristled. Heather's secret was beyond belief. So, for the moment, he decided to do as his daughter wished and keep it to himself.

Heather has told me some fantastic before, he thought, and this is no different.

He had no clue where she got the stories. He didn't rule out the fantasy world of a young child. He certainly didn't want his wife to think that both her husband and her daughter had mental issues.

"Ben, what did she tell you?"

"She just told me that she loved me, that's all."

He grabbed her hand, kissed her, and led her to the ATV.

The police left and wrote it off as a false alarm.

***

A few days later, alone in the house with Heather, he realized that he hadn't seen his daughter for a few hours.

Rianna was in town and he'd stayed home to pay bills.

Time flies when you're having fun, he thought.

He clicked on the curser to pay the last bill when he then heard two gunshots outside near the pool. Automatically he opened his drawer. His pistol was missing. He had other guns though not near the den.

He ran to the kitchen, out the back door and found Heather lying on the ground petting Bingo and Bongo.

He looked around the property.

"Did you hear any gunshots, Heather?" he asked.

"Yes daddy, I shot Bingo and Bongo because they wouldn't play with me."

"You did what? Holy crap, Heather! Where did you get this gun?"

"From your desk. You gave it to me to shoot. Don't you remember? You were paying bills and I asked you for it."

"Heather, you are going to have to stop lying. Give me that gun!"

Ben grabbed the gun from Heather and she backed away from Ben's loud tone.

Then he knelt down by the dogs.

They look as if they're sleeping.

He examined them for wounds. He discovered, when he raised the ears of both dogs, a bullet hole in the exactly the same place. He led Heather into the house and placed the gun back in the desk drawer. He made sure he locked it this time.

"You stay right here, young lady. I will have to do something about the dogs before your mother gets back," he said.

Ben placed the bodies of the two dogs in two large black leaf bags and then drove them to the other end of the property in the woods.

I will bury them later. He went back to the house. I can't understand how she can shoot the dogs and not show remorse, he thought.

He walked into the den and saw his daughter sitting at his huge desk. He sat down to tell her that guns were not a toy and that she shouldn't shoot animals just because they wouldn't play with her.

"Do you understand?"

He thought he got through to her then she said something to make him think she'd taken a serious mental turn toward darkness.

"You're right, daddy, I lied. I didn't kill them because they wouldn't play with me. I killed them because I wanted to watch them die."

My god!

Ben forced his face into 'a concerned father' look.

"Why did you want to do that?" he asked.

"I don't like them. That is why I want to kill you too," she said.

Heather had an equally concerned look about her. Then she lifted the revolver off the desk and pointed it at Ben.

"How did you get that? I locked that drawer."

"I know where you put your key and I unlocked it."

"Heather, put the gun down!"

"Why?" she asked. A broad smile lit her face

"Because, I'm your father!"

Is it a good enough reason? he thought.

She cocked the gun. Ben moved, just as she pulled the trigger. He was out the door and into the hallway as the gun blew a hole through the back of his chair and sent it barreling across the floor.

"Oops, I missed you, daddy. This gun is too heavy."

She cocked it again.

Ben looked from around the corner. He hoped to disarm her. He couldn't see her. He crept back towards the den and heard another shot, which barely missed his ear. The ringing in his ear caused him great pain. He dropped to the floor to discover her hiding under the desk. He saw his beautiful daughter cocking the pistol again. He moved quickly and left the room.

He knew she had four more bullets, and obviously, she did not aim well. He ran to his hobby room, opened his gun safe, and grabbed a rifle.

Scared for his life, he completely lost sight of the fact that he defended himself against his ten-year-old daughter. He only saw a shooter and wanted to kill whoever possessed the other gun. It was only when he had a bead on the den's open door that he wondered if he could pull the trigger if he saw his beautiful daughter walk out of the den.

As if to test him she walked out of the den and held the large gun at her side with the smoke of the last shot still oozing out of the barrel. Ben pointed his gun at her.

"Stop, Heather! Drop the gun! I don't want to hurt you!"

Heather laughed. "You don't want to hurt me? Are you going to shoot me, daddy?" She inched closer to him.

"Put the gun down, Heather! Don't come any closer!" Ben demanded.

"What? This? What are you going to do if I shoot myself in the head like I did my dogs? Do you want to see me die, daddy?" she asked. Heather raised the gun slowly and placed the barrel toward her temple. "I can't miss from here, daddy."

"No! Heather, please don't! See, I'm putting my gun down. Please, dear, don't pull that trigger," Ben begged. He placed the gun on the floor and pleaded with his daughter to put the gun down.

"Ha ha, daddy, I fooled you. I'm not going to shoot myself. I just wanted you to put your gun down, so I can shoot you."

She moved the gun from her temple, pointed it directly at Ben, and then fired.

She missed.

Ben tackled her, taking the gun away, then he removed the magazine and cleared the last bullet from the chamber.

He hit her.

Then full of remorse he picked her up and hugged her to his chest. Yet it was Ben who eyes filled with tears, Heather's reaction was of indifference. Ben believed she had no compassion for his distress. He put her down and they walked to the den's door. She skipped away, not caring about what had just taken place.

Ben heard Rianna coming through the front door. "Honey, help me with these groceries. Honey, are you there?"

Suddenly afraid for her safety as well, he picked up his rifle.

"Ben, what are you doing? And what are you pointing that rifle at?" She struggled to hold onto her groceries.

"It's Heather. I think she's possessed. She shot and killed the dogs and she just fired a few shots at me. Get down, she may have another gun."

He continued to point his rifle toward the back door. However Heather came in through the front door. Rianna started to speak then Ben turned round and pointed the gun at Heather.

She dropped the bags of groceries she carried and jumped at Ben and began beating him.

"What the hell are you doing? It's Heather! Your daughter!"

"Don't you think I know that? Get off me or she'll kill us both."

He struggled to break free of her superhuman grip.

"Ben, she has been with me all day. She has been with me. Dammit! You're having a nightmare or something!"

Ben looked up to see his beautiful daughter in her new dress. She begged her parents to stop fighting.

"Look, Ben! You're scaring the hell out of her. Now stop!" she demanded.

"She's been with you all day? But how can that be? She tried to kill me," he said.

"Yes, she has been with me. I bought her that dress and she did not want to take it off until she showed you. Ben, what's going on with you?"

Ben looked blank.

What happened? Am I going mad? he wondered.

Heather came over to him and said, "Daddy, do you like my new dress? Mommy bought it for me."

"It's lovely, sweetheart. I'm sorry I yelled at you, baby."

"It's okay, daddy, I love you," she said.

"Go play, sweetie, daddy and I have to talk." She picked her groceries off the floor.

"Okay, mommy, I'll go play with Bingo. Is he outside, daddy?"

Ben knew that the dogs were dead and hadn't the heart to tell his daughter. Then both dogs came running to Heather and jumped up to lick her face.

"I think I need help. Do you know anyone?" Ben went to his den. Rianna, with a look of concern, followed. He opened his drawer and saw his Glock pistol. It felt warm to the touch, as if it had been fired recently. He saw no bullet holes anywhere in the den. "Is this gun warm?" he asked.

Riana felt the gun. "No, it's as cold as ice. Why?"

"Never mind. I must be seeing things and now I'm feeling things. I'm not well."

"Perhaps you should lie down. I'll call the doctor."

"No, I'm not physically sick, I need a head doctor."

After he locked up his Glock and his rifle in the safe in the hobby room, Ben decided to take a nap. He kept the key to the safe with him.

* * * *

Rianna, although worried about Ben's health, had her own problems. Her ankle hurt because of her tussle with Ben. She limped into the bedroom to see him. Ben slept. She believed he suffered a nightmare because his body shook and his eyelids flickered violently. She removed his shoes to make him more comfortable.

She went back to her car to gather the rest of her groceries and bring them into the house then sought out Heather to tell her not to bother her father. She'd purchased a new movie for Heather and was anxious to watch it with her.

"Heather! Where are you?" her mother called.

In the bedroom Ben's nightmares woke him up. Something strange afflicted him. He wanted to rub his eyes yet he couldn't move his arms, nor move his legs. He saw Heather at the foot of the bed. "Hi, sweetheart, go get your mother, please!"

"Why, daddy?"

"I can't move, and I don't know what's wrong." He struggled to move his hands and feet.

Heather remarked, "I know why you can't move daddy."

She held up a pair of heavy duty wire cutters, then moved it towards his little toe.

She cut it off.

The pain seared through his nervous system yet he could not yell. Now Heather moved to the other foot and snipped off his other little toe. Only Ben's face revealed the pain. He couldn't move or shout for help. Sweat rolled down his tense face. Heather seemed oblivious as she snipped the next toe, and the next, and the next, with blood shooting out of every digit.

The intense pain made him pass out for a minute.

He opened his eyes to see Heather on top of him and he slapped her across the face. He heard the crunch of bone as the blow hit. She flew off the bed and onto the hardwood floor with the force of it. Blood spewed from her mouth and nose as she screamed for her mother.

Rianna, searching for her daughter, ran into the room. She saw Heather on the floor, holding her nose and sitting in a pool of blood.

"Mommy, mommy, daddy hit me!" Heather said.

"What did you do, Ben? My God! What the hell is wrong with you? Look what you did to her!"

Riana tried to comfort her distressed daughter.

"Look what she did to me! She cut off my toes, look!" He removed the blankets to show his bloody feet, except there was no blood and his toes were intact.

"What? Your toes are there. My God, you could have killed her!" She guided Heather to the bathroom.

Ben didn't know what to think or believe anymore. He raced to the bathroom and apologized. Rianna told him to leave, and he did.

* * * *

Confused and miserable, he got in his car and drove to the nearest bar. The bar patrons knew him. Some of them had relatives who'd died there. They asked about the estate.

"Have you ever seen anything strange?"

That was the most frequent question.

After a few bourbons, Ben talked openly about what had happened at the house. He had an audience of two plus the bartender.

"I closed off the west wing because then, whatever haunted it, would leave us alone. It didn't accomplish anything."

He asked the bartender for another round. His shaking hands grabbed the drink and tossed it down in one gulp. A crusty, unshaven man in the corner had heard the conversation and walked over to the three men.

"You think that closing off the wing is going to stop her?"

"Who are you, old man?" Ben asked.

"My name is Bertram Black. My nephew David died at the manor. He used to live there too, and then his wife killed him with an ax. He's buried there at the house." The old man's voice cracked.

"You're David Black's uncle?"

"Yes, I wish he had never moved into that place. That house is cursed. He told me that he saw things that were not there, and a lot of other strange things," Bertram explained. His words were slurred.

Perhaps it's through drink and grief? Ben wondered.

"My brother, John Black, wrote about him in his last book."

"I know. I read it. He did my nephew justice. That house is pure evil. I know the history of the house because it had been in my family for generations. Only girls named Heather Black are attracted to it because the original Heather Black, back in the 1800s, made a pact with the devil to take souls. Wives have been killing their husbands ever since." He sat down next to Ben.

"I have to leave it. I've been terrorizing my family and now I think I'm fighting spirits. I have to leave!"

"Leave? She won't allow you to leave until you're dead! Don't you get it, man? You're a dead man walking! You can't leave now! If you want my advice, have another drink, your days are numbered."

"I can leave if I want to!"

"No, you can't. It seems that you've already been targeted. Legend says that your body will be found without one of your limbs."

Ben choked on his drink.

"What?" he spouted. "Why?"

"I have no idea, but every husband who died there had a body part missing when the authorities came to collect the body. It's in your brother's book. Didn't you say you read it?"

"I read most of it. I don't remember reading about that. Did your nephew, David, lose anything?"

"Yes, his head," he replied. "I was there when it fell out of the coffin."

"His head? How could that go missing?" Ben asked.

"I don't know, nor do I care to revisit it too many times in my memory."

"I'm so sorry to hear that, Bertram."

"It's been many years but unfortunately I still remember it. I've been an alcoholic ever since. I drink to forget; sometimes it works and sometimes it doesn't."

"Well, none of that shit is going to happen to me or my family. I'm going to leave with them tonight. Thank you, Bertram, I have to get home."

Ben paid the bill and staggered out of the bar. It was midday and the sun shone brightly.

He didn't hear Bertram's words to the other men at the bar. "It's too bad, he's a nice fellow. He and his family will be dead by morning."

* * * *

Ben sped home. As he entered the manor he called out to Rianna; there was no answer. He searched the entire living area of the estate. Rianna and Heather were gone.

Did they leave me? he wondered.

At the sound of barking he peered out of the rear kitchen windows and noticed the dogs playing in the backyard. Heather was not there. He walked to the bar in his den and poured himself another drink. The dogs' barking grew wilder and they howled in the back yard.

He peered through the kitchen window again and saw them near the pool in a fight with a huge black bear.

The bear appeared to be winning.

Ben rushed to the hobby room, grabbed his AR-15 rifle, and ran to the backyard. He took aim at the massive bear and shot. Somehow he missed the huge animal.

"How the hell could I have missed that shot?" he muttered.

The bear continued its attack on the dogs. Ben aimed again. As the bear tore at the dogs he fired.

Again he missed.

The dogs lay motionless.

The bear ambled away from the house, unharmed. Ben chased the bear and pumped four shots toward it. Each time he missed. Now he walked back to the mauled dogs.

They were still alive, although badly mangled. He didn't want Rianna or Heather to see the dogs in their present state so he put them out of their misery and shot them through the head.

Ben placed them in large leaf bags and sealed them tightly, so other animals wouldn't be attracted until he had a chance to bury them later on. He had a déjà vu moment and realized that he had done that once before. Later it proved to be just another illusion.

Would it be the same this time? he wondered.

He walked back into the kitchen. On the counter stood a familiar bottle of wine. It had appeared as if from nowhere.

It was his wife's purchase. The vintage wine was from an auction for $150,000, and a wedding present to Ben. The bottle sat on a note from her. It read:

> Dear Ben,
> I cannot stay with you any longer. I fear Heather's life is in danger. I cannot abide your anger. Perhaps if you submit to psychiatric treatment we can come home, but not until then. I'm sorry that it has to end this way.
> Rianna.

Ben felt overwhelmed with grief. She and Heather had left him and he sat alone in the huge house. He looked at the bottle and wanted to smash it against the wall. Then he picked it up and read the label; Domaine de la Romanée-Conti Grand Cru from Côte de Nuits, France.

The realization of his situation set in.

He thought, No wonder she left me. I have to do what she wants. I'll submit to a psychiatric evaluation and get committed. I will. I will do it to get her and Heather back and to get my life back on track as well.

He opened the bottle, poured a large glass, and toasted to him getting well so he could get his family back. The wine tasted smooth. He drank another glass, and then another. Soon the bottle was emptied and he went to the bedroom to pack his bags. He didn't want to wait another minute.

I'll drive directly to the entrance of the psychiatric hospital to tell them I'm ready to get better and commit to whatever they tell me to do. He vowed.

In his bedroom he went into his closet to get his suitcase. When he came out Rianna and Heather were both on the bed smiling at him.

"I thought you'd left me."

"I did, Ben. We both did although not in the way you think. You see, we're not really here."

"I'm looking at you. What do you mean you're not really here? Are you crazy?"

Or am I crazy? he thought.

"You are such a stupid man." Rianna turned to her daughter. "Isn't he, Heather?"

Heather nodded. "Can we just kill him and get it over with!"

He dropped his suitcase.

"Who the hell are you?"

"Why, I'm your lovely wife and this is your loving daughter," she laughed.

"No, you're not. Your eyes are black!"

"So is my name. I'm Heather Black," she teased.

"You're Rianna Black. She's Heather Black."

"No, your precious wife is dead, and once more, you killed her!" she said.

"Bullshit, my wife isn't dead!"

"Oh, but she is. Your wife is out in the woods in a tightly sealed black leaf bag."

"No, that's one of the dogs. I shot the dogs because a bear mangled them."

"No, you shot her as she sunbathed out by the pool, you silly man!" Ben shook with fear. "Go on. Go see your pretty wife."

He ran to the backyard, started the ATV and then sped toward the bags. He tore open the bag and it revealed his beautiful wife, in her bikini, covered with blood. She had died from a gunshot wound to the head.

Ben got down on his knees and sobbed hysterically. After a few minutes he knew he had to get back to the house because his daughter and her spirit had been captured. He, picked up his rifle that he used earlier and ran to the bedroom.

He said nothing.

He pumped fifteen rounds into whatever portrayed his dead wife. Blood spattered all over the room and the bullets nearly tore her in half. None of the shots hit Heather. He judged he'd saved her and they were now safe. Then the blood-spattered woman sat up and laughed as she put herself back together.

"Shoot all you want," it said. "I'm already dead. You can't harm me, Ben."

As the last remnants of her body magically came back to her Ben noticed she didn't have a thumb. He recalled, in the book, how the original Heather Black had cut off her thumb just before her death.

"You're Heather Black? You bitch! You made me kill my wife! Give me back my daughter and we'll leave this place to you!"

"Your daughter? You think this is your daughter? I believe in his past life he called you Benji."

"John, is that you?" he asked. Tears filled his eyes.

"He can't speak because I won't allow it. Yes, this little cutie is your brother, John. I had to put a muzzle on his spirit because he almost ruined everything."

"John, how could you do this to me?" he asked.

"He had no choice; you see, I control him now," she said. Then she snapped her fingers and Heather vanished. In her place just a blue haze, which dissipated slowly.

"Where's my daughter, you bitch!" he screamed.

"Silly man, didn't you bother to look in the other black leaf bag you left in the woods? You'll find her in there. See, you didn't miss her with your silly gun. By the way, there was no bear."

"Oh my God! I killed both of them?"

He dropped to the floor curled up in anguish.

In his agony, Ben did what he'd contemplated doing many times. He placed the barrel of the gun in his mouth and pulled the trigger.

The gun didn't fire.

"That's not going to do you any good, Ben. The gun will not fire; besides you'll be dead in a few minutes anyway. As you know, it must be the wife who kills the husband, so I placed a demand in her mind prior to you blowing a hole in it. She must have loved you a lot because she resisted me many times. I made her lace that bottle of wine you drank with poison. A fitting end, I believe? It was a lovely present for you. You must be feeling the effects of it by now. I see that you're staggering a bit. Let's see, what shall we take from you? I took Cyrus' right arm, so I guess we take the left leg from you, and as you're taking too long to die - I'll take it now."

Heather rose up and sent a spell toward Ben. She commanded her spirits to sever his left leg. In a flash, he felt the searing pain of his leg as it was ripped from his body. He died a few seconds later, and entered a strange, new state of being. He knew he'd died. He knew he no longer owned a body. Curiously he still felt the remnants of his life within him, albeit short one leg.

He was unaware of the importance of his missing leg. He just knew he had to get it back. Ben had entered the spirit world and under Heather's spell. Although she'd severed his leg she could not keep it hidden forever.

He entered the spirit world.

Dangers loomed.

He didn't see his wife, or his daughter, in this strange realm, however he met his brother, John, or at least a spirit that resembled him. He did not feel physical pain. There were far worse things to plague him. Heather had threatened to remove his memories for an eternity. She'd told him if he ever reached the place where all spirits go a lost memory might mean he'd never see his loved ones again.

The desire to get to that place overwhelmed him, though he, nor any of the other spirits in the manor, possessed the ability to reach their final destination.

Only the living could help with his salvation. They could assist him and the others to break Heather's hold. Until then they remained aimless souls who desperately sought help. At the same time they were forced to obey Heather. She played on their strong desire to be among their loved ones for eternity.

He realized now why all the cryptic messages had appeared to the living. Heather ruled heartlessly over the spirits and the living occupants of the manor. She risked everything, including her own eternity, for everlasting beauty in the living world. She neither knew nor cared about her own eternal soul.

Ben knew where the manor's newest relic had been hidden in the house. He also knew, from Heather's threats, that if he told whoever next dwelled in the manor where she'd hidden his leg, then his soul would be stripped of every memory.

So, he did what the other spirits had done and made up another cryptic message. He hoped that those in the living would understand and solve it.

Only then would Heather's hold be broken.

***

After many calls to the mansion, Rianna's family grew concerned when no one responded to their messages. They called the local police department. However, since the police refused to step into the house, the relatives contacted the state authorities to check things out.

They found the bodies of Rianna and Heather Black in large black leaf bags in the back of the property and the body of Ben Black in the master bedroom in a pool of dried blood. The coroner speculated they'd been dead for many weeks.

The state police gave the property a cursory inspection and decided no one else was involved. They didn't see anything out of the ordinary, other than Ben's missing left leg. They saw no indication of a struggle. Three people had been murdered on the grounds and the deaths added to the Black Manor's legacy.

They investigated but found nothing to indicate a motive for the killings. Initially, they found no evidence about who killed Ben, his wife, or their daughter; nor did they find Ben's missing leg.

During the autopsy it was discovered that Ben had been poisoned though he died as the result of the severe and sudden blood loss. They also determined, through ballistics, that Ben had shot and killed his wife and child. Ben's missing leg remained a mystery.

They finally reported it as an interrupted housebreak with deadly consequences. They classified the case as unsolved.

The family was buried in the cemetery on the property next to all the other Blacks. They weren't related to the people buried there, however it offered the family a free and beautiful place to be interred. Rianna's family said she'd wanted to be buried there and her family adopted the dogs.

Chapter 10
The Last Relic

Three years passed before another couple moved into the manor, except this time the couple wanted to move into the Black Manor because of its past, and not in spite of it.

That couple, Kevin and Heather Black, were young people who lived for adventures.

Kevin, Heather's husband and the youngest billionaire in modern history, created a website that spanned the world, and at the peak of its popularity, he sold it to the highest bidder for many billions of dollars.

A handsome and adventurous man, he sought out escapades that money could not buy. He'd read about the Black Manor in many books and that the property presented the most beautiful home that he or Heather had ever seen. However, it wasn't its attributes that drew them to the massive Virginia estate, the mysteries surrounding it intrigued them both.

Heather had long, straight, raven-black hair, a face that could melt hearts, and a body that made it impossible not to stare. However, she was not just any beautiful young woman, she had the mind of a genius, and whose intellect and power of deductive reasoning made many envious of her talent.

A modern-day Sherlock Holmes she relished the idea of solving the most complex of mysteries. Despite her intellect, she also loved doing 'young girl' things like shopping, shoes, and a heady social life that an endless supply of money could provide. However, most of the time they embarked on exotic vacations to the most beautiful places the world had to offer. Heather, deemed by her friends as a party girl with brains, loved the description and Kevin loved her because of it.

She possessed the ability to confound her friends by figuring out the ending of any movie or book before they'd finished it. She pictured every scenario in her mind at once and through deductive reasoning created the only applicable outcome. Ninety-nine percent of the time she reasoned correctly.

Everyone loved her company although not so much when she spoiled the movie's outcome for them by solving the mystery before they even watched the second act.

Heather also excelled at college. She graduated at the top of her class. She never considered furthering her education because it bored her.

Her motto was, as she told friends, "Education wastes valuable party time!"

The police used her brilliant talents many times for unsolved crimes. Heather found they did not present enough of a challenge and eventually bored her. She constantly looked for new challenges.

She had a sister, Kirstie Patterson, and two very supportive brothers.

Bryan, her older brother, possessed many similar abilities to Heather though he did not have the desire to solve crime puzzles and mysteries. A fearless thrill-seeker, Bryan believed that there were many unsolved mysteries beyond those in the human realm. These were the ones that drew his interest. He loved to investigate larger more perplexing mysteries. To this end he founded a company called Bryan Black and Associates, which specialized in finding evidence of an afterlife.

Heather's younger brother Daniel worked with Bryan in their search for another realm of the human existence. A tireless worker and a computer genius he devoted much of his time to his brother's pursuits.

Sadly, so far Bryan had found nothing to prove his paranormal interest. Many things presented to the company were made-up hauntings and possessions designed to increase sales of products or to sell vacant hotel rooms.

It frustrated Bryan to discover certain homeowners created stories of mystical sightings just to gain notoriety, or being duped into unwittingly assisting a lonely wannabe medium that desperately needed attention. He felt thrilled and honored whenever someone with genuine concerns hired him. Daniel brought up all the ghost haunting that he had debunked and reminded him of the disgust the people held against Bryan for making them look like fools.

"Those people have no integrity," he ranted.

"Well your tactic of always reporting the frauds deters them," Daniel said.

"Yes. I much prefer the type who desperately wants to find reasons why 'things move in the night' with no desire to deceive anyone."

"And they get their answers," Daniel chuckled. "One hundred percent of the time we aim to find out. Even if it is only rusty pipes rattling in the loft space."

"That's exactly why the company uses state of the art equipment," Bryan agreed. "Our camera systems will capture any evidence of a spirit or ghost."

"Didn't you say you were skeptical about their use?"

"I am, however I'm willing to try everything available. If there is a ghost, spirit or any other life force we need to be one step ahead of them," Bryan answered.

Heather and Bryan were always playfully competitive however each wanted the other to be the one who proved that something wonderful existed beyond death.

Kirstie, Heather's very pretty and eternally sweet sister, remained content and happy to be a housewife, to

Brian Patterson and mother to her two young children, Ben and Wyatt.

Her siblings' exploits interested her. Bryan and Heather knew that Kirstie's faith-based beliefs made her skeptical of their interests. Nevertheless, she accepted their need to explore 'the afterlife'.

Kevin studied the manor's past and reckoned living in such a mysterious place would interest Heather. Years earlier, when John Black wrote his book about the strange things that occurred there, Kevin had inquired about buying the film rights for Heather. When the last Heather Black met her untimely death, Heather implored Kevin to buy the estate. Kevin however was concerned about the way the previous Heather Black had met her demise and didn't want to place his wife in any danger.

Once the young couple found out from the solicitor that only a Heather Black could inherit the Black Manor they moved into the place full of expectation and excitement.

For the first ten weeks, they encountered nothing, which frustrated them both until Kevin recalled John Black's book.

"According to the book we have to visit some secret room in the west wing." He held his hand up as Heather almost jumped out of her seat with excitement. "We're not going in there until we're prepared."

"What?"

In reply he handed Heather the book and she browsed through it again.

"Do you think we'll find a few more of those clues on the wall? To tell you the truth, I kind of doubt most of what he wrote in that book. John Black was first and foremost was a fiction writer, however he confessed in countless interviews, that some of his stories clouded that distinction. If I actually see the wall he wrote about then I'll reassess my thinking," she commented.

"Well, we know three of the messages. Can you decipher those?"

"They're perplexing so I'll need more information before I can determine what they mean. In the meantime, do you want to go out to DC with us tonight? We're going to Lulu's."

"Hell yes, I'll go! Is Bryan coming up anytime soon?"

Heather smiled at his eagerness to see her brother.

"No, not yet, but he's champing at the bit to get into the west wing."

"I know. We agreed to spend as much time as we needed to prepare before we attempted it. I believe that everyone went there too soon. If John Black's book is correct we already know a lot more than the others did and can be more prepared. If we find anything we can't explain, then we'll call in Bryan's company. No one goes into the west wing until we do."

"I agree. As far as that first message, you know, 'Ascend to the fourth vertical'?"

"Yes, do you know what it's all about?"

"Yes, I think so. We don't know what we're supposed to find. I think it has possibly something to do with the trees on the hill at the corner of the property or with the staircase, but I'm not sure yet. I just know that we have to climb something. I'm sure John Black understood the reason," she explained.

"Trees?" he asked.

"Yes, trees are vertical and I noticed the small hill on the corner of the property and the few trees upon it."

Heather hung framed photos on the wall.

"How does this photo look? Is it straight?"

"Yes, fine."

"You're not paying attention are you?"

Kevin looked up as she hung another of Kevin's photos on the wall of his den. His attention was with her again. "Couldn't have done it better myself. Now," Kevin returned to the puzzle. "According to his book, he didn't know what the sayings meant."

"It's not that difficult if you break it down. I'm sure he had an idea of what it meant."

One of the ornate grandfather clocks chimed.

"Heather, don't you have to get ready for D.C.?"

"Oh, shit! You're right. I've got to go buy shoes and a new black dress. Thanks for reminding me."

He smiled. "I've known you for quite a while now, so I know you need at least a few days before a social event. The D.C. event is tonight so you'd better hurry."

"That's true. You know me too well. I love you Kevin." She stopped at the doorway. "I'm thinking about going blonde. What do you think?"

"You are beautiful either way. I love your hair as it is now. You went blonde a few years ago. I suppose I'll get used to the changes! Oh, and don't forget that Bryan and I are going to Spain in three weeks for the running of the bulls, even though they nearly got me last year."

"God, I don't understand you two sometimes. You go all the way to Spain, just to run from bulls. I guess it's a man thing."

"Hey. Well I suppose it's a woman thing to go all the way to France just to buy a dress and shoes for the Academy Awards."

"That's different. I had to have that dress because it's so cute and it wouldn't have gotten here in time. Besides, we have those jets for a reason." She paused and then laughed. "Okay, I see your point. Enjoy your bull running. Take care though, I don't want you to get hurt."

***

Kevin read the news reports about both John and Ben Black, and how Ben had bricked up the door of the west wing in an effort to prevent the horrors from happening again. Unconvinced that the door vanished after they went through it, Kevin continued reading the incredible saga.

Ben Black did not get charged with the murders of his wife and young daughter because he did not survive. The fact that someone severed his leg and took it perplexed him. When Kevin contemplated the west wing, combined with the home's murderous past, he worried about his wife being at the house alone. So he discussed it with Heather.

"Please come to Spain with me."

"No, I'm sorry I just don't feel like going there again."

"Well, I don't like the idea of you being in this house alone."

"Do you mean you are afraid of it's past?"

"Quite frankly, I'm not afraid for myself but I am afraid of losing you."

"I'll be fine. We'll talk on the phone every night."

"That's not the point, honey. Did I tell you that they are having a major fashion show at the very hotel I'm staying at?"

"Fashion show? Can I buy something or just look?"

"Okay, you scheming wench. You can buy whatever you want."

"Okay, then I'm in!"

Just as they decided, Bryan called. "Hi Bryan. Heather and I were just discussing our Spain trip. She's coming with me."

Bryan said, "Really, you bribed her didn't you?"

"Yep, I guess I should bring my bank cards, eh?"

"Yes get ready to pop out six-figures."

"I know but I can't resist her, you know that. When you coming up?"

Bryan asked, "Tomorrow, or the day after, we're flying out of Dulles, right?"

"Yes, non-stop to Madrid and I'll have a car waiting to take us to Pamplona."

"God, I'm glad my sister married you. Are we going on your new jet?"

"Yes, got to break it in and get some miles on it. I may buy some more paintings for my collection while I'm there."

"Wow don't you have enough. Heather told me that the house came with a sizable collection already. Do you have room for yours?"

"Yes, there is plenty of room in this place. Wait to you see it. It's triple the size of our house in Santa Fe."

"I don't care about all that, my crew is itching to test out that west wing. I've been telling them about it."

"Hey you'd just better be worried about how I'm going to kick your ass running from the bulls. I've been training all year for this especially since I finally beat you last year."

Bryan laughed. "That damn bull stepped on my foot. That's the only reason you won."

Kevin laughed as he recalled the event with him. "I still can't believe you actually punched the bull in the face after he stepped on you."

"Well, he pissed me off. I gained on you until he stepped on me!" Bryan said.

"I'm pretty sure you pissed him off too. I still remember that look on your face when the bull didn't even flinch from the punch, and you ran the fastest I've ever seen you run that day. Of course, it wasn't fast enough to beat me," Kevin boasted.

"Okay, I'm humbled, but you'd better be on your game this year," Bryan said.

"Oh, I'm ready. Hey, I'm taking Heather this year. Feel free to bring your girlfriend as well. I'll foot the bill."

"I see, you need a cheering section, eh? Shit! Never mind, I might bring my girlfriend. When do we get to explore that house? I've been reading up on it and my group keep asking me about it every day," Bryan asked.

"After Spain, I don't want to rush into it. Heather and I want to check it out first. I noticed that most of the bad stuff happened after the owners visited the secret room. It's like the visit is a sort of initiation into the paranormal world. Whatever is causing all these things to happen has never encountered the likes of me and Heather," he said.

"I bet Heather wants to go into the west wing now. You know she can't help herself when there's a mystery to be solved. I'm surprised that she hasn't already started searching for that room."

"That's why I've invited her to the bull running. At the moment she's cautious and strangely patient however it could change if I weren't around. John Black's book with its gruesome details has probably given her pause for thought. She does get scared, occasionally, you know. She's my whole life, and although she knows it would piss me off if she went there without me, the west wing is tempting. I'm the practical one. I've been doing a lot of planning and I think I'm prepared."

"When do I get a crack at it?" Bryan asked.

"When we've determined that it's safe."

"Safe? Bullshit, Kevin. I don't like going into a 'safe' area. Every investigation we've encountered turned out to be safe. The fucking people who squander our time making up shit just to get a headline. I want to see everything. I want to see the real shit! I'm not afraid of anything."

"I know how you feel. According to John Black, the shit doesn't start until we, or Heather mainly, visit the room. You know the history of the estate. It's all about Heather. She has to visit the room for the fun to start."

"Okay, but I'll prepare anyway. In fact, I want to be in the mansion when you two go to the room. I want to fit you and Heather with GPS tracking and GoPro cameras so

I can monitor you in real time. I love you guys and I want to be there to go in if you can't get out."

"You know, let's bag the Spain trip and start now."

"What? Bag the running of the bulls? Man, are you that worried about losing again?" Kevin joked.

"No, I'm not afraid of losing, but if I get gored and die on the streets of Spain, and don't have a chance to investigate your house, it would really piss me off."

"Hey, okay. Are you bringing the Goth lesbians?" Kevin asked.

"Yes, they're actually great ghost hunters because they don't run when they encounter something that's hard to explain. Just because they dress in black and wear that stupid makeup doesn't mean that they don't know what they're doing."

"They are pretty hot. I'd like to see what they look like without the whole Goth look. I suppose John and Daniel will come up as well?"

"Yes, I want my whole crew. They're all good Kevin, very good."

"I remember the one guy who wet his pants and ran like a girl when Heather and I went on one of your investigations. We were terrified and laughing at the same time."

"Yes, he'll be there as well. We all laughed at that, but that house creeped us out."

They officially called off the Spain trip though Heather was looking forward to the fashion show. There'd be another year, they all agreed.

Heather asked, "Well we're still going out to DC tonight, though, right?"

"Of course, that will be fun." Kevin asked.

I'm all set and my friends have texted they are ready to go as well."

The limo arrived at five o'clock. They picked up Heather's friends, Zorana, Jessica, Brittany, Kristin,

Stephanie, and Ashley. They were the group. All beautiful, all energetic, all successful, and all greatly desired by men from all kinds of backgrounds.

After many hours of drinks and dancing, they were all driven to their respective homes and Kevin and Heather returned to the manor.

***

They woke up at noon after a perfect night in Georgetown culminating in making love until the sun came up.

Kevin called Bryan again to tell him that they were ready to start their adventure and to clean their mansion of its unworldly evil.

It was a straight forward four-hour drive from Virginia Beach to the manor. Bryan rounded up his group. His partners and fellow paranormal enthusiast were John Jackson III and Ronald McAllister.

As a group they promised to walk fearlessly into the scariest places on earth, never flinching if something suddenly moved in the darkness, or if faced with an indescribable entity.

Bryan, Ron and John always moved forward while the rest of the crew moved back, except for the Michelle and Melody who were affectionately known as the Goth lesbians. The scarier the scene the more they wanted each other. Melody Solomon and Michelle Rocker had been caught many times in the throes of passion at the height of a particularly frightening situation.

They were self-described disciples of the undead who were strangely attracted to death and human suffering. They got so turned on to the point where they had to stop what they were doing and have sex when faced with a frightening situation. Bryan and John laughed at their exploits. Bryan's two camera operators did not scare easily however getting turned on by the slightest bit of creepiness sometimes compromised the footage. They usually held it together to get the shot, however, they never ran when the scenario took a turn toward the unbelievable and, despite their other oddities, they made a valuable addition to Bryan's team.

New to the ghost hunting profession, Daniel, Heather's younger brother, prepared for his first foray into a paranormal situation. He was a genius with anything electronic and played an important part in Bryan's plans. He knew how to use each piece of equipment and how to fix them should they ever get damaged. Daniel usually stayed behind and worked on the machines.

Bryan promised him, "This time you can come on the adventure."

The crew arrived at five o'clock in the evening and at Kevin and Heather's invitation, each selected their own room in the east wing of the mansion. Bryan brought his faithful companion, his exuberant boxer dog named Roxy.

Kevin hired a caterer for the seemingly impromptu party that night. The crew feasted from a fully stocked bar and barbeque, with everything served by tuxedoed staff.

The crew also brought their wives and girlfriends. Their invitation did not extend to a stay at the manor. Heather also invited her girlfriends for the evening party. Kevin had arranged all the rooms in the local hotel to be available for two weeks for all their friends. They didn't want their loved ones around in case the power of the witch had been miscalculated.

They drank, laughed, and swam all night long. Daniel didn't drink, so instead of partying, he calibrated all the equipment and made sure everything worked perfectly. He took extra care with the night vision cameras and the GPS tracking devices which he designed to be strapped to Heather and Kevin to monitor them every step of the journey.

Melody and Michelle shared a room. They didn't feel the need to party with the rest because they always felt judged by the other people. No one cared that they were lesbians however the way they dressed always caused comments. Heather assured them that they were welcome in her house. They just thanked her and stayed in their room.

***

The next morning Heather and Kevin were woke by loud noises coming from the living room. They investigated and found Bryan noisily setting up the equipment for Daniel to check out again. There were four large monitors up and running.

After breakfast the adventure began.

Kevin and Heather were both outfitted with a helmet GoPro video camera, with an infrared switch and a small GPS device, so their progress through the hallway could be constantly monitored. They collected their backpacks from the den.

"We're good to go, Bryan," Kevin said.

Once the pair were out of sight, prior to their entry into the west wing, Bryan did a final check to make sure all the instruments and cameras worked perfectly.

When they arrived at the entrance to the west wing Kevin used his claw hammer to tear away the wallboard and once a few bricks were loosened, they fell easily creating an opening. It was fairly easy because they'd started to pry it away the previous day.

Once the bricks were completely removed, an old door was revealed.

Kevin and Heather looked at each other. A myriad of emotions were mirrored in each other's eyes.

"Ready?" Kevin asked.

"Ready," Heather replied.

Keven retrieved the keys from his pocket. The hinges creaked alarmingly loud as they pushed it open and walked through.

Bryan watched the monitor and commented, "Damn, that door must be over two hundred years old. I'm surprised you still have the key. Are you guys still okay? Wait a minute, I saw something, I'm sure. Turn around and focus on the door."

"Bryan, the door has gone. Shit! The door has gone! It's vanished! Bryan, did you get that?" Kevin asked.

"Yes. I see the door. It's right in front of you. We all see it on the monitor. The door is there."

Kevin and Heather looked up and down the entire wall however they couldn't see the door they'd just walked through.

"Bryan, we don't see a door behind us." Heather then spoke to Kevin. "You know, this is exactly what John Black wrote about."

"You guys want to try to come back? Can you bust through the wall?" Bryan asked.

Heather said, "Maybe we should just find the secret room and come back to this problem."

Kevin said, "No, I want to map each room. We have time, and it's going to take more than a disappearing door to stop me. Are you with me, babe?"

"Of course, let's go." Heather led the way up the stairs.

Bryan asked, "Are you guys okay?"

"Yes, we're fine. We're going to go ahead to the first room because we don't know where the secret room is. We're going up the stairs now to the second floor," Kevin replied.

"Okay, we can see directly in front of you. I can't believe how dark it is there. Turn on the night vision so we can see what's ahead of you. Holy shit! What's that?"

Kevin asked, "What? I don't see anything!"

"On the floor leaning against the wall! Is that what I think it is?"

"Oh shit, Bryan! It's a fucking skull!" Kevin pointed the flashlight at the orb on the floor.

Heather shouted out in surprise. "Oh God, it's still got skin on it. It looks like a man. Kevin! Don't touch it! It's gross!"

"I bet this is what's left of Dan Marlowe. Why didn't they remove the bodies?" Kevin remarked. "Okay, we are now walking toward the first door. It has a room number on it, 101."

"What? We don't see a room. In fact, both of you guys are staring straight ahead," Bryan said.

Kevin looked at Heather and frowned. "No, we're moving."

"We're looking at all four monitors and they show that you are standing still and looking straight ahead. Kevin, turn to the left and look at Heather."

Kevin did as Bryan asked. The monitor didn't display Heather. "Is Heather on your right or left?"

"Left. I see her. We're in front of room 101."

"We're not seeing anything. Take your helmet off and point the camera at yourself."

"Okay," Kevin agreed.

The monitor showed Kevin take off the helmet camera off and turn it round. Bryan and his crew stepped back in silence from the monitor. An old toothless woman, her skin a pale white with bright red piercing eyes, appeared.

"Holy shit! What the fuck is that?"

"What's going on there, Bryan? What can you see?"

Bryan said nothing. Everyone focused on the hideous creature on the monitors. They saw it open its mouth and heard it speak.

"Looking forward to meeting you, Bryan Black."

The words finished with a shocking laugh.

Then the monitor changed. They now saw and heard Kevin talking into the camera.

"What's happening back there? Talk to me, Bryan."

"I think we just saw what you're looking for. The witch of the manor just made an appearance," Bryan said.

Melody said, "I think she's kind of hot, in a scary way. Michelle, did you see that?"

Michelle said, "Yep! Want to go upstairs?"

"God, you guys got horny watching that old woman? You two are sick!" Bryan continued to view the monitors.

"Yes, we are. Are you coming, Michelle?"

"Let's go." Michelle grabbed Melody's hand and they hurried off to their room.

"Daniel, how did the cameras do that? Are we missing any of them?" Bryan asked.

"No, they're all are accounted for. That is Kevin's camera. There is no way for that to possibly happen. That's no trick."

"We need to get the rest of our equipment in there," Ronald said.

"Nope, not yet," Bryan said.

Daniel pleaded with his brother.

"I agree with Ronald, bro. We can be set up in an hour."

"We have a plan to stick to and I will not risk my sister's or Kevin's life. They haven't even entered the first room yet," Bryan explained. He peered intently at the monitor. "Kevin, are you two in the room?"

"Going in now, stand by."

Kevin opened the door with the master key. He slowly pushed the door. Something on the other side resisted his efforts. He and Heather pushed the door all the way open and cautiously, gradually, entered the pitch-black room.

"The light switch doesn't work. Or the bulb has blown. Wait and let me plug this nightlight into the wall socket. Okay, we have some light here."

Bryan saw very little with the night vision cameras attached to Kevin's and Heather's helmets. Darts of light from their flashlights cut the darkness, however they supplied little illumination. She dropped the flashlight and fell backward and then tripped on something on the floor.

"Heather!" Kevin yelled.

"I fell over this," she replied. She kicked at the object. "It's a human leg!"

She shrank back and started to weep. Kevin helped her to her feet and held her tightly in his arms.

"It's a leg, a woman's leg," she whispered.

"How do you know it's a woman's leg?"

"It had pantyhose on it and the toes that were left were painted."

"Are you okay to carry on? We could get out of here now."

"No, I'll be fine. It wasn't only the leg that freaked me out. Look, Kevin!"

She pointed her flashlight upward.

The light caught the sight of a decomposing armless and legless body of a woman. She hung in mid-air with no visible restraints or ropes. Kevin shook as he pointed his flashlight all around the rotting corpse.

"Bryan, are you getting this?"

"Are you joking? Daniel passed out and John has blown barbeque all over the place. Look around the room so we can see all of it."

They couldn't reach the body to try and identify it. Kevin found a box and started to climb when Heather let out a bloodcurdling scream. It was so loud Bryan and Ronald had to remove their headsets.

Kevin jumped down. "What is it? Talk to me!"

Heather trembled and whimpered some unintelligible words. Kevin tried to calm her down once again.

"I can't understand you, honey. Calm down and talk to me."

He sensed her fear. Heather couldn't talk coherently but hugged Kevin tightly. "I want…to get…out of here!"

"Bryan, do you see anything?" Kevin asked.

"No, I just heard Heather shout out. Ronald and I are going to get our ARs and come in."

"Don't do that yet, let's see what else happens."

"Wait! What is that? Kevin, look toward that far corner. Use your flashlight."

"Holy shit, Bryan! There's a headless body on the floor!"

"I see that. Look at what's in the fucking corner!" Bryan yelled.

Kevin pointed his flashlight again and saw the silhouette of a woman standing in the corner. The woman looked as if she'd been cut in two with the back half of her body sprawled on the floor. She was just a shell of a woman and yet she stood unaided. Kevin took a few trembling steps toward the figure when outside the room they heard all the other doors opening and shutting.

However, when he turned back to the woman in the corner, she had turning around and Kevin saw her hideously decomposing face.

"Shit!" Kevin said, as he took a few steps back

The woman spoke, "Ah, I see my last relic has arrived,"

"Holy shit Bryan, Are you getting this?"

Kevin backed away and he removed the light from the hideous sight to prevent Heather from seeing it. Kevin was too late and Heather screamed again. It was so loud it moved the dust." The woman in the corner then collapsed as they moved backwards toward the door. Kevin carefully opened it with Heather clinging tightly to him."

Bryan was speechless though reasoned that the corpse was probably held together by wires as an elaborate hoax.

"Kevin, none of what you are seeing is real! I repeat, it's not real!"

"Bryan it certainly looks real. How do you know?"

"Because there's no odor. That many rotting corpses have to be emitting an odor. Do you smell anything?"

Kevin and Heather looked at each other and Kevin said, "You're right Bryan. There is no odor."

Heather looked relieved, and angry.

"Your sister is mad that she didn't pick that up, Bryan."

However, as they were prepared to leave, a foul stench filled the room. It hit them in the face and almost knocked them off their feet. They vomited violently and had to then hold their breath to get out of the room.

"Bryan, there's definitely an odor now and we can hardly breathe! It came all of a sudden like someone turned on a switch."

"Okay, take your time, I assume that the corpses are real?"

Kevin said, "You assume right Bryan. Maybe we should come out."

Heather asserted, "No, Kevin! I'm okay now. Let's just not go into that room again."

"Are you sure sweetheart? You want to go on?"

Heather responded, "Yes, I do besides there is no door downstairs."

Bryan said, "Fuck the door. We will blast the whole fucking wall away if you want to leave."

"No Bryan we'll continue. Heather is the key to this mystery. If we want to clean this house she will have to reach the secret room."

"Okay, but be careful. Some of this stuff I can't explain away."

"Bryan, okay, something else is happening now," Kevin said.

"Yes, I can hear what sounds like slamming doors. Are you leaving 101?" Bryan asked.

"Bryan, we have to go in there. This is getting fucking real!" John Jackson said.

"I agree with John," Ronald said. "Let the three of us go in there. We'll blast whatever it is. We have the firepower."

"No! Didn't you guys do your homework? Do you remember what happened the last time someone called the SWAT team in? Does the name Ken Knies ring a bell?" Bryan asked.

"Yes, I do remember. Something in there took out three armed SWAT members and later ten others," John said. "They had more guns than us, Ronald."

"That didn't happen Bryan. Only two cops actually went in the house and they were killed except one of them killed three more cops outside. There was no SWAT team."

Bryan answered, "So I embellished a little. We still can't go in just yet."

"Okay then, so what do we do? We know shit's going down in there that we can't explain. What do we do, Bryan?" Ronald asked.

Bryan placed his headset back on and said, "We learn. That's what we do. I know Kevin, and I know my sister, they will get some answers while they are in there."

Kevin listened to their conversation then added his own thoughts.

"Thanks, Bryan, you're right. Heather and I will get through this. If something bad does happen, I'll try to give

253

you as much as we can. I feel that when we find that so-called secret room we'll find a way to see the door out of here. We have to get through the wing first. I haven't forgotten there are twelve more rooms on the second floor. For the record, there are three bodies in room 101; two female and one male. I think the head we saw in the hallway belongs to the male. The bodies are in in various degrees of decomposition," Kevin continued, "okay, we've left the room. Wait a minute, I hear something. It sounds like a whispering of sorts."

"Wind?" Bryan asked. "Open window?"

"No, there's no wind in here and no windows that I can see. I need to get closer to that corner. I need to go back in and check the closet for that lectern."

"Don't go back in there, Kevin,"

"I have to. There's a closet in there that I haven't checked."

Heather pleaded, "Please! No! No! What the fuck?"

Kevin stepped back in 101 and again he saw the woman on the floor face down. He moved to the closet and opened it and found it empty. He made his way past the bodies and headed toward the door when suddenly the decomposing woman held her head up and screamed.

"It's too late!"

Kevin heard wild laughter echo around the room. He pointed his flashlight up and saw the torso and head, which still hung in mid-air with one eye out of its socket dangling down her cheek and the other one staring at him in a menacing manner and followed him out the door as he retreated. He shut the door behind him and collapsed to the floor.

"Are you both okay?" Bryan asked.

"Give us a minute, Bryan. I don't think you'll need instruments here. You won't have to search for spirits here, they will find you. Did you see what happened in there just now?" Kevin asked.

"Yes, we all did, but we'll come in when you give us the word."

"You bet your ass we will!" John Jackson chimed in.

"Where's Ronald, Jackson?" Bryan asked.

"He's loading the ARs and getting our shit together," John said. "He's getting ready to kick some ass."

In the west wing Kevin got up and then helped Heather to her feet. They moved to the room across the hall. He opened the door and ran his hand along the wall, searching for a light switch. When he found the plate, he turned the light on. A single bulb lit up over the bed and illuminated the dusty furniture.

"I don't think this has been touched since the nineteen fifties," Heather commented.

The room had a dusty window, so they walked over to it and tried to open it. It didn't budge - age and time had locked it in place.

"Nothing to report in 102, Bryan, other than, according to Heather, it needs a serious dusting and an upgrade. At least there's electricity in this room."

Kevin turned off the light however, at that moment, as Heather looked back into the room, she spied an old woman who appeared to be making the bed.

"Wait a minute. Bryan, someone just materialized," Heather whispered. "Kevin," she grabbed his sleeve, "look, there's another woman over there."

"Holy shit!" Kevin blurted out. "Bryan, there are two women in here and I can see right through them. They appear to be maids."

"Kevin, talk to them," Heather said.

"Hello. Hello! Can you hear me?" he asked.

The two women continued cleaning as if not aware that Heather and Kevin were in the room.

"Bryan, I think I see real fucking ghosts!" Heather said.

"I don't see anything, just a bed and dresser," Bryan said,

Kevin whispered, "Oh yes, they're here, Bryan. I see them too."

When he turned the light on again they disappeared. Then he and Heather walked to where they'd seen them though they sensed no one in the room.

"That's amazing!" Heather said. "Kevin, you turn the light off and I'll stay here."

In the darkness the two ghosts reappeared. They were on either side of Heather. One swept the floor and the other stood by the window. Unafraid, Heather put her arm out to touch one of the ghosts. It passed straight through. Suddenly the apparition stepped back as if aware of Heather and then lunged at her. The other ghost used her broom and smashed the ceiling lightbulb which exploded in a fountain of glass all over the room. The ghost at the window pulled the shade down then floated over to a terrified Heather.

The room now had an impenetrable darkness.

Kevin heard Heather scream in obvious pain. He rushed to where he thought she stood though he could not find her.

"Heather, where are you?" he called.

"Help me, Kevin! I'm up here!"

Kevin turned his flashlight on to see Heather hanging from the ceiling. She struggled to breathe because the lone wire from the light fixture had been wrapped around her neck. Kevin captured her flailing legs and placed them on his shoulders so she could reach up to untie the wire.

"Honey, hurry up. They're trying to break my legs!" He yelled at her through teeth clenched against the extreme pain.

Heather freed herself and they both fell to the floor in a heap. They scrambled to the door. Heather accidently brushed up against the light switch, which caused the light to turn on. The two ghosts disappeared as the window shade snapped back open.

"Look, Kevin, there's no bulb. The light is still on. How can that be?"

"Let's focus, Heather. I believe the bulb is still there. We are being possessed. What we can see is what she wants us to see. Focus on the light and eventually you will see the bulb reappear around the light. Once you see the bulb she cannot haunt your mind. Heather the lightbulb is there."

He said it as if to reassure them both.

"Yes. I see the bulb. I wonder what else she wants to make us see."

"I don't care, let's get the hell out of here! I think my legs are about to give up on me."

Heather managed to open the door and as they fell onto the hallway floor, the door slammed shut.

"Did you get all that?" Kevin asked Bryan. "You saw the ghosts?"

"I got no Caspers on this end," Bryan replied. "You're joking, right?"

Kevin snapped, "I'm not joking, Bryan, there are ghosts in 102!"

Bryan answered, "Okay, sorry but we picked up nothing."

Heather and Kevin had both of their flashlights trained on the door of the next room when Heather noticed Kevin limped badly.

"You okay Kevin? Are you well enough to continue?"

"Something tried to break my legs back there when I picked you up."

"Roll your pant legs up and let me take a look."

Kevin sat on the floor and Heather saw his injuries.

"Oh my God! These are bite marks! Human bite marks! We have to figure out a way to stop the bleeding." He heard the concern in her voice. "Kevin, we have to leave here and get you to a doctor. These look pretty serious."

"Baby, we can't go back yet. The faster we get to that secret room, the better."

"Kevin, we have to leave. In some places your skin is ripped off to the bone!"

"Heather, there isn't a door, remember? We have to get to that room and find out exactly what John Black saw. I can walk, and the pain is going away now. Let's continue. We have to find that room to allow us to leave. I can walk on it," Kevin said.

Bryan saw Kevin's wounds and offered a solution to rescue them. "As I told you before we can get our ARs and blast a hole in the wall."

"Bryan, I don't think it will work. You can give it a try. We're on the second floor, so blast away," Kevin answered.

"Ron and I will get them loaded up and get back to you. You stay where you are."

"Okay, hurry though," Heather begged.

A few minutes later Bryan returned to the monitor with the bad news. "It's no use, the bullets just bounce off the wall. It's like there's a thick steel plate on the whole wall. None of the bullets penetrated it. I'm sorry guys. Hey, Daniel just handed me something. It appears that an entire cleaning crew went missing a long time ago and their bodies were never found."

"Where did they go missing?" Heather asked.

"In the west wing right where you are, but there's more, a five-man crew of exterminators also went missing in the west wing. I wish I'd known this before you guys went in."

"That's okay, I knew about it. John Black wrote about that in his book." Kevin interrupted Bryan's protests. "I know. I know I should have told you. I bet the ghosts we saw in room 102 were part of that cleaning crew that went missing after David Black died. The realtor told me the story way back when the bankers contemplated tearing down the house. They sent in a cleaning crew of twenty and only four came out alive and vowed never to come back to this country again. I have a feeling we'll be seeing the exterminators as well. They also sent a crew in and none were ever heard from again. Okay, enough with the history, we're moving on to room 103," Kevin said.

They got up and walked up the darkened hallway. Kevin leaned on Heather. He dragged his right leg. They began to smell the rotten stench of death as they moved up the hallway.

"Bryan, I can smell rotting corpses again but can't see any bodies yet."

"Okay, keep me posted."

They arrived at the next room and again saw the ghost of what appeared to be more cleaning women. This time they didn't ignore the ghosts and didn't attempt to go into the room. They only opened the door to scan the room with the camera. Bryan said the camera didn't pick up the images, however he said to scan the rooms anyway in case a trace of the ghosts could be found later.

Suddenly, one of the ghosts turned and stared at Heather. She held her head as it's black eyes seared through her mind.

"Kevin, we have to leave them be!" she said.

"Just a few more minutes, Heather. I want to see if they will move anything around. That way we will be able to pick up some activity in the room. Besides I have to check the closet."

"I have strange thoughts. It's like I want to hit the back of your head with this heavy flashlight."

Just as he heard those words, Kevin saw a bright light then darkness as he fell to floor. His camera twisted toward Heather's face and caught her holding a bloody flashlight.

Bryan saw it all on the monitor.

"Heather, what the hell did you do that for?" he yelled

"Do what? I didn't do anything!"

"Look at Kevin! You just clobbered him with the flashlight!"

Heather got down on her knees to help her dazed husband. "Oh, dear God, I remember now. I couldn't resist it. I think one of the spirits possessed me. He's waking up now. Kevin, are you okay? I'm so sorry, I don't know why I did it."

He attempted to stand up though still groggy, wobbled on hands and knees. "You didn't do it, they did!" He pointed to the spirits still cleaning the room. He walked to the closet and opened the door and slammed it shut. "The fucking room is empty with the exception of these ghosts." He grabbed Heather's hand, walked out and slammed the door to room 103. He quickly sat back down and rubbed his head. "I'm still a little woozy. Maybe we should rest a bit before we continue?"

"I'm worried about your legs. Let me take another look at them."

"I feel something moving under the bandages," he said.

Heather slowly removed the makeshift bandages. She shined the flashlight on his wounds and shrieked when she saw maggots oozing out of his obviously infected wounds.

"Oh gross! This is not good. Did you pack any alcohol in your backpack? It may be too late, but I have to try something."

"I have a few minis in there, I think, left over from our camping trip a few weeks ago."

Heather retrieved two small bottles of vodka, then poured them on the cloth and directly onto the wounds. Kevin winced in pain as the alcohol seeped into his wounds.

As Heather retied the bandages she looked up.

"What's that?"

Kevin followed her gaze.

"What? I didn't see anything."

"Perhaps it's my overwrought imagination," she said.

They inspected a few more rooms and continued down the hallway. They were at room 110 when Heather again saw something strange.

"I saw a red beam flicker off the walls. It came from the end of the hallway." She pointed towards the direction they'd entered. "It looked like one of those laser pointers."

Kevin put his fingers to his lips. There were strange noises coming from the far end of the hallway. They both heard angry growls and it sounded as if it was moving towards them. They shined their flashlight into the darkness and saw three angry lions barreling toward them at full speed.

"Kevin!"

The lions roared past them and continued onwards. Afterwards they heard gunshots followed by streaks of light that pierced the darkness and illuminated the hallway for a split second.

"Holy shit! Heather, let's get into this room. Those are tracer bullets. I think someone from the other end of the hallway is shooting at us."

Kevin and Heather took shelter in the bedroom.

"Is it Bryan? He has tracer bullets!" Heather asked.

"No. He would've told us if he'd managed to break through. He said the bullets bounced off the wall."

"Do you remember the police report, when those officers died?" Heather asked.

"Yes, I remember, so what?"

"We both considered it strange that the officer said he mistook the three electrical workers for lions before he blasted them."

"Holy shit! Do you think we're reliving that and it's the cops at the other end of the hallway?"

"I don't know, but if that's the case, then the bodies should be down there. It said in the report, those officers bodies disappeared later. I bet the bodies are still in here."

"Are you sure? Surely the report said that the bodies were blasted out through the windows, then vanished and then reappeared later at the police station?"

"Yes, yet the owner at the time, Maggie, stated that the windows were never broken. I bet the bodies are still here somewhere. I think those three construction workers were found at their homes, not at the police station," Heather added.

They returned to the hallway. Heather saw something lying on the floor.

"What's that?"

Kevin pointed the flashlight up the hall.

"It looks like a rolled-up piece of carpet. Bryan, we're heading up the hallway. I see something lying on the floor. Do you see it?"

"Yes, that looks kind of weird."

Heather placed her hand over her mouth. "Oh dear God! The smell! It's another body!"

"Bryan, Heather's right, it's another body! A woman and it looks...my god her arm's been ripped off! I'm placing the camera over her so you can get some good shots. Do you see her?"

"Yes, it looks like she's been there for a while. When you two get back, we'll have to find out who these people are. I feel like we are doing the police department's job," Bryan said.

"When this is all over we need to get these bodies out of here or level the place and start over," Kevin said.

Heather and Kevin continued to explore each room and found nothing out of the ordinary other than to discover where the electrical installation stopped. They had just left room 112 when Kevin looked back and noticed that all the doors were open.

He looked at Heather. "Didn't we close all those doors behind us?"

Heather shined the flashlight down the hall. "Yes, we did. Oh shit! Kevin! The body on the floor, it's on the other side of the hall now. We didn't move it!"

"What the hell? You're right, we didn't. I have a feeling that this is going to be minor compared to what is ahead of us," Kevin said. "I don't want to backtrack. What's the next room, Heather?"

"112. We were just in 111 there to escape Tracer fire."

They actually searched 111 while they were in there but saw nothing unusual. Kevin did not explain the tracer fire that they just encountered and assumed that Bryan saw it on his monitors.

"Okay, Bryan, we're going to 112."

"Are those doors still open?" Bryan asked.

"Yes, it appears so. What's this? This is room 113! What happened to 112?" Kevin asked.

Heather walked back to 111, and then to 113.

"There isn't a 112."

"Now why did they do that?" Kevin asked.

Bryan interjected, "Why would they skip a room?"

Kevin said, "I think we may have found that secret room!"

Kevin ran his hands along the wall and felt nothing other than wall. Heather ran to Kevin, shaking, and whispered, "Kevin, that body on the floor is moving again!"

"What? What the hell is that? Shit! It's crawling toward us! Bryan, can you see that?"

"Yes, and it's freaking the hell out of us all."

Just as Kevin and Heather were about to retreat further into the darkness, a panel opened up.

Kevin said, "The room! I think I found room 112! Come on, Heather!"

"What about that thing?" She pointed to the crawling body. It continued to inch toward them.

"One thing at a time. I don't think that can harm us. We're looking for this room and hopefully we've found it. Let's find out why this room is so important and get the hell out of here," Kevin said.

She nodded in agreement. "Bryan, we're going in, you with us?" Heather asked.

"Yes, go ahead, we see you. Ronald and John are here as well."

Kevin and Heather entered the room however as they closed the secret panel a bright blue light flashed which temporarily blinded them.

Chapter 11
The Secret Room of Answers

The monitors went black.

"What the hell happened? Where's my feed? Kevin? Heather? Can you hear me?" Bryan barked.

Daniel rushed into the room to check the equipment.

"Kevin, can you hear me? Daniel?" Bryan yelled at his brother. "I need this fixed now!"

"This is unbelievable, Bryan, but everything here is working normally. Their audio and video could be compromised," Daniel explained.

"Bryan, do you want us to try to get in the west wing again?" John asked.

"Wait a moment, bro. I'll try something else."

Daniel tweaked a few knobs and got Kevin's belt camera to work though both of their helmet cameras were still not relaying images.

Daniel turned on his laptop and typed frantically. He showed Bryan the screen.

"They're good. I see them moving. The GPS is still working although, according to my readings, they're inside a wall."

Meanwhile, Heather and Kevin walked around the room as their eyes adjusted from the bright blue flash, and after a few minutes, they saw the sayings that John wrote about. Cryptic messages covered the walls.

"Kevin, this is amazing. Look at this!" she said.

"I can't, something has hold of my feet and I don't want to find out what."

"Holy shit! There is a pair of hands coming out of the floor! They have your ankles!" At first she recoiled in horror, then got on her knees and started smashing the hands with her flashlight.

In the living room, Daniel could see more than Kevin and Heather.

"Bryan, look at those red eyes in the corner. They're watching every move Kevin and Heather make."

They shouted a warning although neither seemed to hear them.

Now free, Kevin saw the lectern and the mysterious book that John had mentioned in his book.

He saw it open to a torn page.

Suddenly, he shook badly.

He read the next page and immediately stopped and went to Heather. The room had started to spin. Both were thrown to the floor. Their flashlights flickered as items from the room were blown at high velocity around in the dark. Something struck Heather in the face and caused a gash.

Kevin yelled through the roaring gusts of wind. "Heather look! There's someone under the blankets in the bed!"

What they saw in the bed was secondary as the wind blew Kevin around and he struggled to get to Heather. However, try as he might, he could not reach her. He noticed the gale force wind didn't blow into the closet where the book and the lectern were so he fought against the wind to get there. He managed to protect his body as the heavy debris flew around the room.

"Heather, I can't reach you! Bryan, can you hear me? Bryan?" he hollered. "Heather, can you hear Bryan?"

"No, my helmet is gone! My head is cut! Kevin, help me!" she pleaded.

"Try to get to the center of the room. It could be our best chance."

Kevin watched helplessly as Heather was hammered with all sorts of objects. The blanket that covered the bed blew off and he saw two dead people, holding hands, on it. Kevin beat the blast of wind and nearly reached the calm center of the tornado when it suddenly stopped.

He moved toward Heather, tripped and fell at her feet. Once again hands appeared from the floor, grabbed him firmly and held him down. Heather, dazed by all the flying debris, crawled to Kevin and tore at the hands to move them away. She broke the fingers off and they turned to dust. Kevin, freed from their grip got up quickly, grabbed Heather's outstretched hand and ran to the closet that housed the lectern. There he found Heather's helmet though the impact had shattered the camera. He also found his backpack.

"Heather, you're bleeding. I have a first-aid kit. Hold your hand to your head to stem the flow." Kevin wrapped the bandage round her head.

"We've got to go back out there, Kevin," Heather said.

"What? We have to get out of here! What we experienced isn't possible."

"Listen, I need you to hold a flashlight on this piece of paper and I need a pen," Heather said.

"What? Did you forget what happened out there? We have to leave. To hell with that wall and this room!"

"It's the reason we came here. I'll be quick. It's important, Kevin," she begged.

"Okay, let's do it, fast!"

Kevin and Heather went to the wall. He held the flashlight up and she hastily copied the passages scrolled on the wall.

"What are you doing," he asked.

"I'm counting, please don't interrupt!"

She continued to write frantically.

Suddenly, an apparition materialized before them, and the red eyes of the original Heather Black scrutinized them. She pointed a bony finger at Kevin.

"You will die! You are my last relic! I will rise again soon!"

A swirl of dust materialized behind her. She thrust her arms forward and the dust particles came toward them with such force that the particles were imbedded in Helen and Kevin's skin.

The pair rushed towards the closet.

"I doubt it, bitch! You've underestimated this Heather Black, and you most certainly underestimated me. We have others about to invade your hellish realm. We will destroy you," Kevin said. "We have evidence of your existence."

He pointed to his helmet camera.

"You mean these?" she asked.

Heather and Kevin's saw a vision in their minds. In the vision Bryan shot at his crew and his employees returned fire. They saw Bryan and his group on the white tile floor with blood gushing from missing limbs. The final vision showed a bloodied Bryan. "She won, Kevin. Don't come back here!"

Those were his last words.

"So, Heather, you kill your husband now, and I will allow you to leave. There's no escape for him from this wing," she said.

"Bullshit. You are the one who will be destroyed." Heather lunged for the apparition. "You killed my brothers! I will get you!"

Kevin held her back. "We have to go, Heather. Did you get what you needed?"

"Yes," she said.

They moved towards the door.

"You two have nowhere to run but by all means, try. I will be waiting for you wherever you go in the house.

Heather Black, you will kill your husband. You are already thinking about it."

Kevin found the doorknob and they ran from the room.

Instantly, their flashlights went out. Kevin reached into his backpack to retrieve his backup flashlight. It did not work. They heard their own footsteps upon the hardwood floor as they slowly walked toward the end of the hallway. They clung tightly to each other. They were scared and tired. Heather squeezed his hand so hard that it went numb.

They felt the wall and moved along it to each room they'd previously investigated. Heather ran into something hanging from the ceiling in the darkness. She freaked out as she bumped into one of the corpses they'd found earlier. She felt blood and bodily fluids leak out onto her. She ran into two more before she ran into the darkness.

Kevin was alone.

"Heather! Stop! I can't see you! Where are you?"

Heather did not respond. He heard a faint screech from the other end of the hallway.

"I'm coming, Heather! I can't see anything. Tell me where you are!"

"I'm right here behind you, dear."

When Kevin turned toward the voice, Heather blasted her fist at his face. He went down, dazed and confused. He looked up, held his nose to stem the blood, but did not see Heather. As he got to his feet he heard his wife moan in the distance again. Then he heard footsteps behind him. He ran as fast as he could through the darkened hallway. He hoped he would get to the end. He arrived at the center of the hallway. He was exhausted. He checked his watch. Thirty minutes had passed. He gasped for breath and leaned against the wall. The hallway seemed to go on forever. He checked one of the doors only to see the number '112'. He had not moved an inch from the secret room.

In the distant darkness Heather still moaned.

"Heather?" he called.

There was no answer.

Scared, not about his situation; his fear was for Heather. It distressed him. He could not reach her. All of a sudden he heard a faint scream and then the sound of something running toward him. A 'something' that screamed. It got louder as it approached.

Kevin did not know it was Heather until she was less than a foot away. She knocked him to the floor then continued running wildly along the hallway. The sound dissipated however he heard something scarier. The voice, this time unmistakably Heather's, called out.

"I'm supposed to kill you, sweetheart. I must kill you. I will kill you. She's making me."

"No, Heather, you can't kill me. You love me!"

This time Heather appeared three inches from his face.

"I will kill you!"

The words were said in a whisper though no less frightening than had she raged against him. She laughed hysterically and then disappeared in the darkness.

Stunned but determined to get to the end of the hallway, Kevin moved from door to door and counted down the room numbers until he got to room 101.

He heard a whimper near the floor so he moved toward the sound and reached out. He felt a hand and grabbed it. The hand grabbed his. He knelt down to see a rotting corpse of a woman. She lifted her head up and he recognized the red eyes. The ones he had seen in the secret room. He immediately jumped back and slammed against the door of room 102. It opened. He fell helplessly on the dusty floor.

He screamed.

"This is not real!"

The door slammed shut. A slow knock sounded on the door. Kevin shot to his feet and prepared to fight. He did not know what or who knocked on the door. He was ready for anything. He pulled the door open and his fist connected with something hard. He saw something fly across the hall. Cautiously he walked toward the entity, which squirmed on the floor and felt around until he felt long hair. The mass moved and Kevin clenched his fist and realized he had just struck Heather, his wife Heather. She seemed to come out of a trance and begged.

"Please don't hurt me."

Kevin got down on his knees and stroked her hair as she cowered against the wall.

"Heather!"

"Kevin! Is that you?" she asked. She reached out for him.

"Yes, it's me! Let's get out of here."

Heather hugged Kevin. "Don't ever leave me Kevin. I'm sorry I ran. Please, hold me!"

Kevin momentarily forgot that both of them were still in the middle of a horror show. "Let's go, honey."

"Kevin, there's no door. I searched and searched for it but there's no door," she said.

"Don't worry. We'll get out of here." Her body trembled against him.

Heather trembled as Kevin carefully walked Heather down the stairs and they stood where the door once was. Kevin reached into his backpack and pulled out a piece of paper along with a book of matches. He lit the paper and it went up in a flash. He then lit another match to show Heather that the door had reappeared. They opened the door quickly and ran into the room. The door slammed behind them.

"What did you do, Kevin? How did the door reappear?"

"Remember when I shook in the room in front of the book?"

"Yes."

"Something happened to me. A vision, or something, I don't know. I was told to read page 31 of that book. Apparently a spell on the ripped-out page continued on page 31. I knew I had to tear it out and burn it."

"Let's go see Bryan. I don't really want to see what she did to them but I have to."

They both shook away the images the witch had placed in their heads and limped toward the living room together.

It was at that point they saw something that gave them hope. Roxy, Bryan's exuberant Boxer, ran toward them. She wagged her shortened tail, barked loudly and looked happy to see them. They were thankful to find no blood on her shiny brown coat. They knew that if Bryan had been injured or dead Roxy would stay by his side.

They entered the room as Bryan walked toward them. "Oh, you are the reason Roxy barked. Where have you been? Heather are you okay? Your head and mouth are bleeding."

"I just need to sit down in a real chair."

Bryan and Kevin helped her to a chair as Bryan peppered both of them with questions. "Kevin, your legs, what are the bandages for?"

"Oh, with all that happened I forgot. I got bitten by something."

"Yes, we have to get him to the hospital. There are maggots on his legs. Kevin, let me look at it again," Heather said.

Kevin sat down and Heather removed his bandages. He had no wounds at all.

"They're gone! Kevin, the wounds are gone!"

Kevin implored Bryan and his group to go to the west wing. Heather looked up as she tended to her minor injuries.

"Are you serious?" she asked.

Kevin ignored her. He continued to press Bryan to go to the west wing.

"We'll be ready in ten minutes," Bryan said.

Heather wondered why Kevin wanted to put her brothers, and the others, in such a deadly situation.

"Kevin, we can't send them in there."

"I know what I'm doing, Heather!"

Heather stared at Kevin then turned to her brother.

"No, Bryan, you can't go in there!"

Kevin suggested they discuss his idea in private. However, once in the bedroom, he attacked her. She struggled to get free. He put his hand over her mouth to still her cries. He stuffed a pillowcase in her mouth and wrapped part of the sheet around her head. Finally he tied her hands to the bed with the silk ropes from the canopy bed.

"I'm sorry about this but I don't have time to explain now. I will be back when Bryan leaves." he said.

He left her there, as she fought against her constraints, satisfied she wouldn't be able to escape.

Bryan, John, Ronald, Daniel and the Goth lesbians geared up. They had their infrared thermometers, infrared motion detectors, particle detectors, EMF meters, ion detectors, and a multitude of cameras, both video and still. They also took an arsenal of weapons and enough ammunition to wage a small war. They worked as a group, and each had a huge backpack full of supplies. Melody and Michelle were the camera operators. Daniel accompanied them in case there was a malfunction with the instruments. Daniel also showed Kevin how to monitor them on the laptop. It showed their location using the GPS tracking system.

Bryan, Ronald, and John Jackson led the way. They brought extra lights because they knew they'd be in pitch darkness.

Kevin saw the door open and then disappear once they entered. Kevin wanted it to happen. He immediately ran to Heather who was still tied to the bed. As he removed the silk ropes and the sheets he dodged her angry punches. He untied Heather and once both her hands were free she slapped him square in the face.

"I deserved that but please calm down, Honey. I'll explain why I did this to you," he said.

"You'd better hurry up, because I'm about to explode!"

Kevin got his backpack and pulled out an old ragged book.

"Is that the witch's book from the secret room?" Heather asked.

Kevin placed his finger over Heather's lips and whispered. "Shh! She may be listening and, if she is, we don't have much time."

He replaced the book in the backpack.

"What are we going to do with it?"

"Hurry, we have to go to the den, before it's too late and all of us are dead."

They went to the den where Kevin promptly removed the book and placed it in an oddly shaped black safe and slammed the door shut. Heather had never seen it before.

"What is this?"

"It's a kiln and a safe. I had it specially made for this book six weeks ago. You see, this is part of my plan. It's digitally linked to someone in the group's GPS. I had Daniel set it up for me a couple weeks before they came but he doesn't know whom it is linked to and neither do I. If whoever's GPS is still for a certain amount of time the kiln turns on and the book is destroyed. It is our insurance policy against her killing anyone in the group, including us."

"That will protect us?

Kevin explained further. "No one here knows the combination to open the kiln and I know she needs that book to accomplish her quest.

"So, you've always believed that the witch of the manor existed?"

"Yes, I have. I didn't want to tell you because you would've assumed I'd lost my mind. There is another thing I learned in that room. One of the spirits trapped by the witch is an ally of ours. It told me that she would force you to kill me."

"I know the history but why are Bryan and the others in the west wing?"

"I found out she wanted Bryan, and others, to help you in your attempt to kill me. I needed them out of the way because I feared that with all that firepower they might succeed. Another thing - there were just too many for me to fend off. Now, I just have you to worry about."

"I see. So she can't kill or harm Bryan or anyone else for fear of the book burning?"

"That's right. Plus, I won't always have to look over my shoulder. Have you had any more thoughts of poisoning me yet?"

"No, not yet, but when I do, I hope I'll be able to tell you. So what's the plan now?"

"Bryan told me that he saw the witch when he monitored us in the west wing. Let's go in the living room and wait for her."

Kevin and Heather watched Bryan on the monitor as he set up his equipment prior to entering any of the rooms. It appeared that he had yet to experienced anything strange because unperturbed he gave out instructions. Daniel was to stay at the entrance door to monitor the group's activities.

"Bryan, can you hear and see me?"

"Yeah. A question - which room had all the bodies in it again?"

"101. You probably won't need your instruments," Kevin replied.

Bryan said, "Yes, I will. How will we find any spirits?"

"They will find you, trust me!" Heather said.

"Hi sis, is Kevin with you?"

"Yes, he's right here. As I said, they will find you."

"I hope they do. Roxy will let me know when they are around, if they exist. We're ready for them," Bryan said.

"You have Roxy there?" Kevin asked.

"Yep, I don't go anywhere without her."

They waited for an hour before the witch made her appearance on the monitor. A blue glow coalesced into a woman's form. An eerie voice was heard.

"Do you think these people are going to stop me? You are destined to be the sixth relic and soon you will be within the circle and I will live forever."

"I don't think so. You see, I know what you need and I have it," Kevin said.

"You have it now but soon your precious wife will supply me my relic. She can't resist my power and all your friends will die."

"My friends will not die! You will not kill my friends!" Kevin shouted.

"My dear relic, I will not have to kill your friends because they will kill each other. They are at my mercy."

"If one of my friends dies you will never be able to fulfill your prophecy because one of them is linked to a kiln, which now holds your book. If that person dies then your book will burn and no one in this house knows who that person is."

"The book? It's hidden within the secret room!"

The walls vibrated with her thunderous words.

Kevin smiled broadly. "No, it's in an oven."

The blue vapor exploded out of the monitor. All the furniture in the room toppled and Kevin and Heather were slammed down onto the fine marble floor.

The witch stood nine feet tall in front of the dazed couple and shook her bony finger.

"Give me back my book or I'll kill all of you!"

"No, you won't, because without the book you'll always look as you do now!" Kevin said.

He rolled towards the fireplace and picked up a large shiny brass kettle. When the witch saw her image she recoiled in horror.

"Take it away! Take it away!" she yelled.

The crystal chandelier shook.

Then as she disappeared she said something that gave Kevin pause.

"I don't need the book to fulfill my prophecy."

* * * *

Heather pointed at the large monitor. Bryan and Ronald walked into room 101. They came out a few moments later. They looked as if they were all ready to vomit.

Bryan wiped his brow. "Kevin, you said it didn't stink in here. It's unbearable. I didn't see a torso of the woman hanging in the air. I saw three bodies, or what's left of them, in there. When this is all over, this room will need to be gutted."

Bryan shed his backpack, told John to cover the other side of the wall and then instructed Ronald to walk down the center next to him. Melody and Michelle followed them with the cameras and Heather and Kevin saw what they shot. Ronald stopped when he spied a man in the darkness. He walked close against the wall toward them.

Bryan and Ron raised their AR-15 rifles and pointed it at the figure.

"Stop!" Bryan shouted. The man continued.

"Stop, old man!" Ron added his voice to Bryan's command.

The man started to moan and groan and then began to laugh hysterically.

"Bryan, that isn't a man. Look at the way he walks."

"One more warning, whoever, whatever, you are, one more step and we'll blast you," Bryan said.

His trigger finger quivered.

It rushed at them and both Ron and Bryan opened fire. Loud shots echoed throughout the wing. The menacing figure slumped against the wall, mortally wounded. Bryan ran to the thing that now lay face down on the floor. Blood poured from the many holes in its body. He turned the thing over and shrank back in horror. Ronald, his partner and friend, who had stood right beside him when the firing began and assisted in the shooting, was now on the floor.

"Bryan…what the fuck are you doing? You…shot me."

"No, I didn't! You shot with me! What the hell is going on?" He watched Ronald take his last labored breaths. "Oh shit, I killed Ron! Kevin, he stood beside me when I shot. He saw the thing too! I couldn't have shot him!"

Kevin viewed the monitor as the horror unfolded. He looked at Heather as if for reassurance.

"Oh dear God, Heather! Did I make a terrible mistake? Suppose she really doesn't need the book? We need to solve this puzzle and fast before the others are killed. Shit! Do you have any ideas?"

"I have a theory. Remember that wall in the secret room?"

"Yes, the one with all the writing on it. I remember."

"Well, I still have the piece of paper. I wrote everything down. I need to go to the cemetery."

She took the paper from her pocket, grabbed a pen and walked toward the door.

Kevin followed. "The cemetery? Why are we walking to the cemetery?" he asked.

"I'll tell you when we get there."

Kevin didn't question Heather further on the subject because he knew that her theories turned to facts after she had a chance to think. Then she'd explain. They arrived at the cemetery. Kevin gasped for air. Heather ran on pure adrenaline. She started to write and then Kevin asked the question again.

"Now can you tell me why we're here?"

"I need to know when they died."

"All of them?" Kevin asked.

"No, just the guys." After a few minutes, she jumped up. "I think I'm right!"

"You're right about what? Tell me what you're doing," Kevin asked. "Heather, hurry, it's starting to rain. We'll get drenched."

"Kevin, listen to yourself! We're trying to destroy evil in our house and save our lives and you're worried about getting wet?"

"Um, you're right! Sorry."

Heather placed the paper in her pants pocket. Kevin's prediction had been right because as they ran back to the house, the heavens opened up. They were soaked when they entered the living room. They didn't bother to get out of their wet clothes and walked straight to the den.

Heather sat at the desk. It was time to explain her theory.

"Do you remember the cryptic messages on the wall? Some were written many times while others just a few. Whoever wrote those told us who they are. For instance, Cyrus Black was born in 1813 and died in 1884, exactly one hundred and thirty-two years ago. The cryptic message 'Ascend to the fourth vertical' pertains to him. It's the same for Michael Black, who was born in 1912 and died in 1955, sixty-one years ago and is attached to the message 'Surrounding the Master, the con to stay holds my soul'."

"I still don't get how you know that. What are the other ones?" Kevin asked.

He glanced over her written notes.

David Black was born in 1972 and died in 1994, twenty-two years ago, and he is associated with 'The vessel of the mind sets the president of the time of people's rights'. John Black, the resident author of the best-selling book, The Manor, is next. He was born in 1952 and died in 2010, six years ago. 'Released from my cage, seek the stilled flow where rainbows once harkened the sun. 9 11 66 45 23 5 28 45' is written six times.

"The numbers intrigue me and I feel they mean something important," he remarked.

"Do you remember reading something about the last chapter of all his books?" she asked.

Kevin took his copy of John Black's book off the shelf. "Yes, I read an article about that. He always left a personal message to his wife in the last chapter. No one cared enough to try. I believe that I read that it's a fairly easy cipher."

"Well, I've never tried and I think those numbers are a key of some sort," she said proudly. "I'll just have to think about it more."

Heather continued with her theory.

"The next occupants were Ben and Rianna Black. Ben Black is John Black's younger brother who was born in 1973 and died in 2013, three years ago. 'Eternity lies within the grand bridges we cross across the keys' is written three times."

"John Black wrote something similar in his book. He didn't count the number of times they were written on the wall though. What's the significance?" Kevin asked.

"Well, each passage appears to be written to correspond to the number of years they've been dead. I'm assuming that the spirits of the dead husbands had to have written the cryptic messages. 'Ascend to the fourth vertical'. I counted exactly one hundred and thirty-two times. I counted the second message sixty-one times, the third, twenty-two times, the fourth, six times and the last, from Ben Black, just three times. They are telling us who they are and what message corresponds to what husband."

Kevin, as always, was stunned by her astounding skill. "Amazing! Now what do the messages mean?"

"Every one of the husbands' wives was named Heather with the exception of one. I read about it in an old police report. It stated Maggie had changed her name from Heather after she graduated from high school. Also, Ben's wife's name is Rianna though they had a child named Heather," she explained. "What does it all means? I don't know yet."

Kevin and Heather were reminded about Bryan and his friends when they heard them plead for help.

"Bryan, we're here," Heather said.

Bryan had taken his helmet off and pointed the camera at his face, which filled the large monitor. "We have to get out of here. There are so many strange things happening to us. I've shot and killed Ronald three times and he killed John twice."

"What? How is that possible?" Kevin asked.

"It's not possible. That's the point. Melody and Michelle have been killed. They were in one of the rooms and we found them sitting on a day bed but their heads were severed and switched. Daniel is missing. John

Jackson, Ronald and I have been shooting at each other for the last eight hours. We keep seeing monsters. Then we find out they're not monsters – they're us. I've been shot three times although when I wake up I have no wounds. I still feel the pain. Roxy is with me. She's no help because she gives away my position with her barking! I can't bring myself to kill her so I'm taking incoming fire. I need to find the door."

Kevin looked at his watch. "Bryan, you've only been in there for two hours, not eight."

"Are you serious? It feels like days since we walked in here. We've been under attack constantly. We never seem to run out of ammunition," he said.

"Well, we're working on getting you out of there, but it may take a while. Hang in there, Bryan."

"Please, hurry guys, I fear most of us aren't coming out of here."

"Ok, will do. We're with you in here."

Kevin patted his chest.

"I've never seen Bryan so sad. I'm ready to put this all together." She stopped and her face contorted with fear. "Oh, my god, Kevin. I seem to have the desire to poison you. I can't control it, but I can tell you about it. It's so weird"

Kevin looked at her strangely.

"It's her. She's put those ideas in your head. As long as you tell me when you have those feelings we can cope." He added, more flippantly than he looked, "From now on I'll make my own cups of coffee. And please make sure you don't point any guns at me."

Chapter 12
Heather's Mind Detour

Kevin and Heather went back to the den, sat down and tried to figure out what the cryptic messages meant. Then Heather seemed preoccupied with the safe that housed the old book. She touched it to see if the temperature had changed.

"What are you doing?" Kevin asked.

"I'm just checking if it cool to the touch. I wonder who the GPS is attached to. It triggers the kiln off."

"I don't know who it is but I believe he or she is still alive. Why do you ask?"

"I'm just curious. You want a beer? I certainly need one," she confessed.

Kevin sifted through papers while she went to get a beer. "Heather, we have to focus. We have to solve this!"

She poked her head back into the den. "We have all the time in the world, Cyrus, I mean, Kevin."

"Cyrus? You called me Cyrus?"

"No, I didn't. I called you Kevin. I'll be right back."

Heather came back with two unopened cans of beer. She popped hers open and drank. However, Kevin noticed something strange. She stared at him when he opened his beer and brought it to his mouth. At the last moment, he noticed the trace of a powder in the crease in the top of the can. He took a pen, scraped the powder from the crease, and showed it to Heather.

"What is this?"

"It's strychnine and I put it there. Wait a minute. I put it there? Oh, Kevin! I tried to kill you! I remember doing it but I don't know why." Despite her strong nature, tears welled in her eyes when she realized what she nearly did. .

"It's okay, sweetheart. I know you didn't mean it, but I'm going to get a beer that I know is not poisoned. I should've added serving beer to the list as well as coffee. I'll be right back."

Kevin took the tainted beer in the kitchen poured it down the sink and then threw the can into the garbage. He retrieved another beer and rinsed the top of the can thoroughly. In the den Heather was on her knees. She played with the combination lock on the kiln to open it.

Kevin calmly placed his beer on the desk. "You're not going to be able to open it, Heather."

"She's in my mind, Kevin. I'm trying to resist her, but I can't. She wants me to open the safe."

"It sure appears that she needs that book. I think she lied about not needing it. Come on, you need to relax. There's a lot at stake here."

"Oh damn! I just realized something. If we solve the riddles won't the witch know what they mean as well?"

John Black assumed in his book that the phrases were written to fool the witch. What happens if she finds out what they mean? Will the spirits then suffer an unimaginable fate, or will she just change the scenario to make the clues mean nothing? Kevin wondered.

The answers to the mysteries seemed a long way away. He wrote down the first message: Ascend to the fourth vertical.

He decided they needed to leave the manor to erase the grip the original Heather had on his wife. He had to get Heather out of the house so he could talk candidly. John Black observed and wrote that his wife's mind was never invaded outside the iron gates of the manor.

Kevin reasoned that if the witch couldn't invade the women's minds outside the gates the witch probably couldn't hear what they discussed.

"Let's go out for dinner tonight," he suggested.

"We can't abandon Bryan," Heather said.

"It will give us a chance to replenish our minds and bodies. We need strength to fight her."

* * * *

At dinner, many miles away from the manor, he asked Heather what the message entailed as the waiter brought out the appetizers.

Heather picked at the bread rolls.

"Well, ascend means to climb something and the fourth vertical could mean anything upright like trees," she suggested.

"On the property there is a small hill and there are trees on it," he said. "What could be hidden there?"

"Or, it could mean stairs." Heather interrupted. "We climb stairs although it doesn't explain what the fourth vertical means. Trees are vertical and I know there are more than four trees on that hill."

Kevin immediately got up from the table. "We have to go back, Heather."

Heather stared. "We're not finished with dinner, Kevin."

Kevin placed a hundred-dollar bill on the table.

He didn't give a reason for the abrupt finish to the evening however so many odd things happened lately Heather didn't question him. They sped back to the manor. He parked the car in the garage and didn't bother going inside the house or close the car door. Heather stared, perplexed, as Kevin grabbed his chain saw off the shelf and threw it into the boot of the ATV from the garage.

"Come on, Heather. Follow me. I want to go to the small hill on our property."

Once at the hill Kevin went to the fourth tree.

Heather found her voice once more. "What are you doing?" she protested. "This can't be the vertical, Kevin."

He started his chain saw. The tree, a five-year-old oak, fell quickly. It took mere seconds before it hit the ground.

"Nothing there," he said.

"I told you the tree couldn't be the vertical."

"It's the fourth tree we saw. Whatever it is, it has to be here somewhere," Kevin explained.

Heather watched as he sorted through the various pieces of the felled tree. "It is the fourth tree. Can I remind you that one is only about four or five years old? You don't think this tree grew here in 1874?"

"Oh shit! You're right. It's not old enough."

"We need to take a walk outside the gates. Yes, I know, we have to leave the manor. Let's go because I think I have the answer," she said.

They returned to the ATV and drove back to the massive iron-gated entrance to the estate.

As Kevin drove, Heather talked. "She's constantly with me but like you I noticed she left when we moved from the manor grounds. Don't look surprised. I know that's why we went to the early dinner at the restaurant. It's the only time my mind is free of her so we have to solve the messages outside the manor. You'll have to do the investigation in the manor. She watches me and intrudes into my mind when I'm there. I need to think about something else."

"What about reciting a rhyme?"

"That's a good idea. Then she won't know what you're doing. I'll solve them, away from this place, and you find whatever is hidden. Promise me you'll never tell me what you find or where you hide it. Keep it out of the estate. Once all the riddles are solved we'll be able do whatever it takes to end this nightmare."

"What about a simple code?"

"Such as? Everything is so strange in the manor."

"That'll do. Use the word 'strange' if the witch is starting to control you and I need to get out. Keep it simple."

"You could also ask me for the name of 'Zorana'. She was my childhood friend as well. I've known her longer than anyone else. So if you think I might be the witch, it's a good question. That is something she'd never know."

***

They ended their walk together and separated once they re-entered the gates. Heather sat by the pool with her computer and researched the estate. As she read, she was reminded that each husband had mysteriously lost a limb. The authorities recorded they could never find them nor did they discover why it had happened. Strangely, the original Heather Black also lost a thumb.

Heather and Kevin agreed they couldn't help Bryan and his group until they solved the puzzles. When Heather watched the monitors she hated to see her brother and friends in turmoil. She, and Kevin, knew they worked to end their misery as well as their own.

Heather suggested one of the clues led her to believe something lay concealed in the staircase. Kevin went on a mission to locate the hiding place. He stood at the base of the stairs and climbed up to the fourth baluster. He pulled it out and he saw nothing. The balusters, thin vertical risers extended from the steps to the banister, revealed no clues. He sat on the stairs and removed it several times to examine it closely however again he saw nothing. He put it back as well as he could because he had to snap off the bottom dowel to get it out.

Kevin wondered if Heather had got it wrong.

Then as he placed his hand on the box newel post to help him up from the steps a brainwave came to his mind. He looked at the massive curved staircase and counted five posts. He walked up the steps and to the fourth newel post and felt around it for an opening or an indication that someone might have pried it open in the past. He found a slight opening between the wood corners. He placed his fingertips into the gap and pulled until it opened. He closed the newel post quickly and then ran to his den to get a flashlight.

He had seen something inside.

He returned a minute later and removed the little piece of wood to peer into the space and then recoiled against the railing the wall on the other side of the staircase. He found the remnants of a human arm devoid of skin and tissue with the exception of a small piece of tendon holding the bones together. He had a great presence of mind and ran to the kitchen to grab an empty garbage bag and a half-full garbage bag. He extracted the bones and placed them in the empty garbage bag. He carefully gathered all the material. There were many finger bones at the bottom of the space. One by one he found them all and placed them in the bag with the arm. He placed the garbage bag into the half-full one. Strangely, no odor emanated from the space.

He replaced the wood on the newel post and then nonchalantly told Heather that he had to take the garbage out.

"I need to get rid of this, Heather. It's starting to stink."

"Okay," she said. "Hey, I found out something strange, but I'll tell you later."

Kevin stared keenly at Heather.

"Very *strange*," she repeated.

Earlier they'd agreed to the code word in case the original Heather Black began partially controlling Heather. He knew he had to leave the manor soon.

Kevin didn't say anything else as she continued reading John Black's book. He walked past the monitors and saw Bryan shooting into the darkness of the hallway and someone shooting back, using tracer bullets. The bright shooting lights barely missed the camera and almost mesmerized Kevin. Then he shook his head and remembered that he had to get the garbage outside the manor. He walked out through the gate without incident. He stowed the garbage bag containing the bones among the trees.

Heather had solved the first clue, although what to do with his find was still a mystery. He placed the real garbage in the garbage can by the road and saw Heather walk towards him as he closed the receptacle.

Oddly she did not walk through the gate.

"Come on, let's go for a walk," Kevin said. He held out his hand to her.

"Come inside, I want to talk to you," she said.

"Can't we walk and talk? Or are things too strange for you?"

She nodded. When he eventually persuaded Heather to walk through the gate she confessed that she'd wanted to kill him again.

"The evil spirit appears more desperate in her resolve," she said.

"It's because you solved the first riddle but it wasn't in the fourth baluster. It was in the fourth newel post."

"What did you find in the newel post?"

"Do you think it's safe for me to tell you? I mean, even out here?"

"I think I have her mind figured out. I can tell when she's haunting me. However, maybe you're right. We'll solve them all and then do what we have to do. We know that each of the dead husbands had missing limbs when they were discovered. Arms, legs, a head, and a rib were missing and never recovered."

"Do you realize? That represents the human form? Two legs, two arms, a head and the ribs," Kevin said.

Heather gasped as she took in the information.

"That's awful," she said.

Before they walked back to the house they made an agreement to turn off the monitors. They were powerless to help Bryan or his crew and seeing their fight distracted them from their task.

Wary of Heather's need to harm him, Kevin waited for Heather to go to sleep. He got up to watch the bed from a distant dark corner of the bedroom. He propped pillows under the blankets to dupe her into the belief he was still in the bed. It proved to be a great idea.

Unknown to him Heather had gone to bed with a twelve-inch butcher knife. He watched as, with her eyes closed, she thrust the knife multiple times into the piled-up blankets. She opened her eyes and then went to the other side. She continued to stab at the empty bed.

When she realized it was nothing but blankets she looked across the room and saw the shadowy figure.

"Nice try you old witch," he said. "My wife's body is strong though not strong enough to overpower me. You'll just have to try again. Get out of her immediately! Or maybe the book will go up in flames now!"

Heather dropped the knife onto her foot. "Ouch!" She sat on the bed and held her bleeding foot.

Kevin went to help and placed pressure on the wound. "It's not too bad, Heather. I don't think you'll need stitches."

Heather blinked as if she'd come out of a trance.

"What the hell happened? Why did I have a knife? Oh, I remember. She wanted me to stab you."

"She needs some part of me. She's short of something – I don't know what."

Kevin laughed though it sounded mirthless to Heather.

"How do you know?"

"I just know I have to be careful and sleeping is a vulnerable time for me. I can't fend you off if I'm asleep. She still haunts you while you sleep, dear."

"We are going to have to sleep separately. I have the feeling that neither of us should sleep in this room. We have an entire east wing so maybe we should select a different room every night."

"Honey, we need to end this tomorrow if we can. I'm tired and I need to sleep now. I think you'll be safe. She doesn't want you dead yet. You have to kill me first and I'm going to make damn sure that doesn't happen," he said.

"I'll meet you in the den tomorrow morning, sweetheart. I love you. Goodnight."

She hated sleeping alone even though she understood her unconscious desire to harm Kevin. She didn't want to harm him.

***

Kevin found a room far away from Heather. He pushed everything he could move in front of the door. If Heather found him she would find it difficult to get to him. The noise would wake him so he could defend his life. He fell asleep though his dreams were very vivid. He dreamt of a cold day in Virginia. He walked to the small frozen pond on his property. Heather skated on the ice. He watched her move across the ice with grace and precision.

Kevin noticed how beautiful she looked as she spun with her long black hair flowing against the solid white background and the snowflakes fell gently to the ground. He wanted to be a part of the idyllic setting so he put on his skates. As he laced them up, he heard her call out to him, and looked up to see her fall through the apparently thick ice. Despite the fact he had only one skate on he rushed to her. She struggled to get free. There was a look of desperation on her face. Immediately he jumped in and grabbed her.

Then something strange happened.

She pulled him under the water. Her anguished face changed to as a smile as he flailed away seeking air.

Kevin woke up in a cold sweat with the memory of his dream strong in his mind. Afterwards he checked to make sure the door remained barricaded. Reassured he fell into a deep slumber.

The next morning Kevin woke up. A long hot shower refreshed him and prepared him mentally to get another riddle solved. In the den he saw Heather. She attempted to open the safe to get the book.

"You won't manage it, Heather. No, it's not my Heather is it? You'll never get it open. You will never see that book again," Kevin said.

"I said that I don't need the book! Heather is getting closer to killing you!" she said.

She stood up to face him. "Your precious wife will supply my last relic."

He appealed to the woman he knew. "Heather, let's take a walk."

"I don't want to walk out there. Let's go for a swim," she replied.

After his dream he wasn't going anywhere near water with her. He tested her. "Where's Zorana?"

"What's a Zorana?" she asked.

He knew then it wasn't Heather. Zorana the name of her childhood friend was the means to determine if her mind had been taken over by the witch.

"Okay, we need to go for a walk. Nice try, you old bitch, now let her go," he demanded.

He took the Heather by the hand and dragged her down the long, finely bricked driveway and through the ornate gates. Heather immediately snapped out of her funk and they sat down on a bench in the adjacent national park.

"Okay, she's gone. I didn't sleep at all last night, knowing that I tried to stab you."

"It's okay, Sweetie. Did you solve the next message?"

"This one is a hard one."

'Surrounding the Master, the con to stay holds my soul."

"I'm assuming that he's talking about a picture frame. 'Surrounding the Master'. The Master is capitalized, which means it's a noun or depicting a person."

"An artist is also called a Master," Kevin added.

"That's it! 'Surrounding the Master'. It is a framed picture!"

"Do you realize how many works of art are in the house? All of them could be considered the works of Masters. Which one is it? 'The con to stay.' What the hell does that mean?" he asked.

"I think that phrase tells us which picture frame we're looking for. Let's see, 'the con to stay'... What is the opposite of stay?" she asked.

"Depart, remove, leave…"

"Leave! That's it!" she said. "Or rather leaves, as in tree leaves. Find a frame with leaves on it. Remember, it has to be a fairly large frame."

"We have to get back. I think I have what I need."

"Hey, wait for me!" she said. She caught up with Kevin and grabbed his hand. "By the way, my friends could visit this weekend."

"No way! We have to clear this house before we invite any more people here. Is it still my Heather in there?"

"It's an idea. They can help us. They are very smart."

"So is Bryan and look where he is," he said.

"You're right! I am so sorry we allowed him to go in there."

"If we hadn't perhaps he, or one of his friends, might have helped you to kill me. It's hard enough dodging your solo attempts," he said.

They entered the gates but this time Heather got in her golf cart and drove to the cemetery.

***

Heather went to gather more information and Kevin looked for a painting that depicted leaves. He knew it would be difficult. The mansion housed well over a hundred works of art. Some were obscure artists, however, most were priceless. Rembrandts, Van Goghs, Monets, and Renoirs decorated the walls of the spacious mansion. Luckily for Kevin the Masters were easy to locate. They adorned places, which had the most foot traffic, so visitors could admire them.

However Kevin found no leaves on any of the massive frames. He searched for a long time. He feared the painting hung in the west wing and he had serious reservations about revisiting the wing.

He searched and searched. Tired and exasperated, he sat on the bottom step of the huge staircase and looked up. There he saw something of interest. A painting, a 1938 Picasso, featured an abstract of a woman sitting in a chair surrounded by various kinds of leaves. Picasso named it 'Femme Assise Dans Un Jardin,' which meant, 'Woman Sitting in a Garden'.

"I hope I don't destroy your beauty. I bet you're a fifty million dollar type of gal."

He got a ladder from the garage. He climbed up and removed the painting and its very heavy frame. He propped it against the ladder and slowly and carefully edged it down.

He noticed a removable panel part on the left side of the frame. When he opened it, it revealed the remnants of a human hand eerily propped up on its fingers. Rotting brown skin still held the hand together though just barely and he saw small bones protruding. Again he noticed no odor. He placed the grotesque left hand in a small bag and attached it to his belt. He quickly replaced the small panel on the back of the frame and then carefully replaced it on its mounting.

He stood back and checked the painting.

There were no signs that it had been disturbed other than the large amount of displaced dust that had accumulated on the top of the frame. He delivered his new find outside the gates and sat it next to the previous find in his own secret hiding spot. He now had two pieces of the puzzle solved although he had no clue as to what to do with the remains of the ex-husbands or how to release them from the witch's power.

Chapter 13
Kevin Gets a Scare

He found Heather in the den eating a sandwich.

His mind, distracted by his newest find and before he could think about the third message, Kevin placed himself in immediate danger.

While he talked to Heather in the den he reached over and took a bite of her sandwich. It was a bad habit although he'd done it countless times before. He noticed Heather smile as he took a second bite. The smiles turned into wild laughter.

Kevin looked at the sandwich. Immediately his body felt the effects of the poison. He could feel pains in his stomach. He ran to the bathroom and slumped down beside the toilet basin. Heather strolled in calmly and sat next to him on the side of the bath as his limp body struggled to stand up.

"Does it hurt?" she asked.

She didn't lift a finger to help. "You really thought that you could beat me? Go ahead struggle. It makes the poison circulate faster."

Kevin had swallowed a half bottle of ipecac before Heather reached to the bathroom. Suddenly, he vomited with such force that it flew at Heather. She didn't budge as the vomit dripped from her face. Kevin blew out the bulk of the poison and felt the lessened effects. Although weak he kept his senses to prepare for the next attack.

It didn't come. He watched Heather collapse on the floor in front of him. She had also taken a bite of the sandwich. He took out his cell phone and called an ambulance.

"You'll have to break the side door down!" he informed the operator. "We're in the bathroom!"

They just sat together on the floor and listlessly stared at each other until the paramedics arrived.

Heather was still alive. Eventually she curled up on the bathroom floor and cried as if aware of what she had done. Kevin realized the witch had taken a chance with Heather allowing her to eat the spiked the sandwich first.

She probably knew that I'd take a bite after Heather, he thought. *Kevin, you've been outsmarted.*

He moved closer to Heather as he heard the paramedics shout out. When they entered the bathroom they saw the couple lying in vomit.

"We've been poisoned. Please hurry!"

The paramedics worked on Heather first since, Kevin informed them, that she hadn't vomited the majority of the poison out.

Soon they were both off to the hospital.

In bad shape, Heather had her stomach pumped, while the doctors decided Kevin was in a slightly more stable condition.

He wanted to stay with Heather.

The poison coursed through Heather's system though it finally stopped its destruction of her internal organs. Two days later she opened her eyes.

For the first time Kevin was able to relax.

"Take a break, Honey. You look so worn out."

"Ok. I'll slip out for a coffee break."

Later Kevin entered her room to find a police detective at her bedside.

"What are you doing here? What's all this about?"

"Mr. Black, your wife confessed that she poisoned you. I need some answers. The nurses reported, that in her delirium, she confessed to poisoning both herself and you and naturally they reported it to the police."

Heather sat up in her bed and repeated her confession.

"I did. I poisoned you, Kevin."

Kevin gently kissed her on her lips and whispered, "Thank God you came back because I can't live without you."

"Mr. Black, we need to talk to you as well," the detective said.

"Get out of here! Can't you see she is ill?"

"Mr. Black, a crime has been committed and we have to arrest your wife."

"Nonsense. I told you to get out. There will be no charges pressed, or do I have to call your captain? I own him and your force, Goddammit! Now get the fuck out of here!"

A doctor persuaded the policeman to leave.

"You can't question her now," he said. The doctor took her temperature and blood pressure. Then he spoke to Kevin. "Ah, it looks like she's finally past the serious stuff. I think she'll be fine, Mr. Black,"

"When can she be released?" Kevin asked.

"I'd say in a few more days, just to make sure. You, however, can leave at any time."

"No way, I leave when she leaves."

"I see. Well. Okay. Hopefully, Mrs. Black, you will be much better tomorrow so we can release you early."

The doctor left the room.

"Kevin, I know what the third message means," she said.

"How can you manage to think about that now? You nearly died."

"My mind is always thinking and I have these messages implanted in my mind. 'The vessel of the mind sets the President of the time of people's rights'. The bust of Thomas Jefferson! It's the Jean-Antoine Houdon in the hallway. Do you know which one?"

"Okay, how did you determine that?"

"The way it was phrased 'sets the President' 'Precedent' is spelt wrong and 'the time of people's rights' he wrote the Declaration of Independence and embraced the concept of individual rights. It's Thomas Jefferson. 'The vessel of the mind' is a head. It's a very expensive sculpture."

"Yes, I know. God, I hope I don't have to break that."

"Just think of it as a replica and hope that it is," she suggested. "Kevin, you should leave and check it out."

"I can't do that. Without you there to distract the witch she will know we've found her hiding place."

"Well, I can walk, you want to bust out of here?" she asked.

A huge, devious, grin lit up her face.

"We can do that. I'll call the service to drive a limo over. I'll let you know when it arrives."

Weak, but strong enough to move, she got dressed. When they were ready to leave they simply walked out of the hospital. No one noticed. The limousine picked them up and they returned home.

Heather said, "Then it's back to our normal nightly routine of retiring to different bedrooms."

"If anything can be considered normal," Kevin joked.

The remark was met with a faint smile from Heather. They walked to the living room and Kevin turned on the monitors though they showed nothing. No sounds of gunfire, no movement and no people. Then Bryan's image popped up on the monitor; bloodied and beaten he struggled to talk however his words sounded muffled and strained.

Heather touched the screen.

"I'm so sorry, Bryan. I never meant this to happen."

**

Meanwhile, Kevin tried to reason how the bust of Thomas Jefferson figured in the story. He observed a tiny opening at the base of the sculpture and started to scrape away the plaster. A few layers down he saw hair. Now he knew the artifact housed a real human head.

"Freaking hell," he muttered, as he peeled away layers from the valuable sculpture.

He didn't know to whom the head belonged. He didn't care. He just wanted to get it into the bag without viewing the face. He opened the base wide enough to get the head out. Afterwards he tried to replace the plaster back over the hole. No luck, it broke off. He hoped the witch wouldn't notice anything amiss. He placed the head in a bag before he looked back at the bust.

"No, I don't think anyone could tell a human head came out of that."

He labeled the bag with the number 3. There were only two more messages left to decipher; he felt confident they were near the end of the mystery. He hid the head in the park and checked on the other two to make sure they were still safely stashed away.

Heather turned off the monitor and then noticed the laptop Daniel had set up for the GPS systems. She was surprised to see everyone in the group move around as if nothing had happened. Immediately she closed the laptop and went to find Kevin. She looked out the window and saw Kevin walking up the driveway. She ran outside to tell him that Bryan and his friends seemed okay.

"Really? This I've got to see," Kevin said.

He opened the laptop and what he saw made him feel uneasy. Kevin looked as surprised as Heather at this turn of events.

What on earth was happening? One moment they were in danger, the next, Bryan and his team were on a Sunday picnic, he thought.

Then, as he began to close the laptop he noticed moving lights in the background form into something familiar.

"It's the Big Dipper and these are constellations. You see them form then disperse to form another." Kevin banged his forehead with the palm of his hand. "God dam it! She's discovered the GPS system! Shit!" he lamented. "I don't know what she'll do now. Maybe we should just give in and tell her what we're doing."

Heather said, "What? Give up? Those are my brothers in there. We can't give up! Wait a minute! My Kevin wouldn't give up! Who are you?" She took a step back from the man.

"What are you talking about? It's me, Kevin."

"Where's Zorana?"

"What? What are you talking about?" Kevin asked.

Heather thought, *Kevin' didn't know the code word, Zorana.*

"Let's go for a walk, sweetheart," she suggested.

"Sure, where do you want to go?"

"I want to go to the park," she said.

She grabbed his hand and started to walk down the long driveway. Kevin stopped short of the gate.

"Oh, dammit, I forgot something at the house. Come on, we have to go back."

"Get it later. I want to go to the park."

"I said we go back now!" He grabbed hold of her arms and marched her back into the house.

"Kevin, what's wrong with you?"

"Where is my relic, bitch?"

Heather acted in an innocent manner. "Relic, what are you talking about?"

Kevin raised his hand and suddenly the bust of Thomas Jefferson flew through the air and then blasted against the wall shattering into a million pieces.

"My relic. Where is it? Speak now or I'll crush his skull with me in here!"

Heather, now certain the witch of the manor had invaded her husband, did not budge. She had no idea what Kevin had done with any of his finds or what they were.

Kevin' took a knife from his pants pocket and cut off a chunk out of his left ear and threw it at her and demanded she reveal the relics whereabouts.

"I will rip his body apart if you don't tell me where they are!" He held the knife to his right ear. "Show me."

"Okay! Okay, I'll tell you. They are near the gate. I'll take you there."

Blood flowed freely down his face as they walked toward the gates. Heather pointed toward the very edge of the property; distracted momentarily as he looked out, she ran full force toward him and pushed his body through the gates. He disappeared before he landed. Heather tumbled to the ground outside the gates. She looked up and saw Kevin standing beside her. He stared at her. She returned his gaze - his ear was intact.

"What are you doing here, sweetheart?" he asked.

"Oh, Kevin, she knows what we're doing. She found the hole in the bust and smashed it against the wall," she said.

"Shit, the next message, what's the next message?" He turned towards the gates. "Come on, Heather," he shouted.

"I'm not sure if it's you now."

"It's me, sweetheart," he said.

"Who was my best friend at school?"

He frowned and then smiled. "Why it's Zorana."

Reassured, Heather held his hand and they walked toward the house.

"We need John Black's book, Kevin. The key is there, I think."

They entered the house to face a barrage of items, which were suddenly thrown toward them. Chairs, tables, kitchen supplies and knives — everything flew in their direction. They hid behind a table that lay on its side and listened to the sound of knives strike the other side. Cautiously, they moved the table and inched their way toward the den. Heather stayed hidden behind the table as Kevin entered the den to grab the book. He noticed the small safe had withstood the gale force winds within the room. Kevin crept out of the den to join his wife.

"We have to get away from here!" he said.

They struggled to move the table against the wind to the front door. The monitor flew violently from the living room and clipped Kevin's fingers. Injured and bleeding he did not let go of the table. The flying objects appeared to search them out.

Eventually they made it to the front door and ran outside. The door slammed shut behind them with such great force that it split in two. They ran down the driveway to the gates and continued on to the park.

Exhausted, they sat on the bench. There was no time to rest and Heather read the next message to be solved. John Black's message with the strange numbers afterward did not appear to stump Heather.

"'Released from my cage, seek the stilled flow where rainbows once harkened the sun. 9 11 66 45 23 5 28 45'. Look, Kevin, he's sending his wife a message. The numbers correspond to the letters in the sonnet to his wife. The first number is nine. Take the ninth letter in the message, F is the ninth letter, and the eleventh is zero. It spells something."

"You are brilliant, Heather," Kevin said.

They deciphered all the numbers and came up with where the witch hid John's relic: F-O-U-N-T-A-I-N. Thankful that he didn't have to go back into the house to get the relic, Kevin looked at the fountain in front of the house. It had not worked in years.

"Interesting," Heather commented. "I wonder if he used the same formula for his secret message to his wife in the last chapter of his book. Did you know he died prior to the book being officially published? What would you say to your wife if these were to be your last words?" she asked.

Kevin considered it. "I'd tell my wife what she needed to do to remain safe."

"Exactly," she said.

"But how can you use these numbers?"

"It's simple. He started out his chapter with the same phrase. The numbers are the code and he wrote the chapter using this code. This is going to take a while to decipher all of it."

"Here, take my backpack, it's got plenty of pens and paper in it. I'll go get whatever is in the fountain."

He took his gun from the backpack.

"That won't do you any good, Kevin, she's a spirit. Guns can't stop her," she said.

"I'm not going to use it on her. I don't have anything to bust up the fountain, so I have to use this."

"Okay, please be careful. Sweetheart, I love you!"

"I love you too. I'll be back as soon as I can," Kevin said.

Heather started to decipher John Black's last chapter as Kevin made his way to the fountain.

He could see items being sucked into the front door.

That's one angry witch, Kevin thought.

Kevin stood in front of the fountain. Perplexed he scratched at his head.

I have no idea what I'm looking for, he thought.

He fired all of his bullets in an effort to break the monument up. Then he started with the butt of the gun and smashed at the turn-of-the-century fountain. He broke the small cherubs along the perimeter of the fountain. There was nothing out of the ordinary.

It took a long time to break it up.

He found nothing.

***

Heather made great progress. She began to decipher John Black's message to his wife. She took a short break and reflected on the last few days.

Her brother and his group were still stuck in the west wing. Even if what she saw on the monitor turned out to be an aberration, she had no idea whether they had enough food and water to survive. Then she pushed everything to the back of her mind and concentrated solely on the puzzle again. She finished the final sentence and read it.

Heather now believed she had all the answers she needed.

They'd already worked out that the relics needed to be placed on the graves of the dead husbands. That would complete their cycle of death. They were convinced the witch would be weakened once the spirits were returned to their graves. It would be their opportunity to finish her off, once and for all.

It had been six hours since Kevin left and Heather began to worry. Then she saw Kevin running, full force, toward her. Then he paused to catch his breath.

"I got it, Heather. It looks like a rib."

"Of course, 'released from my cage'! It's his rib cage."

"Did you figure out the last chapter?"

She handed him a piece of paper. "Read this," she said.

To my darling Heather, I know that by the time you read this I'll have already passed away although this is a necessary step. I didn't discuss this with you because, naturally, you'd try to stop me. Of all the mysteries I've written, this real-life one has consumed me. I didn't tell you this before but I went back to the secret room many times and have contacted the spirits of all the dead husbands: Cyrus, Michael, and David Black. They are trying to get to a peaceful sleep. However, the original Heather Black will not allow it until her fate is met. She seeks everlasting life and beauty, and has made a deal with the devil to realize that end. She needs six relics to complete the spell, with mine being the fourth. The spirits speak in cryptic messages in hopes that someone will understand and break the spell. They speak this way to avoid the wrath of Heather. She's not very smart, from what they tell me.

Go to the secret room and you'll hopefully see one more cryptic message. That will be mine. Find the relics using the cryptic messages, place them on their respective graves, and this horror will end. I still don't know what they mean, although perhaps I will when I'm initiated among them. I hope that I will be able to be strong enough to resist her powers and tell you exactly what the messages mean. I've been told that will not happen. She wants your soul and will get it through your suicide. I wish that I could have delivered my usual love letter to you, however this final warning will have to serve in its stead. I hope that I will have the sense of mind to help you, my dear wife. If not, then a beautiful place exists for us when someone else solves the mystery. I hope to show it to you. They say that love conquers all, and I will test that theory in death.

*With all my love and devotion,
Your loving husband, John*

"So that's what we have to do! Let's get started," he said.

"There's one more message. You're not going to like it."

"I haven't liked anything thus far. Why should this be any different?"

"You're not going to like it because we have to go back into the house. Ben Black's relic is in there.

'Eternity lies within the grand bridges we cross across the keys'.

It's got to be the piano. The 'grand' piano has bridges and keys. Something is there."

Kevin wiped his brow. "Shit! She's not going to let us in there, at least not through the front door. I think I can get in through the east wing."

"I'll go with you."

"No, I don't want you getting hurt. Let me show you where I hid the artifacts, you gather them up, and meet me at the cemetery. There's one thing I thought of. Why can't we just take these to the cemetery and release the spirits?"

Heather replied, "We can't do that because she will just find more Heathers until she reaches six. We have to end things here and now. We have to end her."

"Of course you're right again." Kevin admitted.

Chapter 14
Betrayal of Trust

Kevin walked carefully and tried not draw attention as he entered the east wing. To his surprise, this wing had remained untouched by the witch's vengeance. The Steinway grand piano still sat proudly and prominently in the marble-floored foyer. The foyer had returned to its previous state. He walked to the living room and stared momentarily stunned, because every piece of furniture was in place and every painting hung securely on the walls. There were no signs that anything had happened in the great room.

Even the monitors Bryan had set up were back in their place and operating perfectly. Although, Bryan and his group were nowhere to be seen and when Kevin opened the laptop the lights, that represented the individuals, sadly they did not move. Some indicated their personal lights had been extinguished and some flickered to indicate the battery had failed.

He didn't feel threatened as he walked through the house and there were no signs of anything spiritual or paranormal.

The condition of the house amazed Kevin. He forgot why he snuck in through the back door of his own home. The echo had returned to the mansion. It felt profoundly majestic to his senses. It was a feeling he'd never perceived before. He stared at all the works of art in a way that he'd never done in the past. The valuable bust of Thomas Jefferson proudly stood with no damage to mar its perfection.

What has happened here? he wondered.

He ran his finger over the top of the picture frames, and saw not a speck of dust. A raging fire crackled in the massive six-foot fireplace. He sat on a chair he'd never sat on before and felt a comfort he'd never experience. While he rested on the chair, his eyes became heavy and his worries appeared to leave, one by one.

He sat in a perfect setting, complete with lilting lullabies from the past, which wafted gently through the house. He'd never heard such beautiful music played with such emotion and it even caused a tear or two to fall. He'd never experienced such pure perfection before and hoped that the home's past would be remembered as nothing more than a nightmare. For the first time he viewed the massive manor as a home to be protected.

He felt these things all at once.

Then it dawned on him he ought not to feel this way. He had something to do and regardless of how he felt about the house he had a duty to perform.

Part of him was thankful for the feelings he'd experienced. The house made him reflect back to his childhood and he vowed that once they eradicated the manor's horrific host he would spend every cent he had to get those feelings back.

"Music, singing and love will return to this great manor," he vowed.

The sense of urgency continued as he walked over to the never played Steinway. He searched among the bridge, strings and soundboard for the remnants of Ben Black. He found the leg bones and the foot stripped of flesh in the body of the piano and then, as before, he placed them in a black garbage bag.

He longed to return to the room and sit in the same chair where he'd wait for the concerto to finish. However his natural caution won and he continued on his quest.

There were a few things that he needed from his den. To his horror he saw the safe that housed the book stood wide open and the book, gone.

"How the hell did she get that open?"

He spoke out loud.

It underlined the urgency to get to the cemetery. The picture in his mind, of Heather in potential peril, moved him on. Kevin reluctantly left the house. He glanced back at the warm, cozy home and wondered whether they would ever see or feel its comforts again.

As he returned to the cemetery he sensed something had changed.

It added to all the woes they'd experienced.

The book had vanished, along with all its leverage. All their work to rid the mansion of its horror lay wasted with every footstep. He didn't know how long they had.

Strange thoughts entered his mind on his trek.

I don't want to sacrifice whatever to become just another relic, to be used in a demonic celebration for the immortality of that bitch Heather Black. Or will I be the next aimless spirit bowing to the whims of a cruel spirit hell-bent on preserving her beauty, and not caring about lights of the living beings extinguished to achieve that end?

He saw Heather in the distance. She sat on the ornate marble bench with the four garbage bags nearby.

He took slow, methodical steps and hoped to delay the inevitable demise of his body and soul.

Heather waved. "What's wrong, Kevin?" she asked. "You look so depressed."

"The book is gone. She has it now," he confessed.

"I know, I gave it to her."

Stunned, he allowed her to take the final garbage bag. "You did what? You gave it to her?"

"Yes, I did."

"Why? Why would you do that? How did you get it out of the safe?" His limbs shook as he sat next to her.

"I gave it to her because she asked for it. I found out you are also one for games and puzzles. You fabricated the grand plan for the safe and all the while she knew that the combination lock is not a lock at all. It's a dummy dial.

You knew that the original Heather's powers were vast. You couldn't hide the combination from her so you fabricated an elaborate story. All along she just needed to turn the handle to open the safe. I have to hand it to you it worked for a while. You see, Sweetheart, while you believed I investigated the house, my investigations focused on the safe manufacturer," she explained.

"So, you betrayed me?" he asked.

"Why, yes, I did. You see, sometimes you confuse intelligence with common sense. We lost this fight long before we began, so giving up is the intelligent thing to do. Fighting her is just a ruse with a purpose."

"How could you do this? Heather, I love you! There's always hope as long as we act and think as one entity. We can do anything with that kind of power," he said.

"I do love you, Kevin! I've always loved you and still do. I love you much more than you know but an emotion elicits no more power than that tree over there. It causes us to do irrational things and makes us ignorant to what's really happening."

"That's not my Heather saying that. My Heather embraces the beauty and the perfection of a life lived with me by her side."

"You're right, of course. This is not your Heather talking. I've completely taken over her brilliant mind. However you can have her back. There's no reason for me to occupy her any longer. I have everything I need, except one relic and that will come to me soon. Besides this woman is pregnant which causes me great angst to be inside her."

"She's pregnant? She's pregnant!"

Kevin turned to Heather. "Is it true? Are you pregnant?"

A tearful Heather smiled. "Yes, I am. I didn't want to tell you until all this was over. I didn't want either of us to lose focus and you, knowing that I'm pregnant, would have stopped me from helping. I guess I'm not as intelligent as you give me credit for. I should have told you; maybe then our fate would have been different."

"Well, now that you have told me perhaps things will be different."

As he gazed into her eyes, he noticed a blue aura surround Heather and watched as a spiritual divide took place. The blue aura moved away from Heather and manifested between them.

The original Heather stood and grasped the four bags of relics.

Unfortunately she doesn't possess the rib of John Black, which remains in Heather's pocket, Kevin remembered.

Heather held Kevin's hand and secretly passed the small rib fragment to him. He managed to place it behind him without the witch's knowledge.

Kevin wasn't surprised by the sudden presence of the original Heather Black yet he felt curious as to why she hadn't just killed him on a whim. After all, she had countless opportunities to have his wife do away with him.

"Why am I still here? I know you need my arm to complete your spell but why have you waited this long?

"That's simple. I needed both of you because, my dear friend, I'm an old spirit. I died an old woman and I simply forgot where the relics were. The spirits wouldn't tell me the information to me regardless of how much I tortured them. I guess I gave you a reprieve so that both of you could find them for me," she said.

Her smile revealed her missing teeth. They saw her decayed face. Kevin looked at the spirit of the original Heather Black and then smiled as he hurled the rib toward the graves. It stuck firmly in the topsoil covering the grave of John Black.

"Nooooo!"

She held out her bony finger and beckoned the rib to come to her. It didn't move.

Instead, it sank into the ground. A few moments later, a great green wind blew from the house. The color changed to a bright blue as it shot toward the grave. There the silhouette of the great author, John Black, thanked them.

The original Heather Black looked at Kevin with anger and disgust although strangely she did not appear as angry as Kevin feared after losing one of her minions.

The spirit of John Black offered a moment of calm for Kevin and Heather as temporarily he thwarted the witch's desire to harm them.

"Thank you for releasing me and allowing me to continue my journey. Sadly, there will be no protection for you from me once I'm gone. I'd stay however the choice is not up to me because I'm not real. When the great wind comes it will take me and you will be subjected to the evil of this hag again."

John turned to the original Heather Black.

"As for you, the spirits are weary of your exploits, and regardless of the outcome they'll not succumb completely to your demands. I defied you and showed them how to defy you as well. These good people are not the ones to be concerned about. You'll never live happily again while one spirit exists under your rule.

"Kevin, Heather, I applaud your efforts in ridding humanity of this scourge. I feel the wind upon me and I bid you farewell."

The wind carried his silhouette away and eventually dispersed his essence until he vanished. The witch raised her hands and with the book and garbage bags in hand she uttered these words.

"It matters not that the spirit of John Black has flown because another Black is on the way. Your future son will make claim the manor and his spirit will take the missing spirit's place. I promise you he'll suffer a most painful death. Your death will pale in comparison to what I shall do to him. He will pay for your sins against me."

Kevin stood by the grave of the original Heather Black. He could no longer be silent.

"No, he won't, you ugly bitch! In all your centuries of torturous behavior, and because you believed beauty to be a mere spell away, you forgot something. Two valuable morals. The first is the ability to be among those who care and love you, without demonic promises of beauty and everlasting life, is essential. The true sense of self is only realized when you leave this realm. The people you leave behind will judge you. Their fond remembrances of you linger when you leave this world. You instead have let people see your black heart. You are destined for darkness and loneliness. I don't envy your eternity."

The spirit laughed at Kevin's poetic sonnet to the fate of the old spirit and replied, "You said two things."

"Oh, yes. You have the book and all the power in the world. I admit that I wrongly assessed the book's importance and I should have destroyed it."

The witch interrupted him. "I don't need the book, you silly man!"

"I know that now but then why were you so adamant about having it? I deliberated about it for a great deal of time and then it came to me. You did not need the book itself, however what's imbedded in its back pages horrified you. You never wanted it to be found. However, I did find it!"

The old spirit dropped the garbage bags and opened the book to find a cutout in the back.

"Where is it?"

She saw Kevin smiling. He held up a small white bone, a long forgotten thumb, extracted over a century earlier.

She shouted, "That's mine!"

He casually flicked it on top of the grave of the original Heather Black. She gasped as it sank below the hallowed ground. She lunged toward Kevin, but the slightest movements caused her body parts to break up into dust. Before their eyes she dissolved into the same green aura as the spirit of John Black. Her anguished expression indicated the extent of pain she endured at her end.

They watched, as all that was left was her hands. They faded into dust. Once the dust settled her silhouette stood upon her grave. She didn't appear to have the same exuberance as before. She entered the next phase of her existence as the wind came. Instead of sending her off to the heavens she shrieked as her aura turned black and screwed itself into the dirt. The grass which covered the grave, died instantly.

Kevin held out his hand to his beautiful wife and together they walked toward their home, happy and hopeful for their future with each other.

The trauma seemed to be a distant memory and they vowed never to bring up their fight again as the dialog drifted toward their baby and what to call him or her. The old witch said they would have a boy however her words no longer mattered and held no forecast of what the future held.

"Well, we can certainly rule out Heather as a name," Heather said.

Kevin grinned. "I don't know, Heather is a fine name but I'm sure he'll hate us later for it."

"What makes you so sure it will be a he?" she asked.

Kevin smiled again. "I don't know what it will be, the only thing I do know is that he or she will be ours."

He stopped walking. "Oh damn, we forgot about the other spirits. The garbage bags! We have to release them."

"Can we wait until night time?" she asked.

"Why night time?"

She held his hand. "The colors, I love the colors they emit as they leave. It should be spectacular amid the stars."

"I'm pretty sure that we could wait but what about them? They have experienced many horrors and this day will be their last. I have a feeling that they do not know that they are free. Honey, if you were separated from me in the afterlife even a second would be torture."

"You're right, of course. My natural instincts focused my mind on Bryan and his group."

She returned the graves and Kevin followed.

"I believe that they are fine because whereas she didn't care about the book she did care about what it held. She couldn't risk having it destroyed. Bryan and his team were mere distractions to her."

They sat on the ornate bench and one by one they allowed the spirits to fly toward the heavens. Though not dark they saw the bright colors of the spirits as they ascended upwards.

They walked back to the house among the previously unnoticed wild flowers as their scents filled the air once disturbed; they believed that they were truly free to explore their future without fear.

At their front door Kevin romantically lifted Heather and carried her through the doorway as if it were the first time they entered their home.

Bryan and John met them in the foyer. They talked over each other as they rushed to explain what had happened to them in the west wing.

Kevin and Heather weren't listening to them. They went straight to their bedroom and locked the door. They made love for three hours. The constant knocking by Bryan was ignored.

"He can tell us his story tomorrow," Kevin said.

***

Heather eventually decided to join the rest of the world. She wanted to tell everyone that she and Kevin were to be parents and a grand party was planned to celebrate.

Finally they welcomed Bryan, John, and Ronald back from the west wing.

Bryan proudly announced that they'd cleared the west wing of the evil that possessed it. Kevin and Heather did not mention their part in the journey. They smiled at each other happy to allow Bryan and his team their glory.

"We discovered over fifty bodies. Most of the bodies were on the unexplored first floor. Some were homeless vagrants who used the manor as their home when it wasn't occupied."

It didn't matter to Heather and Kevin now. They'd already decided that the entire west wing would be torn down and rebuilt once the bodies were removed and accounted for.

Kevin noted some missing faces. "What's happened to Daniel and the Goth girls?"

Bryan and John Jackson burst out laughing as Bryan explained the situation. "Melody and Michelle are still in the west wing. When the shit went down with bullets and asses flying everywhere they stripped down and were screwing the whole time. I reckon Daniel is probably in the shadows watching them. I swear they can do it in the strangest of places. I'm sure they filmed it or they had Daniel film it. They'll show up eventually."

John nodded in agreement. "When that door appeared I cried. I admit it! Bryan shot me over twenty times and I shot him at least twenty as well."

"Bullshit, you shot me just five times but didn't kill me once. My shots were grouped perfectly and you died at least three times," he boasted.

"No, Bryan, you killed me three times not John. I got you back when I zombied out and I cut your leg clean off," Ronald reminded him.

Bryan lifted his leg. "I got it back, see?"

"Yes, I can see that but I peed on it before it came back," Ronald said."

"You sick bastard! Don't you know I could have gotten an infection from that?"

"Bryan, something ripped your leg off and you worry about an infection?" Ronald asked.

Bryan looked at his leg and grimaced. "It just bugs me knowing that my leg is tainted by your zombie piss."

"You guys are weird. You are all alive and well. Be thankful for that," Heather commented.

Ronald laughed. "We are thankful for an awesome experience where we got to blast each other and be zombies over and over again. That was killer!"

Bryan and John burst out laughing. "The whole thing is so surreal," they said.

Kevin and Heather joined them in their exuberant laughter.

An hour later Melody joined them. She looked exhausted with her hair splayed in all different directions and her normally perfect Goth makeup smeared all over her face. She struggled to catch her breath.

"What's wrong, Melody?" Bryan and John spoke in unison and grabbed their guns.

"She's chasing me! I can't do it anymore! Help me, Bryan!" she pleaded. "I'm exhausted."

"Is the witch after you? Where is she? I'll blast the bitch!" Bryan said. He pointed his gun toward the open door to the west wing.

"No, it's not the witch, it's Michelle. I can't orgasm any more, dammit! My eyes have a natural flutter now and I can't make it stop. She thinks I have three vaginas and she's hell-bent on destroying all three of them. My legs are jelly and once, I actually wanted to be the real Alice in Wonderland being chased by the Queen of Tongues."

Bryan and the rest of the group laughed as hard as they possibly could as Michelle staggered through the door, nude, with her hair wildly messed up. "There she is! Melody, I'm not done! Come here, my little vagina fest."

"No, Michelle, I've had enough! If I have one more orgasm, I'll explode!" She whimpered as she held on to John. "Make her stop, John. Please, I beg of you!"

"No, Melody, you will not explode until I explode. I will do you right here, right now if I have to."

She saw no one was offering to assist her so she got up and ran wobbly-legged toward the east wing and into her room with Michelle following close behind. Melody slammed the door shut.

The entire group followed them to the east wing and watched as Michelle kicked the door open. "Nowhere to run, Melody. Now, I want all three of them to explode at once. Then we can smoke a cigarette." She looked back at the others. "Why the hell is everyone following us around?"

The door closed and through the door they heard a scream then eventually a loud and audible sigh of complete contentment. Everyone decided to allow the couple their space as they returned to the living room to see Daniel at the table with the monitors. His face was smeared with a combination of black and white makeup that extended all the way up into his hairline with lipstick in various places supplying color to his new look.

"What the hell happened to you?"

Daniel face was lit by a perpetual smile. "It was so dark in there that Michelle couldn't tell who she ravished when I turned off my flashlight. After a few hours, she didn't care that I'm a guy and neither did Melody. I'm pretty sure I nailed one of them but to be honest after a while I ran faster than Melody. In that environment, Michelle is insatiable. My equipment is still in there."

"Are you talking about your dick? Just asking," John laughed.

"No, I'm talking about my other equipment. I think it will all have to be replaced," he said. A serious look was now on his makeup-laden face.

"Forget about that junk," Bryan said. Everyone stared at him. "Well, that's all it is! Junk! I mean particulate indicators, ION, and EMF gauges? What do we really know about the afterlife? How do you know that these instruments can detect the dead? We don't know! Who said that an EMF meter can detect anything supernatural?

"With all the frauds that we've uncovered over the years, not one time, in my recollection, has any of this expensive equipment, detected anything. We just see the flickering lights and think that we've found something. Well, this time we did find something and I saw no flickering lights to warn us about anything. I'm going to rethink my company's purpose. From now on we'll just debunk the scammers. We know what the real thing is like now," he explained.

"Well, whatever you decide, I want you all to know how much Kevin and I appreciate what you have done," Heather said.

***

A month later, all the friends gathered at the manor for the big party. Movie stars and politicians descended on the mansion with the music playing loudly as everyone laughed and enjoyed each other's stories.

Daniel sipped his beer by the pool. A beautiful girl approached him.

"Is this seat taken?" she asked.

Daniel looked up and saw the girl of his dreams, Katy Morgan, the mega star singer and actress. Words were at a premium as she sat down next to him and started asking about his experiences in the mansion.

"I heard you saved the manor," she said. Bryan, John and Ronald stood nearby snickering.

"Yes, I did, and of course my brother and sister helped a little." He struggled find something interesting to say.

"Well, I'm be performing at the Kennedy Center in two weeks. Will you come to see me?"

"Oh, I'll be there, I promise you!" He fumbled with his phone. "What's your number? I've been having problems with programming my new phone but it's a great phone with great apps. I also have the latest Madden. Do you play video games?" He knew he was blowing it by talking gadget-speak.

She gave him a huge smile. "No, I don't know what Madden is and I have very little time for games or gadgets. Please, when you come, leave your gadgets at home. I have my own, and I'm sure you'll find those much more interesting," she said.

Daniel didn't understand what she really meant until many hours and beers later.

The music blared and the people danced in their finest clothes and later Kevin and Heather slipped away.

Kevin had taken Heather to the empty living room, hoping to recapture the moments before his faceoff with the old witch. He realized that when he visited it the first time, though glorious, it did lack something. Now he felt perfection when his wife sat next to him with her head against his shoulder. They listened to the soft music until the relaxing setting caused her to fall asleep in his arms while he stroked her hair. They stayed there for hours undisturbed and he hoped the feeling would last for the rest of his life.

***

Kevin assured the local police department that the strange things that they had encountered in prior years were no longer evident at the manor and they could come in and sweep the west wing to retrieve all the missing bodies.

When the authorities removed the last body, Kevin and Heather continued to reinvent the manor's legacy by cleaning all the artwork in the rooms, fumigating and restoring the centuries-old furniture.

They demolished the west wing to the ground and rebuilt it to the same specifications as the original but the hallways were brightly lit. A multitude of windows allowed each room to be viewed beyond its horrific legacy.

It turned out to be a truly an impressive mansion; for Kevin and Heather it stood as a beacon of their determination.

However mostly, they just considered it home.

The End

About the author

A prolific writer, Gary D. Henry is an award-winning author who has penned twenty novels and touts several works-in-progress. Specializing in the field of horror and mystery, Henry is not shy about blending other genres into the mix. Averaging two to four releases a year, Henry's first publication came in September 2009 with the release of *The Westward Journey of the Nebraskan Wind*. Since then, several of his books have gone on to win awards, such as: *Opulence Among Us*, Honorable Mention at the 2012 Los Angeles Book Festival—DIY award; *Legacy of the Unsung*, First Place in the 2011 Halloween Book Festival—Time Travel Category; *Falling Waters*, Honorable Mention in the both the 2012 Paris Book Festival Award—General Fiction Category and the 2012 Beach Book Festival Award in New York; and the *Abel Conspiracy*, Honorable Mention in both the 2012 San Francisco Book Festival Award—General Fiction Category and the 2012 The Halloween Book Festival Award—General Fiction Category. Recently, Henry has dipped his pen in the genre of short stories after being compelled to write a story about Alzheimer's disease, which claimed the life of his father Ray Henry

Visit Gary online:

Facebook= Gary D. Henry
Author Gary D. Henry

Twitter= @GaryDHenry

Webpage
http://www.garydhenry.com

Linkedin
http://www.linkedin.com/pub/gary-d-henry/45/9b2/0

Goodreads
http://www.goodreads.com/author/show/3414888.Gary_D_Henry

Amazon
http://www.amazon.com/Gary-D.-Henry/e/B006RUM63Q/ref=ntt_athr_dp_pel_1

Made in the USA
Middletown, DE
21 March 2017